Bastian

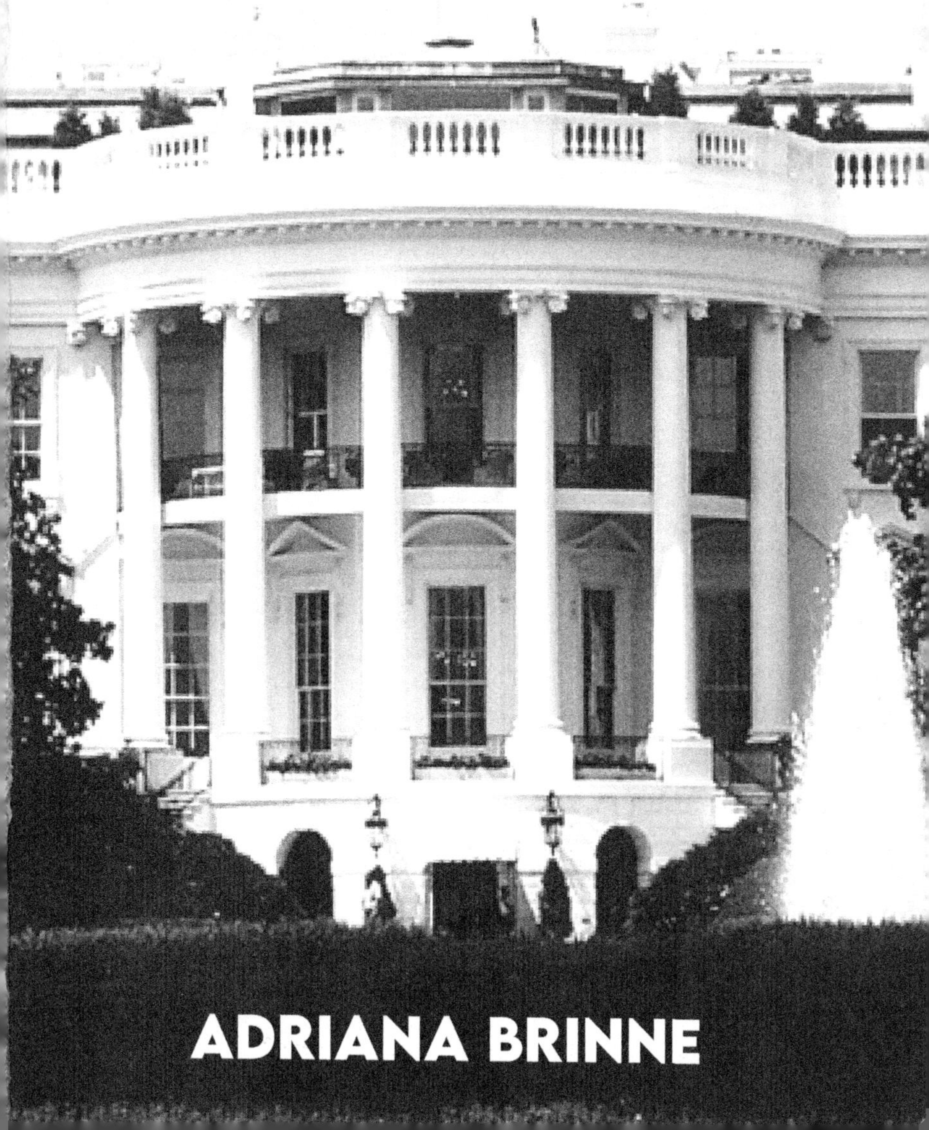

ADRIANA BRINNE

Copyright © 2023 ADRIANA BRINNE

BASTIAN "IN LOVE AND WAR" (UNHOLY TRINITY #6)

Cover Design by Cat at TRC Designs

Formatting by Adriana Brinne

Editing by Elsa Gomes

All Rights Reserved.

This book or any portion thereof may not be reproduced, distributed, or transmitted in any form or by any means, including photocopying, recording, or other electronic or mechanical methods without the express written permission of the author except for the use of brief quotations in a book review.

This is a work of fiction. Names, characters, businesses, brands, and places are fictitious in every regard. Any similarities to actual events and persons, living or dead, are purely coincidental. Any trademarks, service, marks, product names, or named features are assumed to be the property of their respective owners and are used only for reference. There is no implied endorsement of any of these terms used.

DEDICATION

To my brother
I don't say it much but I love you dipshit

PLAYLIST
playlist

Listen to the full playlist on SPOTIFY

"Both Of Us" – Mimi Webb

"The Great War" – Taylor Swift

"War Paint" – FLETCHER

"We Go Down Together" – Dove Cameron, Khalid

"Heartbeat" – James Arthur

"Freezing" – Mimi Webb

"One More Try" – Calum Scott

"Someone Who Loved You" – Teddy Swims

"I Miss You, I'm Sorry" – Gracie Abrams

"Forget Me"(Piano Version) – Lewis Capaldi

"Pains My Only Home" – Zevia

"Nervous" (Piano Version) – John Legend

"To Die For" – Sam Smith

"Hate Me" – Ellie Goulding, Juice WRLD

"Know It's Wrong" – Skylar Stecker

AUTHOR'S NOTE

Bastian "In Love and War II" is the sixth book in the Unholy Trinity series. The story contains sensitive topics that might be triggering for some.

I took some liberties while writing the story regarding politics and the White House history. This, in no way, is accurate, only fiction. Please keep this in mind before starting the book.

I hope you enjoy Arianna and Bastian's journey towards happily ever after. It's power and heartache wrapped in a beautiful, chaotic but sweet package.

Note: This is the conclusion of the In Love & War duet. Please read book 1 before starting this one.

WHAT IS THE UNHOLY TRINITY?

The Unholy Trinity is the most notorious crime organization in the United States of America. It was once run by three crime families who joined forces after a war over Detroit City. They each rule over their own family, but only one controls the entire organization. Currently, the organization is fair game since the Volpe family was extinguished, and the Holy Trinity was taken over by the remaining families and the Irish (O'Sullivan Family). The Nicolasi and Parisi families hold a small percentage of the city, while the other half is fair game to the Irish and Russians.

The Holy Trinity is not pure anymore.

It is Unholy.

The Unholy Trinity is composed of the Nicolasi, Parisi, and from now on, the O'Sullivan family. The Nicolasi family deals in the gun trade, the O'Sullivan family deals in the drug trade, and the Parisi handles the organization's legitimate side, including the casinos and strip clubs.

For years, the three most ruthless crime families of Detroit City ruled together in peace. The Capo fell from grace, and now the others lead by greed and sin.

WHO IS WHO IN THE UNHOLY TRINITY?

NICOLASI FAMILY

Cassius Nicolasi

Andrea Valentina Nicolasi

Lorenzo Antonnio Nicolasi (Capo of the Unholy Trinity)

Valentino Alexander Nicolasi

VOLPE FAMILY

Lucan Tomas Volpe

Cara Mia Volpe

PARISI FAMILY

Arianna Luna Parisi

Kadra Sofia Parisi

Mila Areya Parisi

OUTSIDERS

Sebastian Kenton

Thiago Sandoval (Capo of the Sandoval family)

Dion Arnault

EPIGRAPH

"A relationship is like couture; if it doesn't fit perfectly. it's a disaster." - Carrie Bradshaw

BLURB

To the outside world, I am the picture-perfect politician who leads the country with integrity and morality, but deep down, I know the truth of what hides beneath the surface.

A flawed man with a rotten soul and not-so-selfless intentions.

The Commander-in-Chief.

I am all of that and more.

I am also a selfish man hell-bent on ruining everyone's life, including my own, over the woman who sets my world on fire.

I couldn't risk getting distracted. I couldn't risk another heart.

Another life.

I had one goal, and that was to ruin the Parisi name.

But then she came along, and I learned the true meaning of obsession.

Obsession and love.

I never intended to fall in love with my enemy's daughter, but I did.

I found once-in-a-lifetime love until I ruined it by trying to be a better man.

I shattered her heart and started a war.

I am no stranger to it, and the war for her heart is not one I intend to lose.

I play a dirty game and that she knows too well.

Arianna Luna Parisi is my obsession's name.

A name my world will never forget.

PROLOGUE
Past

"Sebastian," My father sighs before continuing. "You know that what you did was wrong, right, son? Us Kenton men treat people better than that." He looks down at me sternly but still lovingly as we wait outside for security to pull up with our car.

Thank fuck father decided to leave the event early. Socializing with those brainless pricks exhausts me, both mentally and physically.

On more than one occasion tonight, I had to suppress the overwhelming urge to roll my eyes and call them out on their stupidity. Grown men with bird brains and egos as big as their empty heads.

The cold wind hits me, causing me to shiver. Shit, it's cold.

I rub my hands up and down my arms, but even the heavy coat I am wearing over my suit does very little to protect me from this weather. I normally don't mind the cold, but something about the atmosphere today doesn't feel quite right.

Perhaps I am tired, and my desire to get home and away from these people has me imagining this eerie feeling in the pit of my stomach.

Yeah…maybe.

But then there's the night.

Starless but with a full moon.

A small smile appears on my face when I think about how mom hasn't stopped spitting facts about the cold moon all evening. Hell, she even sat down at the table with other politicians' wives and talked about it.

Something others on our table didn't quite appreciate.

Those women are as thick in the head as the men they married.

Most people would find mom's nerdy facts annoying, but not me.

Never me.

She could do no wrong in my eyes.

Nothing

"Mon soleil…" Mom sighs softly in French making me look up at her.

My sun.

I love my mother.

I love both my parents dearly.

They are all I have, and I am their only child, so that makes me all they have. They are stuck with me.

Bless their souls.

And even though they are both successful in their fields and have busy schedules, they always make time for me and do their best to include me in whatever they are working on. Whether that is political business or one of my mother's benefit projects.

Therefore, it is nothing new that I am here today with them.

Our family opened a children's hospital in Detroit, and the purpose of this event is to help raise money for sick children and their families in neighboring communities, but not everyone in attendance has a selfless heart like my mother. No, most people in attendance tonight are here for selfish and self-centered reasons.

But not Vivienne Kenton.

The world should bend its knee to my saint of a mother. She gives, gives, and never asks for anything in return.

Like tonight.

All she asked was for me to be her good boy, but my temper and my tongue had a mind of their own. In my defense, it is not my fault half of the people inside the gala are idiots who only got to where they are because of their money and connections, not their brains. Not hard work. That was proven when the asshole congressman felt attacked when I pointed out how incredibly idiotic it was of him to pass a bill that does nothing for his people or his campaign.

He only did it to kiss the ass of the other fools who are part of the United States Congress. No morals and no brains. A troubling and shameful combination.

Tucking the queen chess piece out of my suit's pocket, I toy with it and count to three in my head just like my mother taught me whenever I felt the urge to say something that to others might come off as hostile or condescending. I believe I did nothing wrong.

On the contrary, I only did him a favor by pointing out his many mistakes. People should be able to take criticism in all forms. Especially people who promise shit they never deliver. Besides, most humans piss me the hell off. I take a deep breath and hold it in for three seconds.

One.

Two.

Thre– Nope. The urge is stronger, so I succumb to it and speak up. "If they didn't want to be called out for their stupidity, then they shouldn't have said or done anything stupid." I try to keep my tone light because the last thing I want is to upset mom, and whenever I act up or say something that most would find offensive, I know that it worries her. Instead of looking sad or worried, mom chuckles, surprising both father and me. "You're one of a kind, sweetheart." She drops a soft kiss on the top of my head and breathes me in. "Don't you dare change, but stay my good boy, okay? Always my good boy."

I ignore the loud crowd of journalists, guests, and their security escorting everyone to their cars safely. It all fades into the background as I concentrate on my mother's beautiful face. Sea-green eyes, framed by thick and long eyelashes, give her a doll-like look. Long, curly black hair that falls like silk around her stunning face.

My mother is the most beautiful woman I have ever met. Her beauty is rare and very much appreciated by others.

So much so that my father has had to do his fair share of fighting with pricks who have once or twice made a move on his wife. If I ever get married, I hope to find someone as beautiful as my mother, both on the inside and on the outside.

Someone warm.

Kind.

Someone who warms me down to my bones.

Someone the opposite of me or the frigid brats I go to school with.

Ignoring everyone else, I keep my eyes trained on my mother's sweet face smiling down at me as if I am everything good in this world.

I am not.

I'm not.

"I won't change." I won't lie. I tell her the truth.

This is who I am. I do not care for anyone who doesn't share my blood. I won't ever change, but she doesn't need to know that. I am the way I am, but never to her.

I also know that she loves me, but my attitude toward life worries her.

I see it.

"Good." She just wants her son to be a good boy, but I don't have the heart to tell her that something inside of me—something broken stops me from being all she wants. Good and kind.

I'm rude, smart-mouthed, and downright mean when I want to be, and I know it scares her.

It scares them both.

Yet they've never made me feel unwanted or unloved.

Feeling my father's firm hand on my shoulder and my mother's gentle one on the back of my neck, I welcome their embrace. They never fail to make me feel like I belong with them.

"How about we get some pizza on our way home?" Father suggests while the three of us watch our SUV pull at the entrance where we're waiting.

Looking up at him, I ask. "Pineapple pizza?" That shit's good, and that's the only kind I like, to my parent's dismay.

Father looks nauseous, and mom just laughs, even though she, too, finds the combination disgusting. "Sure thing, son." Sure thing. That's my father. The greatest man I know.

"Shit, it's cold." My father curses aloud, then a smack follows as mom hits him on the back of the head as she always does whenever he does it. "Aghh."

"Watch your mouth!" Mom frowns, but it does nothing. Instead, Father pulls her closer and kisses her. I avert my eyes, not wanting to witness my parents sucking faces, but deep down, it makes me glad that my parents still love each other very much and that their marriage is not a fraud like half of his colleagues' marriages. I tuck the queen piece back into my front pocket while my parents stand there in their little bubble, smiling, and so in love. Laughing until it happens.

The worst thing a son could ever witness.

"Ronan!" My mother screams, and then all hell breaks loose, changing my world forever.

It all happens so fast that I am barely able to register it.

One second, we're all laughing, and the next, father stands in front of us, eyes panicked, looking around for someone to help, while my mother urges me back, no longer touching me with a gentle touch.

No.

Her touch is not gentle at all but desperate.

"Cours, mon soleil. Cours!" She shouts desperately in my face while I try my best to hold on to her waist and, at the same time, see what is happening in front of me.

"What is going on!?" I yell, already panicking. "Father!"

The crowd parts, everyone crying in hysterics, seeking shelter from the madness.

Why is no one helping us?

Where is my father's team?

"Hide, son." I have never seen my father this way before. His face looks defeated, with tears in his eyes like mom. Tears form in my eyes in understanding that something is wrong. Really, really wrong.

Father smiles through the tears. "You be a good man, Sebastian. An honest man and someone people will follow. You lead by a sample, do you understand? Tell me you understand, son!" No, I don't.

I don't want to be a good man if this is what happens to them.

I don't understand. I want to scream at him, but the words are stuck in my throat.

"I love you, son." He then, for the first time in my life, turns around and gives me his back, dismissing me. I don't have time to contemplate the meaning of his words when my mother gets in my face, peppering my face with heartbreaking kisses and tears. "I love you to the moon and back, Sebastian." I don't get to tell her I love her to the sun and back, if that were possible. I would do it, consequences be damned.

Because in one second, I have my mother's gentle arms gripping my face, and the next, I am being pushed back into the crowd and away from them. Away from my world.

"Mom! Father! No!" I fight against the sea of people screaming and fleeing like cowards, trying to find my way back to them, but it's too late.

Shots ring out.

Screams hurt my ears.

I manage to get myself free and run back to my parents in time to see our black SUV speed away while a man in a black ski mask waves a gun at the crowd as if he's proud of what he's done.

No.

No.

Please, God. No.

Then I see it.

I see them.

Face down on the ground, covered in blood.

Dropping to my knees, I crawl toward them, covering not only my clothes but my hands, too, in their blood.

Blood.

There is so much of it.

Pooling on the ground and spilling out of my father's mouth.

On his blond hair. His white shirt. God, no.

Why?

Why did this happen?

Who would do this?

"Father! Please!" I move to my father, seeing his eyes closed and his chest no longer moving, and I know he's long gone. With a broken heart, spirit, and soul, I turn away from my father even when it kills me.

Then I move toward my mother and find that she's not dead. Her eyes are unfocused but open. Barely able to breathe, I cradle my mother's bloody body in my arms. "Mommy?" I cry out. I haven't called her that since I was seven years old, but at this moment, I feel like that little boy who called out to his mom whenever he got hurt or had a nightmare. The boy that only felt safe when he was in his beautiful mother's arms.

Mom doesn't speak, there's so much blood, but she manages to lift her hand weakly and touch my heart. A heart that is broken and won't ever beat the same. Not if she leaves me.

She taps my chest twice as tears keep falling from her eyes, mixing with the blood on her cheeks. "I love you. I love you both so much." I whisper so only she can hear. "You'll be alright. Just hang on. Please, mom, please don't leave me." I cry, and I scream until my lungs hurt.

What little remains of my heart breaks the moment her eyes close.

"No, no, no. God, no! Mom!" I rock my mother gently in my arms, willing her to come back. To open her pretty-green eyes and smile at me one last time. But she doesn't. She's gone. They both are.

Rage and grief battle out inside of me.

With a hundred people around us, my parents were gunned down like lowlife criminals, and no one did anything to stop the bad guys from getting to us. Not our security team.

Not the press surrounding us that not for one second stopped taking their fucking photos.

And especially not the elite of Detroit.

No one.

They just stood back and watched as filthy criminals murdered my parents.

This was an ambush.

Someone must've known, and they chose to act against my family. Did they do it for money? Was it one of his political adversaries? The sounds of my cries are drowned by the murmurs all around me. I can't make anything they're saying except one thing.

One name.

Parisi.

Loosening my hold on mom, I look down at the blood on my hands and lock the image of them in my memory to never forget what happened tonight. Dropping on my hunches, still holding my mother close, I look up at the dark sky to see the full moon. December 23rd.

The night my world was torn apart, one bullet at a time.

How ironic is it that my mother would sit outside for hours to watch the moon in all its glory, and now the moon got to witness what happened tonight. It's a witness to my mother's broken and dead body.

Rocking back and forward, I let the hate consume me, coursing through my body like a deadly poison.

Grief, hatred, and denial.

That's all I feel at this moment.

"Sebastian." I hear multiple people call my name, but I can't focus on anything but my pain.

"Sebastian."

"Sebastian."

"Sebastian."

My parents taught me to love but Parisi…Parisi taught me the true definition of hate.

Not being able to handle this heartbreak… I shatter.

And then I cry and scream until I pass out.

Until all I see is black.

***

"You did it, man," Banning says from behind me as we both stand watching the craziness all around us. "Kenton!"

"Kenton!"

"Kenton!"

The chanting of my name grows louder, almost frantic.

"Did you ever doubt me?" I mutter.

I made it happen.

After years of lying, cheating, and scheming my way through every social circle where assholes with shit for brains called the shots, and a hellish presidential race, I succeeded.

I accomplished what the young man used to crave more than anything after he lost what he loved most.

What kept his heart dreaming…

His parents.

"Not for one second." My right hand, sometimes asshole but always a loyal friend, replies.

The crowd goes wild, shouting my name and clapping all around me as I am announced as the 47th president of the United States of America.

All I ever wanted…until her.

To be at the top.

To all that my father wasn't able to do because of Gabriele Parisi.

I smile and greet the crowd but it pains me.

The organ in my chest aches.

Smiling hurts.

It's been hurting for months since I made the biggest mistake of my life.

When I experienced loss for the second time in my goddamn life.

This time by my own doing.

Smiling at the people who elected me one last time, I look up at the sky. There's no full moon tonight. Hell, there's not even one single star in the sky. Dark. Empty. Like half of my fucking heart.

"Find your way back to me," I whisper into the night, but my voice is drowned by the loud noises around me. Fuck.

I got where I wanted to be for so long, but it doesn't feel like I thought it would. I know now that nothing will ever feel the same as long as she's away from me.

Looking back at the crowd, I search for her, but I know she's not there. She disappeared as if she was never here to begin with. A ghost. My ghost. Once I got my head out of my ass enough to realize my mistake, I went after her, but the damage was done. She was long gone. My girl. Half of my heart. The irony… My enemy's daughter took my heart with her the day she disappeared and made it impossible for me to reach her. She was nowhere to be found.

"She's gone…" Banning's words back then play on a loop—over and over again. A firm hand brings me back to the moment and away from the painful thoughts of her. Banning. "It's time for your speech, boss." Even the happiest motherfucker I know sounds as if he too lost a part of himself. I never regretted anything in my life until the day I let my fears, guilt, and past hang-ups get the best of me. If I could turn back time, I would. I would go back to that day, drop down to my knees, and beg her to be mine for the whole world to see. But life doesn't work like that. We don't always get what we want. And now I'm here. I became the president who received more votes than any other candidate in U.S. history. The most powerful man in the country. A man who got everything he ever wanted and, at the same time, lost all he ever needed.

Her.

PART ONE

LOVE

& WAR

To say that I was a dumbass would be an understatement. - B

Chapter 1
MONUMENTAL FUCK-UP

Bastian

"Whoever said if you love something
set it free is one dumb motherfucker." – Ben

"I must say that beating your ass at cards doesn't feel as satisfying as it used to when you act like a miserable fuck, Mr. President." The bane of my existence, Sandoval, mocks me as he pushes his chips toward the middle of the table.

Leaning back on the chair, I throw my chips at him, and before he grabs them to declare himself the winner, I show him my cards.
A royal flush.
The highest poker hand.
The fucker laughs as if losing three million and a brand-new white Rolls Royce Boat Tailis nothing.
I guess for men like us it is like losing a tooth.
It is worth nothing.
Doesn't even hurt.
"You are one disturbed individual, Sandoval. How you are so happy when you just lost another family business, a car, and a great deal of money tonight is beyond me." I take a sip of my whiskey and place the glass down next to my winnings.

Even that does not thrill me anymore.

Winning.

It used to.

Oh, it was all I cared about aside from my daughter, but now it doesn't feel the same.

The boss of the Sandoval crime family shrugs and takes a long drag of his cigar before expelling the smoke my way. "It's just material shit, Seb. It all can be replaced or earned back." He mumbles while chewing on his cigar. Taking a good look at my friend, I notice the dark circles under his eyes are less visible, and he doesn't look as terrible as he did the last time I saw him, but the hatred and anger the death of his loved ones caused still linger, only more intense and fresher now that he lost his right-hand man. Rodrigo Valencia. One of the best men he had. A criminal with a good heart. That is hard to come by.

Sandoval only had him after losing his entire family, and now only the shell of a man I once knew remains. Angry. Fuck, at times, suicidal.

We wait in silence for the dealer to finish setting up the table and hand us our cards. One of the many things we have in common is the loss of the ones we loved most, but unlike him, I didn't have to witness my little girl being murdered in front of me.

Nothing could ever make that right.

Nothing.

It's still a mystery to me how his heart still beats after his daughter's stopped. Fuck, just the thought of that happening to me makes my body grow cold.

Thankfully, the ringing of a phone brings my thoughts back from the dark.

Sandoval's phone.

He picks it up and immediately starts to argue with the person on the other end of the line. From the loud screeching, it is obvious that it is a woman. His wife?

I watch him hang up and throw the phone down at the table after calling her a vindictive bitch.

Sensing the mood growing dark, I ask him, changing the topic. "How do you do it? How do you stay with a woman who's sucking the soul right out of you?"

He takes another drag of his cigar and throws back what's left of his drink before sighing. "She's my punishment." The miserable bastard says staring straight at me with soulless eyes then a mocking smile appears on his face. "Besides good women…good women who bring heaven to men like us don't exist."

Good women.

Heaven.

Lighting up a cigar, I take a quick drag, exhaling the smoke upwards. "I had that once." I had that, and I fucked it up. I hurt her, and there's no going back from that, yet I still try. I tried countless times to find her, but she made it impossible for me to do so. "What?" Sandoval asks while looking straight at me with brows furrowed.

"A good girl. The best girl." I find myself getting angry with myself all over, knowing damn well that there is no healing from the scars her heartbreak left. "She was my heaven on Earth, and I hurt her."

A long silence follows before Sandoval speaks. "Are you referring to that pretty blonde prime pussy from years ago?" Raising my head, my grip on my cigar tightens, and I pin him with a look that says, 'say that shit again and you'll find yourself with my cigar shoved inside your eye socket.' But Sandoval could care less about insulting me or anyone close to me, aside from my child. He never goes there nor do I think he ever will. "You know...Seba. What you did to that girl was cold, and that's coming from a cold fucker like me. The whole goddamn world witnessed that girl–" I interrupt him before his words cut me deeper, more than they already have. "Shut the fuck up, Sandoval." I know what I did. I didn't need him reminding me of my monumental fuck up. Besides, the son of a bitch has no moral ground to talk about what happened. The asshole ambushed an innocent woman and her kid. Luckily for them, he got his head out of his ass in time and didn't go through with murdering a world-renowned fashion designer and her young child.

Kids are off limits, and he knows it too.

He shrugs, "*La verdad duele,* Sebastian. Don't blame me for your stupidity and, instead, deal with it." He mumbles while looking at his dealt cards. "Nobody likes a whiny bitch."

Scoffing, I let that one slide because going back and forth with Thiago Sandoval sometimes, no, most of the time, feels like arguing with a child.

One of his men approaches the table and whispers something in his ear that makes him tense. "*Cabrón.*" He growls before whispering something back to his man and dismissing him.

"Problem?" I ask him.

"Nothing that concerns you. Just Detroit filth stinking up my city. I'll handle it as I always do." He says darkly before adding more chips to his bet.

Doing the same, I speak. "Nicolasi or the Volpe family?"

"Both."

It hurts to say the fucking name, but there's no use since Kadra Parisi always stays away from petty dramas between the cities. Her only issue is with New York, from what I have heard.

New York and Philly.

The two cities are run by the Russians and the Irish.

Sandoval, on the other hand, has issues with Lucan Volpe and Lorenzo Nicolasi. One is the son of the man who murdered his daughter, sister, and mother, and the other punk posing as a capo is the one who murdered Rodrigo in retaliation.

Feeling the hassle of the day get to me suddenly, I find myself exhausted and ready to go back home to Washington. Ready to get back to my Ellaiza. I had to leave her behind with Banning and half of my security back at the White House to attend three social events here in Chicago for two of my organizations.

Where I had to put on my best smile and pretend.

I was used to pretending before, but I was numb to it all. I am not numb now, and I feel everything. I have to admit that it is getting to me.

Emptying my glass of whiskey, I show Sandoval my cards, knowing I lost this game. My head just wasn't in it. "I guess I'll be vacationing in PR soon, Seba." My longtime friend shows me his cards, declaring himself the winner, yet he doesn't smile, and there's only a blank look on his face.

"My lawyer will be drawing the papers, naming you the new owner of the resort," I tell him at the same time I stand up from the chair, and the moment I do, the wall of criminals standing guard behind their boss face off against my team of men.

"Always a pleasure, Sebastian." Sandoval puts his hand out for me to shake, and I do.

The fucking irony.

The president of the United States is playing in an underground casino with one of the most ruthless crime lords in the country, who happens to be one of my closest friends.

"See you around, Sandoval." I button my suit, nod once, and head out the door, ready to go back home and leave a city that haunts me behind. The same city where my once-dead heart broke and hasn't recovered since.

"Sundance is on the move. Heading out now. Get the cars ready." My third in command, Nix, appointed by Banning, talks into his wrist to the rest of the team. My secret service team was trained and chosen carefully by my most trusted man, Benjamin Banning.

Therefore, they're all assholes with a shitty sense of humor.

Sundance.

The motherfucker chose Sundance as my security code name the moment I was appointed the chief of command. No amount of threatening did anything to stop him from using the godawful nickname, so now it's stuck. Nix and the rest of my men form a circle around with their hands tucked inside their vests, ready for any threat that might come my way as they lead me out of the Sandoval mansion's back exit. When we do get there and have almost reached the van, a crowd of paparazzi ambushes us taking photos and asking idiotic questions. "President Kenton here. Look here!" One shouts, trying to get past my wall of security. Sighing, I think to myself that some people should pray for brains at night.

"President Kenton! What business do you have with an alleged criminal?" A woman shouts over the noise. I know Thiago Sandoval is a criminal, but there certainly is nothing common about him. Besides, the man might do questionable shit, but he gets shit done for his city more than the elected officials and the department of justice.

How the fuck did they find out I would be meeting with Sandoval? I wonder. The shouts get louder and the questions more desperate while the flashes of cameras are causing a headache. My team gets me outside, and in a minute, we're all climbing inside the cars and speeding the hell out of there. Resting my head back on the leather headrest, I take a long breath. I try my best to keep my meetings with the bosses of each city secret, but tonight someone leaked my whereabouts. It has been happening a lot lately.

The paparazzi and media are being tipped, and they show up everywhere. Every time I go somewhere alone, somewhere something like this happens. I'm only grateful that it never happens when I'm with my girl. She's always safe and away from the media if I can help it, so whoever the fucker is that's been messing with me, at least has the decency to keep my child out of it.

Nix looks over at me from the rearview mirror, "747-200B is ready, sir."

Nodding once, I turn away and look out the car's window as we leave the press behind.

Front-page news again… shit.

Chapter 2
TWO BROKEN HEARTS

Bastian

"She woke up today and chose violence." — B

"Good evening, Mr. President." The twenty-something tank of a man guarding my daughter's door greets me as I approach. "Shaw." I greet back. "Did anything happen while I was away?" I stop in front of my daughter's bedroom door, that's just a few feet away from my own. The White House is a residence with 132 rooms and six levels, which can be overwhelming for a six-year-old child and scary at times, too. This is a fact my daughter has been very loud about, and of course, I always listen. I will always consider her feelings.

Every time. No matter what.

Shaw, the head of her security team, gave me the specifics of her daily activities while I was away. All this while he has a pearl necklace on and one pearl earring. Shaking my head, I point at his neck. "I see she has you playing dress up now."

He smiles sheepishly. "Moonshine can be very persuasive, Sir."

Moonshine.

Ellaiza's security code was given to her by Shaw himself. Sundance and

Moonshine. Terribly corny.

My men are nuisances, and I still wonder why I haven't ridden myself of them. Then I look at Shaw and remind myself that they love my girl. And she needs all the love she can get. Now more than ever.

My chest feels tight when my thoughts wander to a gorgeous blonde with green eyes and a beautiful heart. Fuck.

"Thank you, Shaw. You can make your rounds while I tuck her in." I pat his shoulder and move to open her door, but he stops me. "Sir."

I look over my shoulder at him. "Yes?"

"Ellaiza... she was not herself today."

Turning to face him, I ask worriedly. "What makes you think that?"

The young man sighs and then continues. "She usually lights up everyone's day with her smiles, but today she barely laughed. Hell, she didn't even bust Ares's and Levy's balls today." Shaw steps back, "I don't know. Maybe I'm overreacting, sir." He says gruffly.

Nodding once, I turn the knob, opening my daughter's room. "You worry about my girl?"

"Of course, that's my job, sir."

No, it is not his job. His job is to make sure no threats come her way. My job is to worry about her, but I'm thankful regardless.

Stepping inside the room, my mood instantly brightens when I see my child sitting at her desk writing in her little pink journal. To my utter dismay, my daughter is crazy about the color pink. Everything in her room is either silver or pink, and I know that is all because of the woman who brought me back to life.

When Ellaiza was a toddler, Arianna used to dress her up in pink and only bought her girly clothes so of course, my daughter grew up to be a girly girl, just like her best friend.

A best friend.

The best friend she used to call mommy.

Fuck, I have the sudden urge to vomit.

When the reality of my mistake hits me, I am helpless against it.

Holding back the pain, I smile when my daughter turns around and offers me a small grin. "Hello, father."

Frowning, I walk towards her, snatch her from the seat and take her into my arms. "What have I told you about calling me that? When you turn thirty, you can call me father if you wish to do so, but until then. It's daddy to you."

She sighs dramatically, as if I am being ridiculous. "It's no big deal, daddy." She says playfully, making me smile, but I know she did it to placate me. When did my six-year-old become so wise and sarcastic?

The brat… That's who created my beautiful little monster who sometimes is as sweet as can be, and other times… she gives me a run for my money. How her tiny body holds so much sass is beyond me.

Kissing her cheek slowly, I carry her to bed, and then tuck her in. Taking a seat at the edge of the bed, I push a soft raven curl behind her ear. My baby is so beautiful. She no longer has the baby fat that used to melt my heart when she was smaller, but her chubby face, gentle eyes, and blinding smile remain. What in the fuck am I going to do when she grows up? Maybe I can hide her away and keep her from danger…especially the dangers who have dicks. Christ. She's already boy crazy. It doesn't escape me the way she looks at Shaw. As if the guard hangs the stars for her. *"Tu m'as manqué, mon coeur."* I whisper and watch as her face lights up and a smile breaks.

Fuck, I love my kid.

"Tu m'as plus manqué." Laughing, I poke her small nose.

My daughter is a genius. No, I am not being one of those parents that believe their kids are geniuses just because they learn to walk before most kids.

No, my Ellaiza is gifted.

She skipped a grade when one of her teachers approached me regarding Ellaiza's disinterest in the material she was teaching to the class. At first, I worried that she might have had a learning disability, but no. It turns out my girl was just bored since she already knew the material before the rest of the kids. So, I took her to get tested, and she scored high in the profoundly gifted percentile.

"Shaw tells me you're not acting like yourself. Mind telling me what's wrong?"

My daughter, I kid you not, rolls her eyes at me. "Shaw worries too much."

Laughing aloud with my entire heart, which I only do when it comes to Ellaiza, I agree with her. "He does worry. We all worry. Want to know why?"

"Pourquoi?"

"Parce que nous t'aimons tous."

She gives me a small smile that has my heart clenching. My daughter is a ray of sunshine on most days. Yes, she has tantrums and down days like every kid her age. She might talk like a petty, brilliant thirty-year-old woman, but she's just a child.

A child who's growing up right before the world's eyes.

Shit.

"I love you all, too, daddy." Daddy.

Thud.

Thud.

My broken heart beats for my kid. Slow but steady.

"Now come on, baby. Tell me what's wrong?"

"I don't want you to feel sad." She whispers timidly.

"Why would I feel sad? You can tell me anything, Ellaiza. Anything." I grab her tiny chin and make her look me in the eyes. "I'm the parent, and I can handle anything."

"Like a supervillain?" Leave it to my kid to root for the villain instead of the hero. When I asked her once if she thought I was a bad guy, she shook her head frantically and told me that she always roots for the villains because they love the hardest. Fuck if I know where she got that from, but it warms my heart that she sees the good in everyone.

"Like a supervillain." I agree.

"Promettez-vous?" she whispers.

"Traverse, mon coeur."

A few seconds pass before she gets the courage to be honest with me about her feelings. "I miss mommy." She whispers sadly, and it's a bullet straight to the heart.

I miss mommy.

Crack.

If it's even possible to feel one's heart break, I feel that at this moment.

I did this. Not only to the woman I love and myself.

To my child, as well.

Grabbing her small hand in mine, I give her only the truth. Well, half-truths because I'm a coward, and she wouldn't understand that selfishly, I was trying to be selfless.

I was trying to be the better man.

A good man worthy of both of them.

"She misses you, too. That, I am sure."

"Is she done reaching for the stars, daddy?" Her face crumbles when she asks. Fuck.

I lied the day I told Arianna that Ellaiza was young and she would easily forget. I was an asshole and didn't mean it. That was just the nail in the coffin. Just what I needed for her to leave.

And I haven't stopped regretting it since. And that is my penance to pay. I did keep their memories together alive in my daughter's mind. Not a day went by that I didn't bring up Arianna in conversation or showed my daughter pictures and videos of them.

My daughter knows who Arianna is to her.

Her mother.

That will never change.

Nor time or distance.

I made sure of that.

But as she got older, she started asking questions. The questions that are getting harder to answer every year. Kids her age have their mommies, and she doesn't, so she asked, and I told her the truth.

That Arianna is reaching for the stars. She's away following her dreams, but she will come home.

God, I hope she comes home.

I made this bed of lies and regrets, and now we all must lie in it.

The bile in my throat as I smile through the little white lies has me feeling like the biggest piece of shit on the planet, but I do it anyway to keep my child from pain.

"She will be, and she'll find her way back to you." To us is on the tip of my tongue. "She'll be back, my heart. She loves you too much to not come back. Trust me. Trust her."

Ellaiza smiles more genuinely now. "Okay. I believe you."

"Good." Bending over, I kiss her forehead and linger a second longer, taking in her sweet scent. Pulling back, I notice something silver sticking out from under her pillow. Reaching for it, I see it's a framed photo of Ellaiza and Arianna in Paris. One of the many I took back then.

I had it framed for her even when it killed me to look at it. It reminds me of what I've done.

"I like holding it. Just like Mr. Bugs." She raises her hand, showing me the small pink rabbit Arianna gave her when she was a baby. Fuck, I can't breathe, but I smile anyway. For her. Always for her.

"Let's place it on the nightstand so it doesn't break, yes?" I place the frame next to her night lamp. "There. You can see it every time you close and open your eyes."

Ellaiza nods, looking up at me from the bed.

"Get some sleep." I kiss her one more time and walk toward the door, but before I step outside her room, her sweet voice stops me.

"Daddy?"

"Yes, my heart?"

"Did you kill your speeches?" She asks, sounding so much like the men on her security team.

"You need to stop spending so much time with grownups." I smile back at her. "But yes, yes, I did."

"Next time, I want to go with you." She pouts.

Shaking my head, "You know how I feel about you attending those kinds of events."

"I know you don't want me mixing with brainless do-do heads." She giggles into her fist.

"That is correct. I also need you to always be safe." I am not risking my daughter's safety if I can prevent it.

"You, Shaw, and Ben will keep me safe." Her trust in me. Her trust in my men humbles me.

"You can be my date to the next event." I give in.

She beams. "Promise?"

"Promise."

"Cross your heart and hope to die?" She tilts her head and asks.

I place my hand on my chest, giving her my eyes. "Cross my heart."

"Mad love for you, daddy." My daughter whispers while looking up at me with a smile that reminds me of my mother and eyes the exact shade of my own and my father's.

My heart hurts, but it also beats strong when Ellaiza reminds me of them. "Mad love, my heart."

"Goodnight." I turn her light out and leave.

Hoping and fucking praying that Arianna comes back because, if not, I don't know how to console that shit. My daughter's first heartbreak shouldn't be one I cause.

Fuck.

There are two broken hearts in this home.

Chapter 3
SHAWBEAR
Ellaiza

"My daddy says I am the prettiest girl in the whole world. Under twenty-four, of course." – E

As soon as Dad closes the door behind him, I wait a couple of seconds before getting out of bed and walking toward the windows. Climbing up the steps Benjamin placed in front of the window so I could reach it, I push the curtains aside, and look at the night. From here, I can see the main entrance to the house. Our big white house. Dad's friends are all standing outside on every corner guarding us, so the bad guys stay away. Then I look up at the sky and count all the stars. There aren't many tonight because they're hiding.

Is that why mommy hasn't come home yet? Because she can't reach the stars since they're hiding?

"Where are you, mommy?" I whisper, hoping in my heart that she comes home soon. I don't remember her, and that makes me sad.

I only know her by the photos and videos dad shows me every time I ask about her. Although, sometimes when I close my eyes, I hear her soft laugh. All my friends at school have their mommies. All except Kyrie. He has two daddies.

And sometimes I feel bad because some kids don't have any mommies or daddies, and I have the bestest dad in the whole world.

"Goodnight, mommy," I whisper, before closing the curtain. Maybe she's looking at the sky, too, and thinking of me.

Maybe.

Knock, Knock.

Oh-uh.

Busted.

I run fast towards the bed and dive in under the covers, but before I invite them in, the door bursts open, revealing an amused-looking Shaw.

"Now, I know your dad put you to bed minutes ago, Moonshine."

My silly heart flips every time he calls me that.

It doesn't do anything different when all the others called me that.

Weird.

"Shaw-bear." I try my best to sound grown up, like Chloe, our chef, does every time Shaw walks in the room.

I don't like Chloe.

She smells like onions.

I also don't like onions.

Plus, she's always hogging all of Shaw's attention.

Yes, I don't like Chloe.

My friend, Kyrie, when he comes over always sings the kissing song when he sees Chloe and Shaw together.

It's stupid.

The names don't even sound good together.

Chloe and Shaw.

Blahh.

Shaw moves closer, walking to the bed dressed in his usual clothing.

A black suit with black boots. No tie and no leather shoes like all the other men on dad's team.

Uncle Benji is always yelling at Shaw to follow the clothing protocols, but Shaw never does.

That's why they're always fighting with each other.

It's funny.

He's also the youngest on the team. I don't know exactly how old he is, but I hear Uncle Benji calling him a child, so I'm guessing he's younger than Uncle Benji.

"I brought you something."

Gasping in excitement, I sit in bed, extending my palm toward him.

Shaw shakes his head, pulls out something from his back, and places it in my waiting hand.

A chocolate cupcake with pink frosting.

My absolute favorite.

Not even waiting a second, I take a big bite, making Shaw laugh quietly.

"Dad's going to be mad at youuuuuu," I tease him with my mouth full.

Not very ladylike… but oh well. I love me some cupcakes.

All my happy memories include cupcakes and candy.

Shaw shrugs but says nothing, watching me eat my cupcake.

After I'm done, he grabs the paper cup from my hand and stuffs it inside his pants pocket.

"Was it good?" He asks me while wiping my face and getting rid of the crumbs on the bed.

"Exquisite," I answer truthfully.

Laughing, he says, "You're too smart for your own good, you know that?"

I shrug. "I know."

"Are you happy, Ella?"

Nodding once, I answer. "Now, I am."

"Good." His dark eyes shine just like the stars outside my window. How rare. "Now go brush your teeth and get some sleep."

I get out of bed and head to the bathroom to do as he says, but before I go all the way inside, I turn to him. "You're the best, Shaw. After daddy, of course."

"Right back atcha, Moonshine." He smiles, and my heart does another flip. Settle down, you stupid organ.

Shaw half grins, "And, of course, it's our secret, kid." With that, he leaves.

I don't feel so sad anymore.

Cupcakes are always the cure for a bad day.

Shaw, too.

Shaw makes every day the best day.

Yes.

Chapter 9
PRESS AND PRICKS

Bastian

"The press is a real pain in my ass." — B

"Mr. President, you're on in two minutes." Baron, my press secretary, reminds me as he walks behind while typing rapidly on his tablet. As we both head with Banning leading us to the house's press room, Baron briefs me briefly on questions the journalist might ask. All eyes will be on me, including those of our adversaries in China, Russia, and Iran. How I perform shows the country and the world that voters made the right choice when they elected me.

Today's press conference will tackle updates on all the shit I promised during the campaign trail. An update with gotcha questions on their side meant to catch me on a lie.

Easy on my part.

Terribly difficult on theirs.

They have to get me to slip up, and that won't happen.

I'll go out there, smile, charm my way through the tough questions, give them what they want, and get out.

This is nothing new.

Once outside the doors of the conference room, Baron finishes giving me the statistics and numbers necessary to give the information to the people and then steps aside, allowing me space to enter the room where the press is waiting.

After my horrible experience with Celene, I decided to stop hiring women. Not all women are like that overbearing psycho, but I'm not risking it this time around. Three years ago, Banning dug deep and tracked the IP address where the leaks of mine and Arianna's whereabouts came from, and it all led to Celene.

Not too bright that one. How did I miss that still fucks with my head.

She fed the media shit about all the women who I courted before.

Then when Arianna came along, she got more desperate, and the bitch turned on me. Maybe she could sense that what I had with Arianna was different than what I had with every woman who came before her.

She was also the last one to speak with Arianna when she confronted me outside, asking about the name of the man who murdered my parents.

It didn't take me long to piece the information together.

It all led back to Celene.

Because of her betrayal, I ruined her the same way she tried to ruin me.

Haven't heard from her since.

And if she ever crawls out of the hole she hid in, I'll be here waiting to deal with her for good. I don't handle betrayal kindly, and ruining her credibility and career was an act of mercy on my part because the the alternative would have ended badly for her.

As in five feet under bad.

Baron nods at me once before entering the press room to read aloud my established schedule for the press.

It hasn't started, and I am already bored.

It's the same every time. One side is never happy with my decisions, and the other side just kisses my ass with basic questions to make me look good and not challenge my authority.

The question-and-answer session can last up to 90 minutes, though the length of the daily briefing varies.

That's 90 minutes too long, in my opinion.

Taking a deep breath, I adjust my tie and stride towards the room with my game face on and my charming smile. The smile that got me elected apart from my empty promises. Banning, the asshole, salutes me before opening the double doors and motioning for me to enter. "Good luck, Sundance."

"Fuck off." I cross the threshold of the room when I hear his reply. "I love you, too."

He is one insufferable asshole, but he's loyal to a fault, and that makes up for half the shit he does to test my patience.

The moment I step into the room, taking my place behind the podium, the flashes of the cameras are relentless.

The whole world is watching, daddy. Smile big and make them fall in love. My daughter's sweet and innocent words replay in my mind as I take the room in. It's a small crowd of journalists from different news outlets today. I specifically told Baron that I didn't want the same people asking me questions at every press conference. The White House Correspondents Association assigned seats to every credentialed member of the media today.

No matter how big or small the outlets, they'll all get a chance to attend. That decision won me brownie points with half of the media in the country, which reiterates the fact that it was a successful strategic move.

With my team and the flag of this country behind me, I address the press. "Good afternoon." I smile for the cameras. "Thank you for being here." And so I open the conference with updates on how, during this current term, inflation has gone down tremendously since the last administration. I speak on the low rates of crime and how they are at their lowest. I speak on hate crimes in specific parts of the country and how this united administration has helped fight them with inclusion and empathy. All of these are words from Baron, of course.

Lord knows I can't be honest with the country, or all hell will break loose more than it already has.

I don't tell them that the reason crime has settled in the streets is because the mafia, bratva, and the Irish control them.

The false sense of security the civilians have is all because of them, not their glorified good guys. The men in blue. The cops.

Not even me.

Their chief in command.

The one they look up to for guidance.

I'm a criminal, too, just one who pays for others to get dirty.

After I'm done, the floor is open for the media to get their turn to ask questions.

Here we go.

The usual first questions.

Status of our troops.

I give them the answer they desperately want while lying through gritted teeth. They want me to undo years of fucked-up decisions by past administrations in three years.

My administration agreed to a peace deal that would have US troops out of war zones by June 2nd, and we're sticking to that deadline.

Sighing, I keep my composure when the snarky and gotcha questions start. I answer a couple more from the Associated Press that takes me twenty or so minutes to get through before we reach the end of the conference. Still, before I go, I call on a young lady sitting quietly at the back of the room with an iPad in one hand and her phone in the other, most likely recording the conference. She hasn't raised her hand during the time established nor made any attempt to ask a question until now. "Mr. President. Good afternoon. My name is Nessa Adams, journalist for the Washington Weekly. The last administration severed most of our ties with Europe. What have you done, if you've done anything, of course, to make good without allies again?" She steps closer to the stage with a cunning smile on her face. Not a petty, conniving smile like some of these assholes here, but more 'I'm hungry for the story'smile.

Another gotcha question. After a few times of doing these types of conferences, you learn quickly that most journalists don't care about the state of the country. No.

They only care about getting that one hot piece to break to the media before anyone else. They want nothing more than to catch you in a lie or point out your mistakes. Specialists are the ones that are just starting and need to prove themselves.

I don't blame them.

You must be ruthless to climb ahead of everyone else.

That I understand oh too well.

"I want it known that the United States and Europe are fully united. This morning I had a long conversation with our NATO allies. German Chancellor Weber, French President Dupont, Prime Minister Azarov, and Italian Prime Minister Ricci to continue to strengthen our union and show our overseas enemies that we're stronger now more than ever.

We're also continuing to work with our other overseas allies as well. The Vice President is currently meeting with the Italian Prime Minister in his country." With a condescending yet naturally charming smile, I finish answering her question leaving her no option but to move on to another question.

Whoever says lying gets you nowhere is an imbecile.

Nessa, the young journalist, clears her throat while everyone has their eyes on her. You can clearly see the girl is not amused by my answer or unshakable composure, but the rest of the press is eating this shit up.

The girl, Nessa, continues asking the tough questions no one here had the balls to ask, and while I take my time answering her, I realize she reminds me of someone.

Not her looks, but her take-no-shit attitude.

My chest feels tight like every day since she, and sometimes I find it difficult to breathe. To find my next breath.

"We know you've pardoned five criminals since becoming president. They were high-profile criminals who deserved jail time, yet you got them free and into our streets. Mind sharing the thought process of that decision. Doesn't seem like a wise one."

I smile big and give her half-truths. My version of the truth.

I pardoned them because they're the type of men that don't mind getting their hands dirty to help get rid of the scum of the earth that walk amongst us in high positions of power. I might lie, cheat, and scheme, but I never once hurt someone innocent in my eyes.

In the eyes of God.

And Kayro Cho, Arson West, Adryel Thorne, and Croix Jameson are men this country needs more of.

Trustworthy criminals.

"I believe everyone deserves a second chance." I could care less about giving them a second chance. I just want the best criminals on my side. It always gives me a winning hand.

"Even cops and doctors who murder innocent people?" She asks.

"If you did your research, Miss. Adams, you are aware that both men committed horrible crimes, yes, but horrible crimes were made against them, as well, and our justice system failed them. They failed those countless innocent women Walsh murdered in cold blood. Although I don't condone violence in any form, I do understand that bad things happen to good men that lead them to make hard decisions for the sake of themselves and others." Click.

Click.

Murmurs and flashes all around me.

Ms. Adams grits her teeth but doesn't give up now. She will die on this heel. "What about the man who killed a cop? What about him? Is he excused by your law too? The Pyromaniac?"

"I would recommend you dig deeper, Miss. Adams. You would be surprised what you will find about those four criminals, as you call them. There's always more to the story."

After I'm done answering her questions, Baron lets her know I have time for one more question before I head out.

"You like games, don't you, Mr. President?" The room falls quiet after that question while Baron steps forward to shut the journalist down, but I stop him.

While my heart races like it hasn't for three years.

It's like it is slowly coming back to life. Not completely, but it's a start.

"I do." I don't know what prompted her to ask the question that was not briefed by Baron, but I allow it, feeling something rattle inside of me.

Rather someone.

The girl smiles sarcastically. "Men like you always win, yes?"

Smiling wide, I answer the honest to God truth, "I'm your president, darling. That answers your question." The darling part hurts me, but I throw it in there because my gut feeling never fails me, and something tells me this girl here asking me the same question Arianna did years ago is not a coincidence.

I don't believe in those.

Smiling one last time, I thank everyone for their time and leave the press room with Benjamin and Baron hot on my back. "Baron."

"Yes, sir?"

"I need all the information you can find about Miss. Adams from Washington Weekly's on my desk before the day is over."

"On it, Mr. President."

My mind starts reeling, and all kinds of thoughts pop through my head as I make my way to the Oval Office, with just Benjamin following suit. The guards open the doors of the office, and I step in, only then I'm able to release the breath I've been holding since I stepped out of the press room. Making my way to the window, I look outside and take a second to contemplate my next move.

Could it be…?

Am I just thinking there is more to this than what it is?

Maybe…

After three years…

I searched for her for years, I am still searching. I never gave up even when she tried her best to disappear, leaving no trace for my men to follow.

She made it seem as if she was never on this earth.

Making it almost impossible to be found even with my money and resources. My Arianna is clever, and I underestimated her intelligence and her need to be away from me. No credit history. She didn't use her credit cards. Her name didn't pop up anywhere.

And as cunning and incredibly brilliant as she is, she couldn't have done this on her own.

Someone must've helped her.

All these years, I had an inkling that Banning had a hand in it, but I always chuck it off as being a jealous fuck.

His loyalty should be to me, but what I didn't take into consideration is that I was the one who made him take care of her since she was just eighteen years old.

A bond was formed during their time together, but I was so focused on my loss that I put it on the back burner until now. "You're awfully quiet there, Banning," I speak up after a long moment of silence, still staring out the window. Are you out there? I wonder. "Got nothing to say, boss." He shrugs. I chuckle drily. "That's a first." Banning is not the same man as before. I did that, too. I'm to blame. Fuck. "Are there any updates on her?" A day hasn't gone by that I don't ask, but he never had anything to say. She was just gone. She vanished into thin air like a magic trick.

Black magic she was.

"Still nothing, boss." I used to feel defeated every time he would give me the same answer as now, but at this moment, I feel skeptical, and although the idea that Banning helped her keep her from me pisses me the fuck off, at the same time, I am glad she had someone there for her. When I wasn't. Fuck.

Before I get to ask more, a knock at the door interrupts me.

Sighing, "Come in."

The doors to the Oval Office open, and Baron enters the room. "Mr. President, here is all the information the team gathered on the journalist." Turning to him, I take the yellow envelope from him and walk towards my desk, taking a seat.

"Thank you, Baron. You may leave."

"There's something else, sir."

"What is it?"

"A short clip of the press conference was posted online."

"And?"

"It doesn't look good, sir. The clip was of Ms. Adams' questions, and you look…"

"Spit it out." I bite.

"You don't look all that confident in it, Mr. President." Baron clears his throat. "They made it seem as if you were rattled by the young interviewer."

Looking down at the file, I speak directly to my right-hand man. "Banning."

"Yes, Mr. president?"

"I want to know everything there is to know about the CEO of the Washington Weekly and everyone who works there." For all its worth, I have to give it to him. If he has something to hide, he sure doesn't act like it.

He nods, then steps out of the office.

If I want the truth, I'll have to seek other resources because, one thing I am sure of, Banning won't give out Arianna, not even for me.

"Baron."

"Yes, Mr. President?"

"You may leave."

51

"Of course," He nods, excuses himself, and disappears, leaving me alone with a racing heart and new purpose thrumming through my veins.

Reaching for my phone, I unlock it and search for the video Baron mentioned. It was posted on the company's website. From what I can tell, I've been their most popular topic recently, but what's interesting is the fact that they're fairly new. Launching their newspaper and magazine a month ago. Huh.

Standing from my chair, I walk toward the window once again. I stand there with a big fucking smile on my face because, for the first time in three years, I don't feel like half of my heart is dead.

She promised to show me how it feels to hurt.

Well, here I am, darling.

Make it hurt.

At this time, Arianna decided to act up on her promise of war.

She fired the first shot and instead of being angry, I feel a sense of thrill I haven't felt in three long years.

My girl's come home.

THE GOSSIP ROOM

The youngest president in U.S. history, President Kenton was seen attending a charity event with a mystery woman. Could it be that the President finally found the one after a long trail of broken hearts?

By Kelly Garrett | 04/27/2023 12:12 PM EST

Chapter 5
PRESS AND PRICKS

Arianna

"Sometimes you must be a bitch to remain on top." - A

G I guessed I was no stranger to it. To the way everything felt excruciatingly heavy lately.

Suffocating.

Most days, my breaths were so strained it was a labor to draw them into my aching lungs.

Maybe I knew the feeling, but I was sure I'd never felt it so distinctly as for the last three years.

Looking out my office's window, where the city moves at full speed below me, my mind takes me elsewhere. To a simpler time when all seemed so perfect and real. It was perfect, yes, but it wasn't real.

I can still recall the husky way he said it. "The world is yours. You just have to want it enough to take it." I remember it all. The cold wind on my face and the beautiful view of Paris in the winter. His hot breaths on my neck and his larger-than-life presence still linger. The memory of that day in Paris when Sebastian took me on a hot-air balloon ride is still vivid in my memory, just like every memory I ever shared with him.

The only difference is that now I feel nothing.

That's a lie. I do feel something.

Rage.

Before, those memories would keep me up at night, crying until I made myself sick, just enough to fall asleep and then do it all over again.

Haunting me. Some people say time heals all wounds, but does it really? Because my wounds are still present, and very fucking angry.

Bleeding.

Scarring.

Not yet healed.

Fueling this hatred that has kept my head above water for three long years.

Three years where I went through all the emotions. From heartbreak, abandonment, denial, anger, and finally, acceptance.

Acceptance that I wouldn't be able to fully move on until he felt the same way he made me feel.

Small.

Betrayed.

Hurt.

I don't remember exactly when I fell in love with Sebastian Kenton. There were many instances when it could've happened, but I do remember when I fell in hate with him.

When he shattered me into a million tiny pieces while a crowd of strangers witnessed my pain and shame.

Yes…I remember exactly when he went from the man of my dreams to the vicious monster that was hiding underneath, ready for me to fall so he could sink his sharp teeth into my heart and make me bleed. Bleed for sins that weren't mine to atone for.

The worst part is that the son of a bitch broke me. He broke me to the point I don't care for anything or anyone else. He made a broken heart fall for him and turned the purest of loves into the most vicious hate.

Ruining me for all men because the matter of the fact is I don't see myself falling for anyone ever again. I refuse to give someone the power to end me once and for all.

What my father couldn't do in eighteen years, Sebastian did in a day. In one moment. He ended me, but from that pain, I was born again. And here I am. Older, wiser, and so very angry.

He got to move on with his life as if I never existed and never mattered.

While I was choking on my own tears, mourning their loss, he carried on with his life and all his plans until he made them all happen.

Once the Senator of Chicago, now the Commander-in-Chief. The highest power in the land.

Smiling and promising shit to keep the country eating from the palm of his hand.

Young men aspire to be like him when they grow older.

Young girls swoon over the most handsome president this country ever had—their words, not mine.

Older men kiss his ass as if he's God himself, and don't get me started on the older women and how they view him.

It's nauseating, really.

If only they knew the real Sebastian Kenton. They wouldn't idolize the man so much.

Or maybe they would since this world has gone to hell.

The door of my office closing loudly snaps me out of my thoughts. Sighing. "Haven't I told you that you need to knock before entering?"

"Haven't we established that I do as I please?"

Turning her way, I look at Quinne Jones. Co-owner of the Washington Weekly and the bane of my existence. Quinne has a smile on her face, but it doesn't reach her eyes. It never does, and I have gotten used to it now. There are demons in her eyes that make mine look like puppies.

After my world collapsed for all of Sebastian's world to witness, I only had two people in my corner and surprisingly, one of them was Quinne. We didn't really know each other, not really. We just shared one moment at a gala, but it was enough for me to know that if someone could understand the person that I am today, it would be her.

I sought her out, understanding that I couldn't do all that needed to be done without her, and as much as I appreciate all that Benjamin has done for me. I knew he didn't have the resources I needed to become the woman that I am today.

And, over my dead body would I have accepted Sebastian's charity after all that went down. Turning around, I face the floor-to-ceiling window again. "Your girl did well." Quinne walks toward where I am standing, and we're both shoulder to shoulder as we watch the city below us.

"She did." I agree. Nessa did exactly what I asked of her.

I knew that it would be a challenge, but she proved herself.

She managed to ask the hard questions, and she delivered a message.

I have crawled out of the shadows he shoved me into three years ago, and the game has changed. I am no longer that broken, impressionable girl who fell in love with a lie. No.

I am a woman.

A woman with an agenda and a need to make the sitting president regret ever making me feel worthless. For making me fall in love, not only with him but with life and, most importantly, Ella, and then so cruelly taking it all from me.

The mention of Ella makes my chest tighten with a pain that's too much to bear, so I take a deep breath and concentrate on this dark feeling inside of me. This hate. "So, what's next?"

"Now…" I look her way and meet her eyes. Angry green meets soulless brown. Both hollowed and hurt. That's what binds us. Rage. Smiling cruelly, I finish my sentence. "I make him regret all he did, and once I'm done, there won't be anything left of him but a shadow of the man he once was."

"You do know that hurting him means—"

"I know what I am doing, Quinne." My hate runs deep but never deep enough to hurt her. Never my girl.

Quinne chuckles drily. "Of course."

A moment of silence passes between us as it always does.

With Quinne, I can just be myself.

Cold.

Angry.

Quiet.

Because she's the same except for the quiet part.

She enjoys talking way too much as a mechanism to hide what is underneath. A secret so dark that is eating at her from the inside out.

My past seems like child play compared to Quinne's, and maybe that's why I haven't thrown her in front of a moving car yet. Because I know what it feels like to be drowning, and Quinne is barely keeping her head above water.

"Did you come to comment on Nessa's performance, or is there something else you need?" I whisper gently, sensing she's not being herself today. "Here." She extends her right arm and hands me a stack of papers. Looking down, I ask, "What is this?"

"Take it."

I do.

Reading over it, I find myself stunned.

"Why would you do this?"

"This was never my dream, but yours." She clears her throat and looks away from me.

"Then why help me? Why invest in something you never wanted to begin with?"

Quinne shoots back. "Because this means something to you, and we all deserve a lifeline and this company is yours. I have my own, and someone gave it to me when I needed it most."

Lifeline.

I take her words in.

She's right.

I had nothing, and she used her money and connections to help me get this company up and running. It gave me a reason to get up in the morning and fight.

Quinne gave me that.

"I can't accept this. I won't."

"You have no choice but to accept it, Arianna." Quinne sighs, exasperated. "I'll still be on the board, but this company is now yours."

Knowing this is a losing battle, I give in to her wishes but not before telling her, "I'll repay everything you invested in the company plus interest."

"Wouldn't expect anything else from you." She laughs softly and steps back. "Just...just keep shedding light on them, okay?"

Them.

Victims of a horrible fate.

"I will." I turn back and look at my friend– my ally in the eye, and vow to her that I will respect her wishes and condition, the only one she asked when she started this journey with me. "But you are not to—"

She cuts me off before I can tell her exactly what I feel, but just like me, she doesn't want pity, nor does she want to discuss what causes her pain. Quinne's eyes turn cold once again, and her smile cruel. "He really shouldn't have made an enemy out of you, Arianna. Now give him hell." She successfully transfers the attention back to me.

Knowing vulnerable Quinne is long gone, I nod. "I will." I will show him exactly that. Hell.

Once, he was my heaven, but not anymore.

Now he's exactly what Quinne said.

My enemy.

"I'll be out of the city for a case, but I'm just a phone call away if you need me."

"Same here."

She grins, then turns and strides out of my office as if she's on her very own runway.

Most women would kill to look like Quinne, and most men would kill to spend a night tangled in her sheets, but nobody knows the real her.

I do.

I know the burden she carries and the reason why she hides underneath the facade of a ruthless man-eating lawyer, and let me tell you, it's not pretty.

Not pretty at all.

With the legal documents in hand that declare me the sole owner of the paper and all its areas, I walk towards my desk and take a seat. Placing the documents down, I take a deep breath, allowing myself a moment to breathe. What Quinne doesn't know, and what I try to deny, is that I love that man as much as I hate him, and it only angers me further.

Because nobody understands how painful it is to love someone who destroyed me so thoroughly, I am still picking up the pieces.

I love the son of a bitch, but not even that love can save him from what he created. Whenever I feel myself becoming weak by the memory of his eyes, smile, laugh, and traitorous touch, I recite his last words to me aloud. "Betrayal hurts most when it comes from the person you trust most." I whisper his cruel words while the words echo in my office, taunting me. Then to drive the point home, I open the last drawer on my desk, reach inside and pull out a small black frame. A frame with a photo of the only good thing in my life, even if she's out of reach from me. My Ellaiza.

Smiling at the camera with a face full of pink frosting and her tiny hands holding two chocolate cupcakes.

"I miss you, my girl." The heartbreak and pain that take over me whenever I think about her or see her is the push I need to carry on with what I'll do next. Placing the frame back into the drawer, I close it, keeping her a secret just to myself.

Reaching for the office's phone, I press a button and put it on speaker.

"Yes, boss?" Nessa's sweet voice sounds from the speaker.

"I need to speak with you. Please come to my office."

A second passes before she replies. "I'll be right there."

Hanging up, I lean back in my white leather chair and wait.

A minute later, a knock sounds on the door.

"Come in." Putting my phone down, I turn to see a nervous-looking Nessa step through the double doors of my office. "You did well today." I never compliment my employees or my team.

That is something I just don't do, but I pay them well, and I am never rude. That'll have to do. I motion for her to take a seat which she does, still nervous as hell. "Thank you, boss." Nessa is a young girl, a naive one, but efficient and brilliant. That is all I ask. Their personality traits or flaws are of no interest to me.

Grabbing a notepad and a pen, I jot down contact names and numbers for her before passing the white sticky note to her. "I need to contact each and every single one of these women and try to get an interview with them. Over the phone or in person, I do not care. Most of them signed NDAs, but if you're as clever as I believe you are, you'll find a way around it." Nessa looks down and frowns, but there's also something on her face. A challenge. Good girl. "Count on it, boss. Although messing with the President is one hell of a suicide mission."

Inspecting my nails, I reply in a dry tone. "Nessa…men like Sebastian Kenton think too highly of themselves." Looking at her once again, I smile. Fuck, it hurts to smile. It's been hurting for three years now. Pushing past the pain, I concentrate on the hate. "Men like him are just that…men. Not immortals, and they all bleed the same."

"If you don't mind me asking, why do you hate him so much? Yes, he is kind of a condescending ass and thinks he is God's gift to mankind, but as far as his duty to the country, he has not fucked up yet and has done quite a job of it." That is true. Nessa is all about the facts.

And on paper, Sebastian has done wonders for his people, but I know better. I know him and how he plays. Dirty. Unfairly. He killed me in life, and for that, he must pay. Because I can't forget.

His last words won't let me forget.

"Get me everything you can and fast."

"Of course."

"Good. And Nessa?" The girl had her back turned, all but ready to walk out the door, but she paused and looked back at me to meet my gaze.

"I'm trusting you can handle this."

Nodding, she says. "I won't let you down."

Opening my laptop, I press play on the video of Sebastian's last conference. I watch it till the end, like I've watched every single one of his interviews and appearances for the past three years.

Zooming in on his face, the girl I once was whimpers in pain at seeing him doing so great without me. The lying bastard smiles and makes promises he does not mean, but he does keep them.

Unlike the promises he made to me.

The woman who was born from the ashes of the little girl he broke, hardens herself and reminds me of his famous last words that rainy day back in Chicago, where his world witnessed the death of who I once was. *Betrayal hurts more when it comes from the one you trust most...*

It does. It scars you so deep you won't ever be rid of the reminder.

Sebastian Kenton gave me wings to fly once, and now...

Now, I'm ripping them out of his back until he's nothing but a bleeding mess of skin, bones, and regret.

Furious tears thicken my throat, and I throw the thought of him out of my mind.

He'd taken too much already.

He successfully turned me into an angry, bitter woman.

My hands shake as I reach to close the laptop. "You have no idea the shitstorm that's heading your way, Sebastian. You soon will."

Hardening my heart once more, I lift my head and smile, staring out at the rain that started to fall outside my window.

There's no going back now.

Chapter 6
EXES & O'HOES

Arianna

"Some bitches are all bark and no bite. Me? I bite and fucking hard." — A

"Thank you for sitting down with me today, Miss Vain." Nessa sighs, annoyed by fling #6.

Tall, long, red hair, with a willowy figure and a face that belongs in a fashion magazine.

Marla Vain used to be a well-known pornstar before she landed in Sebastian's bed and elevated her status to the point she is now semi-respectable instead of being linked to the adult industry to put it nicely.

A porn star…

Miss Vain rises from her seat and looks down at Nessa with an air of superiority…as if. How quickly did she forget where she came from and what she had to do to get to where she is or who she had to do.

Rich, powerful, and well-known dick.

I watch through the one-way glass as she leaves with her security guard on her tail, dismissing Nessa completely. With my phone in hand, I type a quick message to my personal assistant, Oliver, asking him to send the last woman in. Trying to get dirt on a President is always difficult, but trying to expose bad behavior from a President who is as beloved as

Sebastian has proven to be an impossible task. Dammit.

Most of the women Nessa has interviewed today only have nice things to say about him, and others just wasted my time trying to get their five minutes of fame while giving us absolutely nothing.

Although, I can still work with some of the details they all shared.

One thing all of those women have in common.

One fact even most women blinded by his charm can't deny.

The man broke things up with them when he got bored. He broke some hearts and egos, too.

They didn't say it exactly like that, but I noticed the bitter undertone and the painful fake smiles.

Now I just need one to expose something that could help me create a crack in that perfect public persona Sebastian has shoved down the country's throat.

And after I'm done exploiting his playboy and heartless side, I'll move to the next.

The shady side of his business.

His criminal friends, partners, and all that he is hiding by being the Commander-In-Chief.

It's hilarious how after Nessa delivered my message, someone from Sebastian's camp tried to make contact, wanting to speak with the one in charge of the paper.

That's when I knew I got him.

What's amusing to me is that he has no idea who exactly the CEO is, not yet. My face hasn't been released since the paper wasn't all that big before, and I used my nonna's middle and last name to go undetected. There's no trace of me.

But now that the press conference gained us more popularity and we're exposed, soon my identity will be revealed but on my terms.

All in due time.

There's a knock on the door next to the double mirror, then Nessa appears with an unsatisfied look on her face. She's eager for information, but no one is truly cooperating, so I understand her frustration.

"These women are so..." she tries to find words to describe the parade of airheads, and I help. "Shallow. Idiots? Brainwashed?"

"Yes, yes, and oh my God, YES!" Her dark brows furrowed. "How can they have nothing of substance to say? Half the interview they spent looking at themselves in the mirror, and the other half just kissed his ass as if that will help them get back in the president's bed." Nessa says with a shocked expression.

I ignore the way the thought of those women fucking Sebastian makes me want to barge inside the White House and stick my favorite black-ink pen on his neck. Instead, I shrug and hand her a notepad where I jotted down the questions I want her to ask the last of Sebastian's fling.

Nessa takes the notepad from my hand and asks, "Do you want me to ask these? You will be mentioned in the article and consequently involved."

Playing with the button on the sleeve of my suit, I reply. "We save the best for last, Nessa. Now make sure that she answers every question. Taunt her if you must, but ensure she breaks and gives us what we want." Nessa knows what went down with Sebastian and me three years ago, not only because she, like me, is obsessed with politics and journalism but because I openly share my story, needing to be transparent with her if I want all of this to work. I need to trust her a little for her to trust me. She hasn't failed me yet.

"I won't let you down."

She nods enthusiastically before stepping back inside the interview room we have here at the newspaper.

I know she won't.

She's eager to climb the ranks, and this is certainly helping her.

Unlocking my phone, I sit back, scroll through social media and open the bird app where Sebastian posts daily updates. I know most of it is bullshit. His press secretary is very efficient in doing the devil's work. One thing that strikes me as odd is that every person on his team is male. The ones working directly with him, I mean. Not one single female is part of it.

There has to be a reason for that decision because he's risking being called sexist in a time where that type of behavior is not only unacceptable but will get you canceled quickly.

I also haven't seen Celene around him, not once. At first, it burned that she was still part of his life after I was gone. They even seemed so closed, but out of nowhere, the spiteful bitch was gone too.

Maybe he used her like he did me and got rid of her or maybe he realized she was a filthy snake.

Bored with the app, I open my email and scroll to the most recent messages. I work on answering them until the last woman walks into the interviewing room. Thylane Bruna.

The one who was with him before me or during? Or who the fucks know anymore. Locking my phone and placing it on the table before me, I lean back in my seat and give all my attention to Nessa and Sebastian's French fling. I have to at least give this one props, even if it irks me. Unlike the other six, she has the decency to be polite to the journalist. Also, just like the rest, she's dressed to the nines. Hair and makeup are done as if the interview is being televised.

She's stunning. That can't be denied. You have to be blind or jealous to do so, and I'm neither.

"Take a seat, Miss Bruna. Thank you for coming in and agreeing to be interviewed by me."

"Is no problem, really," Thylane says in perfect English with a hint of her French accent, making her sound not only charming but exotic with a perfect smile on her equally perfect face. "Anything for my dear Bastian."

Barf.

I feel what I had for breakfast rising back up my throat, threatening to spill out of my mouth. Then Nessa starts with easy and routine questions to make the person being interviewed feel more comfortable.

I zone out during the boring details, taking a glance at her outfit and shoes. For someone who makes all her income from modeling, she has horrible taste.

Besides, who matches a blood-red tube dress with strappy bright yellow heels?

Sebastian's ex-hook-up, that's who.

"Will Bastian be stopping by?" Thylane's voice breaks through my thoughts. Of course, she would look for the first opportunity to ask about him. Then I wonder if they still keep in touch. Are they estranged? What's the situation? And I hate myself for caring.

"I'm afraid the president has more important things to attend to." Nessa responds.

"That's for sure." She laughs. Acting snarky toward Nessa and my company. Asshole.

And to think the media thinks of this woman as a sweetheart.

Please.

She's as sweet as I am a saint.

Nessa clears her throat, the class act that she is, and carries on with the interview. "Can you share how your dynamic was with the president?"

Good girl, Nessa.

Most would start slowly and ease them into it, but the bitch acted as if she were better than us. She would get no special treatment or sympathy from me.

And for the looks of it, Nessa feels the same way.

"Mon amour and I had a very special relationship." Bullshit. Just the fact that she calls him Bastian and not his full name like he allows the people close to him to do, disproves her assessment of their relationship to be one-sided and way off.

"How so?" Nessa leans forward in a strategic move to make Thylane feel as if she's having a normal conversation with a friend. "Were you two together for a long time?" I scoff at that. It's obvious to me that Nessa is playing Thylane, and the woman is so self-centered that she has no clue that she is being played. The parade of women in Sebastian's life only sustains the argument that nothing lasts long for him.

Women are disposable to him.

I am living proof of that.

"We were casual lovers. Whenever one of us felt lonely, we sought each other out." Thylane flips her hair and laughs as if there's an invisible camera in front of her. Oh God, kill me now. "He was the one who always called when he needed… company." I have to give it to her. She might not be the brightest in the bunch, but she's not terribly stupid either. She signed a non-disclosure agreement, and I'm sure her lawyer briefed her on what she was and wasn't allowed to share with us. The country knows he's a dog, and they overlooked that tidbit, but will they turn their eyes when the real him is exposed little by little? I didn't think so.

Nessa keeps asking questions, and I listen intently to her every answer, wanting, no, needing to know more.

"Did you ever want more?" Nessa asks the more invasive questions.

I study Thylane as she takes a second to think about the question. She's clearly irritated by the question, but she holds her composure even though I see through her. She throws her hair over her shoulder and smiles at Nessa as if she isn't fazed by her. "Not really, no. We both agreed we were just having fun and enjoying each other's company."

"Did you see it coming when he ended things?"

Thylane's smile falters, and I take great pleasure in the fact that, slowly but surely, she's breaking. "We both decided our relationship had run its course."

"Were you surprised that he was seen with someone just a day after he ended things with you?"

"I told yo–" She raises her voice but quickly tones it down. Clearing her throat, "I told you it was mutual, and no. I was not surprised he moved on quickly. That's the type of man Bastian is." She laughs it off.

Bingo.

Straight from the mouth of his ex-lover.

Now for the grand finale, Nessa drives the point home.

"Were you hurt when he chose to court a much younger woman who kind of looked like you?" Nessa says sympathetically and professionally.

I chuckle, satisfied when I notice Thylane's right eye twitch. Then she replies through gritted teeth. "Please." She scoffs. "She was just a distraction. Besides, look how that ended." Thylane laughs cruelly. Bitch. I clench my jaw and suppress the urge to take my spike heels and shove them up her pompous ass.

Nessa jolts down everything Thylane is saying rapidly, while the French model is becoming more annoyed with every passing second.

"So, what you're saying is that you were unaffected by him moving on from you so quickly and with someone younger. That's what you're saying, correct?"

Thylane stands, clearly fed up and feeling attacked. Good. Laughing, "That is who Bastian is. He wants nothing serious, and trust me, that foolish girl was one of many." She says with a smile on her face.

Her words manage to penetrate my armor and sting. Fuck does the truth of her words sting, but I smile.

I smile because I got the comment I wanted from someone else's point of view that wasn't my own.

If I gave my side of things, it would make me look desperate somehow in the eyes of the many people who admire him, but if someone affiliated with the president and someone his own age says it, then that makes it look less obvious.

"Miss Bruna, I mean no off—"

"Oh, I know exactly what you meant. I want no part of this. I'm leaving, and you better not use any of this." She points her finger haughtily in Nessa's face before marching out of the room with her bodyguard following behind.

Standing, I button my suit and then step inside the interview room where Nessa is waiting with a triumphant smile on her face. "We got them. She looked pissed-as-fuck, and now we have a statement from someone who had a personal relationship with him."

We got them, indeed.

Smiling back, I tell her. "Well done, Nessa. Add all their comments from today to the article.

Write a draft and send it over so I can edit it before it's published."

"Will do."

Tomorrow his world will get my version of what went down three years ago when he made me look like an idiot. A love-sick foolish girl who was just part of some sick revenge. The world witnessed my pain and still made him the victim.

The son who lost everything at the hands of my father.

I was a victim of his cruelty, yet everyone turned a blind eye to it because the poor rich boy was wronged by the mafia.

They justified his actions and mocked me.

Now, I have a voice to fight back.

A platform that I intend to take advantage of.

Let them see who they voted for.

Because yes, my father was a monster, but Sebastian Kenton is no saint.

Chapter 7
ANYTHING FOR YOU

Arianna

"All that is left of us are broken promises and dust." — A

"Well, look at you, top dog." The comforting sound of Benjamin's voice makes me lift my head and turn my face from the computer screen. Although I don't smile, I welcome my friend. My confidant. The one person who's always been there for me, no matter what.

Benjamin Banning.

I stare at his smiling face, and it warms me. "Benjamin."

"My girl." His smile widens as he steps into my office, closing the door behind him. "I'm so fucking proud of you." Benjamin moves towards where I am standing behind my desk and takes me into his arms, giving me one of his annoying but warm hugs. In his embrace, I allow myself to feel all the gratitude and, dare I say, the love I feel for this man. Although I'm colder than most people, never with him.

He's bigger than the last time I saw him if that's even possible, and he finally finished the left tattoo sleeve that he's been meaning to. He looks even more intimidating now.

He also cut his hair short on the sides and left it a little longer on top. Benjamin is drop-dead gorgeous in an almost intimidating way. A heartbreaker, and he knows it.

He ditched his black-on-black uniform and is wearing dark jeans, black boots, and a sleeveless white shirt. He finally took my advice and started adding more colors to his wardrobe, I think sarcastically to myself.

"Take a seat." I motion toward a chair. He does and then stares at me silently.

"Bossman is pissed as fuck."

"And?" He laughs softly at my 'I give no fucks about what he feels' attitude.

"He wants the name of the person fucking with his public image, kid, and I've steered him away from getting to you for the last three years, but it's getting to me, man." He rubs his face exhaustedly.

Then the truth of this hits me because, in his quest to help me, he was acting disloyal to his boss and friend.

No one could've stayed hidden for so long, especially with the kind of resources Sebastian has, so I couldn't have done it without Benjamin's help.

Every time Sebastian made a move to find me, Benjamin was a step ahead and blocked him, all to get me to this point, but in all of this, he betrayed his closest friend.

Shit.

"I'm sorry."

"What?"

Fuck, the word sorry always feels like acid in my throat. "For putting you in a position where you had to betray your friend."

His gaze softens. "You're my girl. There's nothing I wouldn't do for you. You know this."

How he manages to soften the rock in my chest every time, I don't know, but he does. Ironic since, for so long, he has been my rock.

"I would do anything for you, too," I tell him, vulnerably, and hate it. Ugh, how tedious.

He smiles softly and leans forward with his elbows on his knees. "Would you stop all of this if I asked you to?"

Stiffening, "All but that." Closing my eyes, I breathe through the pain and focus on the hate. Always hate. Because it's the only thing that keeps me from getting hurt.

Smiling sadly, he carries on. "What he did was wrong on so many levels. If I could go back and save you from that pain, I would. I swear to fucking God I would."

"I don't want to—"

He raises his hand toward me, "Just listen, Arianna."

I swallow hard, leaning back in my chair. Nothing my friend can say will change my mind. Nothing.

But then he opens his big mouth. "He suffered. Every day since he has mourned your loss. The fucking idiot paid for his misguided but selfless mistake." Thud. Crack.

How my heart beats after so many attacks is still a mystery to me, but it does.

He mourned your loss.

Good.

The motherfucker not only broke my heart, but he took my girl.

One I can, maybe, possibly try and move on from but the two together? No. Hell no.

"And you should know that he told Ella—" Nope. No. Just the mention of her name is just too much for me to bear.

"Enough." I snap, rising from my seat. Angry, broken, fuck, so broken. "She was my reason, Benjamin! My fucking reason for breathing alongside her fucking father, and he didn't care." I seeth. "No! He didn't care that he killed me that day and buried my heart in front of the goddamn country. Not only did he play me, but he humiliated me!" I try my best to remain calm but it all hits me at once. Breathing harshly, I stare into the eyes of the man who has helped keep my head above water. "He ruined me," I whisper deadly. "He made a fool out of me without a single care about the damage that he would cause. He gave me the world, yes but Christ, Benjamin, I gave him everything I was, and he threw it all away. He threw me away as if I never mattered. Because that's the truth, isn't it? I never mattered." I say through gritted teeth holding back the angry tears that threaten to spill.

Silence falls between us, almost defining, and all I can hear is my heavy breathing. Benjamin's kind eyes pierce me, making me feel like that lost eighteen-year-old he took into his care. "You're holding on to this hate to numb the pain, but it will end badly, kid." Benjamin looks at me with hurt in his eyes, but there's something else there. Something that kills me.

Pity.

"It already ended badly, Benjamin. He broke something in me. Something my father couldn't even reach." I round my desk and stand before him. He stands from his chair too. "Why wait till now to tell me this?"

"Would you have listened before?" He asks.

No.

I certainly wouldn't have.

I was so deep in my feelings that I would have either run back to the man and made a fool out of myself, or I would have spiraled.

I can't do this.

Not with Benjamin.

"I care for you deeply." I love you so much is on the tip of my tongue. I don't say it, but he knows it. God, does he? "But there's no changing my mind, and I would hate for us to argue every time we meet."

Stepping closer, the Viking of a man kisses my forehead and lingers there for a second too long. "I just want your smile back. That's all I want for you." Stepping back, he lifts my chin so he can look at my face. "I miss it."

Christ.

When did I get so lost in my pain that I didn't realize that Benjamin was hurting too?

Selfish…

Always so selfish…

"Will I ever smile or laugh again?" Staring into his eyes, I ask what I've been wondering for three long years.

"You will." He says confidently, but I'm not so sure.

"When?"

"When something is really funny. I promise you, kid."

I nod, swallowing hard.

I doubt that day will come, but he doesn't. Ever the optimist my Benjamin.

"Thank you for checking in." He does. He keeps in touch through email, and sometimes, not often he runs off and meets me in my office. Hiding from view, not wanting to be discovered. He won't have to do this anymore.

I am done hiding.

Benjamin drops another kiss on top of my head, making me feel like that lonely teenage girl again, then steps back, walking towards the door, but before he steps out, he looks back at me. "I'm only a call away if you need me."

Sighing. "You've already done so much. I'll take it from here."

He nods and turns back to the door, but my voice stops him. "Benjamin."

"Yes?" His voice comes out rough.

"Thank you."

"For what?"

"What you've done for me behind your boss's back," I tell him with my broken heart in my hands. He's the only person that gets this. The only one. Now. The one who'd been able to pull me through some of the hardest and darkest days of my life.

"Anything for you, kid." With that, he steps outside, exiting my office and leaving me to deal with the truth of all he said.

I'm heartless and cold, but I can never bring myself to be that way with my best friend.

My Viking.

My protector.

Chapter 8

GODDESS AMONGST MEN

Bastian

"I wish I could open my chest and
show you everything." — B

The words I so cruelly threw in the face of the woman I love most on this earth replay in my mind like an obnoxious loop meant to torment me. Meant to suffocate me.

Betrayal hurts most when it comes from the one you trust most. The words hurt, yes because they are so painfully true. I am aware I have no right to feel angry or, fuck it, maybe I do because my most trusted man has witnessed me losing my godforsaken mind every day since Arianna disappeared. He was right there with me when I fell into a pit of regret and despair when I couldn't find her because she made herself unreachable. Untraceable as if she was a figment of my imagination. She disappeared from my life as if she was never there, to begin with. My nights were cold and dark, with no sliver of her beautiful light. I made the stupid mistake, with only good intentions, yes, but a mistake nonetheless, of pushing her away so she could find herself and be all she ever wanted before she was thrust into the chaos that is my life.

And all along Banning knew where she was.

He had all the answers, and he just let me wallow in self-pity and heart-

heartbreak. Something she never knew. What I didn't tell her.

The painful truth.

In the process of pushing her away, I broke my own heart as well.

Fuck, I broke my child's heart.

When I got my head out of my ass in time to haul her ass back into my life and beg for forgiveness, it was already too late.

Anger coils in my stomach when I think about every time Banning lied to me, but I hold it down and focus on thinking straight. I concentrate on what my next move should be.

Because things have changed.

I promise to show you what it's like to hurt... her words echo in my brain. Closing my eyes, I drop my head back into the headrest of the car and let myself be attacked by memories of her. Her beautiful face lit up with love and wonder whenever she looked at my daughter. The way her emerald-green eyes would pierce my soul, claiming it.

Her soft and inexperienced kisses.

The way her body fit perfectly against mine.

Her laugh.

The way she looked at me when I made her mine. Her trust and her fear.

Fuck, her laugh is what I miss most.

Watching Arianna Parisi laugh was like witnessing a lunar eclipse. Breathtakingly beautiful and rare.

Because she didn't do it often, but when she did, the whole world would stop for me.

Then there was only her.

Motherfucker, it hurts.

If I could turn back time, I would. God knows I would do anything to have the chance to go back and change things, go back to a time when I was the man she loved, not the one I became.

The one she hates.

The one she promised war to.

A buzzing sound coming from my suit jacket snaps me out of my painful thoughts. Tucking my phone from my jacket, I unlock the screen to find several messages from Baron, one after the other. The first one is a link. Clicking on it, it instantly takes me to the Washington Weekly website, where an article has been published.

I usually pay zero attention to useless gossip articles because they do nothing. Well… that is not exactly true. Gossip adds to my popularity, but this one is different.

This is no ordinary gossip site, no.

This article was published by the journalist who has been attacking me for two weeks now. At first, I didn't think anything of it, but now their attacks feel personal.

I should be pissed as fuck. Any sane public figure would feel enraged when someone is trying to sully their public image, but not me. I feel thrilled because, somehow, this seems like it is connected to her.

Call me fucking crazy. I do feel like I have lost my mind, but this feels… right. Scrolling through the article, I have no choice but to laugh.

The president of the United States is a man of many flavors…

Corny-as-fuck if you ask me, but I'll give them C+ for effort.

From what I can read, several of my past flings and one-night stands gave statements. Some of these women I don't even remember.

If I am honest, before Arianna, all those women were just wormholes to get myself lost into, but she changed everything.

That's the difference between these women and her.

Thylane and Marla were the most recent ones.

All these women signed NDAs, but they clearly didn't pay attention to the fine print.

It was stated they were not to talk or mention my name in any public form, especially cooperate in stories to publish in the media, yet they did. Thylane's statement surprised me.

I thought she was smarter than the rest, but clearly, I was wrong because what I got from her interview, makes me look like a heartless bastard who left her for a younger girl.

I make note of contacting my lawyer to handle these women accordingly. Then I read where she mentions Arianna and my blood becomes hotter. She has no right to talk about shit she knows nothing about.

Holding my composure, I carry on reading when I land on photos of that day. Photos of Arianna dressed in all white while the rain fell harshly around us. I close my eyes as shame washes over me, and I allow it because I deserve it.

Her face fuck.

Countless articles were written back then about what happened but this is the first time I read one of them. I was too much of a coward to face the consequences of my mistake back then, but now I see for myself what she experienced. What I did to her. The image of Arianna looking so small and broken would shatter the nonexistent heart of Satan himself. "Fuck," I whisper, not caring that my men are sitting in front of me and might overhear. I keep reading, and it feels like a blow to my heart. One of the many I deserve. This is my track record with women exposed for the whole world to read. If she could live with what I did, then I can take this.

I can take all she'll throw my way.

The article was written by Nessa Adams.

The girl from the last press conference. Before I can give much thought, another message from Baron pops up.

Baron: Viola L. Conti. Washington Weekly CO.

The name.

I asked him to find me the name of the person in charge of Miss Adams and the newspaper she works for.

I let my mind loose to the countless possibilities and the many coincidences. The journalist asked the same questions Arianna asked me the first night we met. *Men like you always win, yes?*

Then I think about the other articles dirtying my name these past few weeks. The haunt. Trying to expose me to the public.

This is a mission, not most new media outlets would consider because it would be a suicide mission and pointless. Yes, this not-so-known newspaper is targeting the president of the United States.

A suicide mission indeed. A vendetta. War.

Only one person that I could think of would think to expose my past 'relationships', and that is a woman scorned. Smiling like a fucking lunatic, I shove my phone back inside my pocket. *Give me all you got, darling. Your war, your pain, fuck, give it all to me.*

"We're here, sir." Nix, one of my guards tonight, says from behind the wheel. Nodding, I wait for the car door to open, and once they do, I get out with a new purpose thrumming in my veins.

Shouts sound in the far corners of the building where the charity gala for the non-profit organization, Purple Hearts, helps support our troops and veterans who are struggling with the aftereffects of their duties overseas after returning from war.

This was one of my father's missions.

To help soldiers who weren't as lucky as him.

Help his brothers and sisters.

Purple hearts troops get all the help they need. Not just economically, but mental health support as well. Those men and women fight for this country. It's only right that we take care of them once they return home and the help given to our troops was not enough in my book.

I might be a heartless bastard, but I will always support what my father stood for in life even now that he's gone.

He believed in helping the ones that aren't able to do it on their own. The ones who sacrificed themselves for their country and their people.

So, tonight we are raising money through the auction of valuable art and it'll all go to the care of our troops.

It is only fair that the rich scum of this country help the ones in need, even if they do it for selfish and self-centered reasons.

Saluting the crowd of paparazzi gathering outside, I smile for the cameras before heading towards the building's entrance. And all the way I think to myself how something has shifted, not only inside of me but all around me.

I feel it.

Her.

A storm is coming.

I feel it.

Somehow, I feel…her.

***

After making my rounds greeting everyone who's anyone in my circle, from businessmen and businesswomen to colleagues and political rivals, I find myself being escorted by my security team, led by Banning, who arrived earlier to secure the building and make sure no one got in without a security clearance from them—towards the stage where

I am to make the welcome speech.

I used to eat up all the attention these events used to gather, but not anymore. After a while, it all became painfully monotonous and downright dreadful.

The Vice President says a few words before it is my turn to take the stage. Adjusting my bow tie, I move forward while my men surround me in a wall of protection. Some are even dressed as normal guests lost in the crowd of people while others are hidden, in dark corners waiting to shoot the first motherfucker who tries something.

I am not risking it.

Ever.

I am not risking her.

The moment I step into the center and am handed a microphone, the blinding lights are in my face. Clearing my throat, I smile at the crowd, and for the first time in a long time, it doesn't feel forced and doesn't pain me. "I want to start by thanking everyone for taking time out of your busy schedules and joining me tonight to not only support the brave men and women of this country who risked their lives every day to keep this country safe from our enemies but to also celebrate the troops currently fighting for our freedom overseas. We are celebrating their courage and selfless act." The crowd claps in agreement, and at the same time, the cameras flash faster. They love this shit.

I might be a selfish prick and do more bad than good, but this is where I act like the man my parents wanted me to be. Even the biggest piece of shit on the planet can agree that our troops deserve better. Fuck, every soldier deserves more than what they get. Soldiers everywhere, not just ours. My father, Ronan Kenton, had the love of a good woman and the resources to get through his war traumas but many aren't that lucky.

That is why this organization was so important to my father and now it is my responsibility to continue his life's work.

I couldn't save them that night, but I sure as fuck can keep his memory and legacy alive. That cunt Parisi didn't win. "Now, remember all of this when you place your bids. Artists from all over the country donated exquisite items from their personal collections for this fundraiser. So open not only your hearts to our soldiers but your wallets, as well." The crowd laughs, eating this shit up. Fucking Baron suggested I throw that corny line in there, but hell, it works. That's what's important. "There is live entertainment and plenty of food and drinks, so please enjoy." With that, the guests are ushered toward their seats while I remain standing for the dullest part of these events. The ass-kissing and interviews to gather more eyes to my charities. *Fuck, but being a nice guy is tiresome. And fuck you too, darling, for making me open the door to feelings and shit.* Watching the small group of journalists move forward, I wait for the first question. It usually is something that has nothing to do with the event and more to do with my personal life.

"Mr. President, good evening. Jean from DC Journal." A woman speaks up first while raising her hand and stepping forward.

"Welcome, Jean." I smile at the pretty older woman, causing her to blush like a schoolgirl.

"It's good to see you again, Mr. President." She clears her throat, visibly nervous. I remember Jean. She takes her job very seriously and asks hard questions but she is never rude or condescending. She is one of the good ones, so I always do my best to make her feel comfortable. "This auction is very generous. The past administration made a lot of promises to the people, and sadly half of their promises went undelivered." That's true.

The last fucker who was in my shoes did shit for the country. That's why all eyes are on me more than usual. They're waiting for me to back out of my campaign promises. "I believe we have a severe problem in this country of abandoning our soldiers when they need us most. There should be more funding and more resources available for them, so it is wonderful that you have started this organization.
Might I ask what made you decide this?"
"Most would believe I started the Purple Hearts foundation for tax payouts or to keep the people satisfied, but that is just not the truth. You see, my father, the late Ronan Kenton, was a soldier who fought overseas to protect this country. A brave man who was honored with a purple heart. He was selfless and honorable, and he believed every man and woman who risks their lives for us deserved better." For a second there, I stop to gather myself when my chest feels tight, remembering my father. Fuck. Taking a long breath, I continue. "He had many plans and goals he planned to make reality before the day of his death, but sadly he never got the chance to see them through. That is why I started the Purple Hearts foundation. Not only for our brave soldiers but for my brave father." Looking at the crowd of journalists, I see Jean wipe a tear. Christ. To lighten up the mood, I throw in. "But I am not that selfless, no. Acts of kindness get me brownie points with my daughter, who at the moment thinks of me as a supervillain with a big heart." I chuckle as the crowd does too, and some even make sounds of awe."Thank you for answering, Mr. President. Keep up the good job," Jean says with a bright smile on her face. Nodding at her, I motion for the man raising his hands two steps behind Jean. "Mr. President. Evening. Robert from The American column."
"Good evening." Oh, I remember this one. The clown who insisted

my supposedly criminal allies rigged the election. As if I needed fucking Sandoval to win over the people of this country. My adversaries knew I already had this election in the bag when rumors of me running for presidency started circulating. I am not being a cocky son of a bitch. Facts are facts. "There are rumors that you will be opening a rehabilitation center for criminals. Is that true, and if so, what makes them worthy of such grace and mercy? One they didn't offer their victims." The asshole adjusts his glasses and steps forward with his recorder high in the air.

In the past, I would agree with the fucker, but this case is different. I don't intend to help the scum of the earth who committed horrible acts against innocent people. Fuck no and the asshole Robert knows this, yet he decided to ask the question anyway and get me to say something that will make me look bad on a night that would've made my parents proud. On a night that does nothing for me but for the ones in need. Looking straight at the male journalist, I don't offer him the same grace and kindness I did Jean. If he wants to act like an asshole, then I'll very graciously make him eat his words. "You have a lot of thoughts about something that you stated is a rumor, Ronald." I purposely call him the wrong name. "I don't speak on rumors but on the truth, and the truth is that all my charities were created to help innocents who were in some way wronged. Men, women, children of all walks of life, ages, sexual orientations, and every single one. You might not understand this, but there are hundreds if not thousands of innocent men and women, who were abandoned and wronged by our judicial system, and most of them were wrongly convicted. But that's another point altogether. If I ever decide to start another charity to help these men and women get back on their feet, I will do so gladly and very proudly, Mr. Hansen."

The look on the man's face is priceless. Fucker knows not to go against a once-corrupt senator who gets really fucking hard by winning arguments and putting people in their place.

But somewhere along the way, I started to believe all the shit that once was only empty ideas and promises. Fuck, now I not only speak for the ones who can't defend themselves, but I fight for them.

Love.

Love, I'm telling you, is witchcraft.

It has me changing my views and acting...less like a heartless motherfucker. I still enjoy playing the rich assholes of this world who love to prey on innocents, but I no longer feel thrilled when screwing good people in the process.

I carry on answering questions until Nyx taps my shoulder and whispers in my ear that the time for questions is up.

Thanking all the journalists, I say my goodbyes and tell them to enjoy the gala.

Turning, I move to follow my men off the stage when a voice stops me.

A voice I still hear at night or when I am alone.

A voice that stops me dead in my tracks and has me freezing, trying to find my next breath. A sultry voice with a hint of anger and resentment but a little bit of hurt, too catches my attention. "Good evening, Mr. President. I do hope there's time for one more question?" Thud.

Thud.

Fucking thud.

Even my heart knows its owner is a few feet away, recognizing her with just the sound of her voice.

Turning swiftly, I step back into the light and search for her in the crowd. As if an angel is parting the gates of heaven, she moves amongst the crowd.

A goddess. My Goddess.

"Arianna," I whisper like a man who has finally seen the light after years in the dark. Like a religion. My religion. The barely beating organ in my chest slowly starts to beat for someone other than my child.

For my woman.

A woman who is currently looking at me as if she wishes to reach forward and strangle the life out of me with the cord of the microphone I am holding in my hand.

I hear the mumbles and whispers all around while I am held enthralled by all the beauty that is Arianna Luna Parisi.

Amazement billows through my spirit when the music in the background shifts and the woman who has been haunting me for nights on end struts my way.

Her honey-blonde hair falls straight down her back without a single strand out of place. Not wavy and slightly curled at the ends like before. The adorable bangs are long gone, making her look even more grown now and not innocent like they did when she was younger.

Her big, pouty lips twist in a cruel smile.

My chest pangs.

Because although it is clear she hates me, that doesn't take away from the fact that she came back. She found her way back to me even if it is just to hurt me. To go through with her plan to make me suffer.

The joy of seeing her again is so full, it is almost painful. But still, I cherish this pain like I cherish every part of her. Time or space didn't change that.

She is so fucking beautiful that I think my heart might explode.

Fuck.

No longer a girl but a woman.

Slowly, my eyes wander over her curvy body with predatory regard.

A breathtakingly beautiful woman dressed in a white suit that hugs every sharp curve of her body. You would think a modest white suit wouldn't make a woman look as mouth-watering sexy, as she does right now but it does. Her cleavage is on full display because the little brat opted not to wear anything under it.

She also teetered on these sex-as-fuck, blood-red heels, the same color as her plump lips, which made my stomach clutch.

The sight of her wearing white with a touch of red twists through me like a knife.

Eyes the color of emerald stare back at me, daring me to refuse her. Clearing my throat, I hold her stare, daring her as well.

To challenge me.

To hate me.

To fucking love me.

To give me all she has, I will carry it gladly.

"You can ask anything, darling." And just like that, we are back to that time. The time when we didn't know when one ended and the other began. The only difference is that beneath all that once was, there is pain. So much fucking pain in her eyes. But I'm a masochist when it comes to her, and I can't help myself. "I am so damn proud of you." Those fiery greens flash with emotions from pain to anger in a millisecond before she clenches her jaw and steps forward with bad intentions. I see the moment she decides to fire back, opening her mouth, to let her venom loose when she's interrupted by the sweetest voice of a little girl barreling towards me at full speed with her bodyguard not far behind. "Daddy! There are like a gazillion cupcakes here. Gimeeee!" My daughter uses

her hungry monster voice, causing the room to explode with laughter. The First Daughter. A sugar addict. Ellaiza wraps her tiny arms around my legs, not tall enough yet to reach my waist. The second she realizes we are not alone, when she burst onto stage, interrupting the press conference, she smiles sheepishly at the audience and waves her hands with a big smile on her beautiful face. "Hello!" Ellaiza says, bouncing on her tiny pink heels. "Thank you for supporting the good guys and voting for my Dad!" She gives them a thumbs-up and a grin. "You all did good." My daughter, so help me God, inherited not only my face, but my charm. Lord, have mercy on me because this little girl sure won't.
The crowd of journalists pick up their cameras and snap picture after picture while smiling and waving back to my daughter.
All minus one.
Arianna.
She stands frozen in place while the world moves around her, staring at my daughter with pain, adoration, and so much love that it has left me breathless. Giving me hope that my girl, the girl who stole my heart, and claimed it for her own, is still there, buried under all the pain I caused. It gives me fucking hope that maybe, just maybe, I can still make things right.
Because I will.
I will heal her heart and do what I should've done the first time around. I will give the woman of my dreams… forever.
Even if I die trying or she kills me, whichever comes first, but knowing her? I'm leaning toward the latter.

Chapter 9
FIRST DAUGHTER

Arianna

"I'll be my own redemption." — A

I once thought it was scientifically impossible for a heart to break. Explode? Yes? Stop in your chest? That, too. Hell, even a medically broken heart can occur. It's rare, but it's possible. But break into a million tiny bleeding pieces and still function properly? No. It was just not factual, but then I thought a lot of things were impossible, yet they happened to me. Scientifically the organ in my chest is beating strong and healthy, or that is what my doctor says. For a while now, I've been experiencing symptoms that resemble that of a heart attack, so I took my ass to the doctor just so he could tell me that there was nothing wrong with me.

Absolutely nothing.

But I know better.

My heart broke when love betrayed me. When the man I loved failed me and I had to pick up not only my pride but the shattered remains of my heart off the ground.

Dramatic? Very much so.

One of the many things I turned into after leaving yet another city and all that I once loved behind for the second time in my life. How tragic. But now… now, it feels different.

I felt out of breath the second my eyes laid on the President of the United States, looking so annoyingly good-looking with his tuxedo, perfect hair, perfect smile, perfect fucking face.

Perfect.

That's the image Sebastian Kenton portrays to the world and I fell for it.

Christ, did I fall hard.

My mistake.

One I won't be making twice.

Because now I hate him with all that is left of me.

With everything bad and ugly.

But I find myself hating myself too because the second he stood there answering questions looking like the picture of perfection and morality, my chest panged, and my breath got caught in my throat, and for a second, I was back to a time when I was just a girl who fell for a larger-than-life man. Just a girl who finally found a home in the arms of someone who made every bad thing that ever happened to her fade away.

And it hurts.

I didn't anticipate that seeing him would hurt this much, and it is infuriating. And as much as seeing him again not through the media lenses but through my eyes, hurts. Nothing hurts more than watching all I ever wanted, standing a few feet away from me, taunting me with the what-ifs. What if he didn't lie?

What if he would've pulled me closer instead of tossing me aside?

So many what-ifs. Now I am standing next to the bar, finishing a glass of champagne, hiding like a coward. One thing I am not, but I am when it comes to him. I've been longing for the day I would stand face to face with Sebastian and show him the woman I became. Not because I need his approval, fuck that, but because I need him to see that even though he broke something inside of me, I am still standing. Yes, on most days, I wish I could turn back time to the night we first met and erase him from my life, but then I remember that in erasing him I would lose the most precious little human in this world. In my world. No matter how far she is. My Ellaiza.

Because as much as I loved her father with all I had, his daughter became a part of me. The purest part. Something I thought I would never have. Gulping down what's left of the bubbly liquid, I place the flute back into one of the trays when a server passes by. Taking a deep breath, I focus on putting myself together. I've come too far to break down now when it has barely begun. Gathering myself. I breathe through my nose and lift my head to take in the people around me. God, I hate these social events that do more for the rich than they do for the ones who are in need. The rich assholes dressed up to the nines in their most expensive outfits, drinking, dining, and kissing ass all night while bragging about their latest purchase, or even worse when they go on and on about the kid they just adopted from a third-world country. Most people adopt children out of the goodness of their hearts, but the ones I've come across only do it to make themselves look less like the rich and self-centered assholes they really are.

Judgmental?

Very much.

I don't even filter myself anymore.

Sometimes being spiteful and judgmental does wonders for your soul.

It's almost therapeutic.

Then I remember I almost had the chance to tear a new one into

Sebastian, but I didn't get the chance. I couldn't. Not with Ellaiza standing there.

Not once since I parted from her have I stopped trying to catch a glimpse of her beautiful face, but I never thought I would get the chance here. Sebastian doesn't usually does not bring her to these kinds of events. This is new, and I was blindsided.

The tyrannical bastard pulled one over my eyes without even knowing I would be there.

"Fuck," I whisper under my breath as I stand motionless, staring at the guests laughing and dancing like they have no worries, as if their perfect lives are always… perfect.

How boring.

Moving slowly, I let my feet guide me, trying to catch another glimpse of them, but neither Sebastian nor Ellaiza are anywhere to be found. The building is packed with security, so I'm guessing getting close to either of them will be a challenge.

A part of me, the masochist in me, needs to see her, even if it will hurt like a bitch to see her sweet face light up for me in recognition.

Her sweet smile.

The one she would give me every time I kissed, held, or gave her a cupcake. All the times I told her I loved her, even when I was scared to do so. It will surely cause me more damage, but hell I am already broken so what's another hit to an already shattered heart?

When I decide to go for it, I feel a tug on my pants, and when I look down to see who is pulling on my very expensive suit, my heart stops right along with the rest of the world. Everything stops, and all there is… is us. "Ella…" I breathe out, feeling my heart ache, but at the same time, beating abnormally slow.

Because that is her effect. My Ella has the ability to stop the world for me. Her beautiful face, the face that changed so much since I last kissed it, looks up at me, rendering me speechless. Her eyes look bigger, and her nose is still adorably cute and small, but her lips look just like her father's. My heart soars when I take in her long curls that fall to her shoulders. Those curls made me fall in love with her, along with her smile. The two missing front teeth are a slap to the face of all the things I missed while she was away from me. Christ, this hurts. I thought I had time. I thought I had to crawl or fight and give one hell of a fight to be able to see her again, and she is here. Here, holding onto my leg with the brightest smile on her face. Smiling at me just like she used to when she was little. As if she knew that she was safe with me.

What should I say? Shit.

Just like the first day I met her, Ellaiza Kenton sneaks up on me, leaving me defenseless.

Does she usually do this? Runoff and talk to complete strangers? My heart races when all that could go wrong with that scenario crosses through my mind.

My mouth feels dry, and my head tries to come up with something to say because lord knows, there are many things I wanted to say. Opening my mouth, I'm about to ask if she's lost, but her sweet voice stops interrupting me.

Angling her face up, she holds onto my leg tighter and turns my world on its axis with the words that leave her pretty mouth next. "You came back to me, mommy. You came back to us!" She squeals in glee, bouncing up and down in her pretty-pink sparkling dress.

She looks so beautiful.

The picture-perfect first daughter.

Thud.

Thud.

Thud.

My heart.

And for the first time in three years, I drop to my knees with a heart full of love.

Full of Ellaiza.

Without giving me a chance to gather my thoughts or catch my breath, my little girl throws her tiny body at me, enveloping me in all that is her. Love.

Powerless, broken, and somehow whole at the same time. I hug her tightly to my body. She called me mommy. I am not dreaming this. Ellaiza looked at me and called me mommy. "Ellaiza…" I don't have the words to express what I feel right now because there aren't any, so I just say her name.

Ella releases my neck and steps back a bit to stare at my face with happiness that shines from within her tiny little heart. "Did you find all the stars, mommy?" Her brows pull together. "Did you reach them all? I know it's impossible to catch stars, but daddy says there's nothing you can't do, mommy. Did you do it?"

"W-what?" I stutter. Never in my life have I been this lost for words. "D-ddo you know who I am?" I breathe out, terrified.

"Of course, silly." The beautiful, clever brat rolls her eyes adorably at me. Shit, it's like looking at a cuter version of myself. "You're my mommy," she whispers with so much love it pours out of her straight into the broken pieces of my heart, breathing life back into it. My head spins while my hands shake. "I don't understand…" I whisper back, with tears that have not fallen for so long, threatening to spill.

One actually does.

"No, don't cry, mommy." Ella wipes the tear away with her still chubby thumb. God, I missed her. I love her. How? How is this possible? She was only three years old when she last saw me. How can she remember me? Has someone kept the memory of me alive in her life?

Perhaps Benjamin? But no...She distinctively said 'daddy'.

But that makes zero sense. Why would he?

Damn you, tyrant...

A soft kiss on my cheek warms me, bringing me back to the now. To her. "I missed you so much, mommy. I'm sorry if I doubted you would come back, but daddy didn't!" She giggles, melting me more than her kiss. "Daddy kept saying that I should trust you. That you were coming back to me. To us!" Her blue eyes pierce through me, then her face grows serious. "Kyrie owes me twenty dollars. He said that you wouldn't come back, but he was soooo wrong." She sasses, tilting her little head. "What's wrong, mommy? Are you not happy to see me? Is that why you're crying?" Pushing my heartbreak aside, I smile big for her. "I've never been happier. God, I could just eat your face." I reply, tweaking Ella's nose, causing her to giggle in the sweetest little voice I'd ever heard.

It's true.

I've never been this happy or this confused at the same time.

And angry, don't forget, pissed as hell.

Because this only means this perfect little girl spent three years thinking that for me reaching the stars was more important than her. Bullshit. I don't understand what's going on, and at the moment, I have more questions than answers, but what I am certain of is that there's no way I'm ever parting from Ellaiza.

Now more than ever.

Now that she is older and thinks of me as her mom, not even Sebastian or God himself can make me stay away.

Because I might be a lot of things God knows I am, but I am not a liar, and I don't break promises.

And at this moment, I'm vowing to do whatever it takes to keep this girl with me forever.

"So silly, mommy." Ella giggles. I grin at her, my heart clutching slightly in my chest, just like it did all those times I spent with her. "I missed you." All laughter disappears as she looks at me with those blue eyes, so much like her father's, that always got to me, making the hollow space in my chest ache.

I take her little hand in mine, "I missed you too, my darling girl."

She bows her head, and I hate it. My Ella should never bow or hide. Never.

"What is it, baby?" I swing our joined hands playfully.

"Will you go again?"

"Never," I vow with my entire chest.

Ella's smile takes over her face, but then her hand slips from mine, and she shifts into the arms of a giant man currently looking at me as if I'm someone he needs to annihilate. Rising to my full height, I step forward, ready to strike the man for daring to take my girl from me, but before I could, he takes three steps back, anticipating my move.

Who the hell is he? My heart is in my throat, and all kinds of terrible scenarios are running through my mind.

Will he hurt her?

Where the hell is Sebastian?

Ellaiza's security?

"Give her back to me," I demand coldly.

Unafraid and giving no fucks about the fact that the beast of a man could step on me if he wanted.

The giant asshole doesn't spare me even a look, his eyes solely trained on the tiny girl in his hands.

"Don't be rude, Shaw-Bear. Say hi to my mommy. See, I told you she would come back!" Ella's blue eyes spark with adoration when looking at the scary-looking man who has more tattoos than the Nicolasi twins, and that is saying a lot because the capo of Detroit is a walking, talking coloring book.

"Mommy?" The man, Shaw-bear as my girl calls him, looks my way with untrusting eyes, and I stare at him in the same manner. Ella grabs his face in both hands and forces him to look at her. That is when I notice how the giant man's eyes turn soft.

What in the–?

"It could be the pope him-fucking-self, and I don't fucking care, moonshine. You don't hide from me. Ever. You got that?"

"Yeah, yeah, no biggie."

"It is a big fuc—" The man, whose name I assume is Shaw, stops himself before cursing in front of Ellaiza. "It is a big deal. If I can't see you, then I can't do my job and keep you safe. Do not do it again."

Ella tilts her head, smiles brightly, and pats his cheek like she's wiser beyond her years. "You don't have to worry so much, Shaw-bear. I don't need protection from mommy. Mommy loves me."

Ella turns to me. "Right, mommy?"

Nodding, I say, *"Plus que la vie elle-même, Ella."*

She gasps. *"Bien, maman."*

Laughing, I look at her and only at her. "Good girl."

I wink at her, causing her smile to grow bigger while I ignore the brooding giant.

"Oh, no." Ella gaps. "Where are my manners!" I swear if I wasn't so emotional and on the verge of tears, I would break out laughing like a mad woman at this girl's antics. God. How much time has passed, yet she's the same over-the-top, silly, beautiful girl with an old soul. "Shaw-bear, this is my mommy. Her name is Arianna." She whispers then. "You should know not to call her anything but her name. She doesn't like it when people shorten it. It's Arianna. My dad says that only he and I can, call her sweet names but no one else." Shaw looks like he could care less about me. The feeling's mutual jerk.

I just care that he has my heart in his arms. Ellaiza.

"Mommy!" Ella exclaims happily, attracting the attention of a few guests that are now looking our way and whispering.

Paying them no mind, I focus on her. "Yes?"

"This big teddy bear is my Shaw! I call him Shaw-bear, and he's my best-est friend after you and daddy, of course." She looks at Shaw as if the man hangs the moon and all the stars for her. Oh, no. I know that look. "He stops the mean people from hurting me. He even broke a man's nose for trying to take me once, didn't you, Shaw-bear?"

Her security, that's who this man is. I should've known by the way he was dressed and assessing the room for any threats, even when he was giving all his attention to my girl.

Shaw nods but remains stoically silent, staring me down, still clearly unsure if I am a threat or not, but I don't back down or bow to anyone, not anymore, so I stare at him in the same manner while Ellaiza stands in the middle blabbering adorably, oblivious to it all.

As she should.

As I stare in awe at my girl, I feel a spark.

A light.

A flicker.

Life roars through me.

Fierce and ferocious.

We stand there while people go on about their evening, drinking and dancing, but then a clearing of someone's throat makes us look at the man currently standing with a frown on his face and murder in his eyes.

"Shaw. Take Ellaiza home."

"Yes, Mr. President."

"No, Dad. I want to stay here with mommy." The way she says it so desperately, as if she doesn't want to be apart from me either, breaks my heart more than it already has but at the same time, it makes it whole again. I can't even explain it.

It's magical.

Just like her father used to do to me.

Stopping that painful train of thought that only leads to more anger and heartache, I put a smile on my face, one that doesn't hurt, and reach forward, holding Ella's hand tightly in mine. "I'm not going anywhere ever again. That's a promise."

Her mouth forms the cutest 'O' shape before she exclaims. "Wow, it's the reals deals." I can't help it. I laugh.

"Yes, baby girl, promises are the real deal."

Then, without warning, she extends her small body, the bottom half still being held by her bodyguard, and her arms wrap around me, pulling me closer. "I really love you so much, mommy. I am so happy you reached all the stars and found your way home. Gosh, dad was right. You are a superhero."

Fuck.

Stay strong.

Kissing her forehead twice, I inhale her sweet scent, then back away, unclasping her tiny arms from my neck. Holding both her hands, I kiss them both and tell her. "I love you so much. I'll see you soon. Okay?"

"Okay!" She blows me a kiss as Shaw, the giant ass, moves with her in arms towards her father. I watch as Sebastian kisses his daughter and whispers something in her ear while never breaking eye contact with me. Tyrant.

Not even the years have changed the fact that he has always been and will most likely die a condescending, tyrannic bastard.

Fuck. Fuck. Fuck. I swear like a damn sailor because this was not supposed to happen. I was ready to tear his world apart and fight for my girl now that I am no longer a defenseless twenty-one-year-old with nothing to her name. But things have changed, haven't they? I agonize about what this all means in my head, but I can't come up with any logical answer. And the sad truth of it all is that I still look at him and feel anger, betrayal, and hurt. So much hurt, and I don't see this torment ending until I make him regret ever treating me as if I was disposable.

Suddenly the room feels too damn hot, and I can't breathe.

I can't think straight.

He always does this.

He managed to suck the air out of a room without much effort.

His mere presence did that.

He turns the tables on me, and it only infuriates me more because I know something inside of me shifted the moment my Ella revealed the reason why I was away from her.

Reaching the stars. The world is yours.

It's too much.

Pressing a hand to my chest, I feel my heart beating rapidly, almost as if the traitor knows the man who used to own is close by.

So close.

So, I run.

Like a coward, I run, leaving him standing in his own little bubble because the painful truth is that I no longer belong with them.

He made that painfully clear.

So yes, like a coward, I move towards the other end of the room where the air doesn't feel as heavy or bittersweet.

Where I'm able to breathe.

Damn you to hell, Sebastian.

I should have expected you would do the unpredictable.

You never played fair.

In life or in games of the heart.

Chapter 10
FORGET ME

Arianna

"Forgive and forget? Fuck that, and fuck you, too". — A

Before I even saw him, I felt his presence. It was as if I had a sixth sense or something when it came to this man. "Are you hiding from me, darling?" His breath so close to my neck causes goosebumps to spread over my skin, taunting me with the fact that he still has that effect on me. Ignoring my obnoxious reaction to Sebastian's closeness, I pick up my third glass of wine of the night without acknowledging his presence. Because when all the techniques I was taught by a very expensive therapist to control my anger failed, I turned to alcohol. It might cloud my judgment, but it does a good job of numbing me.

Because of this man.

Because even when time has passed, when I saw him, it feels as if no time had passed at all. It feels like it was yesterday when I first fell in love with the idea of him. The illusion turned out to be nothing but lies.

A facade.

Yet here I am, drinking to numb myself, to not feel any of the emotions he still stirs in me.

What messes with my head is the fact that this enigma of a man looks the same, yet also not. His black hair is cut short, the curly strands are long gone.

And somehow, that makes my chest ache.

I thought I was ready…

Maybe I fooled myself into thinking the past wouldn't hold power over my thoughts and actions, but here we are. Memories of every second I spent with this man hit me full force until I suppressed them, shoving them to the back of my mind and focusing on the pain seeing him causes. The pain of feeling him this close.

It serves as a reminder that he's not that man.

He never was.

Taking a sip of my glass, I take a deep breath and continue ignoring the man currently standing behind me, waiting for a reaction from me. "Will you turn around and give me those eyes, Arianna?" He says softly and so gently, and that messes with my head. I was not ready for this.

Knowing I can't keep running, I turn around and face him, not at all expecting the sight of him looking at me the way he's doing right at this instant.

No, I did not expect this at all.

I expected a fight.

I expected him to fight back when we started tearing each other apart. Instead, he is smiling and acting as if we are the same people we once were.

We're not.

He made sure of that.

You're not a coward, Arianna…

The vicious little devil on my shoulder whispers.

So, I lift my head and look him straight in the eyes, smiling. It hurts. Why does it hurt when ten minutes ago, I could smile freely with Ella? "What can I help you with, Mr. President?" I ask him. My tone is bored.

His eyes sharpen. "Stop that shit." He seethes, but his eyes do not once seem angry just...sad. Damn you, liar.

I stare at him, trying really hard to hide the fact that his deceiving and sad eyes are having a terrible effect on me. He then takes a step forward, and my eyes instantly look behind him, noticing Benjamin standing back with his eyes trained on his boss. On us. I swallow, looking at him while he gives me a 'you're okay' nod.

And suddenly, I don't feel all that vulnerable. My eyes leave Benjamin's and focus on the tyrant. "Again, is there anything you need, President Kenton?"

"It's Sebastian to you." He whispers, sounding hurt, but I know better. I am just one of the many who fell for his shit and now I pose a challenge to him.

And Sebastian Kenton loves games as much as he enjoys the challenge.

The chase.

The thrill of it all.

I learned that the hard way.

I wanted to remain calm, but now he's pissing me off.

The audacity of this man to act as if I would just fall on my knees the second he got close to me, and all would be right. That I would care about his demands. Fuck that. "You're nothing to me," I say through gritted teeth, hoping that my voice doesn't betray me. Thankfully, my tone comes off as convincing.

He stands tall with both hands inside his slack's pocket, looking confident, strong, and very determined.

"That is a lie, darling. I am everything to you. Just like you are the whole fucking world to me. Heaven, hell, and if there is something beyond that. You're that, too."

Liar.

Liar.

Fuck, stop lying.

Stepping back from him because his mere presence makes me want to break the flute in my hands over his head and cut his Carotid artery with a piece of glass. It also makes me feel things I have no business feeling again for this man.

So instead of being vulnerable or acting on my borderline psychotic impulse that will surely land my ass in jail for life, I place the flute down on the nearest table and then raise my head and stare at him as if he doesn't matter. "You're so full of shit. Step back and save your lies for the naive ones who voted for you and can stomach the farce of you because that is not me. Your lies, empty promises, and meaningless confessions mean nothing to me." I snap, failing at containing my temper.

Sebastian steps closer, minimizing the space between us, towering over me, strong, confident, and really fucking pissed.

Good.

Get mad and fight me, Sebastian.

"You were always a terrible liar." His breath on my face feels like a painful memory. Whiskey, cigar, and mint. His scent.

"And that's where you and I differ. You're a pro at lying." He was. He lies so well, even his eyes do, because something in those blue-gray eyes of his shift from angry to sad, and I instantly feel a pang in my chest.

Damnit. "I see you're not ready for the truth but know it's there waiting for you whenever you are."

"I don't care for your truths, so don't waste your breath, because quite frankly, I do not give a fuck."

Then suddenly, I'm being forced onto his shoes, taking me back to a time I tried really fucking hard to erase from my memory, and this tyrannical, egotistical asshole is determined to remind me of.

Pushing him back, I try to fight him off, but he's much stronger. He holds me tightly in his arms, bringing us closer to where we're mere inches apart. Stay strong… he can't hurt you if you won't let him. "Watch your mouth." He snaps.

Fuck him.

Fuck him for stirring feelings in me when I've been fighting to keep my head above water for so long because of him.

All because of him.

Now, all I thought is not what it seemed, and I do not know what to do but to attack.

Because isn't that what all wounded animals do?

Well, some lie down and die and others fight.

They fight for their survival.

"I won't say it twice, Sebastian. Let me go."

"Not happening, darling." His voice is so tender, so full of lies. I can't breathe. Fuck, it's like a knife to my gut. "I did that once, and it was the biggest mistake of my life. I don't regret anything I've done, before you came along. Not one single thing but that day. Those words I utter to you. There's no chance it will happen again. I suggest you stop hoping for it because you'll be sorely disappointed with the outcome."

"Release me." Christ, let go of me. This hurts. This closeness burns. Set me free from this hold you still have on me. Love. Hate. It ties me to him in every way.

From over his shoulders, I watch as Benjamin steps forward with a frown on his face and concern in his eyes. "You may step back, Banning." Sebastian doesn't look his way when he orders Benjamin. His blue-gray eyes remain on me. "I got it from here." The menacing way he says this freezes me on the spot. He's never sounded so harsh to Benjamin. Not like he does now as a rival and not his most trusted man.

Shit.

Does he know that Benjamin was the one who helped me disappear and stay hidden for these three years?

Looking up, my eyes clash with his. No longer sad or filled with remorse but angry, annoyed, and the one that pisses me off more... Hungry.

The world ceases to exist around us, and at the same time, my heart beat slows, beating softly, almost like a song that only Sebastian knows. God, how corny. "If you don't care about me, darling. If I mean nothing to you, then give me this dance. Unless you're afraid..." His face inches closer, his breath fanning over me, putting me in a spell. The fact that he seems to be caught up in the same spell as me makes me feel as if I, too, still have a hold on him.

The thought irks me just as much as it thrills me.

Because I know better.

My barely functioning heart knows better than to trust this.

Trust him.

"Oh, please Sebastian. What is there to fear? The worst thing you could have done to me... you did." I tell him and I don't miss the way he cringed as if my words slapped him in the face. "One dance." I narrow my eyes, giving in to his demand and ignoring the fact that I still can't dance for shit. Sebastian guides me, not caring that my heels are digging into his leather shoes.

"You take my breath away." He clears his throat. "But you know this already. I bet you're told just how beautiful you are wherever you go." I find it extremely satisfying that he sounds angry and jealous. Because the fact that I have no interest in other people doesn't mean I don't get hit on or approached by both sexes daily. I am not bragging about this fact, but it is that…a fact.

I don't tell him this. Mostly because I don't wish to engage him more than I already have. This night didn't turn out how I wanted it to. "No talking." His hands fall to my back, pushing me closer to his hard body. A shocked breath escapes me, causing him to laugh. A joyous laugh slips from his mouth, causing me to scowl. Those blue eyes of his shine as they did before. When he would laugh at my sarcastic and bitchy remarks. "Tough shit. I miss you. I miss your voice. Now that I heard it again, it feels like I am home. Fuck, darling. I'm home."

He's lying…that's what he does. He lies. Don't fall for it. The reasonable part of me points out.

I scoff, trying to hide the strangled sound of a wounded animal that almost falls from my lips. Home.

Where is home?

It used to be in his arms, but now it doesn't feel like home. At least, not to me. It feels like a battlefield, and this man is fighting on the opposite side. I ignore him, wishing the minutes could fly by so this torture would end. Every second I am in his arms feels as if I'm losing myself all over again. That is the effect of his man. One song. One moment, and I am beginning to fall back under his black magic treacherous spell. Overwhelmed with tedious emotions, I clench my jaw and stare up at him, not oblivious to the fact that all eyes are now on us.

Of course, people will stare.

He's not a Senator anymore but the big boss. The President.
All eyes will be on him, and by association, they'll be on me, too. "You did it," I whisper, not knowing why the hell I opened my mouth. "You became the President."
"Did you ever doubt me?"
What a multilayered question. Did I doubt he would achieve his goal? Not for one second. I don't doubt he'll make every wish he makes for himself come true, but I did and still do doubt his word, but I guess that's the damage he inflicted on me.
I didn't doubt his words when I loved him, but everything changed after that.
"Men like you always win, Sebastian. That is clear to me now."
"Not always, no." He whispers, and his eyes trap me, keeping me hostage. "Sometimes men like me lose, too."
I hate how my chest feels tight when he looks at me as if there's nothing else he would rather see. Lost for words, I keep staring at him as if he didn't just drop a bomb on me. He used to gloat that he always won, and he always would. The man was always on top, and now that he's one, if not the most powerful man in the country, he's not gloating.
Not with me.
Time seems to stop when he bends his head toward my face, his lips inches from mine. A heavy breath gets stuck in my throat when he catches me off guard. "But now this…Arianna." My eyes fall from his eyes to his lips. Perfect, plump, and so very tempting. Fuck, this man really is the devil. A liar. A thief. A seducer. "You once promised a war, and I deserve it. Fuck, do I deserve it. So give me all you got. Fight me. Curse my name to hell and back, but don't you hide from me again." I'm so stunned by the words that just slip from his mouth

that I don't notice his hand coming up behind me to grab me by the back of the neck. "Because not knowing where you were and if you were okay killed me. It killed something inside of me." I remain silent, not knowing what to say. Sebastian's eyes change from sad to determined, and so does his smile. Not cruel. Not a gloating smile but a smile that tells me he's a man with a plan. One I won't like. "I lost a part of me that day. I lost you, but the war for your heart is not one I intend to lose." With that promise, he drops his mouth to mine, taking my lips in his. Robbing me of all breath and logic.

Because that is the only explanation for why I don't push him back. Why don't I break the kiss?

I have lost my mind.

Damn you a thousand times, tyrant.

The kiss is desperate, but completely different from the ones he gave me before.

Desperate as if he's been craving me for so long and now he found me.

You found your way back...

A voice whispers in my head.

An annoying one.

Ripping my lips from his, I step back, fighting his strong hold. Anger swells up inside me again. I want to shove him and make him fall flat on his ass. Or maybe I should spit on his handsome face instead. "Don't ever fucking kiss me, or touch me again, Sebastian."

"There's my girl." His grin is almost endearing. Almost. "It's good to know you haven't forgotten me. Your mouth remembers, as does your heart. Of that, I have no doubt." Determination gleamed in his eyes. "You found your way back to me and I know that when I put my mind to something, I rarely fail. Prepare yourself, *mon coeur*. I intend on making up for the last three years so that we don't spend one more moment without each other again."

Thud.

No.

Thud.

Fuck, no.

Heart… don't be stupid.

Not again.

I freeze, take a deep breath, and do my best to control my rising temper.

I fail.

"Fuck off," I say just loud enough for him to hear and turn and leave his smiling ass behind.

I run.

For the second time that night, I run from the feelings the tyrant in the white house has stirred in me.

Chapter 11
IF GROVELING WAS A MAN
Arianna

"Every corner of my heart is haunted." — A

"Nessa." I stop my junior journalist before she heads back in the direction of her office. She did rather well expressing her ideas to the group today. I must admit I was impressed. That and I'm kind of proud. When she started working with me, she would agree to everything and with what everyone said. Always second-guessing herself, and to avoid conflict or stepping out of her comfort zone she would rather go along with what my other employees said.

Not anymore, though.

Now, she's not afraid to speak her mind and that's the kind of journalist I need on my team.

Someone who takes no shit and goes after what they want.

"Yes, boss?" Nessa stops and turns to me with a tired smile.

I still remember how awkward it was for her the first few times she referred to me as boss, especially since I am younger than her. I got my degree in less time than most college students, so I might seem like I accomplished more than her when we were almost the same age but the reality is that I had a privilege she did not, and I recognize it.

It doesn't take away from the fact that I worked my ass off to obtain all I have now.

Drive.

Ambition.

Dedication and a whole lot of hunger to succeed no matter the help. It got me where I am today.

But I recognize a job well done, and Nessa is working her ass off. There is no doubt about that. "Your ideas were much appreciated, and I am…" God, why is it so difficult for me to give out compliments? Nessa looks at me expectantly. "I was impressed and know that they'll be taken into consideration." Her face softens, then she nods and leaves in the other direction where her office is located.

See, was that so hard? My latest acquisition, a bitch named conscience, taunts me.

Taking a deep breath, I walk towards my office, needing to be by myself after a long morning of meetings. They were all a success. My team and I discussed our game plan for both the paper and the magazine's future. It's been one hell of a week.

After being a small newspaper slash magazine with an average audience, it all changed in an instant.

All because of one man.

An infuriating man with a God complex.

The articles written about him are the most popular ones and are the reason why we gained more exposure. So much so that the company is being added to press conference lists for not only major Hollywood events but more high-elite social events.

This includes the list of magazines and newspapers allowed to attend the White House future press conferences.

It's also because Sebastian re-posted a news article to his POTUS accounts all over social media. Our numbers have multiplied, and so have the amounts of comments, shares, and replies. It's insane how one reaction can change the course of a company for the better.

And as much as I'm happy, because who the hell doesn't want their baby, and this company is my baby, to thrive? The fact that Sebastian made it happen has me on edge. I don't want to owe him a damn thing and this makes me feel like I do.

I don't want my success to be tied to him, but I guess there's not much I can do since I chose to publish articles about him and it was a no-brainer that it would gain popularity.

Still, I rather swallow shit than admit it's all because of him.

Him and his incessant need to meddle in my business.

And that's not the extent of it.

The tyrant upgraded his status from tyrant to stalker.

I won't even entertain the question of how he got hold of my email address because there's no doubt that there's little to no information that he does not have access to.

My inbox is full to the brim of emails from him. Some are short and to the point, asking how my days are going or asking one thing that makes me smile, and others are long letters with the subject line that reads letters from a man in love. I haven't read or answered a single email, not wanting to fall for his shit. He's very convincing. I must give him that, persistent, too, but his attempts to soften me are in vain. Last night, everything happened so fast and caught me off-guard. I imagined a million ways of reuniting with Sebastian Kenton, and none of them ended in a scenario quite like last night's.

He's a smart man.

The most brilliant man I've ever met, and he knows how to play the game just as he plays his rivals. I guess I learned from the best.

I also know that he detests being ignored, and the more I hide from him, it's plainly obvious he'll seek me out. I am aware that the emails and texts won't be the end of him.

Then I think about how things have changed completely. For years, I planned to make Sebastian's presidency a nightmare and expose his dirty secrets, and I still intend on doing that, but now that I know that Ellaiza knows who I am, I need to be careful because fuck, the asshole might use her against me. Knowing him as I do, Sebastian must realize that Ellaiza is the only card he has against me.

And how can I succeed in ruining Sebastian when his kid, my girl, thinks of me as her mother. It all seemed so simple when I believed he erased me from her life and memories.

Ugh.

What a mess.

I also still have no single clue what exactly happened at the gala. All I know is that my girl grew up thinking I was away reaching for dreams instead of being by her side. That her asshole father lied to me when he implied that Ella would forget me eventually, and in other words, told me he was never speaking of me.

Then, that kiss.

The bastard kissed me, and what is most annoying is the fact that even a day later. I can still taste him.

That big, egotistical, selfish prick.

Yet you can't stop thinking about him… the annoying voice in my head taunts me.

But I ignore it as always.

Sebastian's mind has always been a mystery to me. Yes, I thought I knew him before, but maybe there are too many layers that he kept from me. And now I'm not in the mood to uncover the Pandora's box that is Sebastian Kenton's mind.

My phone vibrates in my hand, alerting me to a new email. The man is spamming my work email without care.

Standing in front of the black marble double doors of my office, I twist the knob and open the door. The moment I do, I wish I hadn't.

"Uh, this was delivered for you. I didn't want to interrupt your meeting, so I signed for the packages." My assistant, Oliver, stands next to my desk where there's a large white box with a balcony bow on it. Oliver is my age, good-looking, brilliant, and efficient.

He's been with me since I started the company with less than fifteen employees. He does his work, gives his best, and never asks many questions.

The man is greatly appreciated.

But now all I want to do is rip his ass a new one for allowing this mess inside my office. Stepping inside, I look at everything from dozens of bouquets of gold-plated roses to countless boxes of all sizes spread all over the office. The image takes me back to the night in the Malibu house, where he filled my room with what I thought were thoughtful gifts.

Walking over to my desk, I touch the black bow on the large box. I look down at the box with a frown on my face. "Oliver."

"Yes, boss?"

"Get rid of all of it." I snap. Oliver eyes me suspiciously, probably wondering what kind of maniac would want to get rid of what he presumes are expensive items just from the packaging.

"All of it? What do you want me to do with them? Throw everything away?" Thinking about it, I shrug. "Give them to the employees." Looking down at the box, a shiver runs down my spine, almost like deja-vú. "All except this one."

"As you wish," Oliver says and then moves to take everything away. Placing my phone down on the desk, I move to take off the bow on the box before taking the lid off. "No. You certainly don't play fair, Sebastian." I whisper under my breath so Oliver doesn't hear me.

Inside the box, there is a huge, black and gold globe with the maps painted in gold. Taking it out, I notice some lavender pins and sticky notes.

What the hell...

Bending down, I notice a white note card sticking to the lid.

It's still your world, darling. Can't wait to explore it with you. Where to next?

Yours, even when you weren't here,

Love you always,

Sebastian.

Thud.

Thud.

The traitorous organ beats wildly in my chest not at all concerned that the man is the reason why it's broken.

The man and his lies, and don't forget his selfish agenda.

Dropping the globe back inside its box, I round my desk, taking a seat. Something inside of me tells me that something has changed. Does he... no. Don't be naive, Arianna.

You're a challenge. A game to him.

The daughter of the man who murdered his parents. Nothing more.

He'll hurt you again, and you know it.

Ping.

A message pops up on my desktop screen, and for a second, I think it's another one of Sebastian's annoying messages, but no. It's an email from Nessa.

To: wwceo@mag.us.com

From: najuniorpu@mag.us.com

Subject: Thiago Sandoval - Crime lord (allegedly)

Boss,

I managed to grab some shots from Gary where it clearly shows the president entering and exiting the Sandoval residence in the late hours of the night. I attached the photos for your approval.

Cordially,

Nessa

Clicking on the attachments, it takes a second for the first image to pop up on the screen, and there he is. Not even the night and shadows can conceal Sebastian as he exits a black car with dark-tinted windows and enters the Sandoval residence dressed in a dark gray suit.

Closing my eyes, I push aside yesterday's events and focus on every night I cried myself to sleep, missing them. Hurting for Ellaiza. Searching for Sebastian in the darkest place in my mind, always coming up empty and alone. Sadness takes over me.

Sadness and anger as I think back to that time. Times when I would search the internet while tears fell from my eyes to see him smiling and moving on with his life while mine was in shambles.

No, I can't forget, and I sure as hell can't forgive.

Knowing there's no going back, the anger I feel inside won't subside unless I make his life as miserable as he did mine, I dial Nessa's xtension, and wait for the phone to connect.

"Yes, boss?"

"Publish them." That's all I tell her.

She knows what to do next.

I'm angry. No number of kisses, letters, and excuses can make up for what he did and the pain he caused. The anger inside me has burned for too long, and at this point, I believe nothing, and no one can put it out.

Chapter 12
WAR OF HEARTS
Bastian

"Everywhere I go...
leads me back to you." — A

"Fix that shit, Seba, or I'll have no choice but to get involved." Sandoval has been throwing tantrums all morning, irritating me to the point I am seconds away from cussing out the motherfucker and severing all ties between us and our business.

For fuck's sake.

All this drama because of a news article.

To a rational man who cares about his image, the slandering article would be a big fucking deal, but for me? I could care less. I got the votes even with my reputation, my ties to the crime world, and the rumors circulating about my illegal businesses.

The people of this country were aware of all of this, and they still got out of bed or left their jobs to go to the nearest polls and voted for me.

I was their candidate.

A little gossip regarding my connection to the Sandoval family won't hurt my status all that much.

Yes, maybe it might give my political adversaries something to exploit while criticizing my policies and decisions during my time in office, but they still won't do shit. "Stop with the theatrics, Sandoval. This is not the first time the media has been up your ass, and I assure you, my friend, it certainly won't be the last." I murmur while finishing writing an email. One of ten I've sent today, and that have gone unanswered.

Still, I send them.

Because it's her.

It's always her, and it will always be her.

"Fuck you, *cabrón*. You damn well know this heat on me is not good for business. I can't leave my home without being harassed by reporters asking shit that might get them killed if they keep it up. So, either you manage the situation and get the assholes off my dick, or I'll have to pay them a little visit." Sandoval sounds more than serious, and I know he's not playing anymore. The latest news today was images of me stepping out of Sandoval's home after one of our monthly meetings, where we discussed his underground business and played dirty poker. The news was meant to put a negative light on me. That's what the beautiful vindictive monster that is Arianna intended when she approved the article that was published this morning.

I should be pissed. I should be finding ways to fuck with her like I would any other media outlet who screws me, over but no. Instead, I am overwhelmed with emotions raging from pride, admiration, and fuck, so much love. Not only did she reach the stars, but she made a life for herself. She chose her path and found her place in the world. It led her back to me. I'm more than proud.

I admire her strength and ferocity.

Her thirst to thrive despite her adversities and all the pain I caused.

"Fucker, are you there?"

Sandoval's voice is now graving on my last nerve.

"I'll handle it," I reply to him, while at the same time hitting send on the email. Sitting back on my chair, I look at the picture frame I have of both my girls. The most important people in my life. "You will stay out of it and let me handle the matter accordingly, or you'll give me no choice but to paint your home's walls with your blood, friend or not." I threatened, meaning every word.

Sandoval laughs as if we both didn't just threaten the other's life. That's who he is. The man gets off on chaos. "You don't fuck with blood, Seba. Get the fuck out of here." For her, I do. For her, I will. Every time. I proved it when I paid her scum of a father a little visit. "I sense there is more to this shit that you're letting on, Seba." Sandoval's voice sounds curious.

"I suggest you mind your business." I mumble tiredly.

"And I suggest you get some pussy and rid yourself of that stick up your ass." The asshole continues talking out of his ass.

"Are you done?" I'm bored with this useless conversation.

Sandoval chuckles before saying, "I'm not fucking around. Handle them, or I will." With that threat, he disconnects the call.

Fuck.

As much as I'm enjoying Arianna's attempts to fuck with my life, I'll have to do something soon before she has every made man in this city coming for her pretty ass. Thiago Sandoval might be a friend, but friend or not, I know his family and business come first, and Arianna exposing him is causing problems for him.

And now she's a problem for him.

Fuck, I might have to kill a friend, and that's a shame since I have so few of them. But I would kill the pope, God, and whichever fucker poses a threat to her before they ever get their filthy hands on her.

Knock, knock.

"Come in," I mutter, rubbing my temples. Every time I hold a conversation with Sandoval, the bastard gives me a raging headache that not even whiskey can cure. When the door to my office is shut softly, I raise my gaze to find Shaw standing there with a gift basket in hand. "This was sent to your private residence, sir. It was cleared and it is of no threat to you." I look at what I assume was a neatly packed basket, now a mess of plastic wrap and white decorative paper.

"Bring it over." Although this gift might be nothing special, my pulse races anyway at the thought that perhaps it might be from her. From the woman who's out for my blood. Doesn't she realize that she's in every part of me? My heart and my goddamn blood.

"I must say, boss. You made one hell of a bad impression on this one. Still, this one isn't the worst." Through my years in the public eye, I've been stalked, harassed, and plenty of creepy shit has been sent to my residence. From desperate love letters to dangerous threats.

I have seen it all, and nothing managed to surprise me until this one. Smiling big, I reply. "You're mistaken. This is just my woman's definition of romance and foreplay."

He snorts. "Trashing you and sending you funeral flowers is romantic to you? No disrespect, boss, but you've finally lost it. This woman clearly hates your as—." Looking up at him, I give him a look that has him rethinking his choice of words. He clears his throat, not looking at all sorry for what he was about to say.

Instead of giving him a hard time as I would normally do when Shaw gets too comfortable cussing around me, I reply as I watch him move forward. "Hate and love. Love and hate. It's all the same to us. That's how our story goes."

I focus on the basket placed on top of my desk by Shaw, and from what I can see, there are a dozen of black roses. With a giddiness I haven't felt since she left, I tear open what remains of the basket and take out the items inside.

Newspapers and a magazine.

Hers.

Her work.

Her accomplishments.

Fuck, how I manage to feel both proud and elated instead of offended in this situation is beyond me, but I am.

Hate or love me, I'm still in there.

In her blood.

In her brain.

And I won't rest until I'm back where I was always meant to be.

Her heart.

Looking at the black roses, I smile. I smile because I'm happy. I haven't felt genuine happiness apart from Ellaiza, in a long time, but today I feel as if I'm being brought back to life, and it is all because of the woman who owns me.

Taking the magazine in hand, I flip through the pages in awe of what she accomplished without my help. She is the CEO of a news magazine and a paper.

And I? Her favorite topic, from what I see. She made me the front page of the newspaper and the cover for this month's issue of her magazine.

Bad press, but how can it be bad when it comes from her?

And she thought she wasn't a romantic.

It doesn't get more romantic than this.

My woman even highlighted the best parts of the article for me.

Every quote that makes me look in a bad light…she highlighted for me. Ignoring Shaw's irritating presence, I look at the article that has images of me stepping out of Sandoval's home in the middle of the night. The news is nothing new since more outlets have run with the story before, but what's different this time is the article offers more insight into my relationship with the crime lord.

How Thiago Sandoval has been linked to other crime lords in the States. It mentions the rumors that I know for a fact are true, but the country doesn't. The rumors that Sandoval took out a handful of high-profile politicians, some that were in the presidential race and were my opponents. It makes it seem as if Sandoval cleared the path for me to become president, but the reality is that those men were taken out for other reasons. Reasons that no one but us and the dead men know.

Besides my men, only Arianna knows, to an extent, my relationship with the Sandoval capo. She knows more than most people, and that makes her a threat.

Fuck.

I need to handle this before it gets out of hand and she starts revealing shit that might cause me problems with other crime families I'm associated with, too. I can handle most of them, but I won't risk it.

Risk her.

Roaming through the basket, I notice a small note stuck to a black rose.

President Kenton,

Here's the secret to winning any game…

Play the player, not the game.

-Parisi

Chuckling like a crazy fuck, I shove the note into my breast pocket.

Oh, you play me alright, darling.

I can't wait to play with you, too.

Her pretty green eyes flash through my mind, green and with a new fire that makes promises of misery and trouble—which awakens a dominant, dark part of me.

Bring it, baby.

Oh, she's brought it. That's for damn sure.

The door to my office opens a second time, and a newcomer joins us.

"You wanted to see me?" Banning.

Ah, yes.

There's something that needs to be straightened out now before I continue in my pursuit of forever with a very angry and beautiful woman.

Ping.

Ping.

Ping.

My phone buzzes where it's sitting on the desk.

Text message after message pops up on the screen. I smile, already knowing who they're from.

Picking up the phone, I unlock it, tapping on the first message.

My heart: Dad. I know what's missing in our family.

Smiling at my daughter's text message, I reply.

Me: What's that?

Three dots appear on the screen before her next message comes through. This time it is a selfie of my daughter holding up a drawing of a small dog.

My heart: I need a feeling puppy.

An emotional dog, I'm assuming that's what she's referring to. I sometimes wonder where the hell she gets these ideas from. Then I remember she is my daughter.

She knows what she wants and goes after it even at such a young age.

I was like that when I was a young child too.

I start to type my reply when another message pops up.

My heart: Mommy will totally like a puppy, and you want us both to be happy! Right, Dad?

She's too damn smart and… manipulative.

Me: It's daddy. Not dad or father.

My heart: She sends her third favorite emoticon. A face with rolling eyes.

Brat.

A brat just like her mother.

But she's on to something, and it sparks an idea. An idea and a fire.

Me: Ellaiza, I need you to do something for daddy.

I tell her exactly what I need from her, and not even a second later, my daughter replies.

My heart: I will do it. On one condition.

My heart: *Puppy emoji*

I created a monster. The little brat acts cute now, but I know she'll be a pain in my ass when she's a teenager.

God help me when the time comes.

Me: Daughters don't blackmail their fathers, Ellaiza.

My heart: It's just business… daddy.

Laughing aloud, I send my reply telling her I love her, which she returns before I put the phone back down.

A good man would feel like the biggest piece of shit for using his daughter to get to the woman he loves, but I never claimed to be a good man, and I have always played a dirty game.

And Ellaiza is the one card I have on my deck.

The one person that could help me soften Arianna's heart, and this way, I get to mend all of our broken hearts by fighting for the family both Arianna and my daughter never had.

Because love is Ellaiza.

Love is us.

The clearing of a throat captures my attention.

Turning in my seat, I watch as both Banning and Shaw are looking at me as if I've lost my goddamn mind. Maybe it's because I've laughed more today than I have in the past three years. "Shaw."

"Sir?"

"Leave us." He nods and turns towards the door, leaving me alone with Banning.

I've held off on this conversation long enough, and it is long overdue.

Rising from my seat, I walk towards where he's standing next to the door. Banning was always the one cracking jokes and calling me out on my shit, and that hasn't changed, but lately, he's been quieter than usual. Not quite himself, and it leads me to wonder if it's because he is now stuck in the middle of whatever the hell this is between Arianna, his friend, and me, his boss.

We both stay quiet for a long moment, but then he's the one to break the silence first. "I assume this is about Arianna." He moves closer to where I am with a knowing look. I take the opportunity to truly look at my right-hand man. During these past three years, the man has grown stronger, building muscle on top of muscle. The motherfucker looks like a tank. A tank most wouldn't want to cross their paths. I wouldn't recommend it if they want to live to see another day.

Adjusting my cufflink, I move towards him, meeting him halfway before replying. "You assume right." His eyes search for something in mine. Anger? Perhaps regret? Can he see how fucking sorry I am? "You know."

Looking him dead in the eye, "I do." Clearing my throat, then I ask. "Why did you do it? Why did you not only lie but keep her from me?"

Banning shrugs uncaringly. "There's not much I wouldn't do for her." For a second, jealousy blooms hot and fierce inside of me, but then I remind myself that Benjamin is no threat to me, but he is still a man. A man who got to see and speak to her when I wasn't there.

He didn't fuck up… you did.

"All the times I asked you to search for her, and you came back with nothing…that was a betrayal, Ben." I use his first name because, at this instant, we are equal. Something that looks a lot like guilt crosses over his features, and I'm hit with the same feeling. It would be hypocritical of me to be mad at my most trusted man, who took it upon himself to help Arianna when she had no one. I made him her guardian while she was under my care, and I trust him with my life and the life of the most important people to me.

That doesn't mean I am not mad-as-fuck at myself and him, but mostly at myself.

Betrayal.

That's how it feels.

Banning's face contorts in anger. "I told you she needed more than myself. Didn't I? I told you she was vulnerable, and yet you did what you did. Yes, you wanted better for her, but fuck you, man, for breaking her heart and treating her like every motherfucker before you." Banning snaps, losing all the control he's been holding on to. Finally saying all he wanted to say to me but never dared to. "But most of all, fuck you for breaking Ellaiza's heart in the process."

That he whispers angrily while his eyes shoot daggers at me. "I would do it again in a heartbeat, just so you know. You're my brother, but those are my girls, and as long as they need me, I'll be there." Taking a step forward, he lifts his chin in defiance. Feeling my temper rise, I try to control the anger that his words stirred. The truth is that, in the process of wanting to be the good man, the best man, a man like Banning, I broke the hearts of the two people that mattered most to me.

"You're right. I fucked up, no one knows this better than I do, and the only reason I am not pummeling your face right now for hiding her from me, it's because you kept her safe. You took care of her when that was my job. I love you like a brother, but that's my woman, and no one gets between me and her. I need you to be on my side now. I thank you, fuck, do I thank you for keeping her safe and all you've done, but now it's my time to make up for my mistake, and you know it as well as I do that there's no one else for her but me. No one." I make my point clear, but Banning still looks skeptical but has a good mind to keep quiet, so I continue. "Now listen to me closely because I won't be repeating myself, nor will I keep blaming myself. I'm moving forward." Getting in his face, I tell him how things will go from now on. "I'm trying to repair what I broke, and for me to do that, I need you to be on my side. No lies. No keeping her from me. None of that. Because if you keep her from me again, brother or not, I will end you along with everyone else who tries to keep her from me. With that, I punch the motherfucker right in the mouth and watch him trip backward. "That was for keeping her from me." Stepping back. I adjust my tie, then spread my arms wide. "Take a shot." I'm done talking about my mistakes. I'm done bitching about it. I know what I want and what I'll always want in her. She grew up and found her voice in this world, in her town, without me or her crime family holding her back, but now she's back, and there's no stopping the inevitable.

There's no stopping me.

Banning grins, "Been waiting a long time for this, Mr. President." He mocks and then swings.

Fuck.

The fucker returns the punch right in the mouth. I can taste blood. Using a handkerchief, I wipe the blood off and look at my friend, my best man. "I bet you have."

He hit me with years of pent-up aggression.

Motherfucker.

Now, we're even, and we can move on.

One step closer to her.

To my forever.

I may not be the best man, hell, not even a good man, but she's it for me, and I'd always put her first.

From now on, that's my first priority.

Chapter 13
MAKE IT BETTER

Arianna

"I would burn the world down for you." — B

"Stop hurting her!" I screamed. In fact, I screamed so loud and hard that I felt something give way in my throat, but that didn't stop me. No. It made me scream harder, trying— no, hoping— that the man would stop his ruthless assault.

My scream sounds more desperate and terrified when the image of a woman tied to the wall with a hook around her neck, holding her head straight up and a hunting knife shoved deep into her belly.

The food I had earlier threatens to spill at the horrific sight.

I've known my father to be cruel, but this is inhumane.

This is the mafia… a haunting voice whispers inside my head, reminding me. Not once letting me forget that I belong to this ugly world.

The image of the knife shoved into her pregnant belly will haunt me forever. Andrew, one of my father's men, steps echo in the room while smiling as he approaches the crying woman with another knife. "Oh, God. Please don't," I moaned. "Don't. Don't do it. It wasn't her fault. I made her do it. Hurt me, please hurt me." My cries, as always, were ignored, and Andrew continued his path to Noelia with the intent to keep prolonging her agony. The moment he was close enough, he stabbed her straight through her left thigh. The poor woman screamed, and I screamed with her.

Please, God, if you're there. Please make it stop. My head was a mess and my heart, the one that's been slowly decaying for years, is reaching its limit. There's only so much a person can take before they break.

"This, princess." Andrew, our tormentor, points another knife at Noelia. "This is what happens when you disobey your father." The asshole smiles cruelly, enjoying the fact that he gets to teach me the lesson instead of my father tonight. "Next time you think about poor, defenseless Noelia and how this could be another innocent person in her place. Hell, it could be one of your sweet, sweet sisters." I whimper, like a scared and tortured animal at the thought of this cruel man getting close to my little sisters. We were in our home's basement, where most of Gabriele's torturing happens. Here is where my innocence was stolen from me when I was just a girl. Where I witnessed just how cruel this world is and how little to no voice I had in it. I used to fight back and it only made everything worse for me and the people who dared loved me. That was my place in this world.

Afraid.

Quiet.

Broken.

It was a painful lesson to learn. One my father won't let me forget.

"Just–just please stop. I was the one who asked for her help. She was just obeying orders." I try to reason with him, knowing it is useless. Men like him, like my father, get off on other people's pain.

Their suffering and tears.

"Please, stop. Please stop. That's all you're good for, princess," Andrew mocks. "This is necessary. But, since we're in a hurry, I'll finish up here real quick." He stabbed Noelia three more times, once more in each thigh, and then stepped back to admire his handiwork, while I screamed like a wounded animal, not being able to hold it back.

With each stab, I felt it down to my soul.

Guilt clawed at me, suffocating me.

Stay quiet, Arianna, and no one will hurt you.

Don't fight it. It's a man's world.

The voices in my head repeat it until they drown the screams of agony coming from both Noelia and me.

Then the next thing I knew, I was standing up. My hair was wrenched back so hard that I saw stars. It felt as if it was being ripped from my scalp. It burns, but nothing compares to the pain that the innocent woman was going through because of me. The pain was evident in her posture, as well as her sad eyes when she managed to open them.

Oh, God.

The blood.

It's all over her.

"I've had enough of your screams, Arianna. Toughen the fuck up." With that, my father leaves the shadows and raises his fist then slams it down so hard against my face that my vision blurs. Blackness started to dot the edges of my vision, and the next thing I knew, I was dead to the world.

***

A knock on my office door brings me back to the present and away from the gruesome memories of the past.

"Shit." I breathe out.

Why is it that every ugly memory from my past that I tried so hard to suppress comes back to haunt me now?

I haven't had a single good night's sleep in weeks, but now that a certain tyrant is back in my life, most of the progress I've made has gone to hell. I'm not even blaming him fully for it. I take responsibility for it since I am the one who decided to fuck with him, and now he's fucking with me without even trying.

Turning my head towards the glass doors, I see the intruder. Speaking of the devil. "You've got to be kidding," I mutter, hating that my heart is racing like a lunatic. "Get out." Nope. I rise from my seat the moment I watch Sebastian open the door and enter my office without being invited. Looking past him, I watch a squad of men dressed in black guarding the door while my traitorous employees gather around talking amongst themselves, and some take out their phones, most likely recording their president or snapping pictures.

"Miss me?" Sebastian asks while closing the door with his hip because both hands are busy holding onto a brown bag while the other holds a carton tray with two coffees.

"I miss you as much as a healthy person would miss gonorrhea." Crossing my arms over my chest, I give him an ugly look that causes his mouth to twitch in response.

He chuckles before he says, "You kill me." Then he touches his heart, smiling like a fool.

A gorgeous fool.

Ugh.

"And yet, you're still breathing. Why are you here?" Taking a seat, I have half a mind to call security on his ass, but I know better than to do that because: 1. In this country, the president can do as he wishes and go where he pleases without little to no consequence. It's a losing battle to believe that he will listen to me and leave at his own will.

2. I know my security will feel uncomfortable asking their president to leave the headquarters. Besides, I'm sure most of them would rather lose their job than go through with the order.

"I missed you, and I wanted to see your beautiful face." He stands in front of one of my office chairs with a brilliant smile on his stupid perfect face. "And… I brought you coffee." He places the two coffees on top of my desk and drops the brown bag next. "And treats. I know how much you love these."

Looking down at the bag, I tell him. "Like I would drink or eat anything you brought me. It could be poisoned." I frown while leaning forward in my seat. "You think I would poison you? Come on, darling. Let us be honest here. If anyone were to poison someone, it would be you."

That is true. The only reason I haven't given it much thought it's because of Ellaiza. She surely would suffer if her father were to be murdered. On the other hand, kids are resilient, and she's still young… *You can't kill the man…*

I can if I want to.

You would go to prison.

Orange might look good on me.

If he dies, then he doesn't suffer, not really…

Hmm, that is true.

Too deep in a conversation with the little devilish bitch on my shoulder, I forgot America's nuisance is in front of me, looking at me like Ellaiza looks at cupcakes. The bastard.

"I already had my coffee, and I have no desire for sweets. You can leave now." I look away from him, suddenly finding the tedious papers on my desk very interesting.

Then the asshole laughs.

He laughs in that melodic way he used to that made my heart skip in my chest, but this time around, it only makes my stomach coiled. I remember the sound vividly. The sound used to keep me up at night the first few weeks, hell, the first year after I fled Chicago.

Ignoring me, he moves the coffee cup my way and takes out chocolate cake pops from the bag. "You wouldn't want to break a little girl's heart, would you?" His eyes twinkle with the usual evil glint.

"What are you talking about?"

"Ellaiza specifically asked me to bring you your favorites because, and I quote, "Mommy needs a little bit of sweetness in her life."

Thud.

Fucking.

Thud.

My heart flips at the mention of my girl. This motherfucker is using Ellaiza to get to me, and I am defenseless against it. Contrary to him, I do have a conscience. "If I drink your fucking coffee, will you leave?" I snatch the treat from his hand and take the lid off the coffee cup while Sebastian sits there brushing an invisible lint from his suit, the picture of arrogance and classic beauty. The years only made him more handsome and more of an asshole too.

"You look breathtakingly beautiful when you're angry." He lifts his head, and those blue grays clash with my painfully obvious annoyed ones.

Rolling my eyes, I snap at him. "Cut the corny bullshit."

"Watch your mouth and smile." He replies with a small smile of his own and before I have a chance to react, he is snapping a photo of me. Has he lost his mind?

"What are you doing?" I asked.

"Ellaiza wanted proof that I kept my promise."

He shrugs as if it is nothing. Like taking a photo without my consent is no big deal.

It is a big fucking deal, but again... he's using Ella against me.

Damn you, tyrant.

Damn you straight to hell.

Furious and unnerved by the audacity of him being here, in my space and in my world where he's not welcome–not anymore–I ignore him and I take a sip of the coffee, and I'm surprised that he brought me my usual order.

My favorite.

The moment the flavor hits my taste buds, I find myself moaning aloud. "I don't even want to know how you managed to find out my usual order..." My coffee order is quite unique. An iced chocolate, almond milk, shaken espresso with ristretto in place of regular espresso. A pump of chai, toffee nut syrup, and a drizzle of caramel sauce.

I learned from Oliver that most people, mostly him, hate the taste, but I find it not only comforting but delicious. Sebastian grins while pocketing his phone inside his suit jacket. His eyes never leave mine. "I have my ways. You know this, darling..."

"Don't call me that." I snap, and he rolls his eyes. The condescending ass. "And what you have is Benjamin." I deadpan.

Grinning, he says. "That I do." Benjamin, you gigantic traitor.

A smiling Sebastian sits back in my chair, looking around my office, taking everything in while I try to gulp down the coffee hurrying so he can go on his merry way. Silence takes over the space while he sits looking around my office. White walls, glass doors, a city view, and lots of black and white decor. Simple, classic, and chick.

Me.

I also notice the moment he sees the board of chess sitting on top of one of my tables, closer to the full-length window. "You still play?" I hate the way his voice sounds hopeful and giddy. Something I've never witnessed from him before. Yes, happy but giddy and hopeful? No.

I'm in no mood to entertain his questions or games. I just need him away from me. Far, far away, because at this moment, he is making me feel vulnerable, and that's a dangerous thing to be around Sebastian Kenton. Running my tongue over my teeth, I do my best to remain silent, but the way he stares at me so intensely as if he wishes to eat me alive and keep me inside of him forever, unnerves me so I break the silence, and look away from him. The man knows what he is doing. That's for sure.

"How's Ella?" I blurt out.

Without missing a beat, he answers. "Missing you terribly."

That makes me angry. That I can work with instead of all the other feelings he is stirring inside of me. Turning my face his way, I reply. "And whose fault is that?" I shoot my angry eyes up to his.

Guilt is written on his face, and the smile drops. "Mine."

I should feel ecstatic that he feels bad, and that guilt is gnawing at him but what good does that do me?

"I'm not staying away from her. If I have to fight you to be able to see her, I will..."

"There's no need, darling." Sebastian smiles then reaches inside his suit jacket and pulls out a purple piece of paper, handing it to me.

Getting comfortable in my suit, I study the purple piece of paper in the shape of a heart with childlike writing. My heart skips many beats when I notice it is some sort of invitation from my favorite person in the whole world.

Dear Mommy,

I cordially invite you to my dinner party.

Where: The big white house.

When: Tomorrow night. Eight o'clock, sharp.

Attire: Black tie, not optional.

PS: I can't wait to see you.

PSS: This is going to be sooooo awesome.

Love,

Ella.

Tears well in my eyes while my heart soars with love for this tiny human who has managed to heal my heart twice. A tiny human that is part of the enemy. Part of the man who I hate most, second to my father. What bothers me most is that he knows my weakness is his girl and yet he will exploit it to get what he wants. Then I wonder… What does he want exactly? To fool me as he did years ago? Whatever it is, I find myself losing control every time I see him and it is infuriating as much as it is terrifying. Because every time he's near, I feel like that lovesick fool who believed this man was larger than life. The girl that believed he was everything she needed and wanted in this life. What a fool…

Placing the sweet-as-hell invitation down, I give Sebastian an ugly look, causing his mouth to twitch in response. "What are you doing here, really?" Rising from the seat, he towers over me while I'm seated. Looking strong, confident, and heartbreakingly handsome in his navy suit. I wait for his response as he buttons his suit jacket and steps back. "I can't undo my move, but I can make it better, and this, baby, this is me making it better." Angry at him.

At myself.

At the world.

So angry I don't even feel cold anymore, just this never-ending burn that keeps spreading all over me, more ferocious when he's nearby. It doesn't stop. It's the kind of burn that hurts me.

I always thought that feeling cold was the worst thing a human could be, but this burning sensation is agonizing.

Fuck you. I want to scream.

Fuck you, fuck your empty promises, and fuck your hurtful lies.

Fuck you for showing me how it felt to be loved when I wasn't truly loved.

Not really.

Instead, I mask my hurt the same way he did. The same way I've been doing my entire life.

Understanding my silence, Sebastian nods and turns to leave, but before he's out the door, I speak up, "I'm not stopping. No matter what you do. I'll make your days as president a living hell."

This is what I do.

Love didn't work out for me, so I fight, bite, and claw because anything else is not an option.

Feeling anything other than hate for this man? Is not an option.

A risk I will never take again.

But because the man who once owned my love and now my heart is a masochist, he grins over his shoulder at me, "Give me all you got, love. I was in hell every day your body was away from mine, and I am still in hell every second you look at me that way." A part of me wants to ask him, but I don't. Instead, I look at him without giving him anything, even though, on the inside, my emotions are all over the place. But Sebastian doesn't need to be asked. He answers my unspoken question. "You look at me as if you regret me…"

Hardening my heart, I say. "I don't regret meeting you, Sebastian, because it led me to them," I whisper, disgusted with myself for how weak I sound but I don't stop there. No. "I do regret ever giving you my heart." Hurt flashes in his eyes for a fracture of a second before he masks it, smiling through his feelings. He then turns to leave, but I stop him by saying to his retreating back, "I hate you, Sebastian." I say in a tone dripping with acid.

Without looking back at me he replies. "And I love you, Arianna Parisi. I love you with all that I am." He says it with his whole fucking chest, drops that bomb, and leaves.

He leaves my office while my soon-to-be unemployed team goes crazy taking photos and whispering amongst each other.

I ignore it all.

I ignore the spark that popped into my chest when he told me he loved me. I lock the vulnerability he stirs in me down tight where it belongs.

I ignore everything except this burn in my chest that has left me weak and causes my mind to reel.

I can't undo my move, but I can make it better. So, baby, this is me making it better. His words play through my head like a loop, taunting me but, at the same time, making me feel things I shouldn't. Things that get me hurt.

We're the same.

Two broken pieces that will never be completely whole.

Chapter 19
BREATHE AGAIN

Arianna

"It still wrecks me…

even after all this time." — B

"President Kenton used his public presidential social media accounts to repost an article from the Washington Weekly column where…" Changing the channel, I tried another one but every TV station was talking about him.

Some even mention me.

Turning off the TV, I place my coffee mug on the kitchen counter. This crazy… egotistical tyrant has lost his goddamn mind. There's no other explanation as to why he's giving more publicity to news articles that make him look shady as hell. What kind of politician hoping to get re-elected acts this recklessly? A man with a God complex, that's who. A man who, despite his shady business and reputation, was placed as the most powerful man in the country. Hell, one of the most powerful men in the world.

There's no doubt about that.

"What are you doing, Sebastian…?" I frown down at the paper next to my untouched breakfast. I think I'm one of the few who still reads the paper's physical copy instead digitally.

Today though, I wish I hadn't read it at all. Picking it up, I read the headline: The President and his second chance romance? I roll my eyes at the cheesiness and absurdity of it all. No one couldn't come up with a better headline. Then, to make matters worse, the paper used a photo of us in Paris from the night Sebastian took me to his hotel's restaurant, where I flipped the paparazzi off very elegantly, if I must say.

It feels like ages ago, yet it was only three years. But the girl smirking at the camera with her hands around Sebastian feels like a stranger to me now. Liar…

That girl is you…

Ignoring the annoying voice in my head, I fold the paper, rise from the seat, and walk around the kitchen counter toward the trash can. Throwing the paper in the garbage where it belongs, I take a deep breath and gather my thoughts. I need to be on my A-game today. Because I'll be in my rival's territory, where he has the upper hand.

Ellaiza's dinner is tonight. I'll see my girl again. I'll get to spend time with her and sadly with her father as well. He's only using Ella to get me to comply.

He is smart.

Brilliant and clever, but as long as I don't fall for his shit, then he wins nothing. His attempts to use her against me will be in vain.

Rage flashed through me, but I controlled it.

I turned it to ice in my veins. I'm no longer the twenty-one-year-old girl I once was. I
've changed. I'm stronger, smarter, and most importantly no longer a child. Sebastian Kenton holds no power over me. I chant that last part like a mantra, hoping my mind doesn't betray me like the last two times I've been in his presence.

I refuse to let him get to me. Grabbing my purse and keys to my white Bentley, I exit my cold, perfect, and lifeless apartment. I've been living here for two years after staying with Quinne at her place, and I've yet to make friends with any of the other tenants. It's just me here.

Me and my ghosts.

Taking the elevator because I'm sure as hell not walking several flights of stairs in high heels, it drops me in the parking area. Aware of my surroundings, I hurry to my car and climb inside. It's Saturday, and I took the day off to get some groceries and pick up something for Ellaiza. I can't show up at her dinner empty-handed. My mom taught me a lot of useless shit, but she got this right. Manners.

Turning the engine on, the car roars to life, and I immediately use the console to call the person who, at the moment, knows more about my Ella than me, and it stings. It burns that I need to call Benjamin so he can clue me in on what Ella is into these days.

It makes me angry all over again, not that I ever stopped being angry, but some days the anger is more intense. Like now.

Because it reminds me that I missed milestones that I won't ever get back.

She's a little person, and she has grown and evolved, and I wasn't there.

Fucking Sebastian.

Putting the car on drive, I wait for Benjamin to pick up, and once he does, I'm already out of the parking lot and on my way to exit my building. "Kid."

"I need your help." I breathe.

"What's wrong?" His tone is no longer friendly but alert.

"Nothing is wrong. I just need your help picking up a few things for Ellaiza." I whisper.

Benjamin sighs relieved that nothing is wrong. Christ, I give thanks for him every day. How would life have turned out for me if he wasn't there? I don't ever want to find out. "The little lady is not your typical child." He laughs, and I think to myself of course not. She's gifted, unique, and out-of-this-world cute. There's no one quite like her. Call me biased. I couldn't care less. "At the moment she enjoys getting herself all dolled up, tea parties, and believe it or not, she enjoys fucking chess." What child at that age enjoys that God-awful boring game?" Her father, that's who. I think to myself.

Not much has changed since she was a baby. My girl enjoyed fancy dresses and sweet treats, but the chess thing is new. She's older now and can actually understand the dynamic of the game, whereas before, she couldn't. I bet Sebastian is thrilled to be able to play with his daughter. Something in my chest moves, but I refuse to give it a second thought. Nope. Instead, I ask. "What else?"

Benjamin thinks for a second. "I tried getting her interested in sports, but the kid is allergic to exercise unless it's Shaw. He's the only one who can get Ellaiza to do any type of sport." Shaw.

Her bodyguard.

Jealousy courses through me. I am jealous of a bodyguard.

A bodyguard who my girl so clearly adores and who knows her more than I do. "Thanks for the help."

"Don't be nervous, and don't worry so much. You can give that kid shit wrapped in pink paper, and she'll be grateful and over the moon happy because it comes from you. You're still her favorite human."

Before, I used to end any conversation Benjamin started that might bring up Sebastian and Ella because it was just too painful, so there were a lot of things that he didn't get to say because I wouldn't allow it.

He's saying them now, and I thought I was ready to hear it, but how wrong I was.

It all hits me at once.

Gulping, I reign in my emotions and manage to get the words out. "That is gross, Benjamin, but surprisingly and very disturbingly sweet."

Laughing, he then asks. "I'll be there for you tonight. You hold your head up high, yes?"

Knowing he can't see me but nodding anyway, I say. "Always."

"Yeah, always, kid."

Taking a turn, I wait for the building gates to open, and when they do, people gathering outside bombard me.

Political journalists.

"Wonderful." I mutter. Lowering the window just enough to hear what they're saying, I catch my name.

Fuck.

Driving towards my destination, an incoming call appears on the screen.

This is not good.

"Benjamin?"

"Yes?"

"I'll call you back."

"Sure thing. Love you, kid."

"I know," I whisper back, still finding it difficult to tell him I love him back because the moment I do bad things happen. I'm not risking it.

"I know." He replies, more real. Genuine because he knows.

He knows I love him like a brother.

Like the big brother I never had.

I end the call and answer the incoming one.

Focusing on the road ahead, I wait for it to connect. "Quinne."

My brows furrow when she doesn't respond, but I can hear her breathing through the phone. "Is something wrong? Quinne?"

"I need you to do something for me." The tone of her voice is off and nothing like the Quinne I have come to care for. Instead of replying to her with our usual sarcastic banter, I tell her. "Anything."

She goes on to tell me what she needs from me, and it makes me wish I could turn back time to a minute ago when I told her I would do anything.

I should've thought it better before agreeing till I knew exactly what she needed.

"I was going to go, but something came up."

"It's fine. I'll handle it. It's our company, after all."

Quinne laughs, yet it sounds humorless. "Yours. Get it through that pretty thick skull of yours."

"Uh-huh. Sure." I blow her off because even if the legal documents declare me the owner, to me, it will always be half Quinne's. Period. "I am not responsible for whatever damages might occur to that…man."

"Handle him like I know you can. He's harmless." I can, and if the need arises, I will. "Also, color me surprised when I woke up and saw your face all over social media and my TV."

Yeah…that.

"I knew this could happen."

She laughs. "Yes, but give him hell regardless."

"Always will."

"That's my bitch."

Rolling my eyes, I make a U-turn almost missing my exit. "I don't know what's going on, and knowing you, I might never know but you can count on me. Whatever you need apart from burying a body, I'm there for you." I mean it. She and Benjamin kept me afloat, and I would do the same for them, but something about Quinne has always made me believe that there's more to her than what she shows the world. Her smiles are fake, and she always has a foot out the door wherever she's at. She might not tell me today, or maybe ever, but regardless, I am here whenever she decides to confide in me.

The bitch might annoy me to no end at times, but I do care for her.

Deeply.

"If you won't help me hide the body, at least tell me you're down for the murder." She teases.

"Depends."

"On what?" She asks.

"The murder method."

Quinne laughs. "Nothing too bloody, of course. A hit and run, perhaps?"

Thinking about it for a second, I reply. "You drive."

"So, you can argue that you weren't a willing participant and make yourself seem to the court as another victim of mine?"

Smart Quinne.

"Precisely."

"You little bitch. I taught you well." My twisted friend laughs, and this time it's more genuine. This laugh I believe. "I have to go. I'll be in touch." With that she hangs up, ending the call.

Whatever the hell is happening with her, I know it's not good, but it's up to us to fight our demons.

No one else can do it for us.

That's what life taught me more than once.

Ping.

The sound of a new notification sounds on my car's speaker as I reach my destination.

My favorite kid's boutique.

When I was feeling like absolute shit, I would come here and look at all the things they had for little girls. Clothes, accessories, and shoes that I knew my Ella would rock, and I left empty-handed, just like my heart felt at the time.

Today, that's not the case.

I can give her the world now, and that, for the first time in a while, has me excited like I couldn't explain if someone asked me.

There are no words.

Putting the car in park, I click on Nessa's message to find an attachment linked. When I open it, it's to see the latest article regarding Sebastian. This article has another photo of me and, from what I can read, a story about us.

There's no way.

There's no way in hell this happens out of the blue.

The media witnessed a young girl screaming at the then-senator of Chicago, knowing there was a juicy story back then, but they never published anything.

Nothing.

My face wasn't plastered all over the news. I knew because of Benjamin that Sebastian threatened every media outlet if they so much as posted my name let alone my photograph, and out of nowhere, they did it? I wonder.

I know the magazines, newspapers, and sites have the right to publish a story but somehow he managed to get them off me with whatever trick he had up his sleeves back then but that's not the case now.

Now. My face and my name are all over the news.

I knew this would happen. I even prepared for my world to change for the second time around.

But something deep down inside me, the part that knows Sebastian and how his mind works, understands that this is no coincidence. No.

This is him fighting back.

Very well…

I can handle petty Sebastian.

That I can.

Turning the engine off, I put my Tom Ford black framed sunglasses on and get out of the car with a new purpose burning fiercely in my veins.

Ellaiza.

And bringing her father to his knees. However it needs to be done.

Whatever it takes.

Because I know I will only breathe again once he feels the pain and effects of his betrayal.

Because nothing is working to rid myself of this ache in my chest.

Absolutely nothing.

PART TWO
LOVE & HATE

I'd rather die before I tell you how I feel -A

Chapter 15
HIS WHITE HOUSE
Arianna

"It gives me great satisfaction to witness, my bestie karma, do her thing." — A

God knows I'm trying to stay calm. I'm seconds away from getting my ass thrown in jail for throat-punching a motherfucker. A motherfucker who happens to be part of the secret service. I cringe at my crass choice of words. Hell, I didn't use to cuss this much. Typically, I use the bare minimum when speaking aloud, but in my mind? Yes, I cuss like an angry sailor who's been stuck with seven imbeciles out at sea for far too long. But at this moment, it's tempting. It's been hard to suppress the need to resort to dumb people's words and cuss a motherfucker out. Instead, I refrain from doing that and go for my favorite kind of language. Sarcasm. And there are levels of sarcasm, you know.

For example, some use it to make a situation less awkward, and others, like me, use it as a method to insult others. The fun part? They don't even notice I am insulting them. Evil? Cruel? Perhaps. "At least take me on a date first before hitting first base," I mutter while stretching my arms wide so the security can do a full search for the second time since I've arrived at the White House.

Thank God, I decided to arrive thirty minutes early because security has taken their sweet time, and if I'd come at the established hour, then I would have been late for Ella's dinner, and that is unacceptable.

Anyone with a brain knows that tardiness is a sign of a lack of professionalism. Besides, I can be late to anything but nothing of hers.

Never.

"Look, miss--" The asshole who's been shamelessly ogling my tits for way too long gives me a condescending look while holding onto my Hermes bag. The same bag that has been searched two times by him. He then turns and points to another member of security to hand him the gifts I bought for Ellaiza. The items were carefully wrapped with pink unicorn gift paper, and I will start throwing hands if they mess it up by unwrapping it.

I guess it was my fault I didn't care enough to ask for the protocols to follow when bringing gifts to the White House, and to save myself this headache, I should have, but this man is clearly taking advantage. "If I wanted to murder the president, do you think I would be dumb enough to walk right up to his security with the murder weapon hidden in the presents meant for a kid? Please give me more credit than that. There are a million more successful ways to do it and not so obvious." I smile snidely at the same time the idiot glares my way. "And please make yourself useful and contact your boss. I bet he will appreciate knowing that his security has been paying extra attention to his guest for longer than your protocol requires." There's no humor nor warmth in my tone, just annoyance and a little bit of a bitch attitude.

That I cannot help. The mouth breather looks like he's three seconds away from throttling me.

Oh, how easy it is to piss off mortals.

Then a loud chuckle sounds from my right, making me turn my head away from the dumbass security that's been keeping me here as if I'm a threat to their president, which I am but not today. Today, I have no choice but to play nice.

Mother did say that loving someone was a weakness and a nuisance, and every time I'm obligated to play nice with Sebastian because of Ellaiza, it proves my mother's sentiments to be true.

Love truly is a pain in my ass.

"This is not a tour guest, Barnes. This is the President and the first daughter's guest." Benjamin takes my bag and gift from the asshole. "You're fired. Get your ass out of here." With that, my friend grabs me by the elbow and guides me away from the jerk and in another direction.

"What took you so long?" I side-eye Benjamin while we walk away from the East Wing. As we walk past the theater room, I realize that this place, although it looks grandiose from the outside, is even more epic from the inside. Here lies the history of this country and the many men and their families who have lived here through the years with their own stories. Maybe one day, a woman will sit in the Oval Office.

Maybe.

But for now, we must endure Sebastian Kenton. Oh, how low has the country gone. "I told you to wait for me, did I not?"

Shrugging, I follow his lead through the halls of this enormous place. "I didn't want to be late, and you, my friend, have a bad habit of being late."

"Oh, maybe you're too damn early every time. Have you ever thought about that?" He asks.

"Better early than late." I snap.

"Fine. You're right." He chuckles.

"I know I am." I give him a 'duh' look.

We then walk towards the dining area, where four more security and staff members are waiting for us, when we get close enough, the cream-colored double doors of the State Dining room are pulled open, and the first thing I notice is the wool rug that serves as a carpet that features a border of wreaths surrounding a field of mottled light blue accented by clusters of oak leaves. I also notice that the carpet's design mimics the plaster molding of the ceiling. Then I take in the silk window draperies that are ecru in color, accented with stripes of peacock blue. God, my little sister would love this. Not because blue is her favorite color, all shades of blue, but because her curious mind loved history, and every inch of this place has history.

A pang in my chest reminds me of how deep I buried my sister in my subconscious with everything else that hurts me. But as much as I tried, she always rises to the surface, just like all thoughts of the man who no doubt orchestrated this dinner and the beautiful little girl who stole and keeps stealing all the broken pieces of my heart. Ignoring the hurt that floods my senses, I continue looking at the dining room, not only as a momentary distraction but also because I'm a home decor freak, and I love the renovations this room underwent during the last administration. The last first lady had style, and it shows.

The room has kept the essence of every administration before this one, yet I know by reading an article that Sebastian did order the change of the decor.It seems more modern and classier with gold, white and black tones. Yes, that is definitely Sebastian's doing.

All class and luxurious taste of this man.

"Mommy!" The loud, sweet screeching of a very excited little girl steals my attention, making me look her way, and when I come back down to the reality of this moment, I'm taken back.

The dining table is served as if it is being held for a large formal dinner, and dinner for five has already been served. "You came!" Ellaiza stands in her seat dressed head to toe in pink. Her bodyguard keeps a tight hold on her, so she doesn't fall off the chair.

Looking at my girl I think about how the little sneak not only got me to sit down at the same table with her Judas of a father but also her dog on a leash, who doesn't like me all that much by the way he's staring daggers at me. One shouldn't feel joy when others dislike them, but I do. It's hilarious how, at times, my existence perturbs people.

Is that toxic? Why, yes, but that's me.

Nothing can be done now, nor do I want to change any part of myself.

I offer Ellaiza a small smile. Just for her. Only ever her. "Wouldn't miss this phenomenal dinner you planned for the world." She grins and looks at her father, who I try hard to ignore, although I felt the burn of his stare on me from the second I stepped inside the room.

I also noticed Benjamin has left my side and placed the gifts I bought for Ellaiza on a table in the far corner before heading back over to me, at the same time, I watch from the corner of my eye as Sebastian stands from where he is sitting at the end of the table, comes over to me, and pulls my chair back so I can take a seat next to him and right in front of Ellaiza. I want to argue, but it'll only ruin the little girl's night, and I'd rather suffer through this evening sitting next to President A-hole than watch the brilliant smile drop from Ella's face.

From the corner of my eye, I take in his attire. He's in a pair of dark blue suit trousers and a white shirt with the sleeves rolled to his elbows. The top buttons of his shirt are undone, revealing the taut lines of his collarbone and hinting at his chest muscles.

It should be a sin for someone so rotten to be so damn beautiful.

Taking the offered seat, I feel Sebastian's hot breath on the back of my neck as he whispers. "You look ravishing tonight, darling."

"I know." I clip. I know I look stunning, and I don't need him to point it out. I chose a modest strapless pearl white dress that molds to every curve of my body. It is semi-sexy but not indecent. I paired it with clear open-toe heels, and light makeup with red lips, and my hair is falling in soft waves down my back.

I thought of wearing one of my go-to suits, but I couldn't bring myself to do it. I look cold and, sometimes, downright mean while wearing them, which I love, not going to lie, but for Ella, it felt wrong, so I opted for something pretty and a bit modest without being too conservative.

Yes, so I don't need Sebastian pointing out how good I look, and I also don't need my stupid, traitorous body reacting to this man's words.

Nope.

Sebastian laughs, not the fake laugh he uses in his speeches or events, but the one that used to stop my heart dead in my chest with just the beautiful sound. Bastard.

"Modesty never did look good on you, love." He whispers before sitting back down next to me. Turning my head, I smile sweetly at him, yet it is oh so fake, and then I remain silent. I hope my eyes tell him what my mouth can't at the moment.

A big fuck you.

He smiles right back at me while his gray-blue eyes twinkle with mischief. His eyes lingered for a moment in a way that had heat spreading through my body. I avert my eyes because I can't handle the rising need to fall into those blue depths and lose myself in them. His eyes always did have that effect on me.

"Okaaaay… now that we're all gathered here, and my guest of honor has arrived, we can all dive in." The little diva spreads her arms wide with a grin on her face. Her father and Benjamin chuckle while her bodyguard shakes his head as if this is nothing new. My heart aches thinking about how many of these moments they got with her and how many I missed.

Fucking Sebastian.

I should pick up the pointy knife and shove it deep into his hand. The same one that's suspiciously close to my side of the table.

I can do this.

I can enjoy this dinner with my friend and my girl without having to spoil it by entertaining her father, but, as all egotistical tyrants do, he won't allow being shoved aside and forgotten. No.

"This all looks exquisite, my heart. I bet mommy appreciates that you added her favorites to the menu." I ignore how the way he says mommy makes both my chest and gut tighten with unexplored emotions. Looking at the table, instead of finding a five-course gourmet meal, I find every candy and junk food known to man. There are cheeseburgers, curly fries, and even chicken nuggets right in front of Benjamin. Ella and Shaw's side looks as if a fried chicken place and a bakery exploded in a weird-as-hell combination. Fried chicken and sweets.

Then there's my side. Pizza.

A three-meat pizza, garlic bread, and a side plate of chocolate cake pops. "You and daddy match." Ellaiza teases, causing me to frown and look at Sebastian's plate. That god-awful abomination that he calls pizza. Pineapple. "I see you still have no taste, whatsoever." I blurt out, without realizing that the room has grown quiet.

Sebastian smiles and when he smiles like that so effortlessly, it tugs on a string tied to the deepest part of my gut.

"I beg to differ, darling." He chuckles.

"Arianna." My angry eyes leave Sebastian's, whose eyes shine with victory, and level in on Benjamin, who's sitting on my left. "Yes?"

Thankful for the distraction, I focus on him instead. "Have you met Shaw?" Benjamin motions to the big guy that's standing next to Ella who is devouring her second cupcake since I've entered the room. Ellaiza is a vision of pink. Pure sunshine, my girl. The opposite of me.

I smile when I take in her cute face and how she has pink frosting all over her mouth and even part of her curly black hair. She sure does love her cupcakes.

My heart swells with the knowledge that at least that hasn't changed.

"We've met." Shaw's disinterest has me on edge. What is his issue?

"The bodyguard." I inject.

"Shaw Banning." He introduces himself in a bored tone.

Surprise takes over my expression when I turn to Benjamin.

"Excuse my cousin's lack of manners."

"Nonsense, Benji. Shaw has all the manners!" Ella exclaims from her seat, still munching on what's left of her pink frosted cupcake.

"Ellaiza. We've talked about this. No talking with your mouth full." Sebastian interrupts, scolding his daughter gently but with so much affection in his tone. "Sorry, dad." Ella sasses with her mouth full at the same time rolling her eyes. I almost choke with laughter, knowing Sebastian has his work cut out with her. Good. Suffer, you big handsome lying ass.

"It's daddy to you."

"Yeah, yeah." She dismisses him with a flip of her hand. Smiling, I think to myself how much I love her. How loving Ella has never hurt, nor has it ever made me feel unworthy like everyone else I've ever loved.

Loving Ella is easy.

Effortless and pure.

All that is good in me, or that's left.

I watch in awe as Ella engages in conversation with both Shaw and Benjamin like she's part of them. Like she's a grown-up, and in some ways, she is. She's too bright and wiser than her six years, that is for sure. She's always been an old soul. One I love endlessly.

"Are you not hungry? Should I ask the cook to make you something else?" Sebastian whispers next to me, causing goosebumps to scatter down my neck and spine. I curse him under my breath.

Giving him a droll look, making sure Ella doesn't pick up on my mood. "What she chose is perfect."

"Good." He picks up his utensils and starts to eat his pizza like a proper asshole.

Scoffing, I suppress the urge to roll my eyes.

His fork stops midair. "What is it?" He narrows his eyes.

That's much better. I could always handle petty as hell Sebastian while his softer side always unnerved me and made me feel as if I were in strange waters. Out of my comfort zone. How sad is that I am used to asshole behavior and so out of touch with how we all deserve to be treated. Kindness. Respect. Love.

It will always feel strange to me, I guess.

"Only you would eat pizza with a fork and knife. Would it kill you to be normal?"

"It just might." He resumes eating his pizza, ignoring my critique. It's petty, I know. Most people eat their pizza with a knife and a fork. Hell, I do that too, but the childish part of me wanted, no, need to point out how absurd he looks surrounded by two beasts of tattooed men and a six-year-old while they pig out on junk food.

I take a bite of my pizza, trying to hold back the moan of pleasure that tries to slip out when the delicious taste hits my tastebuds. I haven't had a pizza in three years. I did try once. Benjamin brought me a box from one of our favorite pizza places, but I broke down crying like a fool, so I've been going without it ever since. Until now.

"It's good, mommy?" Ella asks while tilting her head in a knowing smile.

Oh, you're a traitor, my little love. I think to myself while smiling back at her. If I didn't love you so damn much, I would kick your little know-it-all behind.

"It's delicious," I replied.

My girl smiles and then continues eating her sweets while the young man next to her, Shaw, takes huge bites of his fried chicken after dipping it in three different sauces and then licking his fingers like an animal. Cringing, I avert my eyes before I vomit my food. No manners whatsoever. I don't even bother looking at Benjamin since I know he eats like a damn pig, too. I guess it runs in the family.

I love him, but he tests my patience daily.

I continue eating my pizza being careful not to spill anything on myself and staying quiet, listening to Benjamin, Shaw, and Ellaiza talk about everything and nothing at the same time.

The air is sweet here. Not hostile. Not bitter.

It was always this way back then, too. Sweet.

I also feel the heat of the tyrant's gaze on me, but I do my best to ignore it and him. It has proven to be difficult because when he's not looking, I sneak a few glances at him without being obvious.

He's sitting back, drinking his wine with a smile on his face. A content smile. He looks like a king on his throne. I've forgotten how it hurt to look at him for too long.

He shines so brightly even when the bastard is not even trying. The light he exuberates shines from within, but there's darkness too that lingers behind those carefully laid layers he works so hard to maintain. To fool everyone else around him. It fooled me once, too.

I also look down at his strong left hand, the one that is suspiciously close to mine, tapping on the table. For a moment there, I swear I see black ink on his finger, but that cannot be. I once asked him why he didn't have any tattoos on him, and he responded by saying that it wasn't his thing plus he added how tattoos made people look vulgar.

I hate that I think the same way.

What a pair of assholes we both are.

But back to the ink, it can't be, but when I try to look closer, his hand moves from my view making my own eyes rise to meet his blue ones.

Eyes that are shining brightly.

Giddy. Yeah, that's it.

Smiling as if he holds all the secrets to my heart. The same heart he doesn't have access to. Sebastian speaks up, but his eyes never leave mine. "Ellaiza."

"Yes, daddy?"

"Do you want to give your mom the gift you made her?"

"Oh, yes." I turn to look at an excited Ella bounce in her seat before stepping off the chair, bending, and pulling something from under the table. With my heart in my sleeves, I watch her skip my way before dropping a white medium-sized box on top of my lap. "Happy arrival day, mommy."

"Arrival?" I ignore the three men in the room and stare at my girl.

Ella beams. "Yes! Arrival day! Dad says we should celebrate that you've come home."

Thud.

Thud.

My ears ring, and my heart beat slows down in tune with the buzzing feeling in my chest. I don't look Sebastian's way, because, for the first time since I've been back in his world, I'm afraid. Imagine that. Me-afraid of him, but it's the truth, and I'm no liar, nor am I delusional as much as I would love to save myself the sweet pain of this moment.

"Open it, mommy. Come on!" I feel her tiny hands shake my left arm before Benjamin picks her up and drops her down on his lap next to me. Without waiting for another second, I open the box to find a silver photo book with Ellaiza's baby picture on the front. Realizing what this is, I take a deep breath and pray to whoever is listening that not a single tear falls from my eyes in front of these men. I don't mind Benjamin and Ella witnessing me being vulnerable but the other two? I'd rather take a pipe to the head before letting them see me in such a weak state.

Ella's tiny hands help me flip the sparkly pages with photos and messages from not only her but her father, detailing every single stage of her life and moment captured. When I think I'll be fine, that I won't shed a tear, I get to the pages when she was a toddler.

There are countless photos of us together.

Some that I took and some that I didn't even know existed. Sebastian or Benjamin must've taken them without me realizing it.

"You're so pretty, mommy," Ella whispers in awe, making my heart beat stronger.

"Thank you, my girl." I poke her nose like I used to do when she was a baby, and she gives me a soft smile, melting the ice around my heart more than she already has.

I continue flipping through the photo book, looking at all the moments that I missed. From holidays, to birthdays and God, even recitals.

How much she's grown, and it's all for me to see here. How much I missed. I hate this. I hate that I wasn't there and I hate the tyrant next to me, too, for taking this away from me. I also hate him for confusing me with everything he's done that contradicts everything he said that day.

He didn't keep me a secret from Ellaiza. He didn't allow the years to erase me from her mind. Instead, he kept me alive.

I don't realize a tear has fallen until a small finger wipes it away. Feeling embarrassed as hell, I keep my head bowed. I squeeze my eyes shut, releasing two hot tears that burn like lava. Gentle and soft hands grab both of my cheeks. Ellaiza brings my face closer to hers and smiles. So pure. So oblivious to the turmoil inside my head.

The war between my heart and brain.

As if realizing that I'm sad, she rubs her small nose against mine, and it only makes me cry more because somehow, she remembers.

Our Eskimo kisses.

How she remembers, I have no clue. But my heart feels full witnessing how sweet my girl is. The total opposite of her father and me.

"I love you, Ella." Laughing softly, I whisper for her ears only.

Ella whispers-yells back. "I love you a million stars, mommy."

Laughing with my entire heart, I respond. "I love you to the moon and back. A million times."

"Wow!" She gaps. "I think that's how much daddy loves you too, mom. You're soooo alike." Ella's blue-gray eyes, much like her father's, twinkle with mischief and secrecy.

It hurts.

God, this hurts because how I wish it were true.

The hurt girl in me wishes this man loved me for real.

She wishes this would be her reality, but the hurt in me reminds me it is not real. It can't be because I am not ready to admit what this would all mean.

After that beautiful moment with my girl, she goes back to her seat after making me pinky promise that I'll stay the night. I tried to refuse while her sneaky father did nothing to help me get out of it. Not that I thought he would.

It's clear that they're on the same team, and I am left to battle this tyrant on my own.

But who could say no to that precious face Ella makes when she wants something? My heart warmed when she gave me the same puppy dog eyes she would give me when she was younger whenever she wanted more candy or to stay up late with me.

A lot of things have changed, yes, but others are just the same. It's bittersweet.

After dinner, Ella dragged me off to her room while Shaw followed like a trained dog. He stayed outside the door while Ella and I went inside her room, where she's been showing me all her toys and giving me a tour for the past thirty minutes.

Her room was an exact replica of the one back in Sebastian's home in Chicago.

Stars and moons decorate every inch of it.

White and pink is the color palette.

Classic, chic, and very stylish.

That's my girl.

It makes me emotional once again, knowing how time had passed but she was still the little girl I loved more than anything and anyone, just a little bit older.

Her heart, her mind, and her essence are still the same.

"Do you like it?" I look down at Ella, who is grinning up at me with her finger pointing at the ceiling, and I'm taken back in time to the day I first met her and asked her name, and she pointed at the ceiling. Following her finger, I look up, and what I find there has me tearing up. Christ, crying not only makes me look ugly but also ruins the makeup, yet I do. With teary eyes, I look at the ceiling with a big bright moon ceiling lamp with an integrated digital image of Ellaiza and me in Paris with our heads thrown back, completely oblivious to the person taking the picture.

"Beautiful…" I whisper, feeling inadequate because I can't find the right words to describe what this all means to me. It's like a day, not several days to heal most of the damage the last three years did to my heart and soul. That's the power of love, I guess.

Tedious as hell and very painful but oh so beautiful.

Time does not heal all wounds, no.

Love does.

"Mommy," Ella whispers worriedly at me and it has me already on edge. I hate the feeling of impotence I feel whenever she seems sad or distressed. "Yes, baby?"

"Now that you're back. Will you give Dad his heart back?"

All breath seems to leave my body, all rational thought, too. Even words get stuck in my throat. "W-what?"

"Daddy said that you stole his heart, I wonder if you can give it back to him now that you're back. I know it would make him happy if you did since, sometimes, he's not that happy." She whispers. "When he thinks I am not looking, I see him all grumpy or sad."

Fuck.

Tears well in my eyes, but I do my best to hold them back.

"I..." What should I say? What is there to say? I could lie, but I refuse to lie to her, but then my truth is too much for a child to handle, and she shouldn't have to handle it. "I will." Smiling softly while nodding, I hug Ella to my chest and wonder if I lied to myself or her.

Now I have a choice to make.

Do I succumb to my hate for her father and ruin the one person who always loved me no matter time or distance, or do I try to play nice with the only threat to my heart for her sake?

Shit.

Why is everything with Sebastian never black and white?

Nothing is ever simple.

Nothing.

Not even the love I still feel for the man.

Happy, bathed, and ready for bed, Ellaiza hops in the bed making room for me. Of course, I join her, still dressed the same way when I arrived. I promised I would stay because she insisted but as soon as I'm able to leave, I will. Not only to avoid the media shit that will most likely follow if I'm caught leaving the White House as if I'm doing the walk of shame, but also because every second I spend here is proving to be more difficult than I initially thought.

Yes, time and wounds changed me, but every second I'm with them, I feel the old me clawing her way out of the deep hole I buried her in long ago.

Chapter 16
HIS WORLD
Bastian

"Kindness is my enemy." — A

I've always had a strong distaste for the color red. It brings back memories I wish to forget altogether. Besides, the godawful color is not flattering in most cases.

Cases like this room.

The Red Room.

Bright red walls, decorations of all shades of red and antique furniture framed in gold and dark browns.

Not flattering at all.

It's history, and it should be appreciated, some would say.

I don't feel the same. I find it grotesque and the only reason I spend most of my nights here is that the red on the walls somehow ended up reminding me of the color of Arianna's lips. So, if you ask me why I even tolerate the color is for that sole reason. How pathetic is that?

I'm sitting in the dark. The only light coming from the digital clock Benjamin placed next to my chess table, I take a deep breath, and for the first time since I moved to this house, the atmosphere feels right. No longer bittersweet, but…right.

Because that's exactly how it all feels now that she's here–hating me or not– it feels right. Tonight's events play through my mind like an old home movie I wish I could keep forever. How beautiful she looked dressed in all white with that dress that was so tight on her it almost looked like a second skin, tempting me and tormenting me, making me wish I had her for dinner instead of the pizza.

Her hair was what did it for me.

Long, wavy, and framing her perfect face. It reminded me so much of the girl I fell in love with the moment I first laid eyes on her.

Golden waves, green eyes, and ruby red lips.

Perfect altogether, the brat.

And as much as her beauty has me under a spell since that first moment I saw her, and will most likely keep me under for eternity, it's her mind that gets me every time. God, that mind of steel and that sharp tongue of hers, too.

Most men prefer the quiet, soft, and demure ones who light up their world with just one sweet word but not me.

No.

Insults, sass, and sarcasm are what does it for me, and that air of superiority that comes from her in waves.

I have fallen addicted to it.

Then I think back to the way she felt right at home, even when she was visibly nervous sitting there making a million scenarios in her mind as to why she doesn't belong at my table, in my home, in my goddamn world. But she fits right in as if no time had passed. Then there were the tears. I've done a lot of shit in my life wrong, and yes, most of it I don't regret. Not for a second and tears never did move me but the tears coming from Arianna, whether they were happy tears or not, made me want to cut my own heart out and hand it to her on a silver platter. Because there was love in her gaze today, yes, but there was so much pain.

I did that.

But I'm trying to make it better.

Make us better, and I don't intend for her to forgive me easily. She wouldn't be the woman I fell in love with if she did. I expect her to raise hell and give me her worst before I am awarded her best, but that is how I know I am completely gone for this woman. Arianna's worst is still the best I ever had.

Her worst days, her good days, I want them all.

The soft click of the door brings me back to the now. Raising my head, I take a sip of my whiskey and enjoy the burn. Placing the glass back down on the table to my left, I say aloud. "Leaving so soon?" I felt her before seeing her. I don't know how that's possible, but it is.

Because I didn't lie to my daughter when I said that Arianna makes the impossible possible for me.

"I should leave, but I won't." She comes closer, but darkness still hides her from view. "For her, of course."

Chuckling, I look down at the table in front of me and move a piece of chess forward, prolonging the game. I could have made a checkmate twenty minutes ago but I chose not to end it so quickly. Sometimes the long game is more exciting. "Of course," I mumble, trying to conceal how humorous I find her fight. "Couldn't sleep?"

Her voice is closer now. "I was thirsty."

I continue playing my game. "You could have asked one of my men to get you some water, darling." The staff is under clear instructions to treat her as if she is one of us because she is.

Arianna is part of my daughter and me. This is her home. Every place I end up in will always be her home.

"My hands work just fine, Mr. President. I can get it myself." She says haughtily.

"It's Sebastian, to you." Rolling my eyes, "And as you wish." I suppress the urge to laugh at her extremely adorable bratty behavior.

"Don't roll your eyes at me." The woman has supervision or something. I laugh softly. "Right…"

"What?" Then there she is. Standing right in front of me on the other side of the small table like a vision in white with her long hair up in a messy twist, free of makeup, stealing my breath from my lungs. An image sneaks up on me where she is wearing white and walking towards me with a brilliant smile on her face. Fuck.

I can't wait for that day to arrive.

Because it will happen.

There is no way I will walk another day on this earth without her by my side. I don't intend to repeat that mistake again.

"You always see more than anyone else." She saw me for me, ugly, broken, and my asshole ways and all. She saw it all and wanted me anyway and what did I do? I threw it all away without realizing what the outcome would do to us both.

We remain silent as she surprises me by taking the seat in front of me and moving a piece of chess. I don't hide the small smile that forms on my face when I see her sitting down without being forced or threatened. It's her choice, like every moment since the day I let her walk out of my life.

Her choice.

To be here.

To love me. It has to be her choice, and although the road is long and the war might leave me bruised and a little fucked up, no doubt. It will be worth it because she is worth everything.

Everything. "I think we should talk." She mumbles.

Smiling, I say. "I would love nothing more, darling."

"But stop that." She snaps. "Stop calling me darling. We both know I am not, and quite frankly, it makes me want to throttle you."

Shrugging, I say. "If that makes you feel better, then please do." She growls in that cute way she used to when I pissed her off before. "Fine. What should I call you then? Baby? Love?"

She leans forward, and I swear I can feel her hot breath on my face, and it feels like home. "Nothing, Call me nothing."

Shaking my head, I tell her. "That I cannot do."

"And why the hell not? You certainly made it clear I was nothing to you all these years." She spits angrily, shots are fired, and they burn. Fuck, does it burn, but this is better than her unfeeling act. This shows me she cares.

"I lied. You mean everything to me, so no. Don't ask me not to call you darling or my love or whatever the fuck I want because you are all those things to me and more." I expose my queen, knowing it is a risk but I do it regardless because the fire that lights in her eyes is worth it.

"I hate it when you do that." She breathes out.

"What do I do?" I feign ignorance, which only makes her madder.

"You know what. One day, I will win fair and square." She vows, and my heart, as corny as it sounds, does a flip inside my chest. Scientifically impossible, of course, but fuck it, all rational thoughts left me the day I fell for this hardheaded, infuriating, and beautiful woman.

Then her words hit me.

One day, I will win.

One day.

Someday.

She's planning to stick around longer, and that's when I realize I have already won this war, although I say nothing. Because there is no doubt in my mind that she will fight it every step of the way. "I can't wait for you to beat me, Arianna," I say truthfully. The thing is she already won as well. She vows to make me hurt the way I hurt her, and I've been hurting like hell since that day. Miserable when I had all I ever wanted for my life. Ignoring what I said, she changes the subject. "I'm not leaving her. I have no right and no real claim to her, I know, but–"

Interrupting her, I say. "Ellaiza is yours as much as she is mine."

"But that's not true, is it? One day, you can decide you don't want her to be around me anymore and take her from me again. You've done it–"

"I won't." My voice rises, and I hate how she cowers and then tries to mask it. Lowering my voice, I look into her eyes. "Words aren't enough. I am aware of this and I don't expect you to believe me, but I hope my actions, from now on, prove to you that I don't ever intend to keep you from Ellaiza. You might have not been with her physically these past three years, but you were always in her heart. I made sure of that."

"Why?" she whispers, suddenly seeming so vulnerable and young. So much like she used to be. Soft for us only, my ice queen. "Why did you do it? You said she would forget me eventually. What changed your mind?" "I never intended to erase you from her life. Was I a dumb fuck, yes? Did I lie? I did. But what I did not do was erase the woman who made our world so much sweeter."

"I hate you." Her voice trembles.

"And I love you, darling." I breathe out, smiling like a fool.

"You don't, Sebastian, because your love hurts, and love is not supposed to hurt."

Leaning forward, I forget the game in front of me and focus on the part of my beating heart out of my chest. Her. "Real love does, baby," I whisper back. "It hurts and sometimes drives us to make stupid mistakes, but it withstands everything we throw at it." Shrugging, I grin when I watch her eyes fall to my lips. "Ours can withstand anything." Her eyes snap back to mine, angry, hurt, confused, and loving. Because she can't hide from me and I see it. I see her. I always have. How could I not if she's all that's good and bright in my world next to my daughter? "I do not love you, Sebastian." My smirk widens and has her snapping at me. "I don't."

"Liar." I lean closer until I'm able to grab her by the back of the neck and pull her closer to me. "It has always been you for me. It will always be us. We're each other's beginning, each other's end." Then I take her lips in mine, kissing her with all the love, hurt, and need that's been suffocating me for so long. She resists me at first, pushing at my chest where my heart beats for her.

Where my ink bleeds for her.

I find tattoos grotesque and common. Two things I am not, yet here I am, with ink on me. All because of her. She is inked on my skin, marking me, claiming me just as she claimed my heart, making me forever hers.

Because the tattoo on my ring finger is not the only one. I also have the one on my chest that I got with her in mind hidden by my shirt.

Arianna's lips on mine feel like I've been condemned to both heaven and hell. A perfect way to describe my woman.

Heaven and hell.

Ninety percent devil and twenty percent angel.

Perfection.

Magic.

Always has been and always will be.

But that magic soon ends when she rips her mouth from mine, growling like a wounded animal. Standing, she towers over me, fuming but also tripping on her words, letting me know the kiss affected her just as much as it did me. "Don't." Hands clenched at her side, nostrils flaring, she looks down at me, sending daggers straight to my heart with how lost she looks. Fuck. "Don't ever do that again. I am not for you! Never again." She turns her back to me, and fuck if it does not hurt, but not even that can deter me from loving this woman. A better man would step back and not push her, ease slow her into this new reality, but I've proven time and time again that I'm not and will never be the better man. I am just a man madly in love and disturbingly obsessed with this woman. A woman who hates me. The moment she reaches the Red Room's door, she twists the knob, opening but before she exits the room, she looks over her shoulder at me. Hurt. Hurt and so angry, but there's love there, too.

And that's why I keep pushing her because, as long as love shines in her eyes, there's hope for me. For us.

For a future that I thought would never be within my reach. Until her. Until Arianna.

"And stop talking to the media as if you love me. You're only making things worse for yourself." She spits but her words come out unsure. Leaning back on the seat, I reach for the half-empty glass of whiskey and take a sip, needing the burn at this instant. "I'm just telling my truth, darling, and the public deserves the truth, do they not?"

"Bullshit." She hisses.

Smiling, I snap. "Watch your mouth."

"Oh, fuck you, Sebastian."

Laughing, I place the glass back down on the table. "You know, I love the way you say my name."

"You've gone mad."

"I have, Arianna. I'm mad for you." I can't see her face because, from this distance, the darkness has obscured it from my view, again but I can only imagine her pretty face twisted in fury.

"You should be committed. How a man like you ended up running this country, I am not sure." She snaps. "Oh, yes, I know. The people who elected you are just as delusional." She says sarcastically with her hands on the doorknob, yet she hasn't made a move to leave. Instead, she's arguing and enjoying every second of our typical verbal sparring.

Mad, mad love, baby.

Mad, mad love.

"Well, aren't you going to say anything, Sebastian?" Her voice comes off closed off and cold.

I remain quiet, thinking about my next words carefully. Because what leaves my mouth next will set the tone for what's next for us.

A few seconds pass before I break the silence.

"Arianna?"

I watch her shoulders tense, becoming rigid, ready for the impact of my words. It saddens me that that's her usual response. A reflex to guard her heart before she's hurt again.

I will be remedying that, too.

"What?" I almost laugh at how incredibly adorable she sounds. Maybe she's right.

Maybe, I'm delusional.

"You made the world your own. Now it's time for me to do the same."

Scoffing, she replies. "The world is already yours, Sebastian." She scoffs. "Don't be ridiculous."

She is wrong.

"Not yet. Not fully." I whisper, hoping my words penetrate the iron walls that guard her beautiful heart. "Because you're it for me, baby. My world."

A hurt and incredulous laugh slips out on a breath, and I notice her head shaking. "I'm not." Her words come out as a painful breath. "I never was." Sadness laces her words before she blocks me out and exits the room, shutting the door softly behind her.

"You were. You are, and you will always be the whole fucking world to me." I whisper to the empty room, then I empty my glass while her scent still lingers.

On the air, my skin, and in my brain.

Chapter 17

RULE BREAKER

Bastian

"Was I not enough? Was I too cold? Is that why I never measured up?" — A

Entering the dining room area, where we usually have our hot coffee, the newspaper, and breakfast are already waiting for me while Banning and Shaw are both entertaining my daughter, who wakes up every morning at the crack of dawn. The moment I enter the room, I know that Arianna fled after our encounter last night, as I predicted.

I might have pushed her to the point it was too much for her, but it needed to be done. The cards are on her table, and I made it clear I won't stop until she's fully mine. Heart, mind, body, soul, and if there's more, I want that too. All of her.

Every part.

The good, the bad, and all that sass that drives me insane.

"Good morning." I walk over to where Ellaiza is seated having scrambled eggs with bacon and strawberries.

Shit.

The strawberries remind me of Arianna.

Her taste.

I haven't been able to eat one without my thoughts trailing back to her. Bending down, I drop a kiss on my daughter's head and linger there for a moment too long, trying to savor every second. Every damn minute while she's this little. "Morning, daddy." She says between bites. Her two pigtails are perfectly done, not lopsided as usual. Evidence that Banning did not do her hair this morning.

Huh.

"Morning, boss," Shaw mutters, taking a sip of his coffee while Banning nods in greeting. Taking a seat, I take a sip of my black coffee and flip through the pages of today's paper, only to find no new stories about me. Smiling to myself, I direct my question to Banning. "She get home alright?"

He nods once then takes a big bite of his waffles. With his mouth full, he replies. "She got up early and spent a few minutes with the little lady here," He smiles at my daughter with so much affection that it humbles me. "She even did Ella's hair real pretty, huh." He twirls one pigtail making her giggle, and in return, we all smile softly at my kid. "She sure did, Benji. Mommy is da best." She speaks with her mouth full. "Sorry."

Poking her nose, I tell her. "Nothing to be sorry about."

Banning takes another bite of his waffles and then turns back to me. "I drove her back to her place."

She ran.

Things got real, and she ran, and I don't blame her. As I said, I expected it. I don't mind, though. I enjoy the chase, and if I had to, I would spend the rest of my life chasing her. That's how gone I am for the woman.

"Thank you."

"The president just thanked me with witnesses around. Why look at that, cousin...hell must be freezing over."

The fucker looks at his cousin, Shaw, and acts like a silly schoolgirl. The fucker really does test my patience. He is lucky he's the best I have, and my girls adore him. On the other hand, Shaw has the good sense to ignore his elder cousin. Instead, he turns to me after chugging down what is left of his coffee. "Now, boss, I'm telling you, that woman avoids you like the plague."

"Oh, hush, Shaw-Bear. My mommy loves my father. Isn't that right, dad?" Sighing, I nod at my child.

"That's right, my heart." I curl my lip at the two idiots in distaste, and then I proceed to read the newspaper.

"Oh, dad!" Ella bounces in her seat with a half-eaten sausage in her hands and a huge grin on her cherubic face. "I know something you don't know…"

Shaking my head, knowing blackmail will soon follow.

Folding the paper, I place it back on the table and give Ellaiza my full attention. "What do you want for the information?" I cut to the chase because I know my daughter. She loves me, I know this, but she loves blackmailing me, and she loves negotiating even more, even though she has no need for it. I would give her Shaw's heart by cutting it out of his chest if she asked me to.

Ella taps her chin twice and thinks about it carefully before answering. "I want a baby sister."

She asked for a dog last time.

I should've known a kid brother or sister would follow. She's been blabbering for months now about her friend, Kyrie's newest family member. A little girl.

Huh.

"Done."

Both men at the table choke on their breakfast. "Bastian." I ignore Banning's warning tone and offer my daughter a small smile. Proud that she's already a ballbuster. She'll make a great politician or white-collar criminal, I have no doubt. "Spill it."

"Mommy took a plane."

I freeze, and my grip tightens on the coffee mug so much that it could break any second now. I'm always a step ahead, I knew she would run away, I just didn't anticipate her to leave the State.

"Do you know where mommy went?"

"I do." That's all she gives me. I love my daughter. I really do, but she's testing my patience.

"Where did mommy go, Ellaiza?"

"Gweese." She keeps chewing on the sausage.

"Greece?"

"That's what I said." She rolls her eyes at me before adding. "Look!" She picks up her tiny pink phone that I got her for her sixth birthday and turns it my way so I can see the screen. Reaching forward, I gently grab it and look at the picture on the screen. It's a picture of Arianna boarding an airplane, smiling brightly, and looking as beautiful as ever. Giving the phone back to my daughter, I smile at her and then turn to look at Banning, who is looking at me as if I've lost my goddamn mind.

I have.

"Contact Baron and ask him to cancel all my meetings until further notice." Then I look at Shaw. "Get the plane ready." Shaw nods, then he rises from his seat and leaves the room.

"You'll piss her off." Banning warns with a knowing smile on his face. Looking him dead in the eye, I reply. "What else is new?" Rising from my seat, I button my suit. "Ellaiza."

"Yes?" My daughter is lost messing around with her phone, most likely texting Arianna. "I'll get you the dog and the sister, but you need to keep it a secret, yes? I'll surprise her once I land in Greece."

"Uh-uh." Already done with the conversation, she replies.

"Shaw will stay here with Ellaiza and you're coming with me." I tell Banning.

"I want to go." My kid whines.

Walking towards her, I pick her up from the seat and held her in my arms, kissing her face. "You have school, baby. I'll be back before you know it." I promise.

Ellaiza pouts, but like a good girl, she doesn't argue. "Fine."

"That's my girl." I kiss her once more and then turn with her in my arms towards Banning. My friend, the head of security, hangs up the phone and stares at me with a smile on his face. "All clear with the Vice President."

I haven't taken a single sick or vacation day since I entered Office, but I will be taking them now. "Then let's go." Placing Ella down on the floor, I look at her smiling face. "You be good while I'm gone, yes?"

My daughter puts her hands on her hips and raises an eyebrow. All attitude. All sass. I wonder where she picked that up. Arianna. "I'm always good, Dad."

"Daddy." I corrected her.

"Yeah, yeah." She giggles, melting my heart.

With one last kiss to my kid, I head out of the dining room. On my way to Arianna.

I put everything on hold for her.

My duty.

My obligations.

Fuck, even the country.

All for her.

I would cross a thousand oceans and travel a thousand hours if, at the end of the journey, she was there waiting for me.

Chapter 18
PARADISE
Arianna

"Because my way is always the correct way." — A

Santorini, Greece

Two days.

Two days, and I'll be back home. No big deal. I try to convince myself that nothing major will happen in 72 hours, but the sinking feeling in my gut tells me otherwise.

A lot can happen in an hour, let alone in 72.

Relax… I tell myself. I've been on business trips on my own countless times before. This one is nothing special. But this feeling in the pit of my stomach, I just can't shake. "It's all in your head…" I whisper. Yes, maybe I'm just paranoid about all that has occurred in less than two weeks.

The twists of events.

Ellaiza.

Sebastian.

Mostly, fucking Sebastian, who has me second-guessing myself and everything I thought I knew. All I planned for so long.

Yes, that is it.

Nothing more.

Two days and then I'll be back in Washington, but first, I need to get this spread for the magazine, and at the moment, the man I am meeting here is a Latin sensation that's gone international breaking every record known in the music industry.

To me, he is a pain in the ass, but I always put my feelings aside for business. Business is business, and I can act like the guy doesn't salsa dance on my last nerves on the rare occasions we've met. "Welcome to Greece, Miss." The softly spoken, heavily accented words are spoken by my driver. A tall, tanned man with caramel hair and a nice smile. Young, too. About my age. See, this is the type of man I should be interested in, but no. My foolish heart had to fall for the devil himself. An older man and the daddy of all daddies. Okay, that is cringe. I need a drink as soon as possible, I blame it on the long flight.

"Thank you." I nod in gratitude, not missing the way his eyes travel down my body in appreciation. For so long, men's lustful gazes always felt icky. They made me feel like I was an object and nothing more, but this stranger's eyes don't make me feel that way at all.

"Let me get those for you." He murmurs, then grabs my bags, and I watch him place them on the trunk, then quickly come back to my side and open the back door for me. I step inside the vehicle, ready to get to my destination as fast as possible, finish the job, and go back home. I haven't had a vacation in… well, I can't recall the last time I went somewhere for pleasure instead of work.

Taking a deep breath, I watch the magical place around me from the car's window, and we haven't even gotten to the hotel yet. I concentrate on what awaits me when I get there instead of allowing the traitorous memories of last night to plague my mind.

Nope.

That's my problem with Sebastian. He is like a bad cough. He appears out of nowhere and takes a long fucking time to get out of your system, and in most cases, it never leaves.

"Damn you…" I breathe out when my phone pings with a notification.

Ella: Hi, mommy! Benji gave me your number, and I wanted to say hi! So, hi! I miss you already! I hope you have the bestest time while away in Paradise!

The biggest smile forms on my face when I read the text message that came through the moment I found service. During the plane flight, I couldn't check my messages, and no new ones came through.

I type back, while my driver gets me to my location.

I left early in the morning, so early that I knew Sebastian wouldn't be up, so I could make my escape without him noticing. I woke up Ellaiza and told her where I was going and that I'll be back soon. I am glad Benjamin gave Ella my number. Now she will be able to call or text me whenever she wants.

I don't intend to miss anything else. She also made me promise to send pictures religiously throughout my stay in Greece, which I am fine to oblige.

Me: Thank you, my girl. I'll see you soon. xoxo

Me: Misbehave for daddy, okay?

Three dots appear on my screen letting me know she's typing. That kid is texting like a grown-up already. I also knew the paranoid tyrant would give her a phone as soon as she was able to manage it.

Ella: I will!

Grinning, I send her a dozen heart emojis, which she returns with more of her own. God, how is this happening? I don't know how it happened, but I am more than happy I got this chance.

There's nothing and no one I love more in this world than Ellaiza Kenton, besides my sisters, but that's a sad story that I don't intend to dwell on now that I have this second chance. "Umm, sir." I looked up from my phone at the driver. The nice-looking driver looks at me through the rearview mirror. "Ares."

"Excuse me?" I ask.

Smiling, the man says, "My name is Ares."

"Oh, yes, of course." Ares. Sounds fitting for someone who looks like one of those famous Greek sculptures in rich people's homes. "Ares, do you know where I can do some shopping? I need a few things."

Ares' smile widens, "Yes, I do. Do you want to go now or…?"

"If it's possible, yes, I would like to go now." I mutter.

"Yes, Miss."

"You can call me, Arianna." I have no clue whatsoever why I said that.

"Arianna." The way he pronounces my name has a smile forming on my face. "That's a very beautiful name."

My smile has a life of its own. Without realizing it, it widens at the charming man's compliment. Before I go and do something stupid and terribly embarrassing like blush, I turn my head and look out the window, focusing on the beautiful streets. I do need to buy a few things and extra clothing just in case anything happens. I am always prepared, but with the rush of the trip, I could only manage to pack a few items.

I don't mind, nor do I complain or worry much about it. Shopping is one of three of my favorite things to do in this world.

The first is journalism.

The second shopping.

The third is pissing people off.

Pissing him off to be precise.

As always, the tyrant crosses my mind because, even there, he feels entitled to. A tyrant in every sense of the word. Then as I watch the cars pass, and the beautiful city around me, Sebastian's words from last night replay in my head throughout the drive to my next destination.

You made the world your own. Now, it's time for me to do the same.
Because you're it for me, baby. My world.
You were. You are, and you will always be the whole fucking world to me.

***

I'm not a woman who enjoys sunny days, and the heat pisses me off. I am more of an autumn and winter person with a weird love for cold and rainy days.

Some people find comfort in sunny and bright days, but I am the complete opposite.

However, even I have to admit that this is one beautiful day, sunny, but not too hot. Perfect weather for paradise because that is exactly how I would describe Santorini.

Paradise.

It is arguably the most famous of the Greek islands, and it is most known for its whitewashed, cube-shaped buildings adorned with blue accents, steep cliffs, and tangerine sunsets that light up the sky and sea.

Greece was in my top ten countries to visit before I die, and the fact that I am here is still surreal to me. That I get to live this life and travel to so many beautiful places is a dream of mine that I never thought possible.

But he gave me the tools to make it possible, and that is why, deep down in my soul, I haven't been able to stop loving that man.

I hate him, I do, with a passion, but Christ with that same passion, I love him too. Maybe that's why I ran like a scared girl from the White House because I was terrified.

I am afraid that he will get in there again, and this time, I won't survive it. Because there is no surviving a man like Sebastian Kenton.

I tried, God knows I tried.

I also ran because I needed space.

Space to think things through and get my head straight so I can deal with the fact that we both have a little person in the middle who knows I am hers just as much as she is mine in my heart. A girl I will undoubtedly hurt if I ruin her father.

So, I find myself at a crossroads trying to figure out how to let go of this hate and stop unloving this man, so I can move on with my life without blowing up both our worlds. Before, I wanted to make him rue the day he made a fool of me, but that was when I didn't know he didn't go through with his threat of erasing me from Ella's memory.

Ugh, and there's the fact, that little by little, day by day, the cold has lessened inside of me. All because of them and it terrifies me because I didn't lie when I told Sebastian that love shouldn't hurt but the love he claims to feel for me does. What I thought was love hurt me to the point I don't trust it.

Trust him.

Perhaps, I never will.

Taking a sip of the complimentary resort drink, here at the Paradisus, an Ouzo martini, I lean back in the beach chair, enjoying the view.

This place truly is heaven or earth.

The resort is in Akrotiri with the beach right in front of it. In my opinion, a sea view is always appreciated.

Grabbing my phone, I snap a photo of the water and send it to Ellaiza.

Has Sebastian taken her to the beach? I wonder.

She would love it, I know it. No more so that she is obsessed with mermaids and the sea.

"Beautiful, isn't it?" A soft voice whispers from my left. Close, too close. And that voice. The husky, flirty tone I know oh so well.

No.

This can't be happening.

Please don't tell me the devil followed me here. Of all the things that could happen, but my gut did tell me something awful was nearby.

And something awful is here.

Keeping my black frame Gucci shades on, I turn my head and find Lucifer himself lounging in the beach chair next to me. Dressed in all white, with his cotton shirt slightly opened at the collar, revealing slightly tanned skin.

Oh, this bastard.

This gorgeous, imposing, slightly obsessed bastard.

"Where did you come from? No one said your name three times." I huff while he just smiles, irritating me further. "I am not even going to ask how you know I was here because we both know you would be so low as to use an innocent six-year-old child to get what you want."

"I wouldn't call our kid innocent since she got a pretty good deal out of snitching on you." He chuckles, and I am so momentarily struck by the view of him that I almost miss how he called Ella our kid. Shit. I always claimed her as mine in my heart but hearing it from his mouth is a whole other thing. Oh, he's for sure using her against me.

Sighing, I ask. "What are you doing here, Sebastian?"

He shrugs and keeps staring at me as if he can't look at anything else. As if he doesn't want to. It makes my skin prickles and goosebumps rise at the same time. The nerve of my traitorous body. "I thought it was time for a vacation."

"A vacation, huh?" Bullshit. "Don't you have a circus to run and clowns to serve?"

Smiling at my insult, he replies. "The country can survive a couple of days without me."

"Huh."

His blue-gray eyes spark with mirth, taunting me. "What?"

"The fact that your gigantic ego admitted that." The Sebastian I knew would've never admitted that the world, in fact, doesn't revolve around him and that the country can manage a few days without him there. I agree. There is no doubt about it. Sebastian is one man, and yes, he decides a lot, but the house and congress do too. Somehow, he managed to have both in his pocket.

That's a first in US history.

Having both the democrats and the republicans backing you up.

And, of course, he would be the one to do it.

"You look beautiful," The jerk says sincerely.

Determined not to be swayed by flattery, I stare stonily at him. "Get lost." I side-eye him, annoyed that my jabs don't seem to affect him. At all. "Your presence disturbs my peace."

"I do love it when you flatter me." His smile widens. "Besides, I am right where I'm supposed to be."

"You're not right in the head. That's more like it," I reply.

"Oh, darling… I think I am for the first time in three years."

I sighed. "What are you doing here?"

"Joining you."

"No one invited you."

"I did."

"That doesn't count."

Ignoring my last comment, his eyes trail down my body before slowly rising back up. "You fit in here perfectly."

"The beach?"

Shaking his head with a small smile, "In the land of Gods and Goddesses."

"Oh, please. Stop embarrassing yourself, Sebastian. Your charm does not work on me." Rolling my eyes at him, I lie through my teeth and do my best to ignore the way his lustful eyes and flirting make my blood pressure rise and my heartbeat quicken. "If you don't mind, I am trying to enjoy my day. Go bother someone else." I shoo him away, turn my face, and concentrate on my phone.

But then it doesn't last long because the next thing I know I watch from the corner of my eye as he leans back in the chair, getting comfortable. "I think I make you nervous, darling."

Curling my lip, I give him a dull look before replying. "And I think you've lost your mind. You do absolutely nothing for me. Let's get that clear now."

He smiles.

His smile takes over his face while his eyes twinkle, annoying me and melting me at the same time. Damn him because the sight of his smile always twisted through me like a knife. "I do nothing for you?"

"Absolutely nothing." I clarified.

His smile remains, "I think you're lying."

Shrugging, "And I think you're an asshole."

Mature, Arianna. Very mature.

"Tsk, tsk. Now, darling, resorting to name-calling is for academically challenged people, and you're better than that."

"Oh, I know that." Unlocking my phone, I typed a quick email to Nessa. "But insulting you is very satisfying for me."

"I am glad I am still able to satisfy you," he says in that deep voice that makes all of my nerve endings come alive despite knowing this man has always and will always be a very bad idea.

"That's not what I meant." I snap.

"Oh, but darling, that's what I heard." He says in a smug tone. Of course, that's what he got from my comment. The self-centered ass. Why am I still entertaining him? I brought this upon myself, really.

I have a few hours before I have to meet Wizz, the Latin reggaeton global sensation from Puerto Rico, at the resort's restaurant, so I decided to come down to the beach and do some reading and answer some emails, but Sebastian had to appear out of nowhere and dampen my mood with his unwanted compliments and infuriating charm.

"Have dinner with me." He says after we're both silent.

"In your dreams." I snap.

"I spend a lot of time with you in my dreams." He looks at me with a lopsided grin and a brow raised. He lowers his voice, and his tone becomes husky. "Sometimes we talk, other times we argue, but mostly we don't talk at all. Sometimes, I just worship you with my tongue and—" I don't let him finish his sentence.

Nope.

This is not happening.

Sebastian looks at me with that same smug look that tells me he is enjoying this. He wants to push my buttons, and he knows exactly how to do it. Rising from the beach chair, I push my glasses up my hair and stare down at him with a smug look of my own before I drop the entire contents of my glass on his lap.

"Hold onto your pathetic fantasies, Sebastian, because only there you'll get anything from me." I spit at him, ignoring the way he is still staring at me with heated eyes and that obnoxiously perfect grin of his.

His grin widens revealing perfect white straight teeth. "If you say so, Arianna." I am going to kill him.

Curling my lip, I give him a dirty look, annoyed with the way he looks so damn smug, as if he's won something. He has won nothing. "I really do hate your stupid face, Sebastian." Childish? Yes. Do I care? No. The petty remarks always make me feel better.

There is a long pause before I hear the second most beautiful thing in the world. Sebastian's joyful laugh. Looking down at him, I watch as he throws his head back, puts his big, strong hand on his abdomen, and roars with laughter. It was a thing of beauty. It always was, and he knows it too. Now, I really need to get away from him.

Taking off my plain see-through, open-front kimono, I let it fall to the sand, leaving me only in my matching white cut-out, one-shoulder, and one-piece swimsuit. It doesn't go unnoticed how Sebastian's eyes become hooded as he takes me in, but before I give his reaction one more thought, I snatch my glasses off my head and drop them down on the beach chair. Then I turn and walk toward the water and leave him there smiling from ear to ear.I hadn't realized how much I missed the ocean until today. The ocean didn't bring back happy memories, so I went without it, just like everything that reminded me of him.

I missed how the warm breeze felt like a lover's caress on my skin. The water, the sand, and the breeze. It all gave me serenity. Just like him.

So, I walk towards it. Towards that feeling that I missed so much and away from him, but with every step I take, I feel his burning eyes on my skin, hotter than the sun shining down on me, and it reminds me that he's here. That I can't escape him. Even if I try. He's not going anywhere. That much is true.

It also doesn't go unnoticed how easy it is to breathe when he's far away from me.

It's like every time I'm around him, he takes my breath and keeps it for himself.

It is irritating as much as it makes me feel vulnerable.

I keep going, though.

The wind blows my hair in all directions as I walk to the water until it is up to my waist, and only then do I go under, letting the warm water wash away his scent from my skin.

There's nothing like seawater caressing my skin.

When my sister, Kadra, and I were kids, we used to imagine we were mermaids while we were in the bathtub. Playing and dreaming that we were mythical creatures who lived under the sea with fish friends and a father who ruled all merpeople with kindness and grace.

Silly, I know, but it was better than our reality.

Anything was better than our reality.

Even fictional worlds.

Holding my breath, I swim. I swim underwater, going as deep as I'm able to and until I can't hold my breath any longer, and only then do I go up to the surface, taking a big breath as I do. Once I wipe the salty water from my eyes, I look at where I left Sebastian, but he's no longer there.

Maybe he got tired of my shit, finally got the hint, and left.

Maybe...

But then I spotted him.

A vision in white with the sun shining down on his skin tanning it more than usual, and his usual perfectly combed hair messy because of the soft breeze. With his phone in hand pointed my way and a gentle smile on his face.

"What the hell are you doing, you crazy, stupid man?" I wonder aloud.

Then it dawns on me.

The tyrant is standing on the white sand, taking photos of me.

Thud.

Thud.

Oh, Christ, no.

Stop it, you foolish heart. Didn't you learn your lesson last time?

This tyrant with a perfect smile and laughing eyes cannot be trusted.

Overcome with old and newfound feelings, I take a deep breath and dive underwater. Maybe once I go back up again, he'll be gone… but no such luck.

When I resurface, I find him there.

Standing like a Greek statue with a smile on his handsome face that does not falter no matter all the shit I throw his way.

Sebastian is determined to win this.

And for the first time, since all this started, I realize that I'm well and truly fucked.

Shit.

Chapter 19
GREEK GOD
Arianna

"I know better than
my foolish heart…" — A

"*Si, si. Eso me suena cabrón.*" Wizz, the Latino reggaetonero and global sensation leans forward in his seat opposite me with a devious smirk on his face. His stage name is as stupid as his choice of clothing tonight. I am not even going to entertain that mess. Wizz, is a white Puerto Rican male with exotic features. Big lips, curly hair, and a perfect smile. The guy has taken the industry by storm and no one can deny that. People are listening to trap and reggaeton music in countries that didn't even know the island of Puerto Rico existed. "I'll agree on one condition, though," Wizz says.

Here we go.

There's always something with celebrities.

Taking a sip of my glass, I wait for him to ask for whatever it is he wants so I can be done with him. The guy is talented and has a lot of charisma but the fame has clearly gone to his head. We've been sitting down, going through the offer both Quinne and I agreed to, for half an hour, and he has interrupted me more times than I care to count just to brag about his lifestyle. He's rich as hell.

He knows it. I know it, and the world sure as hell does, but a little humility wouldn't kill him, or maybe it just might.

I typically deal with managers or publicists when it comes to artists, athletes, and others in the entertainment industry, but this one insisted on being the one to negotiate instead of his manager, Luisa.

I can tolerate the usual hard-ass managers or pretentious entertainers, but this walking, talking ego has proven to be a challenge.

When he doesn't go ahead and state his conditions, I know it's up to me to get it out of him.

Sighing, I ask. "What's your condition?"

"I'll agree to do the sit-down interview if I'm allowed creative freedom to express myself without censorship and if you promise that bloodsucking viper you call partner won't be present." He means Quinne. The last time we tried to get this dude on the cover of our magazine, Quinne handled the meeting, and by the sound of it, it's obvious why Quinne couldn't seal the deal.

Those two butted heads last time, most likely because Quinne has a short fuse and Wizz is well… too much. "Deal."

I give in because he's the hottest artist and fashion icon at the moment. It would be foolish of me to decline. I also give in easily, so I can be done here. One more second with this guy, and I'll lose brain cells.

Okay, maybe that was too harsh.

True… but harsh.

"Asi me gusta, mami. Much better than that man-hater." He leans back with a smug grin on his face. The superstar wears a burgundy Dolce & Gabbana jumpsuit and matching sunglasses.

Sunglasses at night, for fucks' sake. You see… I try to be cordial but some people just bring out the worse in me.

I bite my tongue, holding back all the things I wish to say to this idiot, but can't because I'm aware that he's the right person to help us reach the younger demographic and expand the magazine, but this moment right here feels like I'm this asshole's bitch and it's pissing me off.

Wizz empties his drink and calls out for another. In the meantime, I take advantage that he is busy looking at himself on his phone camera, and I reach for my phone to read Ella's text that I haven't had a chance to reply to earlier but then my phone starts vibrating with an incoming call from an unknown number. The same unknown number that's been ringing me all day. I roll my eyes and answer. "Give up, Sebastian. Not interested." I hang up without giving him a chance to respond. I quickly save the number as 'Asshole. Don't Pick Up' and quickly finish typing a message for Ella.

Ella: Mommy, I need you to do something for me.

Uh-huh.

I just know this will be a pain for me.

Me: What do you need, Ellaiza?

Ella: Daddy went to surprise you and watch over you because he said black birds will be surrounding you. I don't want anything to happen to you, but I know Dad won't let it happen. Please do the same for him. Okay? He needs more laughter, and I know you will make him happy. Please, Mom.

Ahhhhh. I mentally scream.

The tyrant knows what he's doing and how to get me to comply.

Me: Sure thing, darling girl.

Ella is not here, so she has no way of finding out if I'm a total bitch to her father, and what she doesn't know won't hurt her because, as much as Sebastian likes to use Ella to get to me, I also know he won't hurt her

by telling on me. Ugh, we're horrible people. That's for sure.
But he is one of those people that bring out the worst in me.

"That was cold," Wizz says, crossing his arms.

"The man is a nuisance," I answer truthfully.

My phone buzzes with a new message.

Sebastian persists.

Asshole. Don't Pick Up: I see you have lost your manners, darling.

I ignore him because I have no patience to deal with two idiots at the time.

"*Se me hace que hay una historia ahí.*" Wizz says. I think there's a story there. I've picked up a bit of Spanish from Quinne just enough to understand but not well enough to speak the language.

"Not really." Leaning forward on the table. "Look, Wizz." I hate myself at this moment for the words that came out of my mouth. That god-awful stage name. "I would love to stay here all night, but I'm tired and wish to lie down if you don't mind." Nonsense. There's nothing I would hate more, but I don't say that. Instead, I say, "Do we have a deal?"

He contemplates it for a minute, then nods and offers me his hand. "Deal. My manager will be in contact so we can figure out all the details."

Nodding, I rise from my seat and watch as he leaves. Taking a long breath, I sit back down and empty my glass of Ouzo. I shouldn't drink this much, and I usually don't, but after this day, I need it.

"Is this seat taken?" A smooth and very familiar voice asks.

Took him long enough to appear out of nowhere.

"Yes." I snap. Clearly, a higher being is testing my patience today. Instead of getting lost, Sebastian pulls a chair and sits down opposite me.

"Too bad." Grinning, "You look stunning," Sebastian says with a look of hunger in his eyes. Ignoring his flattery, I say. "So ... this is the way you've chosen to die?" He smiles so big it almost leaves me breathless. Almost. "Oh, but what a sweet death it would be to die by your hand." He gets this look in his eyes, and his grin resembles that of a demon from hell before he snatches your soul. And I know, I just know he's going to say something that will piss me off more than his presence has. "You know…if you were to kill me, I'd prefer to be under and inside of you when—"Rolling my eyes. "You're disgusting."

"Yet… you love me."

"If that's what you tell yourself to feed into your delusion, so be it, Sebastian." I try to calm my racing heart and avoid the way his stare makes me hot all over. I convince myself it is from anger and nothing more.

I hate how hyper-aware all my senses are of him. Not even the salty smell of the sea in the air can get rid of Sebastian's cologne. He still smells the same. "Did you eat?" He asks out of nowhere.

"I have lost my appetite." I level him with a pointed glare, but he doesn't get the hint and leaves. No, he makes it worse. He leans back in his seat and gets comfortable. "Who was that man?" His eyes change from soft to hard in a second. "I've seen him before."

Narrowing my eyes on him, I let my displeasure emanate from me. "Not your business," I mumble, taking in everyone around us. I don't miss the not-so-clever men dressed as locals seated at most of the tables surrounding us. His security team, of course.

Sebastian is known everywhere in the globe now that he's the president, so his team goes above and beyond to keep him safe with measures, like shutting down a restaurant and occupying all the tables so he has a little bit of privacy. How I did not notice is beyond me.

I blame it on being distracted by Wizz and all his nonsense.

But I am noticing now. I glower at him and the bastard grins harder.

"I disagree. You are my business, so who you choose to spend time with is my business." He leans his elbows on the tiny table. His grin is wickedly boyish and sexy as hell.

I clench my teeth in suppressed annoyance. Not only for the boldness of this man but because just the sight of him makes something deep in my chest—the hollow part, the part he broke—ache but at the same time, it burns for him. And it makes me feel weak, and I loathe feeling weak around him because that's when he's able to sneak in and make me feel things I don't want to feel.

I can't afford to feel for him.

"Let's agree to disagree then because I'm in no mood to entertain you tonight, or any night for that matter, Sebastian." Grabbing my small purse, I rise from my seat. "Now, if you excuse me—"

He doesn't let me finish my sentence. Looking up at me without a trace of the cocky smile he was sporting a minute ago, he tells me. *"S'il te plaît."* He whispers while he leans forward and grabs my hand in his. The contact sends a shock of electricity through my body instead of the feeling of repulsiveness I should feel at his touch, but no. I feel the same sensation I felt the first time he ever touched me. As if all I was missing in life to be happy was his touch. *"S'il vous plaît, ma chérie. Ne partez pas."* He whispers, and I detect sadness in his tone. Sadness and regret.

I tell myself I don't care. His pain does not matter.

But then my traitorous heart thuds, "Liar. Liar. Liar…"

Because I am human.

Human and weak for him.

And it did.

I should shake off his hand, tell him to fuck off, and never touch me again. I should cuss him seven ways to hell. A sane woman who's been broken by the man she loved, would do exactly that. But I don't.

I look into those beautiful wolffish eyes of his, and I'm left breathless and wondering if I've lost my goddamn mind. Because that's exactly how I feel when I am around Sebastian. I shake his hands off, at least I do that, but then instead of turning around and leaving him there to deal with his pity and regrets alone… I sit back down, and when I do, the most brilliant smile takes over his face. So brilliant it rivals the starry night tonight. I try to ignore how terribly and unfairly handsome he looks tonight, with his jet-black hair brushed back away from his face and a bit of stubble.

Before, he was always clean-shaven. I have to admit it makes him look older and more distinguished. He's also wearing an indigo blue shirt that matches his eyes, with his sleeves rolled to his elbows, accentuating his strong arms. I used to know every inch of his skin, and now, it's like he's a stranger to me. Sighing, I pull my glass up, signaling the waiter for another. I've been drinking the same thing all night.

He knows by now. If I must endure the agony of sitting right across from the man that not only haunts my past but my present and most likely my future, then I sure as hell will be drinking more than water.

***

BASTIAN

I try with all my power to hold in the chuckle that threatens to spill from my lips as I watch Arianna, in the most adorable of ways, ignore my existence by focusing really hard on that glass of alcohol in front of her as if she finds the glass more interesting than me, which I don't have a doubt in mind she does, but since I am a man who values his life,

I won't. "You really are a menace, Sebastian." Her words come out a little slurred, but not so much that lets me know she's hammered. This is a new side of her, and as much as seeing her in turmoil perturbs me to no end, it gladdens me that she chose to stay with me here at this moment. At least that's a win for now.

Ellaiza is not here, nor did I use her to get Arianna to stay. This is all on her.

Leaning back, I look at her face and take every inch of her like a starving man.

Every second, minute, and hour of every day, I'm starving for her. For her love. For her smiles. For her. "And you are a thing of beauty, Arianna."

"If you start with your corny ass lines and bullshit flirtatious act, I am leaving." The stunning grump mumbles and then takes another sip of her glass.

"Very well," Clearing my throat, I disguise the hurt that takes over me every time she rejects any advance, no matter how innocent, because I know I deserve it. Therefore, I swallow the hurt, and change the topic to something I've been thinking about since I arrived in Greece. Since I saw how the moonlight shone, reflecting her skin and making her look like a goddess. The word falls short when describing my Arianna.

I honestly believe there is no correct word to describe her beauty.

I've seen every side of her, and all of them I love, but tonight she's glowing in a way that's making it difficult for me to find my next breath.

Perhaps, it's the fact that her usual wavy golden hair is now falling in soft curls, framing her face. Curls as in my daughter's ringlets. Making her look less straight-laced and business-like and more carefree. Jovial. Stunning.

Fucking perfect.

Her skin looks sun-kissed even at night, and her face also has a tan. It's also free of any makeup, not that she needs it. She looks beautiful, with or without it.

She's flawless either way.

My eyes roam down her face to her neck, where a delicate chain hangs from it with a small letter E pendant. E for Ellaiza, I presume.

Guilt chokes me, but I do my best to push it down and focus on the enchanting siren in front of me.

My woman, even when she's fighting me tooth and nail.

Clearing my throat, I break the silence by asking her. "Do you know the tale of Hero and Leander, Arianna?" Her eyes narrow, but they also flash with something that looks a lot like curiosity. Arianna always had an inquisitive mind, and that's one of the many reasons I fell in love with her. What attracted me to her. She genuinely loves learning about new places, people, and things. She loves challenges as much as I do. Ironically, she has proven to be my most difficult challenge.

"No, but I am sure you will tell me." She says in a tired tone and adverts her eyes from mine, looking back down at her glass with a blue liquid in it. It still amazes me how the world seems to fade away whenever she is near. My men, most of them, are sitting down at the tables that surround us while others are surrounding the area to make sure no threat reaches us, or even the press. The press as of twelve hours ago, caught wind that I am here on a three-day vacation. I need my men to keep them away from us for the rest of our time here. Looking at Arianna and Arianna only, I begin to tell her the story my mother told me once when I was a young boy. The forbidden and tragic love story of two star-crossed lovers. "Hero was a priestess of Aphrodite.

As such, she was forbidden to have affairs with men. Other versions of the story say that she was simply a virgin." Arianna intrigued with the tale, raises her head and looks me in the eyes, causing my skin to burn just from her gaze. She always had that effect on me. "Hero lived in a tower on the Greek side of the narrow Hellespont straights. Leander was a young man from Abydos, living on the other side of the Hellespont. From the moment he first saw Hero, he fell madly and irrevocably in love." Leaning forward I find myself trying to get closer to Arianna, even if the table between us is in the way. I notice how she doesn't look away from me or tell me to stop. She just remains quiet, urging me with her eyes to continue, but besides that, she gives me nothing. Not a smile. Nothing, not that I thought she would. But she has given me something, though. Her time and attention, and that I value more than all the material things I own. "Hero, with his soft-spoken words and devotion, soon inspired the same love in Hero." Arianna's nostrils flare, and her eyes narrow that bratty way of hers that drives me wild. It shouldn't, but it does. "What happens next?" She asks.

So curious, my darling. "Each night, she would light a lamp, which guided Leander to swim across the Hellespont and spend time with her." "Huh. Then what? I assume there's no happy ending, so get to it, Sebastian." Smiling softly, I do as she says, wanting to share what happens next with the lovers. "One night, however, the wind was too strong and blew out the lamp while Leander was still swimming. The waves were too high due to the wind, and Leander lost his way and drowned." She leans back, a look of disappointment on her face. My not-so-cold queen looks as if she hoped there would be a better outcome than the one I told. "In her grief and desperation, Hero threw herself in the raging sea and drowned as well."

Arianna looks away from me, clearly affected by the story. No, it is not a fairytale, but it is a beautiful story of love and the meaning of forever to some lovers. Without taking my eyes off her profile, I tell her the end. "Somehow, their bodies were found on the beach, in a tight embrace, and that's how they were buried." There's a long silence as she continues looking away from me towards the sea. "Figures. Love like this story is a myth." She mumbles, still looking away from me.

How I hate it when she looks away.

"The story is a myth, yes. But the lesson behind it isn't." There's always a lesson. This I know from experience.

"Oh, please tell me what possible lesson is there of two lovers drowning at sea?"

"It's a tragic story, yes, but it's one about a love that transcends life and death," I mutter and watch as she looks my way from the corner of her eye. I continue, "Hero guided her lover at night, and she became his light in the dark. While Leander swam each night, so he could meet and spend time with her, however long it lasted. And when one was lost to the other forever, the pain was so great she could not bear it. She could not bear life without it, so she ended it to meet him in the next life. Somehow, their love was so powerful that they found their way back to each other, even in death. They're spending eternity in each other's embrace, and that's the lesson, darling. Love is ugly, and sometimes life is unfair, but love trumps the greatest obstacles. Love always wins, even when it feels like all is lost."

I whisper so only she can hear and watch as she swallows and turns her head toward me. I don't mind the teary green eyes cutting me deep. I watch as her eyes flash with every emotion, from hate to hurt, lastly to love and pain. "I don't know what you want from me, Sebastian.

But if forgiveness is what you seek, then for the sake of our girl, I forgive you." She says fiercely, while the warm breeze blows her golden curls in all directions, making her look otherworldly to my eyes. "I forgive you because I can no longer keep drowning in this hate that won't allow me to love her how she deserves. So, I chose Ellaiza. I choose her love over hating you." I sit there in silence, transfixed by the beauty before me, while her words penetrate my heart like sharp knives. Cutting me deep, making me bleed. But I welcome this pain because not only can I carry it, but this is my time to atone for my sins against her. I would sustain a thousand knives to my heart if only it led me back to her heart.

I sit back and watch as she rises from her seat, towering over me. I am a man that always followed Science. The facts are facts, but a lot changed when I met her. I used to believe love, at first sight, was a myth. A thing of fools, but then I saw her, and I fell.

I used to also believe that a heart couldn't break, but mine did. Hers did, as well. But it happened.

Now, this.

My heart is beating so loud inside my chest that I can hear it, or maybe I am just losing my goddamn mind. Perhaps. "Yes, I'll work on forgiving you until I wish no ill will towards you, but if you're waiting for me to love you again, it will be a cold day in hell before that happens." She stares right at me, and for a second, only for a second, I believe her, but then she does that thing she used to when she was nervous.

She tucks her hair behind her ear.

Innocent.

Sweet.

Such a contrast to her usual self lately.

If you're waiting for me to love you again, it will be a cold day in hell before that happens.

It cuts deep, yes, but I know her heart even if she refuses to admit it.

Time didn't change that.

I know she loves me.

She hasn't stopped because a love like ours has a beginning, yes, but it doesn't have an end. Instead of telling her that, like every particle of my being wants to, I tell her. "I will wait forever if that's how long it takes for you to trust me with your heart again."

Her pretty brows furrow, but just as quickly, she masks her reaction, shakes her head as if she's trying to shake my words, and turns.

She turns and leaves me there, with my heart in my hands, refusing it, and each step she takes away from me feels like a punch to my gut.

I did not lie.

I will wait my entire life if I have to.

Then, when I feel like nothing I told her tonight got through to her, she stops outside the restaurant's door and looks back at me over her shoulder. For a second that feels like a lifetime, her green eyes clash with mine, telling me all the secrets that her mouth won't, but then she turns and disappears from my view, and I am left to wonder if I imagined it all because having her back in my life feels to me like a dream.

The dream I've been reaching for three long years, and now it's here, and I fear one day I'll wake up to realize it was only that.

A dream.

Chapter 20
TRUSTING HEARTS
Arianna

"I wanted the world for her." — B

Remember how I said nothing bad could happen in 72 hours? Well, I was wrong. Life has proved me wrong once again because something bad did happen. These two days have screwed me.

Hard.

He got to me.

The tyrant, like a venomous serpent, has slithered into my system long enough to do some serious damage.

He has poisoned my mind. That has to be the reason why I am spiraling. Why I couldn't find sleep last night.

His words played through my mind all night after I left him at the restaurant, looking hurt but determined.

I've been hating him for so long that the thought of forgiving him never crossed my mind until Greece. Until I realized that Ellaiza will always be in the middle. And what happens when innocents get caught in the middle of a war that's not their own?

They get seriously hurt.

And the thought of that cripples me. Although forgiveness won't come easy, I know that for her sake, I'll be able to get there.

I just don't know if I'll ever get to the point where seeing him doesn't hurt me because if I let go of this hate, then all that's left is a lot of hurt and behind that?

So much love.

Buried deep in my shredded soul.

So, yes, a lot can indeed happen in a two-day work trip.

And now this inconvenience.

I should be on a plane back to Washington. Back to my life, my company, and Ellaiza, but instead, I am still in Greece, having to deal with not only Sebastian but Wizz, as well.

I thought we had come to an agreement last night. Meaning the artist, but I guess not, since he wants to meet with me again. God knows for what.

Now, I see for myself why Quinne can't stand the man.

He knows zero to nothing about business, yet he tries to act as he does instead of being smart enough to understand that some artists are just that, artists, entertainers, and not businessmen. Yes, some can be both, but others, like in his case, don't have it in them.

I was planning on catching a plane out of Greece today since my business here ended, but then the concierge at the front desk handed me a written note addressed to me from Wizz, asking me to meet him at the hotel's restaurant again.

So after cursing him and my bad luck for twenty minutes straight, I went back to the room and took a power nap, which lasted about an hour since my mind kept me up. Then, I decided to take advantage of the time I had left here and explore as much as I could.

I took a day trip and visited the archaeological site of Akrotiri. Before coming here, I read online that the fascinating ancient Minoan city is known as Greece's version of Pompeii after being buried by an earthquake. I also learned that some said that Akrotiri was Plato's inspiration for the city of Atlantis. Which is fascinating to think about when you see what was left of the ancient city after the huge volcano, Thera, erupted and blew the center right out of the island of Santorini. The eruption was one of the largest volcanic events ever recorded on Earth, creating a four-mile-wide caldera and sending up an ash cloud 20 miles high. It also set off a 100-meter-high tsunami that battered the coastline of Crete and reached as far as Egypt. By the time the eruption had finished, Akrotiri had been buried beneath a 200-foot layer of ash and debris, and the shape of Santorini had been changed for good. Covered with hot lava and piles of ash, the island was abandoned for centuries.

All this knowledge prompted my curious mind to buy a ticket and visit the site. I needed the distraction and a day for myself to think, but I also wanted to see for myself how the city was uncovered after so many centuries had passed and how it was forgotten for a while until the 1860s.

The archeological site is set in a smart, new building made of steel and wood to let just enough light in but keep things cool and protected. Walkways are suspended above the ruins and take you around the edge of the city. But what's ground level for us is the roof height in Akrotiri.

A pathway leads down through some of the reconstructed houses, where you can see details like an original Minoan toilet and a stone bathtub.

The tour guide explains how during the excavations, remnants of people's everyday lives were uncovered amongst the buildings, and they're what makes the site so fascinating. The ash has perfectly preserved the Minoan way of life, from painted frescoes to hundreds of pots.

These range from drinking cups up to giant storage vessels decorated with geometric patterns. Many of the pots are amazingly still intact, and some even had remains of olive oil or fish inside. You can see some artifacts at the site, but many others have been moved to the archaeological museum in Fira, and some of the best of Akrotiri's frescoes are on display in Greece's National Archaeological Museum in Athens. After taking many videos and pictures to save and send to Ella later, I left the site and headed toward the Red Beach, which was only a short walk from the Akrotiri archaeological site. The moment my bare feet touched the infamous red sand, I knew in my heart that Ellaiza would love it. She was always so curious when younger, just like me.
Looking around the peculiar beach, I set my things down on the sand, grab my phone and start a video call. Greece is 7 hours ahead of Washington.

  Walking towards the crystalline waters, I soak up the warm sun rays as I wait for the call to connect. A sweet, excited, beautiful face takes over my entire phone screen. "Mommy! Hi!" Ellaiza's excited squeals make the smile on my face widen.

"Hi, my love. Good morning." It's early for her there.

Her phone starts to shake as she bounces up and down. "Shaw! Shaw look at mom. She looks like a mermaid. Your hair looks so pretty, mom. You look like a mermaid." The jerk just nods at her but carries on doing whatever the hell he gets paid to when Ella is not on the move.

"Ella, come back to me," I tell her gently, not caring to see her bodyguard. At all. "I'm back. Hi!"

"Hi!" I exclaim happily.

"Huh. You're wearing pink." Her blue eyes, so much like her father's, narrow suspiciously.

Looking down at my pink sundress, I look back at her, grinning. "I am."

"But you hate pink."

I do hate it, but she doesn't, and I guess, in some way, the color doesn't make me sad. Instead, it reminds me that she loved the color, and I love her. Now, don't get me wrong, I despise it, but for her, if it makes her smile like she is doing now, then I'll endure.

Same with her father.

Oh, the irony.

Then it comes to mind that the tyrant must've told her about my likes and dislikes in hopes that she felt closer to me. "It's not my favorite…" I grin at her offended expression. Before she goes on a rant as to why pink is the best color, I distract her, "Look where I am." Flipping the camera, the shot is of the beach now.

"Oh my Gosh!" She yells adorably while her palms go to her cheeks. "You're in mermaid land, mom!"

Mermaids.

I learned from Benjamin that she's been into mermaids lately.

That's why I bought her mermaid barbie dolls and a mermaid costume she could wear for the pool. Laughing, I squat down and show her the sand. "Not quite, baby, but it does look like another planet, doesn't it?" Flipping the phone camera so she can see me. I rise to my full height. "It does. Oh, I want to go there. Please, mom." Her face falls, and I hate it.

"We can come back. Would you like that?" I ask nervously. I don't ever want to overstep, and sometimes I need to remind myself that as much as she feels like mine, legally, she's not.

"With daddy, too?" Ella asks.

Oh, fuck.

This will be my life now, won't it?

It's no longer just me.

Or just me and Ellaiza.

He won't be far behind.

Grinding my teeth, I give her my best smile. "Your father can come, too."

"Yay!" She screams, and the joy in that scream makes my reservations fade away because, God knows, I would do anything for this little girl. I see her bodyguard coming up behind her and giving her backpack and matching pink lunchbox. Ella scrunches her face and pouts when he tells her it's time for school. Knowing she'll give him a hard time, I tell her. "I'm taking lots of pictures, babe, and I'll be back in the States tomorrow. We'll see each other soon, yes?"

Her grumpy face is instantly replaced by a brilliant smile. "Okay! I can't wait!" I smile when she presses the phone to her mouth, giving it a big wet kiss. So silly, my girl.

"I love your kisses!" I do. I miss them. I miss her.

"And I love you, mommy." She speaks.

"And I love you."

"So much?"

"To the moon and back, Ella. To the moon and back." I whisper to her, hoping she feels it. All the love I have for her.

When she says goodbye, I do the same and wait for her to hang up first, but she doesn't. Instead, she says. "Oh, mom, I forgot to thank you!"

"For what, baby?"

"Daddy told me you made him smile a lot, and he's so happy! Thank you!" Her face is so sweet, innocent, and trusting. All that's good in the world. Oh, she has me wrapped around her small finger, and she knows it. Her dad knows it, too.

I made him smile.

Thud.

No.

No.

Don't go there, heart. Nothing good can come of it.

"Anything for you, Ella."

She beams, blows me a kiss, and hangs up.

With a bright smile on my face, I grab my things from the sand and move toward my next destination. I still have time before I have to meet with Wizz, and it would be a shame if I left this wonderful country without really experiencing most of what it has to offer. Grabbing the polaroid camera that I bought specifically to capture memories that I can then give to Ella, I snap a photo of the beach so later I can write a message for her on the back of the polaroid.

"What's next?" I wonder aloud as I scroll on my phone for other sites that are near the hotel without me having to take a cab.

While I'm looking at what might be my next destination before the sun sets, a message pops up on my screen.

I really need to change his name when I get back to the States, just in case Ella gets a hold of my phone.

Asshole. Don't Answer: I miss you.

Me: Just because I said I would forgive you, it doesn't mean you can text me, Sebastian. Unless it is regarding Ellaiza, please refrain from contacting me.

Asshole. Don't Answer: Ouch.

Asshole. Don't Answer: Ellaiza misses you, too. Is that better?

Me: Not really. Goodbye.

I hold my breath when I see the dots appear on the screen, but then suddenly stop. I was a bitch to him, I know, but maybe then he'll understand that nothing will ever happen between us again. It can't. I might still love him, and it bugs the hell out of me that not even the shit he did can kill that love, but I do not trust him.

Not with my heart.

I find myself experiencing local cuisine and winery for the rest of the day, but my heart is not in it. Guilt claws at my soul. Guilt and grief. All because it's becoming almost an impossible task to act like an uncaring bitch to the man that has made it his mission to not only get back into my good graces but my heart as well.

Out of the 8.05 billion humans in this world, why did I have to fall for him? Why Sebastian Kenton?

As I stand on the edge of a marble, white wall, which has the perfect view of the crystal blue sea, a thought crosses my mind.

Because he sets your heart on fire when it only has ever known the cold…

***

Whoever said taking naps is good for the soul was absolutely right. I was never one to take naps since, at first, I was scared of what might happen to my sisters if I closed my eyes, and then the past couple of years, I've been so busy and motivated to build an empire of my own that I never found the time. I found the time today.

Now, I have the energy that is required to deal with Wizz this evening. On the note he left for me this morning, he specified to meet him down at the hotel's restaurant, Myko's, again. And here I am, exiting the hotel's lobby and walking towards the backside where the restaurant is.

I dressed comfortably yet chic tonight. Not for him. I could care less about what he or others think of me.

I always dress for myself.

Because looking good makes me feel confident.

Makes me feel like, somehow, I am in control.

I get to choose how to present myself to the world and that is something I did not get to do when growing up. That's mainly why I chose to leave my hair curly these past two days.

My mother hated my curly hair. To this day, I don't know why but she did, so she used to force me to wear it straight or slightly curled at the ends.

Today, I chose not to straighten my curls and let them fall loose around my back.

I also opted to wear a one-shoulder knot, nude cream-colored dress and paired it with diamond studs on my ears and some minimalist thong sandals to match the dress.

I also added a bit of blush, mascara, and nothing else since my skin is sensitive today after being in the sun all day.

"Good evening." A warm and welcoming voice belonging to an older-looking lady greets me.

Nodding to the smiling hostess, I say, "Good evening. I am meeting someone."

She nods and looks down at the black book in front of her. "Name, please?"

"Arianna. Arianna Parisi." I answer.

"Oh, yes!" The lady exclaims at the same time as her eyes grow suspiciously big. Huh. "Right this way. The boss is waiting for you." The boss? Wizz? Confused, I follow her as she guides me away from the dining area. What is going on? She stops next to a tall man dressed in all black, and I just know.

God, I just know this has nothing to do with Wizz.

Nothing at all. "You are one lucky woman." She swoons, I kid you not, and smiles one last time, leaving me alone, standing next to a giant, strange man. "Miss." The stranger hands me a rose, a gold-plated rose, and nods as a soldier would to his sergeant or superior. Secret service, I have no doubt. If the rose wasn't obvious enough, then the men are. "Your smile makes my day ten times better." Taking the rose, I look at the man as if he has lost his mind, and he looks at me as if he doesn't get paid enough for this shit. Moving forward, another man dressed the same way hands me another rose. "I love how you love my daughter." That one gets me. Taking the rose from him, I nod in thanks and continue down the lighted-up path that leads me to the beach as seven more men hand me more gold-plated roses, and each tells me something they love about me. But when I reach the last man, I stop. "Hey, my girl." His smile takes over his face, but there's a nervousness to it as well.

"Benjamin. You goddamn traitor." I try to muster an angry tone, but I can't. It's almost impossible with this man.

"I am sorry that I didn't warn you." He hands me the rose. "But I did not want to get in the way of you finding laughter again." Taking a step back as if he hit me, I look up at him, trying to understand when exactly I lowered all my goddamn walls to the point so many people slipped through and made it to my heart. It happened, and here stands one of them. "He instructed us to share with you one thing he loves about you, but fuck, let me tell you one of my own. I love your laugh, kid. Your fucking laugh is like a song to our hearts. My heart has been empty for so long that I used to wonder if it only worked to pump blood. If it only did its duty and nothing more, but then you came along and made me feel again. I've lost so much throughout my life, but that asshole waiting down the beach did two things.

He not only gave me my little lady, but he also gave me you."

"God, I can't stand emotions. You've all made me so damn weak."

"Perhaps, we made you human?"

"Same thing to me."

Laughing, he steps aside. "I know trusting again is scary, my girl, but you've always been a fighter. Don't stop fighting now." Benjamin leans down and kisses me on the forehead.

Choked up with emotions, I nod and sidestep him but after taking a few steps forward, I stop.

All these strange men recited ten things.

Ten things the person waiting for me at the end of the path loves about me. My heartbeat slows with each step I take. I should turn around. I should run in the opposite direction, but my feet have a mind of their own, and so does my foolish heart.

Standing on the end path that separates the hotel and the beach, I look back at the ten men standing in line, all looking at me as if they know me. I guess now they do with the little details they shared about me. One of them knows me more than I sometimes know myself.

Taking a deep breath, I bend over to quickly take my sandals off and walk barefoot toward the beach. Looking down at the sand, I notice lavender-colored petals and seashells creating a path down the beach.

My pulse is racing now, and my mind is reeling, but I walk toward... him.

Once I'm halfway to the end, I feel it.

An ache I've carried around in my chest for years splinter painfully.

Turn around and get the hell out of here, I urge myself. Stop being such a masochist.

But I couldn't.

The desire to see what he planned was too great.

A table for two with lit candles forming a heart around it and twelve, or maybe thirteen, bouquets of gold roses. It's a scene taken straight out of a fairytale book. The same Ellaiza loved so much when she was a baby. The moon reflects on the water beautifully as the breeze blows softly around me. I took the last steps, and there he was. That horrible ache bloomed hotter as I stared up at a larger-than-life Sebastian. Dressed all in white, looking like the God of thunder, Zeus himself, surrounded by only beauty. And even with all the beauty surrounding him, he is still the only thing I see. When I reach the table, he offers me his hand and smiles widely.

So irresistible. "You're here." He says in awe, with a wicked smile. "Please don't insult my intelligence. Of course, I am here. You tricked me." I intended to sound cold and detached, but somehow, neither happens, and he notices, too, by the twinkle in his blue eyes. "Owner? Really, Sebastian? Do you own the world?" I take his hand, aware of the shock of electricity that runs through my body. With his help, I take my seat and wait for him to take his.

Sebastian was immune to my aloofness.

It reminded me that when Sebastian Kenton wanted something, he got tunnel vision. There was no one as determined as this man. The thought exhilarated me as much as it frightened me.

His blinding smile turns into a devious smirk when he says, "Pretty much, yes." He laughs when I roll my eyes at him. "But I do apologize for leading you here under false pretenses, but desperate times call for desperate measures."

Tucking a curl behind my ear, I tsk. "Humility was never your strong suit, Mr. President."

"Neither was it yours, my darling." He laughs, and I swear Sebastian was the type of man who could smile at you and make you feel like the only woman in the room. Hell, in the entire globe.

I thought I became immune to it, but I guess not.

We both fall silent after that, and I focus on listening to the waves crashing, trying to shake the nerves that have taken over my body since I sat down. Noticing there's a glass of wine next to my plate, I chug it down, hoping it helps me feel better.

"I hope you're hungry." Sebastian breaks the silence, pointing down at my plate.

"Not really." I'm lying. I'm starving, actually, and the food in front of me smells and looks terribly delicious.

"Since you don't wish to eat, perhaps we should talk instead?" He whispers before taking a sip of his glass, looking smug as hell.

Narrowing my eyes, I pick up my fork and poke the food like a child would when they're not sure if they'll like it. "What is this?" I look at Sebastian.

He smiles and speaks. "Moussaka."

"Okay…. What is this Moussaka made of?" It smells delicious.

"Three layers of goodness." I watch as he takes a bite of his plate first. Searching his expression for any signs of distaste, I find nothing but a pleased look. "Made with sauteed eggplants, minced meat in sweet-spiced tomato and bechamel sauce on top." Taking a bite of my own, a moan slips out the moment the savory goodness hits my tastebuds. Delicious, indeed.

We dine in silence, but even the silence is loud between us. It always was. Before, we didn't need words to communicate. Sebastian's eyes said it all, and I see nothing has changed. Is this real?

I wonder as I watch him eat quietly without taking his eyes off me. The problem with betrayal is that you can forgive, but sadly, you never forget. The doubt lingers and taunts you until you're left to wonder what's true and what isn't.

That, my friend, is… trauma.

The bitch.

"Here." Sebastian's voice breaks through my torturous thoughts. He hands me a white envelope, which I immediately take. Curiosity gets the best of me.

"What is this?" I look at the envelope, and it's addressed to me.

"A very unique young man with an odd name and an atrocious sense of style left it for you at the front desk," Sebastian says cheekily. Frowning, I think to myself. Wizz? As if reading my mind, Sebastian continues. "I must admit I acted impulsively, which I am finding myself doing a lot lately." I almost laugh at his annoyed face. He looks like a child. "I introduced myself this afternoon when he was being escorted by his security, and we got to talking."

You and… Wizz got to talking? What about?" I sit back and wait for whatever he's going to say as I drink my third glass of wine of the night.

"You, of course, and your business with him. I must say your magazine could do better." The pompous bastard says with a smirk.

"Seba—"

He chuckles, "It was just an observation."

"One I don't care for. Now, what did you want with the guy?"

"Just wanted to get to know him better. Benjamin says his music is pretty good. I might give him a listen."

"Oh, please spare me, Sebastian." I try to hold back the laugh that threatens to slip from my lips.

The man is a nuisance, a completely obnoxious menace when he wants to be. Sighing, "The little fucker was around you, so of course, I was curious. That's it all."

"Uh-huh." Tyrant.

"What?" He asks, then takes another sip of his wine.

"You turned out to be quite the liar, Sebastian." His eyes flash with fury before he quickly conceals it. I hit a nerve. Good. At least I've not lost all control.

"I needed a way to get you to meet me, and that kid served as the perfect opportunity. I knew if I asked, you would refuse, so I used him, knowing you wouldn't refuse his invitation." He shrugs like it's no big deal. Of course, for him, lying and manipulating it's nothing big. "Open it." He points to the envelope in my hands.

Trading the envelope, I open the letter inside to find a written statement from Wizz with the tracklist of his upcoming album. What the hell? I was expecting to have him on the cover, and that would be more than enough for my newbie magazine, but this will put us above all others. No one has yet to obtain the tracklist or the name of his next album, and he chose to announce it through us.

This is major. This is just…

"I really am so fucking proud of you." Sebastian looks at me with pride and a wide smile. "What you have done and created on your own in such a short amount of time is incredible. You were meant for great things."

Gulping, I shrug. I still don't know how to handle compliments. I shrug them off like it's nothing, but deep down, it warms me.

It makes something in my chest ache.

Thank you.

No one believed in me before you.

Thank you for giving me the tools I needed to progress in life.

I wanted to say that, but I stopped myself.

Instead, I do what I always do.

I deflect.

"I don't care," I say childishly, like a petulant brat. Playing with the glass of wine, I look up at the sky. God, it's so peaceful here, and how ironic it is that there's a war inside of me.

One side tells me I should give the man in front of me hell for hurting my heart, and the other tells me that I won't ever fully be whole if I'm away from him.

"How is it that we always meet under the stars?" Sebastian's voice cuts through the agony inside of my head.

Still looking up at the sky, I ask. "What do you mean?"

"The night I lost my parents was the night you were born, and there was a full moon then. Same with the first time I saw you and the first time I made you mine."

The planetarium, he means.

The moon and some constellations were shown there while we spent the night together. Memories I buried so deep inside my brain hit me at full speed, and I am left with no choice but to allow it.

It's like I'm that girl again. The girl who thought the man in front of her was the moon, stars, and all that hid in the dark shining so bright.

He was everything to me. Dammit.

Staring into those blue-gray eyes of his I could get lost in forever, I try to calm my racing heart, but nothing works. Not counting to three or the breathing techniques I was taught in therapy. Nothing. "Why am I really here, Sebastian?" Setting the statement down on the table next to my plate, I blurt out.

"I don't want you to be anywhere else." He answers without breaking eye contact.

"Bullshit. Try again." I snap, unable to process the mess in my head. A part of me believes him, and the other is deadly afraid to fall for his games again. "What do you want from me?"

"I want your love." He answers.

I inhale and exhale slowly, feeling the sting of his words. "You had it, and it meant nothing to you. Try again."

"I want all of you. Your love. Your heart. Your time. Your good days and bad days. I want to be your passion. Your first choice. Your main reason for breathing." He says hoarsely while his eyes search for something in mine. "You were all of that, Sebastian." I let him see all the hurt his lies caused. I let him see the mess I am now. "You were all of that to me and more, but you threw me away like I meant nothing. Just like everyone I ever cared about has done."

Hurt flashes through his eyes. "I lied about a lot of things, yes. But never about loving you. Baby, never that. Please understand that all I wanted for you was better. I wanted you to—"

Hitting the table hard, I lean closer, feeling all the emotions coursing through my veins, clouding my judgment, or maybe it's the alcohol. Maybe both. "Don't you see it? All of this. The things you say. The things you do. It hurts." Hitting my chest, where my heart beats. "It hurts here." Then with the same hand, I touch the side of my head. My temple. "And here." I choke out. "Because you broke me. You broke me so terribly that I don't know what's true anymore. I struggle every day to trust not only myself but everyone else." I grit out. Hurt, so hurt. Before my tears fall, I storm off towards the seashore, barefoot and embarrassed.

Embarrassed about my outburst.

I don't know what to believe anymore.

The feel of the warm water touching my feet calms my heart, and the breeze helps me breathe easier. The beach has always had that effect on me. Feeling Sebastian at my back, the same way I feel the wind on my face, I let the tears fall when he whispers in a broken voice. One I've never heard before. One I wish to never have to hear again. "Fight me. Tear my heart out. Rip it out of my chest and watch it bleed down at your feet if that's what you wish, but don't run away from me. Fuck, baby, don't run away from me." His chest rises and falls rapidly, and I feel him at my back. "Don't turn your back on me, please."

Finding my voice, I reply. "Funny since you're the one who turned your back on me. You're the one that didn't fight."

"If I could go back, I would choose differently. I would have chosen love instead of acting out on the crippling fear that was consuming me. I could handle the world badmouthing me and speculating shit they know absolutely nothing about, but when I saw you get hurt because I wasn't quick enough, I felt like that young boy who had everything he ever loved ripped out his hands so cruelly. I was afraid."

"The Great Sebastian Kenton afraid?" I scoff painfully.

"Terrified, darling." He whispers. "Then I heard what you told Ellaiza that night, and you know, these are not excuses, believe me, but maybe you can understand why I did what I did, however stupid it was."

Turning, I face him. My heart racing when I see his solemn expression. What did I miss? "What are you talking about?" I search his eyes and watch him cringe.

"You wanted that for her, and fuck, I wanted the world for you." He breathes out and looks up at the sky while I look at him.

"I didn't want you to end up like my mother and then regret me later. I didn't want to watch you die in my arms as I did her. I was afraid. So fucking afraid to lose you, and in the end, I lost you just the same."

Grabbing his neck, I force him to look down at me while I rise on my tippy toes. "You were all I had," I whisper brokenly. "But what hurt me most was realizing I wasn't all you had. That I was so easily forgotten." Tears, stupid, frustrating tears, sting my eyes. "You weren't the only one scared. I was too, but I chose to put all my faith in you. I chose to believe we would be alright, but you didn't. You walked away and now look at us. We're broken. Never to be the same again." His blue eyes flash with determination.

"We can't turn back time. We won't ever be the same. This I know but we can be better." Our lips are a whisper apart. Our noses are so close they almost touch. "We can be better." He repeats.

We stand there, chest to chest, with only the moon, stars, and the serene sea, and I wonder if maybe this all needed to happen for me to finally be in a place where I no longer had to fear raising my voice and making my own choices. Maybe in his own misguided way, he gave me my wings back when I thought he ripped them off my back. Because yes, I've been dead for three years, but I also managed to conquer my fears, speak my mind, and make all my dreams come true. Still, I would've traded it all in a heartbeat for those three years with him. With Ellaiza. With Benjamin. With the life I once had with them. In a heartbeat.

Because nothing meant more to me than them.

Nothing.

And the fact that he heard my conversation with Ellaiza and thought that's what I wanted. That's all I cared about. It hurts me more than he will ever know.

"After what happened… after the things I said and did sink in, I knew I fucked up and tried to find you. I looked everywhere. Had my men searching everywhere, but you disappeared. I had to live without you for three years, darling. That was my penance. I was too late."

Christ, this is all too much.

This is messed up.

"I don't know what to say or what to think." Emotions clogged my throat, and I met Sebastian's searching gaze. "I'm lost."

"I'm not. Not anymore," he said quietly. "I'll do whatever it takes to make this right." He kisses my nose so sweetly that it makes a tear fall from my eyes. "Because you're my person, and I don't deserve you. Fuck, lord knows I don't, but I want you anyway." Sebastian looks gutted when I don't say anything, but determination burns in his eyes. He sighs and continues. "I know some say that you need to be whole to fully love someone, but that's utter bullshit to me. I am not whole unless you love me, Arianna Parisi. You complete me." He shrugged in exasperation. "You. Are. Everything."

"Sebastian—"

"Everything."

"Just stop." I try, but he doesn't.

"And I don't know when exactly it happened when you became a vital part of me," He's breathing hard like he's been running. "No, fuck, I know exactly when it happened. It was the night Ellaiza got a fever, and I was so scared. Fuck, I was out of my mind, and then I walked into the room expecting the worst, and the most beautiful sight greeted me. You looked so young, so pure on the floor, holding onto my daughter as if she meant the entire world to you. You stole a piece of a heart I only saved for my daughter that night."

His words are undoing me. Word by word. "Then there were many times when you would stand up to me and give me all that sass unafraid. Then your smile. The first time you ever laughed at something I said, I felt it in my stomach. You gave me butterflies, darling. Me. A Bastard like me who never had butterflies in my life. But you gave me that, and even now, with so much hurt and hate in your eyes, you still have that effect on me and that will never change. What I feel down in my soul for you will never change."

My tears spilled free before I could stop them.

Sebastian reached out to cup my face and brushed the salty drops with his thumbs. He bent to rest his forehead on mine. "One day, you'll believe me," he promised before pressing a gentle kiss to my forehead.

I don't know if it's the alcohol in my system or all that was said that is clouding my judgment, but the next thing I know, I am pulling Sebastian's face down and claiming his lips as mine.

All my sadness and frustration became a fire inside of me that I didn't know how to expel. Apparently, my body had decided exactly how it wanted to release all that pent-up anger and regrets. Part of me needed this. To feel anything but sorrow. Another part wanted to brand me on him, to ruin him as he ruined me.

So I kissed him. And he kissed me back.

Lips, tongue, hunger. Ferocious, biting kisses that stole our breaths. I pushed at his peacoat, shoving it down his arms without breaking our kiss, and then we fell to the sand. Hands pawed while lips and tongues searched for any naked spot they could find.

We lie there in the sand, trying to find our way back to who we once were. Naked, so very naked.

A pile of bleeding hearts wrapped up in heartache, pain, and regrets.

Chapter 21

IT'S A GIRL

Arianna

"I don't want to be the cage that keeps you

from being free." — B

I didn't use to be this way. No matter the circumstance no matter how difficult they were, I would have faced them head-on and never run away like a little coward but when it comes to Sebastian Kenton, lately, all I seem to do is run away. Run and agonize over every decision I have made since he's been back in my life, and to make matters worse, he hasn't contacted me since my last night in Greece. Since the day I so foolishly gave in and had sex with the man. On a beach! On a freaking beach with his men not far away.

Not only did I do the walk of shame in front of them, but I ran out of there with white sand between my ass cheeks.

Christ.

That is not who I am.

Not anymore.

After leaving Sebastian on the beach, I ran to my room, took a quick shower, and then found myself being driven to the airport. An hour later I was exiting the country and leaving Sebastian behind, but all throughout the flight all I could see were those eyes. His eyes.

Determined.

Bright.

Not cocky.

No vindictive. Not at all.

Just… alive.

A look that takes over when he's with his kid. How he used to look at me before.

But now I am back in the states and nothing.

Radio silence.

Not one call.

No messages.

Nothing.

Zero, zip, zilch.

That's not the worst thing. Not at all. The worst thing is that it bothers me. *Why hasn't he reached out?*

I am losing control, and I can't stand it.

It makes me weak, and being weak around Sebastian is the worst thing I can be. It's dangerous.

"You're fine," My brain tries to assure me.

"No, you are not." My heart argues.

See? My brain and heart can never be on the same page when it comes to that man.

Because of all this turmoil, I ran.

I panicked, okay?

I want to blame the night we spent together on the delicious Ouzo cocktails, but that would be a lie, and although I am acting like a coward. I am not a liar.

I got caught up in the moment.

You little liar… the disturbed little devil on my shoulder singsongs.
Shush, I snap back.

"Parisi." The barista calls out my name and hands me my coffee.

"Thank you." Walking towards the exit of the coffee shop, I notice a small crowd of paparazzi and journalists outside the small shop. I sigh and prepare myself for the chaos that will break the second I step a foot outside. Since I got back I've been harassed by the media wanting to know about me and wanting me to comment on my relationship with the president, which I refused, of course. As if I'll ever give my competition anything to use against him or me, for that matter. Besides, Sebastian is mine to mess with and mine alone. *You don't want anyone else hurting him… do you*? I ignore the little voice inside my head and move quickly through the flashing lights to get to my car with my head down. If they as much as get a hair out of place, I'll sue their asses. I can handle being followed and hounded with questions, but I won't tolerate anyone putting their hands on me.

Once I reach my matte-white Continental GT Bentley, I take off my black frame sunglasses, breathe in and hold it for three seconds before releasing the air. I do it three more times. It helps to drown out the noise outside. I can handle the press. It never bothered me, not even when I was young and knew nothing of this world. Yet, Sebastian didn't trust I could handle it. I must admit that what he told me makes sense. I have my own trauma, but I never had to witness the horrible murder of my parents at such a tender age. Parents that he loved more than anything. I also never realized that the great Sebastian Kenton.
The fearless and all-powerful man that I came to love more than life was terrified. Terrified of having what happened to his parents happen to me. When I think of what my family did to his, it makes me

nauseous, and all I see is red. Innocent people lost their lives. A boy lost everything. "Shit. Fuck you, Gabriele." Wherever the hell you are. I hope you are suffering. I hope you never find a peaceful moment until the day you die, and when that happens, I really do hope you burn in hell. Turning the engine on, I wait for the car to roar to life, and then I am hightailing out of there on my way to work. Like every day since I've arrived, I look through my Fairview mirror and spot a black car tailing me. It took me a while to catch up to the fact that I was being followed, not only here but in Greece as well. Now everywhere I go, men are hiding in plain sight and following me. His men. It would've been obvious if he had assigned Benjamin, so he did the opposite and assigned someone who isn't usually seen or pictured with him. That's why I missed them before, but after Greece and yesterday spotting the handsome man from Greece, Ares, if I'm remembering correctly, I pieced it together. A robotic voice sounds from my car's speakers, interrupting my train of thought. "Incoming email." My heart stops when I hear that. Like every time I get an incoming message, I wonder if is irom him.I usually wait until I get to my office to answer or read work emails, but this time I don't. With one hand on the wheel and the car steady, I tap the screen to have a look at the email address. I instantly feel disappointed when the email is not from him, but when I take a second look, my heart stops in my chest. From: stelinainthesky

Stelina.

I must be hallucinating this because how? How did she find me? Why now?

I shouldn't read it. I should not put my heart through more agony, but I'm a masochist when it comes to my sisters. My love for them is greater than my hate for my father, and I guess that's how I know he didn't win.

But then this could be a trick. How do I know it is truly her?

Tapping on the message, the voice in the car reads it aloud. *"Is it one day yet?"* One day.

Someday.

"Mila…" I breathe out her name in a broken whisper. Mila. My stelina. How I've hurt you… because after three years of torturing myself with her letters, I've come to realize how much I hurt my baby sister. She did nothing wrong, nothing, and for my survival and hers, I ultimately ended up hurting her. I am not perfect. I am who I am, and I never tend to make excuses for my actions, but hurting my sister is something that has haunted me for so long, and now having her reach out with something only she or our middle sister would know has me feeling hopeful.

Hope that maybe I wasn't so horrible after all.

Maybe my coldness and my actions haven't caused her to lose faith in me.

Stop loving me.

A tear falls, but I quickly wipe it away.

I am no longer that girl that was silenced and made to behave. I am no longer someone held back by powerful men.

No.

I stayed away because I felt like she was better without me. Without being reminded of so much pain, she, as always, my beautiful little star, so brave and compassionate, made the first move.

Now, I can either ignore her message and carry on with my life with half of me missing, or I can finally do what's right and make amends.

Amends and make myself whole again.

And I won't ever be whole without her.

Hitting the gas pedal, I race to the office with a new purpose.

It dawns on me how Sebastian did the same to keep me from him. Keep me safe from his world out of fear and because he wanted more for me. Ironic that's the same case with my baby sister. We do stupid things for the ones we love, and we also do very stupid things when we think they're better off. *You, stupid, stupid man. I love you...* I think to myself. There is no way he has nothing to do with this.

He loves to be all over my business, after all.

***

"Boss...I tried to stop them from entering, but..." Oliver, my assistant, cringes when I raise the hand that is holding the coffee up to silence him. I hate excuses. Either you do what you're told or stay silent. "I'll handle him. Hold my calls and cancel my morning meetings." I mumble, walking past him. Not caring for the whispers and the flash of the cameras in my space. Once I'm in front of my office's door, I turn and look around the room, seeing my employees talking amongst themselves instead of doing their jobs. Women giggling, men taking photos of Sebastian's secret service sneakily. Sighing, "The last time I heard, this was a place of work. Now I suggest you put your phones away and carry on working before you find yourselves standing in the unemployment line." I mumble, satisfied when they scatter to do as they say. I don't run this place from fear but respect. Nodding to Oliver, I let him know that he may leave, which he does a second later. Turning, I come face to face with a smiling Benjamin. Sighing, "Your boss is like a bad rash that never goes away." His gentle eyes crinkle at the corners every time I say something he finds amusing, just like his boss. Most people cringe or roll their eyes at me when I'm honest. Nowadays, people get offended way too easily, so is refreshing to find people who get me and are not so easily offended. That is why I always felt at home with them.

Never felt judged or made to feel horrible for the way I was wired.

They get me, and I get them.

Maybe that is why it felt like death when I lost them.

It was like losing the home I never had before Sebastian, Ella, and Benjamin. "You're glowing, kiddo." My friend says with a knowing grin. Oh, great. Of course. He knows he was there. I mentally cringe and narrow my eyes at him. "Shut it." I pass by him to find the other guard, the silent and moody Shaw standing by my office's door with his usual bored expression. Now that he's not wearing a long sleeve shirt, his full sleeve of tattoos is on full display. "Shaw."

"Ma'am." He nods before opening the door to my office. Asshole. He damn well knows that I am around his age. Giving him a warning glare, I step inside my office, and the moment the door clicks shut behind me, the loud sound of horns startles me. At the same time, a pop sounds, and pink confetti explodes everywhere. What…

"Mommy. Mommy!" Ellaiza screams, running to greet me where I am standing paralyzed at the door. Pink balloons float around my office with pink roses and teddy bears all over the place.

In the corner of my office, next to my table with the chess set, stands Sebastian, dressed impeccably in a light gray suit and a pink tie.

The same pink as Ella's dress.

"What is going on?" I ask, confused, looking down at Ella, hugging her closer to me as she holds on to my midriff and stares back at her father, who starts walking our way with a gentle smile on his stupidly handsome face. *"Tu es magnifique, mon amour."* His blue eyes roam my body, and suddenly, I am taken back to Greece. To the beach. Fashes of our entangled bodies on the sand and the echo of our hisses and moans hit me. Nope. A child is in the room.

Ignoring the heat creeping up my neck, a reaction to Sebastian's hot gaze, I ask instead. "I don't understand. What is going on here?" I never know what to expect from the man, and he takes me by surprise every time.

Every. Single. Time.

A high-pitched bark makes me turn and when I do, I spot a tiny ball of fur. A dog with a pink vest is peeing on my white rug. Holding back the thousands of cuss words that come to mind, I fake a smile and look at Sebastian with a look that says 'You opportunistic bastard. Stop using Ella to get back into my good graces.' He only chuckles and shrugs unapologetically. Ignoring the beautiful tyrant, I focus on Ella. "You got a dog!" I feign excitement for her because what else can I do? Hurting her with the truth is not an option. Not to me. Never.

Baby girl nods excitedly, causing her perfect curls to bounce in the cutest ways around her face. "His name is Cupcake!"

Frowning, I ask. "Cupcake?" I look at Sebastian, who is now standing a foot away from us. "The dog is a boy?"

A boy dog with a pink vest and a name like Cupcake. Poor ugly mutt.

"He is." Sebastian nods, looking down at the dog who has finished ruining my perfect and very expensive rug and is currently chewing on my Gucci shoes. With a fake smile on my face, I try to get him off me without letting it show how displeased I am with the new little member of the Kenton gang. "That's enough, Cupcake." Sebastian comes to the rescue and picks up the little nuisance. "Daddy got me Cupcake for being the best informen. Right, Dad?"

Informant, she means. Oh, you clever little darling.

"It's Daddy to you, Ellaiza." He narrows his eyes lovingly at Ella. "And yes. The best informant there is."

I am caught off guard and not for the first time today, by the two of them looking at me with identical grins and an evil glint in their eyes.

Oh, I know that smile.

That is the smile of two tyrants who conspired against me.

Knowing that going against them is futile, I ask instead. "Why the pink balloons if the mutt is a boy?"

Ella gasps. "That's rude, mom!" Her blue eyes grow big before she looks at me like an adult reprimanding their child. Her sass is a thing of beauty, really. "Not mutt. Cupcake." She corrects me.

"My apologies." I offer her a gentle smile. A genuine smile. "Cupcake." I don't like dogs. Hell, I dislike most animals, but there's something about dogs and cats that creeps me out. I don't say that to her, though. The small dog with a pink vest makes her happy, so I just suck it up and deal with it. "Issa okay, Mom and…" She looks up at me with a sheepish, dimpled smile. The same as her father's. My weakness. Shit. "The pink is a surprise, but first, we eat!" She takes my hand and guides me toward the small seating area inside my office, where a sweet picnic setup waits for us. "We're having a breakfast picnic, mom. Are you surprised? Do you like it? Are you happy?" She hits me with a million questions and I can't help but laugh at her cuteness and eagerness. Bending down, I grab her face, squishing her cheeks together, and drop a kiss on her nose. That makes her smile wide. God, I love her smile. I truly believe Ellaiza's smile can heal any wound. "Look, dad!" Ella jumps and down while staring at her father with a mischievous grin. "Mommy's laugh is back!"

"I see, *mon coeur,* and what a beautiful laugh it is, yes?" My stomach flips when I turn to look at Sebastian and find him already looking back at me with a tiny dog trying to bite his hand and a soft look on his face. A million tiny bugs flip their wigs inside my stomach, and I can't help it. I can't. Most days, Sebastian's charming side is hard to ignore but the two of them together? That's an impossible task. I am bound to lose that battle. "The most beautiful!" Ella nods, then plops herself down on the leather couch I have in my office on the far right and takes me down with her. "This is going to be the best date!" My girl smiles at her father while I look at him, as he puts the dog inside a tiny pink dog bed, then sits back on the couch lazily, looking carefree while confidence oozes off him in waves. His intense eyes find mine and hold me hostage. It was a betrayal, the way my heart calmed when he looked at me. How my breathing leveled out just at the sight of him. I wonder if he feels the same when he looks at me. Lately, I've been wondering so many things. For example… Does he love me the way he says he does? Or am I just a challenge? I know how much he loves challenges, but it all quickly vanishes from my mind when he looks at me as he is doing right now. Clearing my throat, I break eye contact and use Ellaiza as a shield. As an excuse to not deal with my chaotic feelings toward her father. "So, a date, huh?"

"Yes!! Dad says we take the people we love on dates!" Ella frowns, looking between us, and I just know that whatever will come out of her mouth next will be catastrophic to my heart and my self-preservation. "You're my dad. Right, dad?"

Sebastian smiles softly down at his daughter before nodding. "That's right." Ellaiza turns her little head towards me next. "And you're my mom, right, mommy?" The way she says mom disarms me. I do not know whether Sebastian has told her the truth about who her real mother is. All I know is that she's mine. She has always been mine, and that is my truth. So I smile and poke her nose. "That is correct," I whisper, making her smile.

I am caught off guard and not for the first time today, by the two of them looking at me with identical grins and an evil glint in their eyes.

Oh, I know that smile.

That is the smile of two tyrants who conspired against me.

Knowing that going against them is futile, I ask instead. "Why the pink balloons if the mutt is a boy?"

Ella gasps. "That's rude, mom!" Her blue eyes grow big before she looks at me like an adult reprimanding their child. Her sass is a thing of beauty, really. "Not mutt. Cupcake." She corrects me.

"My apologies." I offer her a gentle smile. A genuine smile. "Cupcake." I don't like dogs. Hell, I dislike most animals, but there's something about dogs and cats that creeps me out. I don't say that to her, though. The small dog with a pink vest makes her happy, so I just suck it up and deal with it. "Issa okay, Mom and…" She looks up at me with a sheepish, dimpled smile. The same as her father's. My weakness. Shit. "The pink is a surprise, but first, we eat!" She takes my hand and guides me toward the small seating area inside my office, where a sweet picnic setup waits for us. "We're having a breakfast picnic, mom. Are you surprised? Do you like it? Are you happy?" She hits me with a million questions and I can't help but laugh at her cuteness and eagerness. Bending down, I grab her face, squishing her cheeks together, and drop a kiss on her nose. That makes her smile wide. God, I love her smile. I truly believe Ellaiza's smile can heal any wound. "Look, dad!" Ella jumps and down while staring at her father with a mischievous grin. "Mommy's laugh is back!"

"I see, *mon coeur,* and what a beautiful laugh it is, yes?" My stomach flips when I turn to look at Sebastian and find him already looking back at me with a tiny dog trying to bite his hand and a soft look on his face. A million tiny bugs flip their wigs inside my stomach, and I can't help it. I can't. Most days, Sebastian's charming side is hard to ignore but the two of them together? That's an impossible task. I am bound to lose that battle."The most beautiful!" Ella nods, then plops herself down on the leather couch I have in my office on the far right and takes me down with her. "This is going to be the best date!" My girl smiles at her father while I look at him, as he puts the dog inside a tiny pink dog bed, then sits back on the couch lazily, looking carefree while confidence oozes off him in waves. His intense eyes find mine and hold me hostage. It was a betrayal, the way my heart calmed when he looked at me. How my breathing leveled out just at the sight of him. I wonder if he feels the same when he looks at me. Lately, I've been wondering so many things. For example… Does he love me the way he says he does? Or am I just a challenge? I know how much he loves challenges, but it all quickly vanishes from my mind when he looks at me as he is doing right now. Clearing my throat, I break eye contact and use Ellaiza as a shield. As an excuse to not deal with my chaotic feelings toward her father. "So, a date, huh?"

"Yes!! Dad says we take the people we love on dates!" Ella frowns, looking between us, and I just know that whatever will come out of her mouth next will be catastrophic to my heart and my self-preservation. "You're my dad. Right, dad?"

Sebastian smiles softly down at his daughter before nodding. "That's right." Ellaiza turns her little head towards me next. "And you're my mom, right, mommy?" The way she says mom disarms me. I do not know whether Sebastian has told her the truth about who her real mother is. All I know is that she's mine. She has always been mine, and that is my truth. So I smile and poke her nose. "That is correct," I whisper, making her smile.

"And this is a date!" She exclaims.

"Yes." Sebastian chuckles. "It's a date."

Where is she going with this?

Ellaiza then smirks at both of us. "Since you're both on a date, then you love each other," Ellaiza says, rendering me speechless, but not her father. No. Never him.

At the same time, I open my mouth to try to explain to her in a way she could understand, her father replies. "Yes, we're very much in love."

Snapping my head back at him, I narrow my eyes while he leans back on the sofa with a wicked grin on his face, takes a strawberry from the food container, and takes a bite out of it. *"You taste like strawberries..."* I remember how he used to say that every time he kissed me on the mouth and my...

No.

Get your head out of the gutter...

You are going to pay for this little stunt, Sebastian. I smile sweetly at him while he just chews and wags his eyebrows. The gigantic ass.

He then turns his attention to his daughter. "Ellaiza..."

"Yes?" Ella replies with her mouth full.

Sebastian leans forward and wipes Ella's face with a white tablecloth napkin. "Don't you have a gift for your mom?"

Your mom...

I've never had or will have a better title.

Not mafia princess nor boss but Mom. Ellaiza's mom.

"Oh, yes!" I watch in amusement as Ella hops off the sofa, runs towards one of the pink teddy bear arrangements of flowers, pulls a white envelope from it then hurries back to me. "This is forever, Mom." She whispers with so much love reflecting in her eyes that I'm overcome with emotions just at the sight of her sweet smile.

Taking the envelope, I smile at Ella, and from the corner of my eye, I watch her father looking at both of us with a smile of his own. Tearing the envelope, I take out the stack of papers inside and open them. Suddenly my past, present, and future collide. Everything seems to fade as time stills. At this moment, it feels like all I've been through and all that has happened has led me here. It's as if all I went through made me stronger. Stronger to love her. To love this family. As if this is where I was always supposed to be. Here with them.

With a little girl asking me to be her forever.

Adoption papers.

"Will you be my mommy forever?" Ella whispers almost self-consciously. With teary eyes, I look up from the papers and meet her loving eyes. I look at my world. My girl. My best friend. "Forever, my baby." I take her in my arms and squeeze the life out of her, peppering her face in kisses and soaking up the feel of her warmth as she giggles like a crazy person. "You have always been mine, Ellaiza Kenton. Always and forever." She pulls back and looks at me with those puppy eyes, so much like her father. "Always and forever." Ella smiles at me and then at her father. "You were right, daddy. Mom loved our present!" My girl kisses me on the cheek once more and then pulls back and goes to the ball of fur playing quietly on his dog bed. Overwhelmed with emotions, I lean back on the sofa and stare at Sebastian. I have no words. No words to explain what this means to me. I never dreamed something like this would be possible. For him to share his daughter with me. I release a deep breath that feels as if I've been holding it forever. For three long years. This changes everything. Every single thing because I won't ever have to fear losing Ellaiza ever again. She's mine. The moment I sign these papers, she will be legally mine too.

Staring at those intense blue-gray eyes, I search for answers because Sebastian's eyes always tell me the secrets his mouth won't.

We remain silent, just staring at one another, no longer on the opposite side of the world. How can we when a little love will always be between us? My darling girl. Ours. I have lost the war. *But have you really?* The little voice inside me whispers. I haven't.

Not really.

Yes, I have battle wounds, but, in the end, it all feels insignificant. So small.

Because look at all I've won.

My Ellaiza.

Clearing his throat, Sebastian looks me in the eyes. "You don't trust me, and I understand that words do very little. Words are just words, but actions speak louder. So this is me proving to you that I'm in it for the long game. I am giving you not only my daughter but my heart."

"I-I don't know what to say." That's a first. I'm lost for words.

"You don't have to say anything." He hands me his handkerchief, and taking it, I wipe my eyes. Not caring that I am crying like an idiot in front of him. Looking at Sebastian with tears in my eyes, I whisper, "Thank you."

He smiles widely with gentle eyes. Always gentle. Always so sweet. This damn tyrant is making it difficult for me to fight this feeling. "You are most welcome, my love." My love.

My heart has no business freaking out every time this man calls me his love and tells me that I am beautiful, but somehow the organ in my chest has started beating back to life little by little since Sebastian reentered my world. Yeah, I lost. I'm gone for this man. *Here we go again.*

While I contemplate all the ways my life has changed in the past week, Sebastian's deep voice breaks through my mind, bringing me back to the now. *"Mon Coeur?"*

"Oui papa?" Ella responds while munching on a piece of chocolate cake. We really should stop giving this girl so much sugar.

"Tu aimerais passer la nuit chez maman?" Sebastian asks his daughter in perfect French if she would like to spend the night with me. "Wouldn't that be fun?"

"Oui oui! J'aimerais bien, papa." I am amazed by how well Ellaiza speaks French. Her pronunciation might not be as perfect as her father's, but she's getting there, and she is only six years old. I always knew she was special. So perfect. Ella's big blue eyes search mine when she asks next. "Are you happy, mommy?"

I look at her and then at her father and take in their hopeful smiles, and I share with them one of my own.

A smile that doesn't hurt.

One that comes easy when I am with them.

All my reservations, fears, and past hangups with Sebastian slip away in this moment.

"I am the happiest I've been in a long time," I whisper to her, my voice breaking a little.

It's the honest-to-God truth.

How is it possible for a person to have so much power over me? Sebastian taught me how to love, how to hate, and somehow his daughter, blood of his blood, has taught me how to forgive.

Maybe I can find happiness again. "Oh, you disgusting little fu—" Sebastian rises from the sofa, catching himself before he cusses the mutt who is currently lifting his small leg, intending to ruin my white rug.

Benjamin's and I's discussion from a while back comes to mind.

"Will I ever laugh again?"

"You will."

"When?"

"When something is really funny."

And I do laugh again.

I throw my head back and laugh as I watch a small dog with a pink vest pee all over the president of the United States.

Perhaps Cupcake and I will get along just fine…

Chapter 22

WORLD NEWS

Arianna

"I could have been selfish and kept you from running wild and free." — B

Ella sits on my kitchen stool while decorating a dozen heart-shaped cookies. She wanted to hand them out to her security guards. Her loyal friends, as she calls them. The way they all treat my girl with so much tenderness and care makes my heart happy because it means they really do care and she's not just their boss's kid. My sisters and I didn't have that, but I'm so glad my Ella does.

Her head is bent low, and her small tongue is sticking out as she decorates the last cookie on her batch. Shaw's cookie.

It also doesn't escape me how she paid extra attention to his cookie.

Her innocent crush on him makes me nervous because her tiny heart is bound to break when she realizes he is not for her. He is too old for her and besides, he's not the man I dream of for my girl. She deserves a Disney prince not the moody and asshole villain.

He has heartbreak written all over.

When the time comes, I'll be here to help guide her through the disappointment of her first crush ending badly but for now, I'll just do the best I can to shield her from that day.

Leaning forward in the kitchen, I watch Shaw, as he stands guard near my penthouse window. All ten guards on Ella's detail are here tonight keeping her safe and guarding my place.

I see Sebastian doesn't play when it comes to her.

He has doubled her security since she was a baby, which I appreciate.

Looking at Shaw again, I notice how he hasn't sat down since he arrived two hours ago, even when I told him he was welcome to take a seat anywhere he wished to, but he refused.

I didn't press the issue.

I let him be.

Now he is standing in the corner babysitting Cupcake. Ella's dog is taking a nap on his very own cupcake-themed bed that I got this afternoon for him. I also got the mutt everything he needed for when he came to stay here with his owner, my girl.

Anything with a pulse besides my sisters bothered me and had no value to me. Until the needy pup with a pink sweater named Cupcake gave me one pitiful look and bark, and then I was done for.

He was black and warm.

Yeah, just like someone I know, he gave me one sweet look, and I was gone. Besides, who says no to a small mutt with a sparkly sweater on? Even if he looks extremely grumpy. His owner is a big bully who dresses him in pink is hilarious to me.

He at least barked and urinated all over Sebastian, which gave him all the bonus points in the world. That made me dislike the small creature a bit less until earlier in the evening when my Ellaiza insisted I hold the damn dog. Now, I have another living thing to care for.

Great…

"Wow, mommy. You reached all the stars!" Adding a few black sprinkles on my white frosted cookies specially made for Benjamin and some for Sebastian per my girl's request, I ask Ella. "What do you mean, baby?"

"Well, your office is so big, and daddy says you're the big boss." Her smile widens, and I can't help but smile at her enthusiastic mannerisms as she spreads her arms wide. "And look at this place, mommy. This is every fashionista's dream home." She sighs, reminding me so much of myself when I first entered Sebastian's home back then and saw the huge walk-in closet he had made just for me. I looked just like my little mini-me looks right now.

"You know, Ella…" I drop the kitchen knife and stop to stare at her while she looks up at me. "Stars are great and all, and so is all I've accomplished, but nothing means more to me in this world than you, okay?"

"Oh, I know." She grins, but then her smile drops, making my heart stop in my chest.

Grabbing her chin, I ask. "What's wrong?"

"Will you… will you go again?" She asks, looking so small that it makes me want to wrap her in my arms and never let go. So I do just that. I take her in my arms and give her small head a gentle kiss. "Never. I am here to stay, and that's a promise, Ella."

"Pinky promise?" she sticks her little finger up, and I quickly wrap my own around hers.

"Promise. Forever." I whisper.

"Forever." She repeats.

I pull back, releasing her with another quick kiss on the head. "Now, how about we give you a bath and then make some popcorn and watch the mermaid movie?" When she was a baby, she was obsessed with all things Frozen, and now Frozen is long forgotten, and she's into the older princesses. The mermaid movie is all she talks about lately. Ella nods enthusiastically, "This is the best mommy and daughter date ever! Dad is missing out." She says that, and suddenly, my mind goes to a very dark and dangerous place. A place inside my mind where a little green monster resides. One who vanished for a while alongside my love for Sebastian, but now it's back, and pissed at the thought of Sebastian with someone else. I hate that my mind went there the moment he suggested Ella stay with me tonight. I know he wanted us to spend more time together, and I feel like shit for instantly thinking the worst. Damn, tyrant, you mess with my head too much.

And that's why he needs more time to grovel because what example do I show my girl if I let heartbreak go unpunished? Let him grovel a bit first while I sort out all these confusing emotions.

Cleaning the kitchen and the mess we made quickly, I watch as Ella climbs down the stool with a heart-shaped cookie in hand and runs toward Shaw. With my heart in my throat, I watch, ready to rip his own heart out of his chest and give it to my girl if he so much as makes her feel anything less than extraordinary.

But then the giant tattooed man does something that makes my heart flip inside my chest. Something that makes me not want to maim him just yet. He drops to Ella's height and takes the heart-shaped cookie. The one she spent ten minutes on and smiles at her. In the time I've known him, he has never smiled at another living thing, not even his cousin, Benjamin. Only Ellaiza. Only a heartless bastard would be immune to her charms. Her father's charm, might I add. How did the man know that cookie was the one she deemed most special, I don't know, but it sure makes my girl smile from ear to ear. And for that, I am grateful to Shaw Banning.

***

"I love it so much!" Ella exclaims while looking at herself through my phone's camera. I laugh because she used to love taking photos of herself when she was a toddler, and I guess that much hasn't changed. After I ran her a bath and got her into her purple pajamas we came back down to the living room and sat on the couch, eating popcorn and watching her favorite animated movie. Well, she did the watching while I did her hair and answered some emails. Work emails and the one email I've been agonizing over for the past two days. Mila's. While sitting on this couch so blissfully happy that I could burst at any second, I emailed my sister back.

I didn't know what to say.

What else is there to say but I am sorry? Therefore, I replied with a yes.

A yes! To her email asking me if one day is here.

Because yes, one day is here, and I am so tired of living with regrets and pain.

I don't want to live that way anymore.

So I conquered my fears, pushed aside my regrets when it came to my baby sister, and messaged her back. Looking down at Ellaiza sitting on my lap, I smile as she keeps taking selfies of herself and both of us. "I am glad, baby."

"You're the best hair stylist, Mom."

Nonsense.

She gives me way too much credit, but I take it regardless.

I take everything my girl has to give and treasure it.

I brush her hair one last time and she's good to go.

I put her long curly hair into two space buns like I used to do when she was younger and let two strands fall around her face. "Thank you, baby."

Once the movie ends, Ella grabs the remote and exits the movie app, and searches through the cable channels like an expert. Lord, this child is like a grown woman stuck inside a tiny body. How she's so smart, I have no clue.

Yes, you do…

I ignore the small voice inside my brain who suddenly is Sebastian's biggest fan and cheerleader. Traitor, like my heart.

"Look, there's, daddy!" Ella jumps in my lap, excited to see her father on TV.

Huh…so he wasn't with another woman like the twisted, vicious little green monster tried to make me believe.

I'm losing it.

I truly am.

"He looks so handsome, doesn't he, Mommy?" Ella looks up at me with a mischievous grin that has me rolling my eyes playfully at her.

"He is…alright. I guess." I mumble and hear someone scoff in disbelief behind me.

Looking over my shoulder at Shaw, I narrow my eyes and watch as his eyes shine with amusement.

Rat…

Ella leaves my lap and goes to sit on the carpeted floor closer to the TV. There is no doubt in my mind that Ella is Sebastian's biggest fan, and he is hers. Their bond is truly beautiful.

A man who lost so much at such a tender age can love as deeply and fully as Sebastian loves his daughter. He loves her with all his heart, and I never doubted that not even when I thought the worst of him.

Grabbing my laptop from my coffee table, I open it and go through some emails I missed from Nessa.

Clicking on the most recent one, I divide my attention between the email and the man on TV with a crooked grin and a dangerous voice. Sebastian looks perfect as ever, dressed in a black three-piece suit and a lavender tie. Odd choice for him since I've never seen him wear anything but black, white, and gray. His black hair is brushed back, and his eyes look brighter.

More alive.

Christ, he's so beautiful. It hurts to even look at him.

His beauty should be a crime. It really should because look at all those women in the crowd losing their minds over him.

All needy. Wanting more of him, and it irks me. So I focus on Nessa's email instead.

Subject: Crime organization involvement in politics.

Boss,

I've attached some old articles I dug up from old newspapers of the murders of Ronan and Vivienne Kenton for you to look over. I think there's something here we can use. The late Ronan Kenton had to be in bed with the Detroit crime families for him to be gunned down the way he was, and now his son has the same ties with another known crime boss. We can expose his hypocrisy to the world, and there's proof. Let me know if I should proceed with writing the piece for next week's paper.

Best,

Nessa Adams

I read through the message and click on three of the articles she attached to the email while bile rises in my throat. Has my hatred for this man led me down this road? A road where I exposed his greatest pain to the world. When I open up the wound that his parents' murders left him.

Looking down at Ellaiza, I can't help but feel guilt choking me. These are innocent people who died at the hands of my own family. So much hatred, my God. It all started with my father, but looking at Ellaiza, who has gotten off the floor and is now walking towards me with a blinding smile on her face, I know the cycle ends with me. I can't do this. I can't hurt him. I can't, and maybe that's where he and I differ.

He hurt me to give me what he thought I needed to be fulfilled in this life, and I was willing to break this man all in the name of revenge.

Noted, I didn't know he had broken my heart to save me from what his mother went through. From ending up the same way she did. Giving up her dreams for an older man and losing her life years later.

Watching him through the TV, looking serious as he talks to the crowd, I make my choice.

I let go of the hate and choose love instead.

I choose them.

Typing a quick message to Nessa, I let her know she can trash the article because I won't be publishing it in my paper.

Not now and not ever.

"Oh, mommy! Listen!" Ella's sweet and excited voice breaks through the noise inside my head. "That lady with the microphone asked daddy about you!"

With half of my heart sitting next to me, I watch Sebastian. The President smiles widely and seals my fate forever. The beautiful, clever, and opportunistic tyrant.

"The love of my life." His voice booms around my apartment, echoing through the speakers.

"Ahhhh!" Ella jumps up and down as she watches her father while I sit there, not being able to look at anything else but him.

"Three years ago, I made the biggest mistake of my life when I hurt the woman of my dreams. Mind you, I thought I was doing what I thought was best for her, but I made a mistake, and I lost her. But life gave me another chance and she's back, and she's mine. She's my person."

Thud.

Thud.

Thud.

Fuck.

"What…" I whisper at no one, staring at him as he looks so heartbreakingly beautiful, professing his love for me to the entire world and claiming me as his for everyone to know in the process. There's no way I'll be able to escape this man now or the media storm his love confession will surely cause. "You crazy bastard…" I grin the same way he is grinning at the crowd.

So cocky and sure of himself.

So…him.

With that, he leaves the crowd going nuts after he exits the stage, and the live footage ends, surely making our situation world news.

Ella's loud sigh makes me look at her as she falls back on the sofa with a grin and little hearts in her blue eyes. "I can't wait for a charming villain to confess his love for me on TV, as daddy did."

Laughing, I tickle her belly enjoying the sweet sound of her giggles. "Villain?"

"Yes!" She breaths, holding onto her belly, stopping me from tickling her more. Her blue eyes meet mine, and a determined look that reminds me so much of her father takes over her expression. "Villains love the hardest, and they are misunderstood."

"Where did you get that from?"

"Daddy." She shrugs as if her father's word is the law. I guess to her, it is. "Your daddy is not a villain, baby. He is just a butthead sometimes." I grin when she giggles at my use of the word butt to describe her father. "Dad said he is the villain, and you are the hero who saved him, so I want that. I want to save a villain like you saved daddy."

Okay…. I am about to press her for more information when a rough voice interrupts me. "Time for bed, moonshine."

Ella lifts her body off the couch and turns to Shaw. I rise from the sofa and give him a look that has him narrowing his eyes back at me. I sometimes wish I could call the guy some of my favorite insults, but thoughts of Ella stop me every time. She won't like it if I give the moody asshole a piece of my mind, but that doesn't mean I don't call him every cuss word known to man at his back or under my breath.

"Five more minutes." Ella negotiates with a grin his way.

His eyes leave mine and look down at her, softening. "That's what you said an hour ago. No more minutes." He says, but since I love pissing idiots more, I tell my girl while looking at his reaction.

"Ten more minutes, and we go to sleep, yes?"

Ella sighs and jumps into my arms and gives me all the kisses while I look at a pissed-off Shaw and offer him a big triumphant smile with a silent and very satisfying…fuck you.

Chapter 23

ROYALTY

Bastian

"I can't afford love." — A

Three weeks later...

"She will be pissed, you know that, right?" Banning says from where he is standing next to the Oval Office's window. "Now more so after your corny ass confessed your eternal and undying love for her on national TV. She has been stalked by the press every day since. You have lost your mind, motherfucker." My head of security breaks the peaceful silence I've been enjoying for the past three hours while I've been going over a few documents Baron left for me this morning.

Now, Benjamin has joined me to test my patience and sour my mood because he is bored.

The overdramatic idiot.

Do I text, call, and message her hourly? Yes.

Do I show up at her place uninvited to tell her good morning and that I love her? Again, yes.

Do I send flowers, candy, and gifts to her place of work and home? Yes.

Since when did courting the woman you love become stalking?

And people say romance is dead.

Sighing, "Do you have anything useful to say to me, Banning? If not, there's the door." I mumble, ignoring his last comment. So I told the world who Arianna is to me. I did it and I don't regret it for a second. Let them know she is mine because make no mistake that is what she is. Mine as much as I am hers. Besides, they've been whispering and speculating about her for weeks, years even, now they know not to fuck with her. I partly did it for that purpose. Everyone needed to know she isn't just anybody, and she's not to be fuck with.

"Now, now, don't get your panties in a twist, boss." He laughs, then walks towards my desk but doesn't take a seat. Instead, he looks at me like a creepy fucker. I feel his stare until he speaks up. "Thank you." Looking up from some legal documents that have been sitting on my desk for far too long, I ask. "For?"

Banning looks me straight in the eye. "For making her smile again."

"You don't have to thank me for that." Leaning back on the leather seat, I say. "Because I don't plan on ever stopping."

"Good because if you do…" I grin, waiting for him to finish his threat. "She'll cut out your balls and keep them for herself."

Chuckling, I rise from my seat and button my suit jacket. "She already has them, Banning. That is nothing new." It is the truth, and what is the point in denying it? She not only has my heart, mind, and soul in her hands, but my damn balls too. And the proof is in the way she has consumed my every thought since the second I laid eyes on her. Now all I do, every decision I make, I have not only my daughter in mind but Arianna as well. "Is everything handled?" I ask, moving towards the door, itching to get to her. We haven't had a moment alone since our night in Greece on the beach. . Fuck, I can still hear her soft moans and feel her long nails scratching my back as I drove in and out of her. From the second I saw her naked body, I haven't stopped seeing it since.

I can't unsee her.

Whether it is her crazy perfect naked body under mine, her stunning face looking up at me with tears in her eyes, or her crooked smile when she tells me off.

All of it.

I can't unsee any of it. Not that I want to.

It's funny how you always remember where you were and what you were doing when something pivotal happens in your life. Every moment I spent with Arianna since the first night we met, I remember. I remember all of it, and that night we spent together when I made her mine after having lost her for so many nights and days…something changed. Pivotal. Monumental. You name it. Since that night, I've been chasing forever like a madman on a suicide mission.

And tonight…tonight, I am done taking it slow.

I have wasted enough time.

"Yes." Banning nods and moves to trail behind me as we leave the office, heading toward my next destination. Her. "Good." Stopping, I turn. "I need you to stay with Ellaiza tonight."

"Absolutely not."

"I am not asking you." I need him to stay behind with my daughter. Whenever I travel out of the State, I can sleep better knowing it's him with her when she wakes up and doesn't find me there. She knows I'll be traveling tonight and that I'll be there early in the morning before she wakes up, but if something happens, I feel better knowing my best man has her back. "It's a big event, boss." Banning tries again. "This is not how we do things, and you know it."

"It is how we're doing it tonight. I'll be fine." I shrug his concern off.
As long as I am with her, nothing can touch me, and if it does…it'll be worth it.
Every second spent with Arianna Parisi makes me feel like a struggling man winning the lottery. As if all is alright now that she's here.
Yeah, nothing can touch me when she's near.
Nothing has the power to hurt me.
Only ever her.

***

ARIANNA

Ping.

The third email of the day from Sebastian appears on the screen. It has been two weeks since he stood in front of a big crowd and on national TV and told them I was the woman he hurt and the one he loves with a crooked and very cocky grin on his face as if he couldn't care less that he put us both on blast more than he already had.

If I am being honest with myself, a part of me, the one that died when he looked me in the eyes and said the hurtful things he did when he broke my heart, came alive when he told the world I was the love of his life. And every day since, he has sent daily emails quoting famous men in love through the decades. Today's quote is from Rosemonde Gerard.

"Each day I love you more, today more than yesterday and less than tomorrow." A bit corny, but still…it moved me. Everything he says touches my heart deeply. From quotes to messages asking me how I am and telling me he loves me.

Flowers. Chocolate.

My morning coffee. He is relentless and very dedicated.

I will give him that.

"You look like a million bucks, mommy!" Ellaiza gasps in shock the second I flip the phone camera so she can see me fully clothed. We've been FaceTiming for two hours straight as the team I hired to help me get ready for tonight do their magic on me. "Thank you, my baby." I smile at her and laugh when she places the phone on her vanity table and starts to imitate all that is being done to me.

The hair.

The makeup.

Nails.

All of it.

If I am being honest there are a thousand and one other things I would rather be doing than getting ready to attend one of the shallowest galas to ever exist. Okay, I don't want to be ungrateful because only the crème of the crème of Hollywood and social elites get an invitation to this specific gala, and the fact that someone like me got one blows my mind.

I am also well aware that it is mostly because my face has been plastered all over the news and social media since the most powerful man in the country put me on blast when he told the world he loved me. It still feels surreal to me. All of it.

The adoption papers.

The love confession on national TV.

Sebastian and I becoming a trending topic.

It all feels like a dream. One I'm too afraid to wake up from.

So yeah, the organization in charge of the gala knew what they were doing when they extended an invitation after Timeless Magazine named me one of four successful women CEOs this year. I don't care much for titles or kissing ass at social events, but I did decide to attend when Quinne reminded me that the exposure will help the company grow even more than it has in the past month. And if I have to endure an evening with shallow and self-centered celebrities, I will. It's nothing new to me. Besides all of this… the prepping, the glam session, and the gala take me back to my first and last event of this magnitude. The one I attended with Sebastian. Now sitting here, three years later, I realize how much things have changed. How I've changed, yet a lot feels the same, as if no time has passed at all.

"Ella." I cringe when the hairstylist burns my scalp while straightening my hair. For tonight, instead of waves or curls, I chose to have my long blonde hair straightened to perfection and added hair extensions for more volume and length. My hair falls down my ass, making me look almost like Rapunzel with how long it is.

"Yes?" My mini fashionista applies glitter gloss and pops her lips three times like I did when the makeup artist was applying my nude lipstick. Laughing softly, I ask. "Are you feeling this dress?" Grabbing the phone from the vanity, I point it toward the gown hanging on the metal rack for her to see. Since it was a last-minute invite, I didn't have much time to shop for the perfect gown for this occasion. This gala is all about fashion more than the art they showcase. Now, seeing the dress, I am not so sure about it. Ugh. This is why I dislike dealing with these types of events and also why I find last-minute invites incredibly rude. Give people the courtesy to find the right outfit in advance and not two days before the event. "I would love it if it were pink, mommy, but you will be the most beautiful princess there. Do not fret!" Oh, the way this girl expresses herself… hilarious and oh-so-sweet. Melting, I offer her a soft smile. "You always know what to say, kid."

"I know. I'm the bestest."

"You sure are."

She giggles while I grin at my little sweet and sour girl. One moment she can be extremely sassy and hilariously rude, and other times she's the sweetest kid.

Knock, knock.

Looking away from my phone, I look at Oliver, my assistant at the door holding a big black box. "This was delivered and it's addressed to you, boss." He's been a God-send, helping me maneuver all these people here tonight.

"Oh, mom, you gots a present!" Ella screeches. "Let me see! Open it."

Laughing, I stand from the chair and place the phone back down on the vanity so I can open the box so Ellaiza could see.

Taking the box from Oliver, I stop to see that it is a matte black packaging from House of Arnault. One of the most expensive high fashion brands in the world. I know my fashion, just like I know journalism. House Arnault was created in France and is now a household name. A billion-dollar brand that belongs to Dionysius Arnault. The grandson of the initial designer.

I also know that House of Arnault is currently— Andrea Nicolasi's brand—only rival.

A whistle sounds from behind me, making me turn to look over my shoulder. I watch Vanni, the makeup artist, look down at the box in awe. "That brand is expensive as fuck. I need to sell a liver to afford as much as a belt from that line, and even then, I think I'll be short."

Snorting, I turn back to the box.

"Open it, Mom! I'm waiting." Ella says impatiently.

Loosening the black bow, I find a note.

You are made of solid gold, Arianna. It is only fitting that tonight you're dripping in it. I love you to the sun and back. A million times. - S

Thud.

Thud.

Damn. tyrant, why do you have to be so sweet?

"Who is it from!?" Ella asks.

"Your father."

"Daddy has it bad, mommy. He has mad, mad love for you. Now, open it!"

"Yes, ma'am." I roll my eyes playfully and open the box, and when I do, I am taken aback when I see the most stunning fabric. Taking the gown out of the box, I smile from ear to ear because this dress is ridiculously stunning.

Perfection.

Gold.

"Oh, wow," Vanni says while everyone else in the room stares at the dress.

"Mom."

"Yes?" I turn with the dress in my hands and look at her.

"Thinking about it now. I'm not feeling the other dress."

"Oh, aren't you now?"

Ella smiles sheepishly. "Nope. The gold one is more you."

"How so?"

"Oh, silly!" She rolls her eyes at me like she's grown. "Because gold is the color of queens."

Oh, my...

Yup.

This girl.

This girl owns me, and so does her tyrant father.

I've come to accept my fate.

"Oh, there was something else." Oliver interrupts, making me turn his way. I look at him expectantly, then he grabs a golden rose out of his suit jacket and hands it to me with a small blue box with a note.

Tonight is yours, and so is my heart. Here's a token to remind you what you mean to me, and here's to many more memories to add. - S

Opening the smaller blue box, I know just by the color that the item is Tiffany Co. I'm left speechless again. Sebastian has given me countless material things throughout the time we've known each other, and although I am grateful for them, I don't care for expensive things. Not like most women do, but when it comes to him… Sebastian's gifts always have a meaning. A sentimental value, and that is what I treasured most.

The beautiful gold charm bracelet to someone else might be just that. Jewelry. To me, though, it is everything.

Our story is being told in the bracelet in tiny gold charms.

Running my thumb over the bracelet and each charm, I find myself speechless. The only one who gets that reaction from me is Sebastian.

My heart skips a beat when I take in the Eiffel Tower charm for our trip to France. Our first trip together. Then there's a charm of a little girl for Ellaiza. A snowflake for what I assume is how we met in winter, or perhaps it's because he came to love my cold exterior. A queen chess piece and a rose. I laugh when I see the pizza charm and then so many more charms that remind me of us. A story about us.

And just like that…the last of the ice that protected my damaged heart from this man break for the second time allowing love to pour out.

Putting the bracelet on, I turn and face the group of stylists. They all watch in curiosity and some even in envy. "Uh, I assume you won't be wearing the original gown…" Karol, the stylist who helped me choose the accessories to match the dress, speaks up.

Smiling, I nod. "Change of plans."

"Yay, mommy. You will look so beautiful! I can't wait to show all my friends at school the pictures! Make sure to take lots okay? Take lots of pictures and send them to me!" She points her little finger at me through the camera, making me chuckle. "Will do, my baby." Walking back to my seat, I take my phone and give Ella all my attention.

"Oh, mom! I forgot to ask you for something!" Ella presses her face to the phone with an evil glint in her eyes. Oh, no. Here we go. What will she ask now?

"What do you need?" I ask as I take a bottle of water from the counter where all the makeup was placed and take a big sip.

"I want a baby sister!" The moment her request slips from her mouth, I choke on the water. Breathing through my nose, I let Oliver know I am alright and turned back to Ellaiza, who is looking at me with all the seriousness in the world. What to do? What to say? How to put into words that I don't care for more children and that she's more than enough for me? I should tell her that. I should be the grown-up here and be honest with her, but instead, I choose the easy route. Her father's route.

I negotiate. "How about instead of a sister, I get you another dog?"

She immediately shakes her head no.

Huffing, I ask. "How about I let you eat cupcakes for breakfast, lunch, and dinner?" And the award for greatest mom goes to me...

For a second, Ella contemplates it. Yes, cupcakes! Cupcakes always do the trick. "No." I guess not this time.

"Baby..."

"Yes?" Ella looks at me with so much hope in her eyes that it has me flustered and lost for words.

Sighing, I give in because I don't know how to say no to this kid.

"Okay, you can get a sister, but… in the very and I mean very distant future," I tell her. There. I didn't specify that the sister had to come from me. Let Sebastian deal with that, but then the thought of him having a child with someone else makes me murderous. It has me seeing red. Shit.

Ella…playing me just like her father. How is it that I ended up with rotten people…

Cause you're rotten to the core… the annoying voice inside of my head taunts. I don't argue because, deep down, I know it's the truth. I found my people. Just the same as me.

Taking a deep breath, I look at Ella on the screen of my phone, smiling so big. How could I not give her the world if she asked for it? "Je t'aime, mam." My sweet, little devil whispers with a crooked smile.

I should be annoyed that she got me to agree to a kid, but instead, I feel love.

So much love that nothing else matters. Not really.

"*Je t'aime*, Ellaiza." I reply. "I need to hang up so I can finish getting dressed. I'll send you lots of pictures before I leave, alright?"

Ella nods, looking adorably cute dressed in a blue gown with her curls brushed to one side and lip gloss on her lips. Even at six, my baby is a stunner. Poor Sebastian. He has a hard road ahead with Ellaiza and the attention she will attract when she gets older. *Good. Karma.*

"Okay, mommy. Sending you all the kisses and all the luck tonight!" She blows me a kiss, and I make a show of catching the kiss and touching my cheek with it.

"Forever, Ellaiza." I smile.

"Forever, mommy." She smiles back. After saying goodnight and promising to take her on weekly mommy and daughter dates, we hang up, and

I finish getting ready. Once the team finishes their work on me, I stand and put the gown on. Turning to look at myself in the mirror, I admire their work. My hair falls like golden silk down my back, and my makeup is perfectly done with a bold look, which is a black cat eye that highlights my green eyes, giving me a mysterious look, or so the makeup artist says. I, on the other hand, think I look like an evil fairytale villain, and that's fine with me. Looking down at the charm bracelet on my wrist, I smile, feeling like a million bucks dripping in gold and all because of a very tyrant man.

Chapter 29

GOLDEN GODDESS

Arianna

"We don't think we're better than everyone else. We know we are." — B

The Met Gala, otherwise known as the First Monday in May, is held at the Metropolitan Museum of Art in New York, where the guests will descend upon a red carpet in celebration of the museum's new exhibition, Timeless Art: An Anthology of Fashion, which will serve as an exploration of fashion through all five periods of history. The display will be presented across 13 of the American period rooms in the museum, and feature design works from Milli Lars, The Jonas Sisters, Alya Kypa, and one anonymous artist called V.M. The artist is crazy talented, and his art is being sold for millions. No wonder he was invited to showcase his art in one of the most famous galas in the world. This night is not only to raise funds for the museum but also to display fashion of the early 19th century through a modern lens. If you, by some luck, get an invite to the Met, you have to make sure to bring your fashion A-game. After all, the gala has a long history of creating memorable outfits that are seen around the globe.

This is surreal.

Little me would have never thought she would get this far. Not in this lifetime at least. But here I am.

On one of fashion's biggest nights.

You go, bitch. Show them how it's done. The little devil on my shoulder whispers, oddly giving me a confidence boost, which I needed when the anxiety started to creep in.

Taking a deep breath, I stand tall at the top of the stairs, ready to walk down when suddenly all fashion chaos begins. First, I see the flashes, and hear the noisy crowd of paparazzi on the right, trying to capture the perfect picture. They are relentless. Perhaps there is someone famous behind me, but when I turn, there is no one there. It is just... me. They're talking and taking pictures of me as if I were one of the A-listers.

When a man dressed in all black nears me, I tense but then remind myself that there's a lot of security here tonight, and although the gala is highly publicized, the media inside the event is regulated. Hell, they even forbade everyone in attendance from posting on social media for security purposes.

I pose, trying to show every angle of this masterpiece of a dress. I noticed some celebrities took the theme and ran with it. While some look ridiculous but if they feel good, then more power to them. I, for one, feel just like my baby, Ella, described me.

A billion bucks.

The gold dress fits me like a second skin showing my curves and a bit of cleavage, making me look exotic but not trashy. And when the flashes of the cameras hit my dress, it makes it look like liquid gold.

You're solid gold... Sebastian's words from so long ago play through my mind as I stand there for the country to judge me based on what I am wearing. Nothing matters, though.

I could care less if tomorrow I wake up to have made the worst dressed list because that man-the man I should despise but clearly can't, made me feel like the most beautiful queen in the world, and he is not even here. Sebastian makes me feel like royalty, and to a woman like me, that for so long felt like she didn't measure up, it means the world.

I stand for ten minutes posing for the cameras when I see her.

When I see a ghost from my past. Well, technically, she's been very present lately since her face is plastered all over this country, almost as much as Sebastians'. The heir to the Valentina Co. empire.

Turning, I remain stoic as I watch Andrea Nicolasi standing tall and elegant. Looking like a picture-perfect, life-size barbie dressed in a see-through red gown and her hair pulled back in a high ponytail, looking stunning as always and secure in her skin. Looking at her, I notice how everyone gravitates toward her like the sun.

But who wouldn't?

Her smile is warm, and her posture is graceful and inviting. A total contrast to myself. It's funny how we kind of look alike-apart from me being a few feet taller-yet on the inside we couldn't be more different. Whereas my eyes are the color of emeralds, hers are the same golden shade as my dress. Her eyes twinkle with happiness, and her smile is genuine while I am the queen of the RBF. Resting bitch face. I should turn my back and head to the spot set up for interviews as they told me to do once I finished the carpet, but instead, I stand looking at a person I did wrong. A person who reminds me of all the ugly parts of me. At this instant, I wish I were like most women.

Kindhearted women would approach and make amends with Andrea, but I'm not that type of woman. I don't hold grudges, but I just don't care to pretend to be someone I am not.

Feeling eyes on her, she turns her head and the smile falls from her face, for a second before she recuperates and puts her A-game face on. Cameras flash all around us while celebrities waltz past us getting their pictures taken hoping to make the best-dressed list tomorrow.

Andrea's eyes grow big when she spots me standing on the other side of the carpet, then she hides her shock with a smile but is not friendly, just cordial. I, on the other hand, just nod, acknowledging her.

There's a silent understanding between us.

We will never be friends, but at least from what I saw in her eyes...we are not enemies either.

I turn my back to her, but not before, I catch a glimpse of her confused expression. What? She thought I was going to walk over there and throw my arms around her as if we were good friends. As if I wasn't the bitch who told a gossip site her mother's cause of death?

I am not a hypocrite.

I am a lot of things, yes. Cold? Yes. Bitchy? That, too. But a hypocrite? Nope.

Slowly making my way towards the sidelines, where fashion correspondents are holding the interviews, I plaster a friendly smile on my face and hope to all that is holy that it doesn't translate as being fake. That's the last thing I need. So, instead of pretending, I think of someone who makes me smile with pure joy. Ella. I think about how she's probably back at the White House watching me on her tablet with Benjamin and Shaw. That does the trick because the next thing I know, the interview is going excellent. The correspondent, Suzanne, from Vogue, starts with questions about me and me only, which I appreciate. She asked me who I was wearing, and I told her House of Arnault, and she went crazy when I did. I guess she's a fan of the Frenchman and his brand.

I bet she's mostly a fan of the man more so than the brand. Can't really blame her, though.

She then moves to ask me how it feels to be featured on Business Magazine's most successful women of this year, and I tell her how it still hasn't sunk in. Honestly, I am trying to be humble, but it's utter bullshit. Yes, it is a dream come true for me. All of it, but I'm damn proud of myself and all I have accomplished on my own and all I have done with the help of my partner, Quinne, and my tyrant, Sebastian. I don't tell her that because most people dislike overconfident women and try to make them look conceited and frivolous. Because that's the world we live in now. They expect us to celebrate our wins in silence, and if we dare share our accomplishments, some might take it as bragging.

The girl carries on asking me more questions about how someone as young as me started a newspaper and magazine company in such a small amount of time. She asks in disbelief, not in a bitchy and envious way, which I appreciate because then I don't have to be rude or cold towards this girl that could very well trash-talk me on the magazine she works for. Before, I did not care if what came out of my mouth offended anyone, but with the company, I know it's not wise or a good business move, at least not yet.

"You are not only successful and brilliant, but you're so stunning, girl!" I cringe at her overly friendly tone but quickly mask it with a blinding smile. "But apart from all that, you seem to be all over social media lately with your involvement with president Kenton. Have you seen what the media is calling you?" I don't want to talk about Sebastian with this girl. With anyone, really, but how do I get out of this without letting my usual bitchy attitude loose, which typically gets me out of plenty of uncomfortable or unnecessary situations.

Leaning forward and with a smile on my face, I reply the best I can. "The president and I have a long history together, but tonight is not about him." I keep a fake smile. "If you don't mind, I don't–"

"Come on, Ari. Can I call you Ari?" She laughs, still with her overly nice act. Shit, I feel the bitch inside of me coming to the surface, wanting to tell this girl that, yes, I do mind her calling me that. How horrid. I had a feeling the interview would go south soon enough. They always want more than what you're willing to give. It comes with the territory and this business, I understand it too well, but I am not giving anything away. Not about him or our complicated history and relationship. Clenching my jaw, the smile on my face is starting to hurt. I need to cut this interview short before I say something I won't regret. "Sure." All this hassle is in the name of business. No wonder business moguls sell their souls to the devil. The devil seems like someone I would enjoy more than this girl with these questions at the moment.

"They're calling you the heart of the president." She giggles. She honest-to-God giggles like a small child, leaving me stunned. I've read the papers. I know what they're saying about me and us. How we're the western royals. "It's like a fairytale romance. Like the Royals, but here in the States!" She exclaims happily.

There we go...

And now it's time to cut this interview short.

Keeping my smile, I do my best to evade the question. "Yeah, his supporters seem to really care for president Kenton and his personal life. It's kind of...sweet." Yuck, the words burn my mouth like acid. It's not sweet to me, but I understand people feeling as if they know him for how open he is about most things. I can't fault this girl for doing her job either. It would be hypocritical of me to do so.

Making a show of looking at the other reporters down the line, I tell her. "Thank you for your questions. You're doing a fabulous job tonight." I throw that last part in because, although I am not as friendly or friendly at all, like her, I value hard work and I know her job is hard work, even if people don't believe so. It's not easy to interview and ask hard questions, even when you feel like the scum of the earth asking them or when people are rude as hell to you for doing your job.

The girl looks stunned, and then nods, thanking me.

Smiling one last time, I walk back to the red carpet, ready to continue with the rest of the night.

No more interviews.

I tried. I really did but I am no longer in the mood to endure them.

All of a sudden, I am taken aback by the loud murmurs, all around me and the sudden erratic behavior of the photographers. One of those famous billionaires or reality TV stars must've caught their attention. Okay...and that's my cue to leave. Looking around for the ushers, I notice more men dressed in black than they were before. There is one I recognize anywhere now.

Ares.

Of course, Sebastian would send his security.

I wonder if he was invited.

He didn't say anything to me the last time we spoke, and it is unlike him to not show up like the devil wherever I am.

He has a bad habit of doing that...

Oh, please, you foolish brat. Your heart stops every time he surprises you and catches you off guard.

Who wouldn't when they're being stalked by the devil?

You are delusional...

Shush.

Yeah, I am losing my mind if I am standing on a red carpet dressed head to toe in House of Arnault, ready to be ushered out of the interview section and talking to myself. But then I know for sure I am losing it because a shock of electricity runs through my body, making me feel as if something monumental is about to happen.

What is going on?

Turning away from the direction I should be heading in, I watch as the crowd at the top of the carpeted stairs parts, and a second later there he is. The most beautiful man there ever was and most likely will ever exist. Dressed in all-black Dior.

The President of The United States is attending this Gala for the first time. My handsome devil stands tall and overlay confident in a black suit while his eyes are trained on me and nobody else with a perfect crooked grin on his face.

Thud.

Thud.

There goes my traitorous heart.

I stand there frozen as he makes his way through the crowd, while his men surround him, but still give him room to walk. Is it possible for one man to steal the air out of this place? Logic will tell you no, but then again I tend to lose all logic when he looks at me the way he is doing tonight.

The small crowd around us buzzes with excitement, and the flashes of the camera go crazy.

"Well, look at you." Sebastian's husky voice makes the hairs on the back of my neck rise. *"La plus belle reine du monde."*

Snap.

Snap.

Snap.

Flashes all around us.

But all I can see is him. All I can feel is him.

Only him.

As we stand facing each other, it feels as it has always felt when it is just the two of us. As if the world fades, and all noise quiets.

Looking up at him as he looks down at me, I offer him a smile. Not the smile I gave the fashion correspondent minutes ago, no. But a smile that tells him I find comfort in his presence now that he's here. Of course, he wouldn't stay away. One thing that's certain is that Sebastian Kenton is as obsessed with me as I am with him, and sadly, time didn't change that fact. It only heightened the feeling. "You're stalking me now, Kenton?" Chuckling, his eyes never leave mine. God, tonight they look more gray than blue. Do you know that deep gray on a cloudy day when night nears? That color. Unique. Comforting. Beautiful. Him. "I am." He shrugs unapologetically with that precious grin of his that makes him look like a hungry wolf. "Besides, you're my woman, and I'll always be where you are." He smiles smugly at me when I roll my eyes. "Vous êtes fou." His smile widens from ear to ear making him look so beautiful it freaking hurts to look at him. "Je suis fou de toi." He rasps.

Crazy for you.

Back at ya, tyrant.

There's no point in denying it. I am sick. This has to be a sickness because not one thing about this love is logical.

Not one thing. "I still hate you, you know." I rasp when he comes closer. Sebastian's smile doesn't falter as he bends lower to where our noses touch. "You can't fool me, my beautiful little liar."

He whispers, and his hot breath, a mix of mint, cigar, and cologne, brings back so many memories. Old and new. "That heart currently pounding as strong as a winter storm is still mine, and we both know it."

"Shut up," I growl playfully, not wanting to admit defeat, and admitting I still love him is like conceding the war. Foolishly, I convinced myself that's the issue here, but deep down, I know that I am afraid to speak my feelings aloud because, once I say it, it all becomes too real.

Looking into his eyes, my breath hitches when I feel his arm come around me, pulling me closer to his body until I don't know where he starts and I begin. We're perfectly intertwined, just like our hearts used to be once upon a time. Just like they still are…

His eyes are intense, his voice raw. "I told myself at first that if I gave you the time and space, you would come to terms with what is so clearly right in front of you." He leaned closer until his forehead was on mine. "But then, as expected, you're so fucking stubborn. I understand why. Trust me, my darling. I do. But then last night I realized that I've wasted enough time as it is. I love you. You're my heart. My soul. My all. I'm so fucking in love with you, Arianna, that it physically hurts to be apart from you. All those years, it hurt, but I bore that pain because your dreams mean everything to me, but now you're here and it still hurts." He sighs, kissing my forehead. "Put me out of my misery, will you, darling?" I feel tears well in my eyes, but I hold them back because there's not a chance in hell I'll cry in front of the world a second time and especially when I have seventy-five dollars worth of mascara on. Blinking the tears away, I say the only thing that comes to mind while looking up at him with a devious grin. "How about you suffer a bit more, yes? I'm not quite done with you." I lean back, and my smile widens when he playfully narrows eyes at me with a promise of bad, bad things.

Bring it on, tyrant.

My enemy. My rival.

My equal.

Mine.

That's all that comes to mind as he holds me in his arms. "Fuck, you're so perfect. How I got so lucky, I do not know, but fuck if I'm not thankful." He growls. He seriously growls like a starving wild animal.

Then the neanderthal does what he does best.

He gives the world a show.

One second, I am looking into his intense blue-gray eyes, and the next, he grabs me by the neck and brings his mouth down on mine. Kissing me as if we've been apart for a long time. As if he could suck the life out of me with just one kiss.

Deep.

Intense.

Soul shattering.

Kismet.

Us.

Chapter 25
I WILL DIE FOR YOU

Bastian

"She put stars in his eyes." — Ben

Even after so many years since I was a young boy accompanying his parents to shallow social events it still feels the same. The air was filled with arrogance, stupidity, and people without substance. Mind you not everyone's the same. I don't get off on generalizing humans but most celebrities I have met tonight have yet to convince me otherwise.

Mom and Dad made the evenings of socializing bearable back then until I lost them. Then it was just me and the woman who was hanging on my arm that day going to these types of gatherings as a means to an end. But now things have changed. The only silver lightning is the golden goddess in my arms. Arianna.

Looking down at her, I am left speechless. Just like every time I look at her. Even when she looks annoyed, she is the most stunning woman in this room. My God what a beautiful creature she is. Every day she looks more perfect than the day before if that is even possible. She looks breathtaking wearing the gold Arnault dress I chose for her. There were a few gowns that caught my eye when I was searching for the perfect fit for her and when I saw the gold dress, I knew it was the one for her. It had her name written all over it.

As if it were made for her.

Gold, glamorous and sensual.

Her.

My otherworldly beauty.

Then there are her eyes. I never thought women's eyes were sexy until this woman. Arianna's eyes tell the stories her lips won't.

Even when she was an eighteen-year-old, standing on Malibu's beach, with her head held high as her entire life changed, her eyes told me more than her bratty mouth did, and even now, it tells me all I need to know.Because even when insults slip from her perfect mouth, her sweet emerald eyes– eyes that shine more than the lights all around us– tell me a different story. She loves me, but she's terrified, and it breaks my heart that I did that, but as long as there's breath on my body, I will not stop showing her just how much she truly means to me. My entire world, right along with our daughter, because this woman embraced my girl and loved her as her own. She loved Ellaiza so much that she didn't have to be told twice before she signed the adoption papers.

Now, you might think I was being selfless when I decided to share custody of my daughter and in part I was. We both know Ellaiza is mine, just as much as she is Arianna's, but the selfish bastard in me also knows that Arianna adopting my child ties her to us for a long time. And even if Arianna hadn't forgiven me, at least with Ellaiza in between, I could keep her in my life forever. It was a shitty thing to do but sometimes shitty things must be done in the name of love or war. In this case… both. Like tonight with me showing up at the gala.

I could not for the life of me miss this pivotal night of hers.

Some moments stay with you forever until you're in your grave, and even then, you take them with you. I share many moments like that with her. Tonight is one of them.

The second I got word that Arianna was invited to the gala, I knew I would do whatever needed to be done to be there for her. Including getting on a plane and following her here.

Because looking at her now, glowing radiantly I am certain I made the right move.

And even when I know she must have felt out of her element, at some point on the red carpet, she never let it never show. Arianna was the most beautiful woman in a sea of A-list celebrities.

There is no competition.

None.

And this is not me saying it because I am irrevocably and hopelessly in love with her but because it is the truth. No woman has ever or will ever compare.

"You know… this isn't as fun as the photos on social media make it seem every year." She looks up at me with a grin on her face and no longer sad eyes. *That's it, darling. Smile at me. Laugh with me. All with me.* "I much rather be watching a mermaid movie or baking cupcakes with Ellaiza and the mutt."

"I was told that you and said mutt developed a bond." I tease her about the dog, loving the fire in her eyes when I do. "Bond is a strong word…" She rolls her eyes when I laugh. I can't stop smiling when she is around, and that's how I knew that there was no curing me of this obsession. There is no stopping it, either.

She grumbles at the same time I swing us side to side. "Do not be extra, Sebastian." She holds tighter to my shoulders while I spin us around while *John Legend's Nervous,* the piano version, plays in the background. After ten minutes of fighting me, she gave up and got on my feet. The woman is a menace on the dance floor and has no interest in learning to dance, which I do not mind whatsoever since I prefer her dancing while on my feet. Laughing, I hold her closer, forgetting that we're in a room filled with people and not alone. That's what she does to me. She stops the world, until there is only us. Magic.

My Arianna is magic.

"That existential feeling when you're staring at the stars." My hands tighten on her back as I draw her closer, and like a fool, I sing along to the song, loving the way she tenses for a second before relaxing in my arms. That is it, darling. Fall into me. It's fair since I have been falling from the first day I met you. No, I have been falling since before I knew of your existence. Of that I am certain.

"You old fool." she hisses, but there's a hint of humor.

"There's a hurricane in my head…but the lightning in my heart makes it worth it." I watch as she slowly lifts her eyes, clashing with mine. Green eyes that shine so bright and radiate warmth. How she thought otherwise is beyond me. *"Yeah, I still get nervous…"*

Her smile softens, and so do her eyes. "Since when do you listen to modern music, Sebastian? I thought you didn't listen to anything from this century." I laugh at her adorable way of telling me I am old as fuck. Brat. Mine. "I heard it by chance at an event I was attending, and every single lyric reminded me of you."

"You're so obsessed with me. It's sick, Mr. President." She tries to sound unaffected, but the pink on her cheeks tells me my words had an effect. My strong, brave, and sometimes mean as fuck Arianna is blushing, and what a beautiful sight it is. Right up there with my favorite sights.

My woman throwing her head back while she is laughing or when she's about to fall apart in my arms when I make her come undone for me.

"I love you." I remind her as I do every time I see her. And although she doesn't say it back. I know. Her sweet eyes tell me just how much.

Time ceases to exist when I hold her in my arms, dancing to the beat of the slow melody…her eyes on me. "I hate you, Sebastian." She whispers… so vulnerable and so brave because after so many hits to her heart, my brave little fighter has raised the white flag by admitting this. Because when she says hate, we both know she means love. "Good. Give me all of you, *mon amour*." I kiss her forehead gently and stay that way for a second.

"*Idiote*," she rolls her eyes and gives me a crooked smile.

"*Votre imbécile*."

Arianna looks up, all jokes are forgotten, and tightens her arms around me. "Yes…"

And that's that.

We spend the rest of the dance ignoring the world around us as I sing her a love song. Because the lyrics are more than accurate. I could fall forever for this woman. She also makes me nervous. Imagine that. Me? The most confident motherfucker. The president of the United States. The son of Ronan Kenton. Nervous.

I feel nervous every time the woman in my arms looks at me.

Because when she gives me those fiery green eyes, all I feel is her.

I am no longer my own.

I haven't been for a long time.

I am hers.

Just like she is mine.

I just need to set it in stone.

"One more song and we're leaving." The grumpy beauty standing on my Gucci shoes mumbles.

Nodding while smiling like a damn fool I reply, "One more song, and we go home."

That is another thing…

How do I make the most stubborn woman I know give in and move into my home like she was always meant to?

***

ARIANNA

"You made quite the show tonight, Mr. President. Expect to be all over tomorrow's news…" I hold onto Sebastian's arm as he helps me walk down the stairs that lead to the back door of the building. No main entrance for the president.

I can't help but smile when he shrugs and says, "Fucking love that the world knows you're mine."

Trying hard not to laugh, I reply. "Psycho, watch your mouth."

We take the last steps before Nix, Sebastian's guard, opens the back door for us, leading us outside the museum. Sebastian turns and roughly grabs me by the neck and kisses my lips softly before pulling back.

"Yours." He breathes out after stealing the air out of my lungs.

Yes.

Mine.

But I am not admitting that. At least not yet.

The warm breeze hits my face as soon as we're outside while the night obscures us a bit, giving us the privacy, we need to make it to the waiting cars so we can head out of there. Sebastian's guards form a barricade around us so they can shield and protect us from any threat that might come our way. I was aware Sebastian's life was in danger everywhere he went because as much as people love him. Some don't quite agree with him and those are the real threats. Sebastian is not only the most powerful man in the United States but he's also a threat to other countries. To our enemies around the world. Apart from the fact that my tyrant loves to piss people off with his honesty and condescending behavior, of course. My hand instinctively tightened around his and whatever he sees in my face softened his expression. As if he read my mind, he speaks up while we move towards our vehicle, holding me close to his body. "Make no mistake, Arianna. I'd burn the fucking world down before I let anyone hurt you."

My heart flails in my chest at his declaration.

I stare at him for a beat too long before I murmur, "It is not me I am worried about."

His smile turns soft. "Are you worried about me, love?" He looks cocky as hell.

I flip him the bird and roll my eyes, making him laugh.

What an odd…odd…man.

Once we're almost to the black vehicles lined up waiting for us, I feel something slip from my wrist and fall to the ground. Shit. Sebastian's gift. Our sweet memories. Looking down, I watch as it falls into a puddle. Shit. Pulling my hand from Sebastian's, I bend and reach for it. In other circumstances, I would leave the bracelet in the dirty water, but this bracelet means something to both of us.

I don't want to lose it.

I should have left it alone.

I should have not let go of Sebastian's hand and gotten out of the barricade because, the next thing I know, he is shouting at me with fear in his eyes. "Arianna, don't!" The scene starts in slow motion, but then it's too fast. I am unable to register what is going on. For a moment, I think I am stuck in a nightmare. That is until Sebastian tackles me from the side, taking me down so hard that my arm lands funny, raw pain shooting from my fingertips to my shoulder blade. I feel a sharp pain when the back of my head hits the ground.

I cry out in agony, and that's when I realized that Sebastian wasn't getting up.

He stays down on top of me so long that I start to panic. Pop. Pop. Pop. "Do not move," Sebastian's dark, angry voice growls. I close my eyes as silent tears start to slip down my cheeks. "What is going on? Are you okay? Oh, Christ, Sebastian, are you okay?" I scream afraid and in pain, tears clogging my throat. But he doesn't answer me. Instead, he stays exactly where he is, and that is when I register what is happening. Sebastian's security team hovers, protecting us while others leave the barricade and spread out with their guns in the air. Shooting at whoever is behind the attack.

No.

This is not happening.

Not to us.

We are under attack and if something happens it will be my fault.

It is all my fault.

"Sebastian!" I yell when he doesn't get off me. Oh, God, no. He's not responding.

Why is he so quiet?

It feels like an eternity when the loud noise of gunfire disappears and Ares helps Sebastian off me, and when he does, the shooting pain in my arm intensifies so much that I vomit on myself. My eyes go down, and my head starts to whirl as I get a good look at my arm.

It was odd. I'd never seen my arm contorted like that before, but as bad as that was to see, nothing will ever hurt as much as the sight of the man who owns my heart and soul on the ground with blood on his chest and neck. The stubble covering his cheeks looks too black against his paling skin.

Pushing through the unbearable pain, I push away the men trying to keep me from Sebastian. I claw and scream in agony with blood, his blood all over my gown and my arm in so much pain. Nothing compares to the pain I feel when I look at Sebastian lying there, looking up at the sky with a somber look on his handsome face. Nothing will ever hurt more than this moment right here.

"Sundance, down. The president was hit! Move, move, move, move!"

"Help! Get him in the car and drive to NYU Med."

I tune everyone out, his guards, the media circus near us and the pain currently shooting up my arm. I crawl closer to Sebastian and fall next to him. With my good hand, I put pressure on his wound. He was hit in the chest.

Someone fucking shot him in the chest.

Rage and grief as I have never felt before consume me, and I wonder if this is how he felt when he watched his parents being gunned down for everyone to witness his pain. "Baby... baby, look at me. Stay with me. Do not close your eyes." I am bawling my eyes out and the sight of his blood makes me want to throw my guts up more than the shooting pain in my arm. Blood pools in his mouth when he tries to speak. Tears fall as I watch him try to form words, but the blood makes it impossible. "I–I" He croaks, but I stop him. He is losing so much blood.

"No, don't say anything. You'll be fine, okay?" My hand, the one that's not broken, keeps holding pressure as his eyes turn sad with pain as if he knows what will happen next because he has lived it once before, but no. No, we are not our past. This is not how it will end.

A cry of pain slips my mouth when I see him lift his bloody hand and tap his chest twice, pointing weakly toward me. "I know. I know. My heart is yours, too. So hold on. Hold on!" I try to hold my fear back, to reassure him that all will be fine. Frantically, I look at the men around us who are spreading out with their guns raised while others are speaking into their wrists. "Help. Get him help!" I release a sigh of relief when I hear the distant sound of sirens. Turning to Sebastian, I offer him a smile. I smile while on the inside I'm slowly dying. "Help is coming. Don't close your eyes, baby. Okay? Don't close your eyes. Please…Hold on." I whisper as tears fall rapidly from my eyes.

My chest aches when he tries to speak, but he can't get the words out. "Tell E-ellai–" More blood spills from his mouth onto me. Staining my gold dress with red.

Please, God.

Please, don't take him from me.

Not him.

I didn't mean it.

Fuck, I did not mean for this to happen. All the times I wished him bad things, I didn't mean it. "You tell her yourself, Sebastian. You are not leaving me! Do you hear me? I am not done fighting with you yet! I–I love you so goddamn much, tyrant. Please hold on." I scream when I am being lifted from the ground, and paramedics and more of his guards are lifting him onto a gurney while they strap an oxygen mask to his face. All the while, he smiles at me softly, trying to reassure me. Even when he is on the brink of possibly dying, he keeps a reassuring smile for me. My beautiful, sweet when he wants to be, tyrant…

It will all be okay. It has to be. He is the strongest man I know. The most powerful. He can move mountains. I truly believe that. He will be okay. I tell myself that, trying to convince my bleeding heart, but then I watch from afar as the smile falls from his face. Sebastian closes his eyes and it feels as if I, too, was shot in the chest.

Fighting the agonizing pain I scream at the top of my lungs when I am being held back and watch the paramedic lift him into the ambulance. "Don't leave me!" Trying to get free from the arms keeping me from the man I love. I scream until my throat hurts. "Please don't leave me again!"

Please, don't leave me.

I didn't mean it.

War.

Hurting you.

Hating you.

I'm sorry.

I love you.

Don't leave me.

But then the pain takes over, and the world goes black.

PART THREE
LOVE & US

What was life before him? - A

Chapter 26
LIFE AND DEATH
Arianna

"My stupid heart won't let you go." — A

The constant beeping sounds of a machine wakes me up from the deepest sleep I've had in years, but when I try to open my eyes, I feel a little groggy and there's a sharp sting on the back of my head. And why do I feel as if I have been run over?

Everything is blurry when I manage to fight the fog and open my eyes. Once my eyes find focus, the first thing I see is white.

White ceiling, walls, and furniture.

And the room is so cold.

Why is it so cold?

"Hey there, kid. Stay down." I recognize Benjamin's soft voice as he pushes me back down onto the bed gently.

"Where am I?" I look down at my bandaged arm and then up at Benjamin in confusion. "W-what happened?" I croak out when my throat feels like it's burning, as if I smoked three packs of cigarettes.

"You're in the hospital," Benjamin says.

The hospital...

That's when it all comes back to me hitting me at full force. Hurting me. Annihilating me.

The gala.

Sebastian showing up.

Us dancing while he sang along to a John Legend song like a fool while my heart was beating so hard, trying to get out of my chest and fall at his feet. The feeling of peace I got while he held me as we danced like no one was watching and then… Then the gunfire and the blood.

So much blood.

And his eyes…

Those blue grays I love so much were smiling through the pain.

Smiling so I wouldn't feel scared.

Oh, God.

"Sebastian!" My eyes are wild, and my heart is racing, I try to get up, but Benjamin holds me down with a somber look on his face. No. No. Please, God not him. Not my tyrant. "Calm down. You'll hurt yourself." He pins me to the bed, so I don't hurt myself. "Fuck, kid, please calm down."

With my good hand, I grab his. My eyes blur with tears as I ask in a voice so low I think he doesn't hear me, "How…" Clearing my throat I try again. "Is he…?" I can't finish the sentence. I can't, but Benjamin doesn't need me to. My friend's eyes turn sad but before I lose my mind with the thought of the man I love leaving me forever, he puts me out of my misery. "The motherfuckers got him. Two bullets to the chest. The doctors were able to remove the bullets, but some fragments hit the heart and caused damage to the fine arteries. He also lost a lot of blood. The doctors did their best, but the rest is up to him now. He was moved to the ICU. Fuck, he…" Benjamin looks away from me, swallowing hard. I know that face. He is beating himself up, most likely for not being there.

"What is it?" When he doesn't look my way, I snap. "Dammit, Benjamin. Tell me!"

His sad and angry eyes fall back on me. "The Doc said we need to prepare for the worst."

A sob of agony escapes me. "I want to see him. Take me to him." I let go of Benjamin's hand, and try to get up from the hospital bed, hissing in pain when I put too much pressure on my bandaged arm that's up in a sling. Yet, nothing hurts like the realization that Sebastian might leave me. This time for good. "Please," I croak, my voice cracking. "He is all alone." It hurts, fuck it cripples me. He needs to know that I am here, and that he'll never be without me. Not as long as I am breathing. This love? The love I feel for him? Refuses to die, and nothing could finish the job. Not misunderstandings. Not the threats of war. Not the years or the pain. The lonely nights and all the times my heart bled for him. Nothing and while he was lying down on the ground looking up at me with only love in his eyes and touching his heart to let me know that he loved me… I knew I could never kill this love.

Nothing could.

"He is safe. Trust me. No one will get to him." Benjamin stops me from getting up fully. "But you need to rest, my girl."

"What I need is to see him. I need to tell him that I—" My voice cracks some more. "He needs to know…" I take a deep breath. He needs to know that I love him. That I am sorry. That I need him to stay and Ellaiza needs her father. I need to make sure the tyrant bastard understands that there is no chance in hell that he'll leave me a second time. "I didn't say it back…" I rasp, while my fight gives out.

"He knows. Trust me, Arianna. That man knows. I don't think a sane man would do the shit he does and follow you across the world if he didn't know he was loved in return." Benjamin nods in understanding but still doesn't let up.

Looking up, I see the pain in my friend's eyes. The pain and the… fear. "I'm scared." I allow myself to admit it aloud, not caring if it makes me seem weak. The truth is that when it comes to Sebastian Kenton… I am weak. "He needs you to be strong, alright?" Benjamin says while grabbing my hand and squeezing it gently. "But please, my girl, stay down and rest. Apart from the broken arm and hit to the head, you were severely dehydrated, and the nurses had to run some tests. The doctor will be back, and once you're cleared to go, I promise I'll take you to see him myself."

Sighing in defeat I lie back, annoyed that he won't let me get up from this god-awful depressing bed. I look away from him at the giant window where rain is falling rapidly. Christ, even the weather is in tune with my mood. "I can't…" I whisper. "I can't be strong when I know it was my fault." I sob quietly, trying to hold back, but it is a losing battle. I hate showing emotions because I was taught more than once that crying was a show of weakness, and it did nothing to me. However, at this instant, I need to let it out. I need to cry for the man I love more than anything and for the little girl who is at home waiting for her father, unbeknown that he is fighting for his life.

I am not a religious person, but ever since meeting Sebastian, I have found myself praying more than I care to admit. I send a silent prayer to whoever the hell is willing to hear me up there to keep Sebastian safe. To give him the strength he needs to beat this.

Please, God…

"It was not your fault." Benjamin says gruffly while squeezing my hand in reassurance.

"Do not try to make me feel better, Benjamin. If I hadn't broken the barricade of protection for a damn bracelet, this wouldn't have happened. The bastard was waiting for the opportunity, and I gave it to him when Sebastian put himself in the line of fire to protect me. I did that. I might as well have pulled the trigger myself."

Gentle, strong fingers take a hold of my chin, tipping it up. "The only one to blame is the motherfucker who did this, Arianna, but if you're looking to blame someone then blame me because I wasn't there for him. For you. I didn't protect either of you, and that's on me."

Benjamin, like me, would rather have all his teeth pulled out than admit defeat or admit that he made a mistake, and the fact that he is doing it now, lets me know he's beating himself up hard for this. That I just can't allow.

Not my Benjamin.

He is the most selfless man I know.

"Stop." I breathe out, staring into his eyes. I have never seen the Viking of a man look this way before. He is furious, yes, but there is sadness mixed with guilt there, too. Helplessness. "You were where you were supposed to be. You were protecting the most important person in mine and Sebastian's world, Ella." I make sure that he reads the truth of my words in my eyes. Sebastian told me once that my eyes were the windows to my soul, and they never lied to him.

I hope Benjamin can see the sincerity in them now.

My friend nods, but I can see clearly that he is not convinced.

He then lets go of my face and takes a step back.

I meant what I said. He is not to blame. He did his duty.

He kept my Ella safe back at the White House. Then I think of how she could've been there to witness her father lying on the dirty ground, choking on his blood. Shivers run through my body. Opening my mouth to reiterate that even if he were there, the outcome most likely would have been the same since it was me who messed up and put him in a situation where he had to cover me with his body from the bullets, a soft-spoken voice interrupts us. "Good. You're up." A pretty redhead with brown eyes and a sweet smile enters the room, approaching me in a white coat. "I am Dr. Sexton, and I've been treating you, Arianna. How are you feeling?"

"Fine. There is no need to keep me here." I tell her a bit rudely. "If you can clear me to go…" I muster a smile when I notice she is taken aback by my rude tone. Dr. Sexton sidesteps Benjamin, who doesn't, for a moment, leave my side in full bodyguard mode, and checks me out with a stethoscope first.

"Take deep breaths for me, please."

I do.

Then she moves to my chart on the end of the bed and looks it over. "When you arrived, we treated your head wound, and thankfully, it was superficial. As for dehydration, salts, and fluids were delivered through the vein and absorbed quickly. Your levels are up, and you'll be back on your feet in a couple of hours, so please rest." The doctor smiles kindly at me. "See? All good, take me to him now. I promise I'll be back in this bed as soon as I see for myself that he is okay." I try again with Benjamin, and he looks away from me to the doctor. Benjamin always did have a hard time telling me no. Holding my breath, I look back at the doctor when she clears her throat. "Miss Parisi, although your situation is not serious and you will, in no time, be released.

I do recommend remaining calm and trying not to stress. It is not good for the baby."

The...what?

I swear a pin can be heard falling to the floor when the room grows silent. I can even hear my heart pounding and my ears ringing.

I look at the woman, confused and as if she has lost her mind. "Baby?"

Dr. Sexton nods with a big smile. "When you were brought to the ED, we had to run some blood tests quickly to determine the reason why you were slipping in and out of consciousness. At first, we thought the head wound caused some trauma, so I ordered more tests to make sure all was okay. The bloodwork and HCG showed you are indeed pregnant."

Out of nowhere Benjamin laughs loudly, making me look up at him, still in a daze. "You are pregnant! That fucker will be out of his mind when he stops fucking around and wakes his old ass up." I know Benjamin is talking, but it's only background noise at this point.

Pregnant.

Looking down at my stomach, covered by a hospital gown, I feel the urge to, once again, pass out.

A kid.

Another kid.

I didn't lie when I told Ellaiza that she was more than enough.

I never gave children much thought since in the world I lived in back then, children were just pawns.

Who would want to bring a child to a world where they would know pain and hatred before they're able to speak? Before they know what love feels like?

"Arianna." A gentle hand touches my shoulder, bringing me back and away from deep in my head. Looking up at Benjamin I notice he looks worried. "Where did you go?"

"What?" I ask, confused as well.

"You zoned out for a moment there. The doctor wants to do an ultrasound to make sure everything is fine with the baby."

"The baby..." I whisper.

"Yes, mommy." He grins.

I narrowed my eyes at him.

I am pregnant.

I knew that damn trip to Greece was trouble…

"I know it's a big shock…" Dr. Sexton speaks up.

A big shock?

She has no idea.

"Not even a week ago, I hated this man with everything in me, or so I convinced myself, and now I am pregnant with his spawn. If this isn't a bad soap opera, I don't know what is," I grumble, sounding more annoyed than I feel. Dammit, I don't know how I feel. So many emotions, thoughts, and things happening all at once.

Dr. Sexton smiles softly, not a trace of judgment in her expression. I remain silent while she exposes my flat belly, and spreads a clear and cold gel on my belly and pelvis area. "This won't hurt. I just want to make sure all is right and how far along you are." Can't be much since I spread my legs for the devil weeks ago. I look towards Benjamin who is following all the movements the doctor does, while petting my head as if I were a dog. The only reason I let him is because, with all that is going on, the gesture gives me comfort.

Damn… girl, he put a baby in you before he put a diamond on your finger…kind of slutty of you. The little bitch of a devil on my shoulder cackles. You're a baby momma.

I don't believe in old traditions or any traditions for that matter, so the realization that I will be an unwed mother does not bother me at all. On the contrary, it gives me pleasure to know my mother would be so disappointed in me. The firstborn Parisi princess spread her legs for a man that is not her husband and is now carrying his child.

Submissive princesses do not do that.

Not in the world my mother lives in.

I am brought back and away from my thoughts when Dr. Sexton moves a handheld probe over my stomach. "The gel helps the probe transmit sound waves. These help us get a clear view of the baby on the ultrasound machine." She gently explains every step, which I'm grateful for. I never thought I would have this life. A dream job. An education. A beautiful girl to call my own. Loyal people and friends who care for me, like Benjamin and Quinne. I never would've imagined a man like Sebastian or getting to build a family with him. That was not in the cards for a mafia princess, but here I am.

And I wish I could feel blissfully happy, but all I can think of is Sebastian fighting for his life and being on his own while I'm here. Of him not going home to his daughter or never meeting this baby.

"Isn't it a bit early? I've heard ultrasounds are mostly done after seven to eight weeks." I blurt out.

The doctor nods while moving the wand over my pelvis. "Yes, but this is just a precaution since you took a hard fall. It's just to make sure everything is okay." She smiles and then points toward the ultrasound monitor. "You won't see anything clearly in four weeks, but see that tiny dot there?" I look at the black-and-white image and spot the tiny dot. "Yes…"

"I can't see shit," Benjamin mutters crassly and leans over me to get closer enough to see better.

Dr. Sexton laughs. "That is the gestational sac." Without taking my eyes off the screen, I ask what that is because I didn't study medicine, and I don't know what the hell she's talking about. As if reading my thoughts, she explains. "The gestational sac is a fluid-filled structure surrounding an embryo during the first few weeks of embryonic development. It is the first structure seen in pregnancy by ultrasound as early as 4 to 5 weeks of gestational age and is 97.6% specific for the diagnosis of intrauterine pregnancy."

"Huh…" That dot on the screen will develop into my baby. A baby. Suddenly I feel nervous. I've excelled at most things in life, but this is uncharted territory. Pregnancy. All that comes with trying to keep a baby alive. I didn't have that opportunity with Ella.

I am pregnant. This is happening.

Then I think of Sebastian and how I might be doing this all alone if he doesn't get the fuck up. Oh, God. Not only did the man make me his baby momma, but there's no chance in hell I will be a single mother. Not because there is something wrong with that but because I refuse to live without him. "I will be here every step of the way. So will the boss. He is one stubborn motherfucker and not even death can keep that obsessed motherfucker from you. Trust that." Closing my eyes in pain, I take a deep breath when my brain and heart register Benjamin's words. He always knows what to say when my mind instantly goes to the worst possible scenarios. The doctor clears her throat and hands me a black and white photo of the tiny blob that was just on the screen.

Mine.

Mine and Sebastian's.

That's life.

A new life while its father is fighting for his.

Taking the photo, I hold it close to my heart. "Don't worry. All will be fine. You'll see." Dr. Sexton says, offering me comfort, and for that I'm grateful. She then finishes cleaning me up and leaves me alone with Benjamin. Once, I thought my heart was beyond repair. Too much damage. Too hurt. To love someone other than myself.

Then he came along and changed everything.

Because my heart loves hard now. So much so that it has grown to hold more than one person in it. At this moment, it has split in three.

A part is with Ella, the other with Sebastian in the ICU, and now…now there's another with the tiny little piece of heaven currently growing inside of me. Swallowing past the lump in my throat, I look up at Benjamin. "Please take me to him." Whatever he hears in my tone and sees in my teary eyes makes him finally give in.

He sighs and then helps me up from the hospital bed carefully. I think whatever the medics gave me for the pain is working because I haven't felt anything but numbness when it comes to my physical health. My emotional state is another thing altogether. There's no medicine to help me with that. None Dr. Sexton would prescribe anyway. "Careful," Benjamin whispers once my feet touch the floor. "My legs are fine, Benjamin. I can walk."

"Shut up and let me help you."

For the first time since meeting the Viking of a man, I do just that. I shut up and let him help me without giving him a hard time. I don't have the energy to fight him anyway. All I want to do is stand by Sebastian's side. Please…

Please don't take him from me.

Not him.

Never him.

Not again.

I don't think I'll survive this time.

***

The second I enter his room, my eyes instantly well up with tears at how tragic the air feels in this room.

"This was not necessary at all, Benjamin. You are so extra sometimes." I grumble when Benjamin pushes the wheelchair towards the bed where the strongest man I have ever known is lying, fighting for his life. The moment I am close enough to touch him, I do. Taking his big hand in mine, I choke on my tears.

I have suffered a lot throughout my life but nothing like this. "You said we had forever…" A large ball clings to the back of my throat, and I don't hold the sob that slips from my lips at the view in front of me. Sebastian lies on the hospital bed with tubes in his mouth and nose. Bandages covering his naked chest. Even his slightly golden skin is pasty and his beautiful face is too colorless. He looks as if he's giving up. Leaning forward, I bring his hand to my mouth and kiss it, feeling dead inside and tired. So very tired. After I cried my eyes out upon hearing about Sebastian's slim chances of survival, I haven't been able to stop crying. The only reason I don't crumble is because I know him. I know my tyrant. "I am so sorry, baby," I whisper not caring that Benjamin is witnessing this. "I should have known better. I should have never let go of your hand. I am so sorry. Fuck, just open your eyes, Sebastian. Open your eyes and tell me I was an idiot in that condescending way only you can pull off." I laugh through my tears, remembering all our fights and silly arguments in the past. It all seems so pointless now that we're here in this heartbreaking moment. "I didn't get to tell you just how much I love you, Sebastian. I think I loved you before I even knew what love was." Taking a deep breath, I carry on, holding onto his hand and looking at his pale face. "I never told you this but that night back in Detroit on the plane track was not the first time I ever saw you. No. The first time I saw you was when I was a young girl. When I was waiting to be seen by a shrink per my nonna's insistence. In the waiting room, someone left a newspaper on the table, and you were on the front page." Taking a deep breath, I squeeze his hand, needing his strength and the feel of him to continue. "I was so young and so angry, and then I saw you, and I thought to myself how intimidating yet so perfect you looked and how powerful even through the pages of a newspaper. One thing I remember was how your eyes didn't match your smile. You had a crooked grin, but there was no light in your eyes, just like in mine. There was an emptiness in them. The same emptiness that I saw when I looked at myself in the mirror, and somehow at that moment, looking at your eyes, I didn't feel so alone. It's stupid, I know." I chuckle, embarrassed, even though he can't see or hear me. "Then the second time I saw you, I was angrier than ever, but your eyes… your eyes were no longer so angry or empty. Then I thought to myself that maybe the anger I carried for so long could fade away. Maybe my eyes could shine like yours did and maybe I didn't have to feel so damn empty all the time. Even though I was scared out of my mind of letting you in, I did. The anger faded away every second I spent with you, even if I didn't realize it then. I no longer felt alone or angry. I felt alive for the first time in my life and you did that. You breathe life into me with one kiss, touch and smile at a time. Right along with Ellaiza. You not only gave me life but you, also gave me love. So much love, even when I hated you, I felt your love, so open your damn eyes and come back to me. Love me." My voice cracks when his eyes remain closed. "Come back…"

I don't miss the click of the door behind me, letting me know Benjamin slipped out. Maybe he can't handle all the heartache in the air. I sure as hell can't. It's suffocating me. The machine tracking his heart activity is the only sound in the room as I sit there holding onto his hand, looking at him afraid to close my eyes. Afraid that at any second, he can slip away. My dream can slip through my fingers.

Because that is exactly who this man is to me.

Love and hate.

My dream and my nightmare.

The good and the bad.

Sebastian could never be just one thing.

My eyes leave his face and travel down his neck to the bandages on his chest, and there I see something I hadn't seen before, not really. He always had it covered, and the time we were both naked, it was dark. I could barely see his face. Now I see it, though.

A tattoo of a wolf.

It was big, not just a small tattoo on his body. No, this one looked so real, so lifelike and big, that if you were standing far away, it could pass as a real-life wolf on his chest. The nose and mouth of the wolf stretched from Sebastian's collarbone down to his muscled chest. It is very intricate and well done, and oh-so-beautiful. Hauntingly so. Then I see the eyes of the wolf. So lifelike, piercing through me.

They were my eyes.

Tears fall from my eyes when I remember how I used to think of myself as a lone wolf with only myself to count on, but then he crash-landed into my life, and I found my pack.

He gave me that. He has given me so much.

Now, he gave me life again. A little life.

"Sebastian…" I whisper, kissing his hand without looking away from the wolf on his chest. "You need to wake up. I…" Taking a deep breath, "I'm pregnant." Deep in thought, deep in my pain I almost miss the squeeze of my hand. Gasping, my eyes leave his chest and rise to his face, and I swear my soul almost leaves my body when I see blue-gray eyes looking back at me. Piercing my heart just like the wolf on his chest.

He is awake.

He came back to me.

To us.

Smiling wide, I laugh softly. "A baby," I whisper, shaking my head. "Can you believe it, Tyrant? We made a human. You and me. As if the world needed more of us." I tell him playfully. I hold my breath for what seems like an eternity when his eyes crinkle at the corner, but not in pain, no.

His eyes are smiling at me.

My strong and brave man has not given up.

He squeezes my hand, and I feel like I am finally waking up from this nightmare. I let go of the breath I've been holding and feeling, and it all starts to feel right again.

"I love y–" But then, as if fate hates me, the monitors start going off, and Sebastian's eyes roll to the back of his head.

No.

No.

Don't leave.

Stay with me.

Hold on.

"Help!" I scream at the top of my lungs. "Someone, please!" Holding tightly to his hand, I tell him. "I am here, baby. I am here. Stay with me. Please, fight." I rasp.

"You need to leave, miss." An older man, a doctor, tells me as he moves, quickly checking Sebastian while he is still trashing.

"Sebastian! What is going on?" I scream at the nurses gathering around him. "Someone please tell me..." I cry out.

A sweet-looking young nurse smiles apologetically at me. "Loss of oxygen to the brain... I am so sorry you need to step out." My hand slips from his when I am being pulled back and escorted out of the room. No. I rise from the wheelchair, refusing to leave him alone. "The war is over, baby. Come back to me." I whisper once he's blocked from my view, and they work on him. Once he is out of sight, I fall against someone's chest and sob so loud that my heart feels like it's losing a battle, along with Sebastian's. Twenty minutes later, the doctor comes out with a sullen look on his face and the news that the man who owns my heart has left me.

JUNE

Dear Sebastian

No one likes a martyr. Please...wake up

Yours always

Arianna

JULY

Dear daddy
I miss you
I need you to scare all the monsters under my bed. I need your hugs and kisses.
I miss you daddy
Please wake up

AUGUST

Dear motherfucker

Get the fuck up. We miss your moody ass

PS That fucking dog was a terrible idea — Banning

Your other half

SEPTEMBER

À la claire fontaine m'en allant promener
J'ai trouvé l'eau si belle que je m'y suis baignée.
Il y a longtemps que je t'aime, jamais je ne t'oublierai
Sous les feuilles d'un chêne, je me suis fait sécher.
Sur la plus haute branche, un rossignol chantait.
Chante, rossignol, chante, toi qui as le cœur gai.
Tu as le cœur à rire… moi je l'ai à pleurer.
J'ai perdu mon ami sans l'avoir mérité,
Pour un bouquet de roses que je lui refusai…
Je voudrais que la rose fût encore au rosier,
Et que mon doux ami fût encore à m'aimer.

Darkness is all around me, covering me in it, but then when I feel myself walking away from the light, I hear it. The soft, melodic voice of an angel. Have I died and gone to heaven? But that cannot be since men like me won't ever see those pearly gates. More like the burning red ones, yet in this desolate darkness, the voice of an angel sings to me the French lullaby my mother used to sing to me every night before bed or when I was feeling rather clingy.

As I was walking by the clear fountain,
I found the water so lovely I had to bathe.
I've loved you for so long, I will never forget you
Under the oak's leaves, I lay and dried.
On the highest bough, a nightingale sang.
Sing, nightingale, sing, you who has a joyous heart.
Your heart is made for laughing... mine can only cry.
I lost my love without deserving it,
Because of a bouquet of roses, I refused him...
I wish the rose were still in the bush,
And my sweetheart loved me still.

My angel with a sultry voice sings to me, and I have no choice but to follow. I walk in the dark until I see it. A bright light. Some would say I should stay away from the warm light, but my feet have a mind of their own, leading me closer to it. Once I reach the light, the voice singing to me does not sound so far away, and my body is no longer freezing but… warmth takes over me.

"Sebastian…" the sweet voice of the angel leading me to my apparent death whispers. "Come back to me. Come back to us…"

"Daddy! Wake up. Super villains don't sleep so long!" Trying to fight the darkness, I concentrate on the sweet voices and only two voices.

All of a sudden there is a ringing in my ear.

And I'm no longer able to hear them.

Why can't I hear them?

I'm slipping away.

The darkness is fading.

I don't want to go.

I want to stay here listening to the beautiful voice singing to me, but I'm losing the fight.

I'm slipping away, falling until the light covers me completely.

I found my way out of the dark.

I found my way back to them.

To my loves.

To my life

Opening my eyes, I'm greeted by green ones, the color of emeralds, smiling at me. "You came back to us…" The angel with golden hair whispers while leaning over me. This must be the light I followed out of the darkness. Her.

My angel.

My light.

My savior.

Arianna.

Finding my voice, I tell her. "Did you ever doubt I would?"

Then the sweetest sound of her laugh surrounds me as I fall back under.

You came back to us.

You came back to us.

I came back for you…

For the three of you.

Chapter 27
BABY DADDY
Arianna

"This love is bigger than us."- A

Three months later

"Please! Help him!" My voice is raw from screaming at the doctors begging for answers and pleading with them to save Sebastian's life. No one is giving me answers.

The image of him with a tube down his throat and his eyes rolling to the back of his head when he started seizing will haunt me forever.

I don't understand what went wrong.

He was right there with me.

He opened his eyes and smiled at me.

He came back to me.

One of the nurses, a male with a pretty great poker face, stands blocking Sebastian from view before he shuts the door in my face and I am no longer able to see him.

I let go of his hands again.

"Please, Benjamin. Tell them! I need to know what's wrong with him. Please." I've never been more scared. I fall back into Benjamin's arms, letting him hold me and give me the strength I need right now, but he *stays quiet, not really knowing what else to say. What is there to say? I clearly heard one of the nurses say there was no pulse and the doctor saying that he flatlined. I've watched enough Medical series to know what's happening here, yet I still can't believe it. I just can't. Not my Sebastian.I silently sob, falling apart in my best friend's arms, and wonder what life would be like if I lost half of my heart. Forever.*

Because what was life before Sebastian Kenton?

 Nothing.

Empty. Colorless. Just like it would be after him. Cold. Dark. Desolate.

"Mommy! The pancakes!" A sweet voice screeches at the same time as a high-pitched bark, bringing me back from the heartbreaking memories that still plague me whenever I let my mind wander to that time months ago. Looking down at the cooking pan, I indeed burned the pancakes. Shit. Making sure that I lower the heat on the stove, I grab the burnt pancakes with cooking mittens, drop them on the dog's plate and place it in front of Cupcake. "*Bon, appetite,* mutt." The ungrateful little ball of fur barks at me while my kid yells, "Mommy!"

"Oh, he loves it when I call him mutt, baby. It is our thing." I wave Ellaiza off as she looks at me offended that I gave her dog burnt pancakes. Shit, can dogs eat pancakes? I need to google that before I end up killing my daughter's pet slash friend. Taking the burnt pancakes off his plate, I throw them in the trash before grabbing dog treats and giving them to the dog. "Good, mommy." Ellaiza praises me the same way she does the dog when he learns a new trick. Brat. I roll my eyes and ask. "Are you sure you can carry the tray? It's a long walk, you know. Let me help."

"No, I can do it." She smiles at me so brightly that it's contagious, and I find myself smiling back at my girl. It's been a hell of a time for both of us, but the sun came out after long months of complete darkness.

Months where I and everyone else around Ellaiza had to lie to spare her feelings and keep her innocence intact a little while longer. After her father was shot outside of the gala, he managed to be conscious for barely sixty seconds before he flatlined two times and ultimately fell into a coma. The doctors said he lost too much blood and oxygen wasn't reaching his brain, even though he was stable. No one knew exactly what caused it. All I knew was that the heart of the man I loved stopped two times, and mine did the same alongside his.

They managed to bring him back twice before he fell into a coma. A coma he was in for three long months before he woke up miraculously at the beginning of September.

We were all walking zombies going through the motions all those months Sebastian was in a coma. The world burst into chaos when it witnessed its president being shot on all the news TV stations and the internet. We not only had to deal with Sebastian's condition but also with the shit storm that followed.

The country witnessed its leader fall, and panic started to rise. The Vice President stepped up and served while Sebastian was unable to carry on as president. What pissed me off more was that, while the country was going through dark days, our enemies overseas celebrated Sebastian's fall as if he was already dead. I guess it comes with the territory of being the leader of one of the most powerful countries in the world. While all this was happening, Benjamin and I decided to tell Ellaiza that her father was sick and sleeping to get all his strength back. Luckily she is young and she did not question the lie although I felt like shit for lying to her. I wanted to keep her innocence intact for a while longer.

My sweet girl read to her father every night and kissed him too, hoping that like Snow White he would wake up with a true love's kiss.

That's how kindhearted and lovely our Ella is.

I don't know what I would've done if Sebastian had taken longer to come out of the comatose state.

The loss of him was weighing us all down.

"Daddy's birthday is coming up!" Ella exclaims while adding three strawberries to the plate of fruit she prepared all by herself.

"It is." Not so soon, though. Sebastian's birthday is in February. I grab another tray and place a coffee and a glass of orange juice onto it. "What do you think we should get him?" With all that has been going on it slipped my mind. The last birthday I was truly happy, hell, the only birthday I had an ounce of happiness I spent it with him, Ellaiza, and Benjamin, and he made it so special.

Before, he used to make every day special for me.

Now, I get to return the favor.

Ellaiza and I move through the house with two trays of food and a small dog trailing behind. "I don't know! Dad has everything." She huffs and throws her hands in the air in exasperation.

"He does have a lot, yes. But you know what he doesn't have enough of?"

"What?" She looks excited now.

"Your pretty pictures," I tell her while I hold the tray with one hand, and with the other arm, which is no longer in a pink cast, I support Ella's back as we climb the stairs. "You know how much he loves those." I wink when she beams.

"Yeah, my drawings are the best." Not so humble, my sweet girl. "Hey, how's baby sister today, mommy?"

Baby sister.

Looking down at my growing belly, I smile. "Baby is very active today."

I still don't know what the sex of the baby is. I'm scheduled for a check-up next week, and there I'll be able to find out the sex if I want to.

I'm in the second trimester, and although my belly is not huge, there's a bump that's growing every day.

Growing my unborn baby.

Throughout this pregnancy, I've been going through it. At first, I was terrified of something happening to my baby since I was not in a good headspace with all that was going on with Sebastian, but as the weeks passed, I learned to take care of myself and be strong for not only Ella and Sebastian but for my baby as well.

Baby Kenton is now the size of a banana, according to the first-time mom's book I've been reading every night. The same book tells me that my baby's fingers and toes are well-defined. Their eyelids, eyebrows, eyelashes, nails, and hair are formed, and teeth and bones are becoming denser. It says that the baby can even suck their thumb, yawn, stretch, and make faces.

I must admit that although this hasn't been the most blissful experience and it certainly has had its challenges, I am looking forward to seeing my baby and listening to its heartbeat.

I still can't believe there's a human inside of me.

My little human came into our lives to fill us with joy and more love. Because although a lot has happened, I am forever grateful for this little miracle inside of me. Ella and I carry on talking about the baby because, lately, that's her favorite topic, and it also has helped distract us from what was happening.

"It smells delicious." Benjamin sniffs the air the second while we climb the last step. "Is there some for me, ladies?" Benjamin makes a move to grab a pancake, but I slap his hand away.

"There's more downstairs. Help yourself, Benjamin." Smiling, he opens the double doors and allows us inside the room he's been guarding all morning.

"Bonjour, papa," Ella yells happily as soon as she enters her father's room with an infectious smile. Following her inside, I stop when I was standing on the threshold and stare. I stand there, and just take a second to take everything in. Before, I used to live a very fast-paced life because nothing had meaning, not really, and I missed a lot of moments that could have filled my heart with joy, but now I don't take the little moments for granted. I don't take love for granted.

Because of this love I feel for both of them. Hell, even for Benjamin. The love I feel for all of them comes once in a lifetime, and I almost lost that love. Now, I protect it with all I have.

"Bonjour, mon coeur." He says to Ellaiza.

Thud.

Thud.

Thud.

Closing my eyes, I take a deep breath and let the comforting sound of his voice wash over me. Soothing me. Assuring me that all is okay in the world.

Ellaiza's laugh.

Sebastian's voice.

As long as I have that, I know all will be well.

"Bonjour, mon amour." Opening my eyes, I smile and stare at Sebastian hanging onto a metal rail doing his daily physical therapy. After he woke up, he had trouble going back to normalcy, and therapy has helped with that. He can stand and walk on his own, but he is still unable to do some movement without being in pain.

He's almost healed… almost, but he's taking every precaution so he can speed up the process of recovery.

Sebastian, to me, is young, but he won't recuperate at the speed a twenty-year-old man would. Something I told him yesterday, which prompted him to give me the finger. That fact that I finally admitted that I love the man more than anything and that I thank God every day that Sebastian didn't kick the bucket doesn't change the fact that I love pissing the man off. "Good morning, tyrant." I greet him at the same time Benjamin shuts the door behind me. I move towards the coffee table, placing the tray down, and Ella follows suit. I don't miss the little growl that slips from her mouth when she takes in Sebastian's home nurse and full-time flirt, Kim. Laughing under my breath, I pat Ella's hand, which in turn makes her relax a bit. Only a bit.

"Comment est mon bébé?" Sebastian asks with a crooked grin as he slowly walks toward me, completely ignoring his nurse now that we are here. You know, I am trying to be good. I am trying hard, but sometimes the man loves to test my patience, like right now. Where the hell is his shirt? Narrowing my eyes, I take in his raw beauty and the giant wolf on his chest. The wolf with my eyes. I haven't asked him about it. Same for the tattoo on his ring finger because, well, it hasn't come up. I had other things to worry about, but now that he's on full display for this woman's eyes, it's giving me an odd sense of satisfaction and possessiveness to see that he marked himself with something that reminds him of me.

Nurse Kim clears her throat like she always does when I am in the room, looking away from Sebastian, I glance at her. Kim is pretty, there's no doubt, and the only reason I haven't thrown her obnoxiously sweet ass out is that, apart from flirting, she manages to do her job right.

Besides, I have nothing to worry about.

This man can't seem to look at anyone else but me. Looking away from her, I roll my eyes at Sebastian, making him smile when I respond. "Our baby." That smile. It rivals most of nature's unexplained phenomena. I vividly how he looked at us and smiled the night he woke up from the coma, and he hasn't stopped smiling since. I swear the sun rises in Sebastian's eyes when he smiles, and I can't look away. Not that I want to. We stand there, smiling at each other like two damn fools, and I have never felt more at home than here with him. In his space and his heart.

Ugh, Sebastian's romantic slash corny disease is contagious.

But there's no denying that things have shifted between us. I was still wary, a bit guarded, yes, but every day I try to leave my past reservations behind and be more open… more loving towards him. I am still allergic to corny behavior, but I am trying to be more understanding of the fact that this giant tyrant of a man, at times, can be one needy ass baby. So, yes I am trying… but Rome wasn't built in a day, and my turning into a hopeless sap won't happen any time soon either.

All I know is that I never want to go through what I went through in the last months again.

I don't want to be without him.

Ever.

So that is why I am here.

In his life and in his world when I once swore to burn it down.

But the second he put himself between me and two bullets, I came to the realization that I, along with his daughter, am his world.

Feeling gentle hands on my stomach, I can't help but feel warm all over. He does this three or four times a day. He puts his hands on my stomach and just smiles from ear to ear. Sometimes Ella does the same. I told them they wouldn't be able to feel the baby kicking until at least the sixth or maybe, seventh month and they both shrugged me off telling me they just wanted the baby to know they care.

That the baby is loved beyond measure.

Sebastian's words, to be exact.

"How are you feeling?" I hand him a plate of fruit while Ella sits like a proper lady with her phone out, taking photos of us. The little diva not only enjoys taking photos of herself but of others as well. Mainly us, Benjamin, and of course, Shaw.

Sebastian grabs me around the waist and pulls me closer to his body until our foreheads are pressed together. I sigh at the same time as he says. "Better now that you're here." He gives me a quick kiss and pulls back, looking down at me with bright eyes. Smiling. Laughing. Loving. Dammit, I am sick in love with this man. "Now that you're both here." He releases me and looks back at the two trays of food we brought for him then his eyes fall back on me. "I like this domestic side of you, darling."

Narrow wing my eyes, "Don't get used to it. It was your daughter's idea. Right, Ell—" When I look at where I last left her, she's no longer there but on the other side of the room where nurse Kim is packing her stuff. That's when the little monster I created shows her claws. She's been waiting for this moment since she entered her father's room to find him shirtless and with his very obviously smitten young nurse. "Excuse me," Ella says.

Kim turns with her bag in hand and looks down at Ella as if only now realizing she's there. "Your dress is very short," Ella states with her brows furrowed, making the most adorable angry face. The one she makes when she's really really mad. Oh, no. Here we go. Bending, I grab my mug and take a sip, already knowing my kid will say something that will make my day. A second later she does.

"I think I can see your butt, and maybe even your va—"

"Ellaiza!" Sebastian turns and interrupts his daughter before she goes any further.

"What?" Ella turns to us with her hands raised in questions and a confused look. "I wasn't going to say anything bad, daddy. I was just going to say that I can almost see her vagina."

Sebastian groans.

I, on the other hand, take a second sip of my tea and sputter and choke on it as I try not to die from laughter.

Nurse Kim rolls her eyes and steps back. "Oh, what a sweet girl you are…." Ella rolls her eyes and puffs up her chest. "I know." Ellaiza says, with all the confidence in the world.

Kim smiles, but it's clear that it pains her. She bends down to pinch Ella's cheek.

Ella slaps her hand away and frowns with annoyance. "You can go now."

Good girl.

I can always count on my Ella to spook them away.

I snort not very elegantly, which makes Sebastian look my way, and his shocked expression turns soft before he says. "Thank you, nurse. I think that will be all for today." He says coldly, without the warmth he reserves for Ella and me.

"Of course, Mr. President." She says through gritted teeth while holding a sickly-sweet and fake smile all the way to the door. "Same time tomorrow?"

Sebastian grabs my hand and guides me to the couch while motioning for Ella to follow. Without looking away from us, he replies. "Someone will be in touch. Good day." And that's that. Yikes. I sometimes forget that this man is as rude as I am when he wants to be.

Cold too. The only time I see him act genuine is when he is with the people he cares about. Everything else is forced kindness, fake, and downright mean.

Kim lifts her head, pulls her shoulders back, and turns, exiting the room while mumbling under her breath. Most likely cussing at us. Oh, how I love it when people don't have the balls to say whatever they feel to my face. "Ellaiza… you can't treat people that way." Sebastian sits down on the couch in between us.

"Why not? You do." Ella smiles up at her father like the precious little diva she is, making me laugh.

"She has you there, Mr. President." I mock while taking another sip of my tea. God, how I miss coffee. Another thing I had to sacrifice for this little tyrant, apart from wine and well… my figure. Sebastian turns his face and narrows his eyes at me, but there's only mirth in his gaze. I stick my tongue out at him, and I enjoy how his eyes turn hot when I do. Then I start to feel hot all over when he gives me the look that tells me he's hungry but not for the food down on the coffee table.

No.

Hungry for me.

It's been a while since we've had sex. Since Greece and then with him acting like sleeping beauty, well… it's safe to say that it's been a long while. "You know, Ellaiza, I think mommy's jealous."

"Oh, please. Jealous of her?" I laugh, but I can't hide the fact that, yes, I am jealous. I am jealous of everyone that gets near him but he is too. I just hide it better while he is painfully obvious and does not care even a bit that he acts like a jealous fool. "Do not be ridiculous, Sebastian."

"Yeah, daddy. Don't be ridico—" Ella has trouble pronouncing the word, so I help. "Ridiculous."

"That!" She smiles at me and then at her father. "Mommy is the prettiest in the whole world. She doesn't feel jealous."

Smiling proudly at my girl. "Thank you, baby."

"You're welcome, mommy." She smiles and then leans back on the couch and continues typing on her phone.

"See! You bore her, Sebastian." I grin when he roughly takes my chin between his fingers and steals a kiss. "Tyrant." I breathe out when he breaks the kiss and looks down at me with a crooked grin and that damn dimple on his chin.

So hot and so handsome, my baby daddy. Sometimes, it's annoying how perfect he is. It honestly should be a crime to be that perfect.

"Brat." He leans forward, grabs a strawberry, and pops it in his mouth. He chews and grins. "I miss the taste of strawberries." His eyes wrinkle at the corners as he smiles.

I blush.

I blush when I realize what he means when he says he misses the taste of strawberries.

He misses my taste.

"You're so filthy, Sebastian," I mumble, trying hard not to give away how hot he makes me feel. Hot all over, but especially between the thighs. Bastard. Perfect, beautiful bastard.

"And you love it." His crooked smile makes my heart beat faster and causes my stomach to flip. "Just like I love how possessive of me you are. You're so sexy when you're jealous, baby. That does it for me." he teases.

"Shut up," I try hard not to laugh, but it's almost impossible with this man. "You've always been like this." He mutters.

"Like what?" I ask.

"Crazy jealous when it comes to me as I am when it comes to you.

Remember when the French waitress was hitting on me back in my restaurant in Paris? You put her in her place quickly." He grins, pleased with the fact that I lose my head when it comes to women thirsting over him. Women or men. It does not matter.

"She's lucky I didn't break a plate on her face," I mutter, remembering how small that girl tried to make me feel while at the same time acting so sweet toward Sebastian.

"Such anger..." He tsks. "Admit it." He nudged me. "You are crazy about me..." I eye him seriously. "Like you need reassurance, Sebastian." His eyes turn soft, and his smile takes over his face. That perfect smile stayed on his face throughout our family's morning breakfast and throughout the day. And I wonder if it would be too much to ask for him to keep smiling at me like that for the rest of my life.

Chapter 28
ROMANCE OF THE CENTURY
Arianna

"I looked for you every day and every night." — B

"Thank you all for stepping up," I tell my team through the camera of my laptop as I recline in one of the baby's rocking chairs. "Wizz's feature on our magazine brought us a new wave of readers with more exposure. I couldn't have done it without you all. Now let's keep this same energy for the next issue. Brainstorm all your ideas and I will be taking suggestions for next month's cover and issue." I finish up my video meeting with the team by pointing out a job well done. Wizz's cover not only gave us more exposure than we had before, but now up-and-coming artists are looking to be featured in our magazine while our newspaper has taken over the political side of the industry. Apart from these past months being hell on me, at least business has been good. Because my second baby, my company, is always good to me. Unlike the little tyrant currently causing havoc inside my womb. This trimester, although all is going smoothly with the pregnancy, Baby Kenton decided to mess with my routines, and there's nothing that pisses me off more than not being able to show up at work because I look like death.

This morning, I was woken up by the need to puke whatever little was in my stomach. I jinxed myself when I celebrated how smooth my first months were going, and now, I not only have cravings, I suffer from lack of sleep and morning sickness.

Now the issue is that I could only keep two things down, chocolate and tea. An odd and not very nutritious diet for my baby. So I suffer, trying to eat the foods that make me nauseous but are rich in vitamins and nutrients for the mini tyrant but then after, I find myself suffering with my forehead plastered to the toilet as I puke my guts out.

The things you do to me, little tyrant.

You bring me so much joy but a lot of trouble too.

You are your father's spawn.

Ping.

A new notification pops up on my computer's screen.

An email from my sister Mila.

My mood instantly brightens when I read it.

Since that first message she sent so many months ago, we have exchanged emails every day since. At first, I felt extremely awkward because so much had happened between us but none of it was her fault, and Mila had the ability to make everyone feel comfortable with her sweet, kind, and sunshine nature that could be transmitted even through her words.

We've talked about the present, focusing on that instead of all the ugly that separated us.

I messaged her I was sorry.

She replied that I had nothing to be sorry about and that she once dreamed of the life I have now for me.

Sweet and pure, my baby sister.

I also know that she's still in Detroit and under Kadra's care. I once asked if she wanted to one day come here to Washington and be with me, and she replied that maybe one day, but as of now, she needs to remain in Detroit.

I also asked if she was safe, even though I knew Kadra would go to war with both Satan and God themselves for our baby sister. Mila reassured me that she was okay but that she had a mission. I asked what the mission was, and she just replied that one day she'll tell me while we were sitting in a Paris cafe. That night I cried my eyes out. Blame it on the hormones or just the fact that I was bursting with happiness because someday is here for me and Mila at least.

She also told me that she's been following my social media and that she is so proud of me. I tear up at that, too, because all I want for her is to have a life as I do. I want her to experience the world, and in the mafia, she won't have the same freedom. Not when she's stuck there in the middle of a war between territories. I also know that I can't do anything about it because taking a mafia princess from a boss is considered treason and has cause for death.

I can't ask Sebastian to get involved, even though I know he would in a heartbeat, but there's so much at risk. Messaging my sister back, I close the computer and place it down on the white carpet on the floor. God, I love that carpet so much that the little mutt, Cupcake, is forbidden from entering this room. Baby Kenton's nursery.

My heaven inside this historic and bland house.

Mila pointed out that my baby will be the second child to be born in the executive mansion in its two hundred and eighteen years of history. There have been more kids born, of course, but only one was the child of a sitting president.

Now, my baby will be the second.

Already making history, my little tyrant.

Looking around the nursery, I can't help but smile.

Ellaiza chose the theme, although her father had to convince her that we shouldn't pick pink for the color palette because we still don't know the sex of the baby. I honestly could care less if it's a boy or a girl, and I know Sebastian feels the same way, but deep down, I worry how Ella will feel if she gets her wish.

Will she remain excited, or will she feel left out, or as if she's being replaced by another girl? Will she feel like the attention is all on her baby sister? But that's nonsense because I know my girl, and her heart is pure. Without meeting this baby, she already loves her or him so much.

When my stomach growls in hunger, I sigh. I am craving nothing healthy. I pick up my phone from the white wooden nightstand next to me and text Sebastian.

Me: Your spawn is in the mood for chocolate.

I don't expect him to immediately reply, but then I see the 'seen receipt' and the three dots.

The man is supposed to be in his first press conference since the shooting, which is being held here in the press room. He has a message to convey to the country, and Baron, his press secretary suggested it was time. I am so proud of Sebastian.

So damn proud for fighting for his life and coming out stronger than ever. There's a fire inside his eyes now that didn't burn quite as brightly as it does now.

The asshole who thought he could snuff that out of him was severely mistaken, and I hope karma gets his ass before Sebastian does.

No, wait.

I hope the bloodthirsty demon that lives inside of Sebastian gets the bastard and makes him regret ever thinking he could get away with hurting the President of the United States. The man that is my heart.

The immediate reply comes through. Now before you start cringing at Sebastian's contact name on my phone, you should know I had no say in the matter. The tyrant did that himself, and every time I change it... he manages to change it right back to Daddy. It has been a long and tedious battle, and I gave up because the man is determined to take over my life, and I am gladly letting him.

Daddy: White or dark chocolate?

Gross.

The thought of eating white chocolate has me wanting to throw up again.

Me: Neither. Who even likes dark chocolate?

Daddy: I and 34% of the population.

Of course, he would love that god-awful taste. He loves pineapple on pizza, after all.

Me: You're one odd man, Sebastian.

Me: Milk chocolate…

Daddy: What is the magic word?

Me: Fucking now, Sebastian.

Daddy: No. That's not quite it.

With a smile on my face, I laugh at the absurdity of our text conversations lately. It goes from us sending strange facts about foods, the baby's nursery décor, and him flooding my phone with love quotes. The gigantic sap. Opening the camera app, I snap a quick selfie of me flipping the man off and send it to him.

Daddy: Fuck, you are perfect.

No. I look like hell, yet he never fails to remind me how beautiful I am to him.

Me: I look like a mental patient who hasn't slept in two decades. You are just biased.

Daddy: I am biased, yes, but I also think my baby is making you lose brain cells, darling.

Me: Our baby, Sebastian. I am the one giving birth to her.

Daddy: So you finally admit you think it's a girl.

Me: I admit, nothing. I am just going along with Ellaiza's wishes.

Daddy: For our sake, that baby better be a girl…

Daddy: I'll get you the chocolate, darling.

Me: Thank you, Sebastian.

Daddy: You are welcome, brat.

And that's how our conversations go lately. Too good to be true. Sometimes, I feel like things are too perfect… but then I remind myself that I can't live in fear of what might happen. That's no way to live, and it has just made me miserable in the past. For Ella and Baby Kenton, I am trying to break that cycle and just enjoy the little moments. Like now. Here, in the quiet and peaceful room of my unborn baby. Rubbing my protruding belly, I look at all the decor. All I've worked on for months while Sebastian was in a coma. Decorating, the baby, and Ella kept me from losing my mind with worry. I was still worried, of course, but I had motivation keeping me from falling into a deep state of grief and misery. "You are one lucky, baby…" I whisper, touching my stomach lovingly. I never thought I was mother material since I didn't have a great example. I did love my sisters with all my heart, and I knew that love, even though it hurt. Loving them back then, hurt, but then Ella came along and showed me that I was capable of that kind of love, too.

A love that did not hurt.

Ellaiza might not have my blood running through her veins, but she is my daughter in every way it counts. She taught me how to love fiercely, and that is how I know I'll be a good mother to this little one.

Because of the beautiful little girl who chose me to be her mother.

The same little girl who spent day and night in this room with me, helping get it ready for her sibling.

I chose the color, but she chose the theme.

Brown teddy bears and the moon.

And I thought it would be perfect not because the moon is the English translation of my name, no, but because the moon means something to Sebastian, and it also meant a lot to his mother. I wanted that beautiful bond they shared when he was a young boy to be present here in our baby's room, just like in Eliza's room.

So the entire nursery is painted white with gray furniture and brown teddy bears all over.

In the crib's bedding. A teddy bear lamp on top of the nightstand. On the changing table.

It's cute, and it's perfect for this baby.

At first, I was bummed that I couldn't go all out and decorate the walls and ceiling like I wanted because, well, not much can be done to the executive mansion, but after Benjamin, Ella, and I finished the nursery, it all came together beautifully.

There was one missing piece to make the room perfect, and it was delivered early this morning after Sebastian left. Benjamin helped me put it up, and now I cannot wait for both Ella and her father to see it. Picking up my phone again, I take a quick shot of the giant teddy bear that sits on the floor next to the nursery's window and post it on social media.

I stopped posting for a while, not wanting Sebastian to track me down by using my social accounts, but after all that has happened, I find myself posting more of my life there. I have an even larger following than before, but I honestly don't post for the audience. I now post for my sister, Mila. So she can be a part of my life even if she's just seeing me through a screen or a post. The second the post is up with a teddy bear emoji as a caption the notifications from my followers pop up in large amounts. The world still doesn't know I am pregnant, and I am planning to keep it that way until I can't hide it anymore, but it has been fun to read the news articles that speculate and lie about our lives. I might be in the same business, but I swore to never publish something that hasn't been fact-checked or confirmed. Once I see the heart notification from my sister's account, I smile and place the phone back down on the table.

"You're so beautiful when you smile, darling."

I gasp when the father of my sweet spawns startles me. Grabbing my chest, I breathe out. "Dammit, Sebastian. How long have you been standing there like a creep?"

"Long enough." He smiles, enters the nursery, and shuts the door behind him. I narrow my eyes at him when I notice he has ditched the cane which I point out a second later, and he just shrugs, walking towards me with confidence no one but he possesses, wearing a full three-piece suit. He looks so handsome and so alive. So mine.

"I do not need a cane to walk. You are being irrational." So I forced him to use the thing so he would have help and didn't put too much pressure on his body. Sue me for caring. Although, I enjoyed the way he cringed when he saw the offending item. He gave me an ear full of how that shit made him feel old.

I did enjoy that, I won't lie.

"You are so vain, Sebastian." I shake my head at him.

"And you are a bully, my darling."

Shrugging, "You know what you were getting into…"

"I did." He smiles wide, leans down over me, and places a kiss on the top of my head. "You smell like strawberries…" he sniffs me like Ella does her mutt.

"You really need to stop sniffing me, Sebastian. That's just weird." I scrunch up my nose.

"As weird as you watching me sleep at night when you're supposed to be getting sleep yourself?"

Oh, so he noticed.

Giving him a bored look, I tell him. "I am making sure you don't leave me with two kids and an ugly dog to fend for myself." I try to make a joke out of it, but my fear transmits.

Sebastian drops to his knees and forces me to look down at him. That's when I noticed a medium-sized white box that he placed on my lap. "I am not going anywhere, love." He says this with such ferocity and sincerity that I can't help but believe him, even knowing he can't control that. Not when he has enemies gunning for him.

Smiling, I nod, not wanting to dampen the mood. "What's this?"

"Open it and see." He gently taps my nose, and I never thought that would make a woman like me swoon, but dammit it does. Everything this man does makes me feel like the heroine in a romance novel. Very cliche, I know.

Crazy curious, I open the box to find a black chocolate heart inside.

"Sebastian, you menace."

Offering me a crooked smile. "You did ask for chocolate…"

"I did, but this is too much."

"Nonsense." He hands me a small wooden object. "My heart, go ahead and break it."

Once, I would have taken this chocolate heart that symbolizes his beating one, and smashed it on top of his head, but now… now, I just want to treasure it. Treasure him.

Smashing the chocolate, I notice something sparkling inside. This man…

Using my hands, I break some more pieces of chocolate until I find what hides inside.

A necklace.

My necklace.

The one he gifted me so many days and nights ago that I left behind, not wanting anything that reminded me of what I thought were lies.

The diamond necklace with a snowflake pendant.

The difference is that now instead of one snowflake, it has two.

Two beautiful diamond snowflakes.

Strong hands touch mine as I hold the necklace, trying really hard not to cry. "Two little snowflakes for our children…"

Damnit.

There goes a tear.

Ugh, I blame these hormones and Sebastian's ability to make me cry with pure joy.

Sebastian takes the necklace from my hands, stands, and hovers over me. "Pull your hair aside, darling."

I do, and he works on placing the necklace on my neck.

"There." He stands back and watches me with so much love and heat in his eyes, there's always heat when he looks at me. "Perfect."

Placing the box filled with broken pieces of chocolate on the floor, I rise from the rocking chair, I stand on my tippy toes and give him a quick kiss before smiling up at him. "I do love diamonds…" 'Not more than I love you' is on the tip of my tongue.

He grabs me by the waist and pushes my body closer to his. "I love you."

Melting, I smile at him and save this memory in my mind forever. Moments like this one make me believe all that I went, all we both went through, was worth it because it led us here.

To this moment in time.

To where we were always meant to end up.

Each other's arms.

"And I love you, Sebastian…" It's the first time I've said it aloud to him while he was conscious.

"You better." He says playfully.

"Don't ruin it with your obnoxious cockiness." I snap.

"You love my cockiness, Arianna. You don't fool me."

Rolling my eyes at him, we are both silent, just holding each other until I remember to ask him. "How did the press conference go?"

"Great, as expected." He shrugs, smiling like it is nothing. I guess to someone with Sebastian's confidence, standing in front of the press while millions watch is nothing.

"Are you close to…"

Knowing where I am headed, he answers. "I delivered the news that the man who shot at us has been found to give the country peace of mind."

"Did you really find him? "I narrow my eyes.

He gives me a 'are you serious' look. "Did you doubt I would?"

"Not for a second." It's true. I've come to learn that Sebastian can make anything happen. It wouldn't surprise me if one day he moved a mountain with just one thought. That's how magnificent he is to me.

He kisses me softly and then looks down at my stomach. You can't really tell that I am pregnant with the long sleeve oversized shirt, but you can feel the tiny bump. "What will you do?"

"Do you really want to know?" He asks.

"I wouldn't be asking you if I didn't. Tell me."

"I'll make him and whoever else was involved wish they never pulled that trigger."

"Good." I hiss. I usually don't wish innocent people ill, will but this time I made an exception.

We both stand there grinning like two comic book villains... Oh, what a match made in purgatory we are.

"You are vicious, darling." He smiles arrogantly at me while gently rubbing my stomach. He's so whipped for this kid already.

"I am." It's true. I am ruthless and vicious when it comes to the people I care about, now more than before, because I no longer feel trapped. I have a voice and the means to fight back.

His eyes turn soft then he steps back from me and looks around. "The nursery is coming along beautifully."

"It is..." I say proudly, waiting for him to notice the new addition. Suddenly becoming nervous because what if I overstepped? What if he doesn't want the painful reminder?

I hold my breath, staring as he has his back to me, looking at the three large frames hanging in a straight line on the wall that's in front of the baby's crib.

The frames hold three photos.

One is a portrait of Sebastian and Ella.

The other photo is of the three of us, plus Benjamin in Paris.

The last one, though.

The last one I recruited Benjamin to help me with this because I could not for the life of me find a picture of them.

It is a family portrait of young Sebastian, at maybe six or seven years old, dressed in a full suit, looking dashing as always, while his parents, Vivienne and Ronan Kenton, embrace him lovingly.

When I look at that image of the three of them, I feel the love they all had for each other.

I see what true love and family is…

I see what I never had until Sebastian.

I stand there looking at him as he remains silent for a second too long before he turns his head and looks back at me with a look that freezes me in place. Then he abruptly turns, giving me no time to prepare before he takes me into his arms and seals his mouth over mine, taking every single breath and keeping it for himself.

When he pulls away, his eyes shine bright like two stars. "You're incredible. Thank you…" He says roughly, his tone holding many emotions.

Instead of agreeing with him, as I would normally, I tell him. "I was thinking…if we indeed have a baby girl, we could name her after your mother."

"Vivienne…" he breathes out smiling from ear to ear.

Vivienne Kenton.

Named after the woman who gave so much love to her only son. The son who grew up to become the man I love most in this world.

I thought long and hard of names for girls one night while I was watching as he slept. Somehow, it never occurred to me to think of boys' names. But then Vivienne came to mind, and when I researched the name, it sealed the deal.

Vivienne derives from the French word Viviana meaning 'lively.'

From the Latin word Vivianus–meaning "alive."

Perfect for the little human growing inside of me.

My heart once felt like it was dead inside my chest, but here I am now.

Alive and so very blessed.

Loved.

Nodding. "Vivi for short. It has a nice ring, don't you think?"

Sebastian nods in agreement. Then bends down, grabs a piece of chocolate, and hands it to me. "Perfect for her. Now feed my baby."

Rolling my eyes playfully, I take the chocolate from his hand and pop it into my mouth. With my mouth full, I say, "Ours, Sebastian. Our baby."

"Ours…" He breathes out before kissing my lips again.

Ours has never sounded better.

Chapter 29

HANDSOME DEVIL

Bastian

"Tell me how you hate me." — A

"Looking sharp, Mr. President." The rough accented voice of one of Thiago Sandoval's men, Armando, greets me as soon as I step foot inside the dirty, rundown building where he usually handles business when he's in the city. And when I say handle business I mean as in someone is getting whacked. "*Armando, ¿cómo estás?*" I replied in perfect Spanish. The man grins. "*Todo bien, jefe. Ya veo que tu español ha mejorado.*" Picking an invisible lint off my suit jacket, I shrug. "*Un poco. Quiero poder mandar al carajo a tu jefe en su idioma natal.*" Laughing, he steps back, moves towards the side doors, opens them, and shoves a man with his hands tied behind his back and a hood over his head into the room. His black clothes are covered in blood and filth. "Be nicer to the boss, si? He sent you a welcome back to life present. Well... what's left of him." Shrugging out of my suit jacket, I hand it to Banning and signal him to stay back as I step farther inside the room, towards where Armando has the man my team has been searching for months. Inhaling, I notice that with every step I take further into the room, the putrid smell of torture becomes stronger.

Fuck, it reeks of blood, urine, and excrement.

"The boss had fun with this cunt before handing him over. Apparently, Hank here makes enemies everywhere he goes. Enemies that were way too willing to give him up." Armando walks over to me and nods. "Here you go, man." He shoves the silent man to the ground. "Pick your poison." I silently walk over to a table on the left, where there's a rope, a gun, and a butcher knife.

I've been daydreaming about this moment since I woke up from the coma. A coma this son of a bitch put me in when he shot at me in the chest. I lost almost four months with my child and Arianna because of this lowlife, and as much as that infuriates me and fills me with hate towards this useless cunt, the thought that he aimed a gun towards Arianna's direction enrages me more than the damage he caused me. It has me seeing red.

Choosing the butcher knife, I turn back to the man kneeling in the center of the room. He's shaking his head, but the hood prevents me from seeing his face, so I remove it. I remove it so my face will be the last thing he sees before I send him straight to hell. The second his eyes register who is standing before him, his eyes grow big in recognition and… fear. Annoyed by his muffled screams, I pull down his gag.

"You motherfu—" No. I refuse to listen to this stupid cunt. Pulling the gag over his mouth again, I almost laugh when the imbecile falls face down and tries to wiggle his way across the floor. "Kevin Voight…" Tsk. I stay in place, just watching the snake slither across the room, trying to escape as if he could. As if I would let him walk out of here with his life after he endangered the life of the woman I love. "I could ask you why and who paid you to come after me, but you will only lie to my face. And I hate liars. Besides, we both know why you did it. Croix Jameson correct?" The man screams, but again the screams are muffled by the gag. So I continue playing with my prey.

"You're a cop, yes? Fifteen years on patrol. Squeaky clean record? A good cop. A stupid man but a good cop. You're also a man who disagrees with my decision to pardon the life of the criminal who murdered a fellow cop, correct?" Voight screams quietly, but his heavy breathing is the only indication that he's listening. "So you took it upon yourself to track me down and shoot at me. Shoot at my woman..." Walking forward, I kick him in the side, knocking him to his back. "You aimed your gun at me where I was standing with an innocent woman who had nothing to do with my decision, and you pulled the trigger and opened fire, not caring if she was a casualty." The fucker screams, and it only makes this all the much sweeter. I do not enjoy blood.

But I am a man who enjoys spilling the blood of anyone who hurts Arianna. It brings me great pleasure.

And this fucker intended to hurt my woman, and for that... Well, he must pay.

I take in a deep breath, crouch down, and slice the man's neck from ear to ear. I watch the blood squirt all over both of us. His body now convulsing before movement ceases completely.

Standing to my feet, I hold out the knife to Armando, and he smiles at me. "Always good to see you, Mr. President." He nods and gets to work on disposing of the body while I turn to Banning and smile from ear to ear. "Fuck, that was quick, gruesome, and quite a show, boss." Banning laughs, then hands me my jacket. I shrug it on and pass through the metal doors that lead outside. Once, I stood back as criminals handled the darker side of my business and did the torturing themselves, but for her...For Arianna Luna Parisi, I am the judge, jury, and executioner.

Forever holding an unmatched power. Looking down at the blood staining my white shirt, I smile.

This is who I have become. All in the name of love.

When I climb inside the waiting car, I feel a buzzing in my pocket.

Reaching inside my suit, I pull out my phone and see a new message notification.

Speaking of the beautiful devil.

Wife: Where are you, Sebastian?

Smiling like a fool, I text her back.

Me: Why are you awake this late?

Wife: Why are you out this late?

Me: Needed to handle business.

Wife: I suppose it has nothing to do with your presidential duties by how late it is.

Arianna is not naive nor is she weak, and both sides of me never scared her. Not even when she was an eighteen-year-old girl.

Not once was she afraid of the things I was capable of.

That is one of the many reasons why I love this woman.

She is similar to me.

In almost every way.

Some say opposites attract, but that was not the case with us.

I am her, and she is me.

We fit.

Perfectly.

Me: Go to bed, baby. I'll be home soon.

I find myself amused when I see the little three dots that tell me she's typing a message. They appear and disappear for almost a minute before a message pops up.

Wife: Stay safe and come home.

Wife: White heart.

Pocketing my phone, I feel the scars of my attack. Before the shooting, they would have made me want to send her ass away from my world and keep her safe where no one could hurt her, but that is just not possible now.

I'm too far gone, and she is now a permanent fixture in my world.

I'll do whatever is necessary to keep her there and safe.

Whatever it takes. Even get my hands fucking dirty and bloody whenever someone as much as look at her the wrong way.

***

Once I arrived at the White House, I found her sitting quietly in the theater, room watching the late news. This is something she does a lot lately. She either stays up watching me sleep or watches the news until she can find sleep.

It's becoming a habit and one that concerns me.

I know she worries even when she put on a brave face for us all. She doesn't need to do that with me, but she does it anyway, and I love her all the more for it. Closing the door gently behind me, I step inside the room, walking towards where she's seated on the big cream-colored sofa, looking so stunning, that I am left with no choice but to admire her beauty.

I have never met anyone more perfect.

More effortlessly beautiful.

Even more, now that she is glowing with my baby inside of her.

My baby.

I never wanted nor cared for children, not really, but then Ellaiza happened, and she turned my world upside down in the best way.

But that was it. It was supposed to be just us.

Then this perfect creature with golden hair, emerald eyes, and the most beautiful heart burst through the ice walls around my heart and made a place for herself. Now, she is giving me that gift inside of her belly. Another child.

Our baby.

"Did you have fun?" her sultry voice makes the hairs on the back of my headstand. Fuck, I am so horny for this woman, and the fact that she is pregnant with my baby intensifies the constant need I have for her.

"Not, really. No." I say with a smile on my face.

"You stained your shirt." She points a beige nail at the blood stains on my white shirt with a bored look on her face while raising a perfect eyebrow at me.

"So I did." I don't look away from her face, enjoying this quiet moment between us.

"Did he scream?" She mumbles, her eyes now on my face.

"Like a pig for slaughtered." I reply truthfully.

"Huh." Her green eyes narrow.

"What is it?"

"You usually bring me a souvenir when you go out terrorizing people. Has the romance fizzled out already, Mr. President?"

Laughing, I place the white box I have been holding behind my back since I walked inside the room on her lap. "Never, darling."

Arianna's eyes grow big when she looks at me and then down at the box on her lap. It's quite comical. "The last time you went out at this hour you brought me back my father's finger. Is this another body part, Sebastian? One was enough." She asks with a small smile on her face. See? Deviant.

Unafraid. Mine.

Getting comfortable on the sofa, I lean back and point toward her box. "Open it."

A moment later she does, and then her eyes come back to mine when she spots what's inside.

"A car? You got me a car?" She holds up the keys to her new White Roll-Royce Phantom.

Shrugging, "Banning mentioned something about a push present."

She throws her head back and laughs and that right there has always and will always be my favorite sight. "I haven't given birth, Sebastian."

Reaching forward, I move a strand of golden hair that stuck to her lips, and instantly I become hard as fuck, when her breath hitches and her eyes grow intense. "I like spoiling you. Sue me."

Her eyes go soft, and as much as I love forever Arianna, I am addicted to her sweet side, too. It only comes out when she's with our daughter or when it is just the two of us, and like the possessive fuck that I am, I prefer it that way. "You've given me so much already." I sit, watching as she moves from her spot on the sofa and straddles me. My hands instantly go to her naked thighs. She is wearing one of those long shirts she loves so much, and that shouldn't get me this hard, but she makes even a simple, large shirt look sexy as hell. Leaning forward, I place a soft kiss on her lips before pulling back and staring into those green eyes I love so much. "Not nearly enough."

A moment of silence passes between us before she speaks again. "Are we safe here?" The anxiety in her tone makes me sick and pissed. It makes me want to go back in time, and kill the fucker more creatively and painfully for causing this fear in her. "I'll kill anyone who blinks at you wrong. Does that make you feel safer? "The fear fades and is quickly replaced by curiosity. "Would you kill more for me, Sebastian? I thought you hated blood." I do hate blood.

It reminds me of shit I wish I could forget.

Grabbing the back of her neck, I bring her mouth closer to mine. "With a passion, but I love you more."

"You are so obsessed, Sebastian. It is kind of sad." She mocks playfully and pats my wolf tattoo. A tattoo I got the same night I broke her heart. If that doesn't say obsessed, the one inked on my ring finger does.

Then, in a swift move, she leaves my lap, sits seat next to me, and spreads her thighs. That's when I see she is not wearing panties.

Fuck.

I feel my mouth go dry as she spreads her thighs even wider. "You are still recuperating, so be gentle." She whispers.

I'll be gentle, yes, but because of the baby, not because I was shot months ago. If it were only that and there was no baby in her, I would impale her with how long it has been since I stuck my cock inside of her tight and hot walls. "I can be gentle," I promise.

Rising to my full height, I unbutton my slacks and lower the zipper while she watches with heat in her eyes. I am obsessed, yes but so is she. Lowering myself on the sofa on top of her, her legs automatically encircle my hips, and she lifts them so that she is pressed against my very hard erection. "Are you horny for my cock, darling?" I tease.

Then, like the vicious little brat that she is, she clamps her mouth down on my carotid, causing me to curse and jerk. I take it back. Vicious Arianna will forever be my favorite side of her although her sweet side that doesn't happen a lot makes me hard as fuck too. "Shut up and fuck me, Sebastian," she hisses.

Well if she's that hard up for cock…

Rearing up, I spread her thighs wider and notch my cock at her very hot and wet entrance, and without warning, I slam into her with one quick thrust of my hip.

Fuckkkkkkk.

Inside her tight pussy will always be my favorite place to be.

Because just like every time, she feels tight and goddamn heavenly.

The heat and tightness of her pussy around my cock cause my eyes to roll back in my head.

My head falls backward, and I groan, long and loud.

Almost as if she was responding to my moan, she follows with one of her own. "Go deeper," she breathes out. "Please, Sebastian."

"You're so tight. So perfect and mine, darling." I pull my hips back until the head of my cock is the only thing left inside of her, then thrust forward, filling her so deep, hard, and fast that her body jolts with the force of my thrust. Her unbound breasts underneath her oversized shirt jerk and jiggle with each thrust, making my eyes take in the sight before me.

God, she's a vision.

Her gorgeous bare pussy taking every inch, and her breasts, now bigger because of the pregnancy, bouncing with each thrust.

She jokes that I am obsessed with her.

It's not a joke but a fact.

I am addicted to her.

Obsessed to the point this obsession will one day lead me to madness.

I am sure of it.

Gritting my teeth, I try to hold off on coming like a prepubescent punk with his first taste of pussy. Because the way her green eyes look, as if she is so dazed and confused that she could be high on something has me wanting – no needing to go over the edge and lose myself in her.

"Fuck, your cunt drives me wild, baby," I say when her eyes meet mine. "You are such a good girl when you take my cock." I praise her. "My good girl." Three years of celibacy can make a man go crazy and say stupid shit while in the heat of the moment.

Her teeth bite down on her plump lower lip, and I can't stop myself from jerking at the sight.

"That's it. Be my good girl and touch my pussy," I instruct. My pussy. Because it is mine, just as much as it is hers. Like a good girl, she does what she's told. I watch in filthy fascination as her fingers travel down her rounded belly until she slips them all the way inside of her, making me groan like a sick fuck. Out of my mind with need and lust, and strung up on her, I grab her hips and pound her hard and fast.

Her moaning turns to sharp squeaks, and then I can feel her pussy rippling, letting me know that she is just as close as I am.

"I am close," I hiss. "Get there, darling. Play with that pretty little clit and come undone for me, yes?"

I pound harder, watching as she rubs her clit faster with one hand, and with the other, she plays with a pink nipple. The sight does it for me. One second my balls feel tight and then I groan, filling her with a few deep, hard thrusts, shooting my release deep inside of her.

"Ugghhh," I grunt. "Take my cum." I ride the high of ecstasy watching as Arianna lets go.

"Oh, God," she wheezes, eyes rolling back in her head so hard that the whites of her eyes show. "Oh, fuck, Sebastian."

I grit my teeth and pulse inside of her, emptying so much cum into her that, if she weren't already pregnant, that would have done it.

Fuck, so hot.

Nothing has ever felt like this.

No one has ever made me lose my mind while in the thrust of pure adulterated passion like my woman.

When we both come to a jolting stop, panting and spent, we stare at each other. "I told you to be gentle," she whispers up at me with a crooked grin. My otherworldly vixen. "You almost broke me…" I pull out, and then look down between us to watch my release leak out of her onto the white cushions. A sick sense of satisfaction courses through me as I watch my cum leak out of her hole. Mine.

Always mine. "You make me lose my mind, woman," I growl, reaching forward and swirling the milky substance around her opening before dragging it to her clit.

She jerks as if she is too sensitive to touch, and I pull back watching her with a grin. My cum inside of her is the sexiest sight I have ever seen.

She sits up, tugs her sweatshirt down low, and takes my lips in hers, biting softly.

"Can you go again, old man?" she grins with a raised brow.

I like her pregnant and needy for my cock. Needing what only I can give her. "I'll show you old…" With that, I gently maneuver her until she's on her knees on the sofa and get her to choke on her words.

And my cock…

Then I fuck that sass out of her three more times.

That'll show her old.

Chapter 30
WRAPPED IN LOVE
Arianna

"It will always be you, for me." — A

Two months later

Have you ever felt true peace? I didn't know how that felt until I met Sebastian. I had short intervals of happiness, yes, but never peace.

Now, here in his world, all I feel is peace.

Autumn is almost over, and as the seasons change, so has my body. Growing a human inside of me. A human who will be here in the winter.

"Beautiful! Yes! That's the one!" Micha, one of the photographers that work for my magazine and creative director, praises me as I stand in the middle of the east garden room dressed in all white.

For this occasion, I chose a white crisscross top and a matching skintight, long skirt while my huge belly is on full display. I look almost angelic and so does the decor around me. Sweet, tender, and yeah a bit over the top. There's a lavender background behind me, while everything else is white and silver. There are dozens of gold roses at my feet and some golden rose petals are in between my golden locks making me look as if I were from another world.

Heavenly even.

A maternity shoot.

In my defense, it wasn't my idea. My team is to blame for wanting me to be featured on the cover of next month's issue of my magazine, Vive. They came up with the argument that working moms and pregnant women should be showcased more and praised in the media. That's how they convinced me to do this, plus Oliver let it slip in front of Ella, and of course, she begged to be part of it as well.

I couldn't say no.

So now I am here.

I'm six months pregnant now, and my belly can't be hidden by clothes.

This will also serve as my pregnancy announcement, I guess.

But I am not going to lie. I can't wait to see people's reactions to the news of my pregnancy. I'm having the president's baby, and we're unwed.

Oh, the glorious scandal.

"Mommy, gosh, you look like an angel!" My girl gasps bringing me back to the present. My glam team did a wonderful job with this look. I didn't want to look over the top, showcase my natural beauty, and that's what we did.

My long golden hair is curled at the ends while the hairstylist gave me curtain bangs like I used to wear when I was younger. Every day I feel more like myself.

As if parts of who I once was are slowly coming back to me.

Turning my head, I smile at Ella who, like me, is dressed in all white and has gold-colored roses in her hands and hair. My kid is so beautiful.

I thought I knew what beauty, was but then I met this little girl.

A little girl who knows my heart.

Who owns my heart just the same as her father.

"Thank you, baby." I smile, and at the same time, gold petals fall from above me. Micha captures the moment, screaming like a crazy man. Feeling the moment. "Come." I urge her to join me because none of this would mean anything if she weren't in the photos.

I carefully pick her up and place her on my belly. She then wraps her tiny arms around my neck and gives me Eskimo kisses while Micha captures the moment with his camera. "Hey, mommy." Ella takes a strand of my hair, twisting it in her tiny finger.

I know that sweet tone.

It's her 'I want something' tone.

"Yes?" I reply, suspicious.

"Can we go eat cupcakes and macaroons later? Baby sister is craving sweets."

Raising her higher, I ask, "Oh, is that right?"

"Yes!" She tilts her head, and her grin widens into the sweetest smile.

How can I say no to that face? Easy, I can't.

"Fine," I growl and pepper her face with kisses, making her giggle.

Yeah, that sound, it's what life is all about.

Her and her father's laugh make the world stop for me.

'Call it what you want' by Taylor Swift blasts through the speakers the team brought with them as we pose for ten minutes straight. Then my baby decides to make my bladder its personal plaything, and now I need to go to the bathroom. Setting Ellaiza down on the floor, I turn to Micha to tell him that it's a wrap, when the double doors open and Sebastian walks in dressed in a black suit, with his black hair pulled back and grin that makes him look like my very own devil who has come to take the soul right out of my body.

Yummm... The thirsty devil on my shoulder whispers as I watch

Sebastian walk in, sucking the air out of the room as always.

"Dad." Ella runs toward her father, and he effortlessly picks her up.

"Daddy." He corrects her at the same time he tickles her belly. Sebastian moves forward until he reaches where I am standing and looks at me, as if he's hungry. As if he wishes he could eat me alive. No one has ever made me feel the way Sebastian has without saying a word.

He sets my body aflame just by looking at me.

With Ella and my growing belly between us, he kisses my lips softly. "Hey, baby," he said.

"Hi." I breathe out while he smiles wide.

Damn you, tyrant.

I can't get enough of you.

"Oh, that one right there! Yes! Perfect. Don't you guys dare move!" In Sebastian's arms, I turn to see Micha with the camera trained on us. "What a beautiful family."

"Micha! Take all the photos with daddy!" Ella screeches, bouncing in her father's arms and holding onto my neck. Sebastian's eyes melt when he sees our daughter's excitement then his gaze lands on me at the same time his hand touches my belly. For a second, my breath is being held hostage as I look into his blue-gray eyes. Then it happens as if sensing that its father is right there, the baby kicks.

It kicks, and the subtle movement feels like a dozen butterflies spreading their wings inside of me. So sweet. So pure.

We both look down in amazement at where Sebastian's hand is touching my belly. The flash of a camera goes off capturing the moment Baby Kenton made its presence known.

"Well… I guess this one also takes after you." I tease.

"How's that?" Sebastian rubs my belly while kissing Ella's cheeks.

"This baby is not even born and is already stealing all the attention." I huff. "There's a beautiful mini tyrant inside of me." Sebastian laughs, not at all bothered by my comment. Instead, he looks proud. Rolling my eyes playfully, I pat his suit. "Now, if you don't mind, I need to go to the ladies' room."

"Uh-oh. That means little sister is being a nuisance." Ella gasps comically and then laughs like a crazy person when her father tickles her stomach, making us both laugh in return with her.

Baby kicks, laughs, and love.

Us.

All wrapped in love.

Our eyes hold as he gives me a slow and gorgeous smile.

Everything else has stopped around us.

It was just us.

Smiling at each other as if we're the only people in the room.

As if we're all the other wants to ever see.

Yup, if it wasn't obvious before. It is now.

I am terrifyingly in love with this man.

***

"Yummy, yummy." Ella munches on a strawberry macaroon as we make our way back to the White House after spending half the afternoon sitting in a cozy, rustic, and very pink cafe that took Shaw almost half an hour to find. I should have known something was up when a secret service agent had no clue where the cafe was located.

Isn't ihis job to verify the address and the safety of the location beforehand? This time he did not do that.

"You want one, mommy?" I suppress the need to gag when Ella offers me a strawberry macaroon.

My baby, like her father, has horrible taste in food. When I decline, she shrugs and then shoves the entire thing in her mouth, making me laugh at how adorable she looks acting as if she has no manners and dressed as if she were British royalty. We are both wearing matching outfits per her request. Leaning back, I keep my eyes trained on the driver's side where Shaw is busy focusing on the busy street ahead of us, and then I whisper to Ella. "Spill it, kid."

She side-eyes me with a suspicious look on her face. "Spill what?" She asks, with her mouth full and her sticky hands raised in the air.

She's as cute as she is clever.

"I know this sudden craving for sweets of yours was an excuse to get me out of the house." It has to be. The tyrant has not left my side in months, and now he was more than eager to let us out of his sight? I call bullshit. "So tell me… what is going on back home?" Ella side-eyes me, giving me attitude, and I would be proud as hell if it wasn't aimed at me. "I don't know what you mean…"

Sure you don't… Ella can't usually keep secrets, but this one she's keeping to herself.

"Fine, be like that." I sass her back but smile so she knows I am not mad at her. Not at all.

I just hate not knowing what's going on and Sebastian loves to surprise me. I've never been big on surprises but now that's all there is with this family. Surprises.

"Oh, mommy, don't worry! You will love it!" There. She let it slip, but instead of giving her grief about it, I just throw my head back on the car's headrest and smile all the way back home.

***

"Surprise!" White and gold confetti explodes all around us as we enter the main room.

"Yay!" Ella jumps up and down next to me holding my hand and pulling me further inside the room. "Surprise, mummy! We gots you!" Holding her hand, I stand there, taking in the room, which has been transformed into what seems like a baby shower.

White and gold balloons float on the ceiling, while in every corner of the room, there are brown balloons in all sizes in the shape of teddy bears.

The color theme is gender-neutral, with gold, white, and brown.

The phrase 'Oh, baby' is everywhere in the room.

On one of the walls, there is a beautiful photo backdrop that reads 'We Can Bearly Wait' in watercolors. On the other end of the room, where the window is situated, there is a beautiful set-up with cream, white and brown bouquets of balloons with a giant teddy bear and four pieces of baby shower blocks with letters that read 'baby'.

And lastly, in the center of the room, there's a small table with a tall white cake with an adorable teddy bear wearing a gold crown and holding onto the moon as the cake topper with a sign that read 'Baby Kenton.'

What... this is so beautiful.

So sweet.

"How about it, kid? Do you approve?" Turning, I watch as Benjamin smiles proudly at me while holding his phone up, most likely capturing this moment just like he has captured all the important moments since I came to him. Amazed and left without words, my eyes move around, taking in everything they did, and then my eyes fall on Sebastian. Dressed impeccably as always, standing next to a tower of presents wrapped in gold, white and brown paper.

I didn't think to throw a baby shower never crossed my mind since my only friends and family are standing right here in this room, and I can count them with one hand. But if I had planned it, this would have been the theme I would have chosen. They did this.

For me.

For Baby Kenton.

I smile when Ella lets go of my hand and makes a run to the cake table, where a dozen cupcakes are waiting for her. She's in sugar heaven.

Cake pops, cupcakes, macaroons, and more.

She picks a cupcake and starts munching on it as if she didn't stuff her face barely an hour ago.

"I…" I swallowed hard before successfully getting the words out. "I love it." Smiling at Benjamin and then at Sebastian, I whisper. "So much." I am touched that they did this for me. Three men and a baby girl went to all this trouble to celebrate me and my baby. Tears well in my eyes as I think of how lucky I am. How much life has gotten better in just a couple of months. How loved I am. Damn, hormones. The hormones and the baby have turned me soft.

Benjamin steps forward, kisses me on the forehead, and looks down at me with gentle eyes. "I'm so fuckin' proud of you, kid."

"Proud?" My brows furrowed. "I got knocked up, Benjamin." I joke.

Laughing, he shakes his head at me. "Look at the family that you created for yourself. Look how far you've come, and fuck, look at that sweet smile." He, too, smiles from ear to ear. A dimple shows on his cheek, giving him a boyish look. "Look at you, little fighter."

That does it. A tear falls from my eye, and I quickly wipe it away, feeling embarrassed. "I love you, Benjamin."

There, I said it, and it didn't kill me.

"See? You finally said the words, and it didn't kill you." He jokes, reading my mind.

"Don't push it…" I narrow my eyes with a small smile on my face. He laughs, lovingly pokes my nose, and walks away toward Ellaiza, who has her phone out and is most likely taking pictures for me to post on our joint social media account. My little social media addict.

'If You Love Her' by Forest Blakk's version with Meghan Trainor, starts to blast from the speakers. A second later I am being lifted by strong arms that I know so well and placed on top of black loafers. Sebastian."Hello, beautiful." He smiles down at me as he sways us to the beat of the song.

"Well, hello, sneaky." I teased. "You were busy today."

Chuckling, he asks. "I take it that the tears in your eyes are because you like the surprise?"

"I love it," I tell him truthfully.

He pulls me closer until our lips are only a breath away."I love you." He says fiercely. My stomach flips when he says it, or maybe it's the baby. "I love you more…" I breathe out.

"Impossible." Happiness dances in his eyes.

Grinning, I tell him. "Let's agree to disagree then."

He laughs and that also makes my stomach flip and my heart beat faster. He's more than my best friend. Forever and then some, and I choose him over and over again. I sing along to the song in my head while in Sebastian's embrace. He moves us in place as the song plays on, and Ellaiza dances around the room while Benjamin and Shaw stuff their faces with baby-sized food. Joy fills my heart.

"Hey, darling?" Sebastian kisses the side of my head.

"Yes?"

"Will you go on a date with me?" He asks, and I swear if I didn't know him, I would think the pink staining his cheeks is because he is blushing.

"A date?" I ask with wide eyes.

Holding me tighter, he smirks. "I intend to get forever with you… right."

Forever.

I find myself blushing as well when I look up at him. "I'd like that."

Smiling wide, he nods and pulls me closer.

"Sebastian?"

"Yes?"

"Can we eat now?" As if on cue, my stomach makes a crass grumbling noise. Thank God for the music. No one heard.

I've been meaning to go to the buffet set up in the corner after I smelled the delicious scent of barbecue wings. Lately, my cravings are all over the place.

"Yeah…darling. We can eat." Sebastian laughs.

I grin.

And that's what we do the rest of the day.

We laugh, eat, and well… love.

Corny, I know.

But hey, that's love.

Chapter 31
JE T'AIME

Arianna

"If we go down then we do it together." — A

The next evening, I find myself walking into what looks like a classic French bistro-style restaurant instead of the White House's dining room.

The last time I was in a French-style restaurant with Sebastian was in Paris. The vibe there was fancier and more elegant, while this setup is more casual and relaxed with a cafe-style atmosphere.

This is so incredibly thoughtful of him.

Lately, I barely left the house and if I am honest tonight, I was in no mood of being around strange people in a crowded restaurant. This sweet date is all I need.

The lighting is soft and illuminates the space with warmth at the same time the moonlight enters from the windows.

In the middle of the room, there is a round marble pedestal bistro dining table with a pedestal base. From all the way here, I can see the table is decorated with lit candles and red roses. In fact, there are red roses in every corner of the room. Sebastian never fails to shower me with not only material stuff but also roses and candy.

The man knows me so well.

As I move farther inside the room, soft music starts to play in the background, and suddenly, a feeling of deja vu takes over me, reminding me that I've been here before. The feeling takes me back in time to those blissful days in Paris.

A date.

This is his idea of a date now.

Once, he would have gotten a jet and flown us to Paris for the night, but now that I am pregnant, he's been more careful and even a bit more tyrannical, which I don't really mind. Not at all.

Since I can't fly, he brought my favorite city to me.

"Bienvenue à Paris, mon amour." Sebastian's husky voice washes over me as he enters from the side door. As if my imagination conjured him, he comes closer dressed in dark gray slacks, and a white long-sleeve dress shirt with the two top buttons undone, revealing golden skin, and dark ink. He is looking dashing as ever with a smile on his face and suddenly I am very grateful to Baby Kenton for not acting up tonight. This afternoon I wasn't feeling so good and I was close to throwing on my favorite oversized t-shirt and putting my hair up in a messy bun because I had no energy to get all dressed up. So close really but then after a long nap and a chocolate bar the little tyrant inside of me behaved just enough for me to enjoy this dinner with his father.

Tonight, I opted to dress comfortably but still elegantly, choosing a maternity solid-rib-knit black cami dress and I paired it with clear, single-band heels because although I had to give in and start wearing godawful maternity clothing, there's no way I was going to give up my heels. That's where I draw the line. I gave this baby my body. I sacrificed both my work and sleeping schedule for him or her, too.

Hell, I am even eating foods I've never eaten in my entire life for this kid. The heels? I am not giving them up. Nope.

Half of my hair is up in a messy ponytail, while the other half falls in soft waves down my back. In my ears, are diamond studs, matching perfectly with the gift Sebastian gave me. The two snowflakes' diamond necklace.

I feel beautiful tonight. The look Sebastian is giving me now makes me feel beautiful, too. Desired.

Loved.

Throughout the day, I had butterflies dancing around with my baby in my stomach. This is not the first time I have had dinner with Sebastian, but something about this time feels different.

I intend to get forever with you right. His words replay in my mind.

Forever with Sebastian.

"C'est beau..." I breathe out in wonder as Sebastian takes me in his arms and kisses me senselessly. God, I love the taste of this man. Mint, whiskey, and cigar. I moan aloud when he swipes his tongue against mine.

Perhaps it's the hormones.

Breaking the kiss, he smiles and helps me to my seat. "You look stunning, but you know this." He whispers.

"I do, but it's sweet of you to point it out." I grin when he rolls his eyes playfully. Taking his seat, he says. "I never thought sweet would be an adjective you would use in a sentence about me, darling."

Raising my glass of water, I take a sip before replying. "There's a lot of sweetness underneath that cocky and asshole-ish exterior, Sebastian." I roll my eyes at him when he grins. "Touché, darling."

Shaking my head at him, I look down at the table to find mini-French appetizers. My stomach growls, and Sebastian laughs, passing me a one-bite appetizer. "I see my baby is hungry."

"We've been over this, Sebastian. 'Our baby.' I narrow my eyes, taking the small piece of bread from him and popping it into my mouth. "And starving, actually," I tell him with my mouth full, all decorum goes out the window when I'm hungry sadly. Laughing, his eyes shine when he looks into mine. "I meant you, Arianna."

Oh…

I blush.

I seriously blush like a lovesick fool.

Trying my best to disguise my reaction to him because the cocky bastard finds great pleasure when he makes me blush or swoon, I quickly change the subject when the delicious goodness of the flatbread hits my taste buds. "What is this?"

"Socca. It's like a rustic flatbread and pancake rolled into one treat." He replies, while taking a bite himself. French cuisine is truly one of the best. Simple yet elegant. My type.

Wiping my mouth with a white cloth napkin, I point to the next plate. Damn, I'm hungry tonight. In my defense, I've been craving junk food all day.

"Those are French cheese puffs." He places the small plate in front of me. "They are made with cream puff dough that yields a crisp outer shell. Inside, there's a soft interior loaded with cheese."

And that's how we spend the next half hour. Me stuffing my face, and Sebastian explaining all that is going in my mouth while watching me eat.

A bit later, the servers come out to refill our drinks, water, and iced tea. Since I can't drink, Sebastian is being sympathetic and has iced tea with me.

I do miss wine, though.

So much.

A delicious and odd-as-hell-looking pizza is placed on the table between us. Sebastian whispers something to one of the servers before turning back to me. "What was that about?" I ask curiously.

Leaning forward, he cuts into what looks like a chocolate pizza and serves me a piece. Damn, that looks good. "Maurice asked for the recipe." I blinked. "How would you know it? Why didn't he ask the chef?"

"Tonight, I was the chef." He shrugs as if it's nothing.

"You can cook?" My eyes narrow. "No way."

"Yes, way." He smirks. "Take a bite. It was my mother's recipe."

His mother's recipe…

I was going to tease him about how you don't serve pizza in French cuisine, but the fact that he cooked all of this today for me and even shared a plate his mother used to make, warms my heart. Taking a bite, my eyes almost roll to the back of my head with how delicious it is. "May I ask what prompted you to cook French appetizers and pizza?" I smile softly at him, enjoying the way he eats his slice as if he's reliving a warm and sweet memory. "I wanted you to enjoy dinner without feeling nauseous." He takes another bite. "I know how you have a weird chocolate fetish." He teases. He's not wrong. I love chocolate like Ellaiza loves cupcakes. I swear I can eat chocolate all day and in all forms.

A fact Sebastian never forgets. It's sweet of him and sweet Sebastian will always be my favorite.

No, that's not true.

As much as I enjoy his tender and sweet side that he shows only to me and Ella. Savage, cocky, and downright disrespectful Sebastian takes the number one spot of my favorite sides of him. It's sick, I know.

Oh, well.

We eat in silence for a couple of minutes before I speak up. "Hey, Sebastian."

"Yes, love?"

"Tell me something no one knows about you."

Wiping his mouth with his napkin, he leans back in his chair, the shadows of the candlelight dancing on his face. Irresistibly gorgeous and the man knows it. With laughing eyes, he says. "I am obsessed with you." Rolling my eyes, I take another bite of the pizza. "Everyone is aware of that, Sebastian."

He chuckles. "That is true." He thinks about it for a while before his expression goes from soft to serious. "After my parents died, I didn't fear death. In fact, at one point, I welcomed it." My heart stops in my chest. He must've seen something in my eyes that make him soften. "That changed now."

"You're afraid of dying?" I place what remains of my pizza on the plate and take a sip of the iced tea suddenly feeling thirsty as hell.

"I am now, yes." He smiles tenderly. "Once Ellaiza came into my life, I had a new purpose and a new outlook on life. It was not just me. I had to live for my child. Then you came along and now our baby. Therefore, yes, I am terrified of dying because I don't ever want to be without you three." He breathes out.

"You're immortal, Sebastian." I try to lighten the mood. My own heart is beating too damn fast inside of my chest just at the thought of Sebastian leaving us. "You came back to life twice. I wouldn't worry about dying." He chuckles, then leans forward on the table and takes my hands in his. The instant our hands touch, I feel a shock of electricity. "How about you… what is something no one knows about you?"

I think about it for a second before I confess.

"I am afraid of the dark," I tell him, embarrassed, yet Sebastian doesn't mock me. "I know it's silly for a grown woman to be scared of the dark, but I am." I shrug feeling a bit vulnerable. "When I was little, I used to sleep with a nightlight until my father found out and told me to grow the fuck up." I laugh without humor.

Sebastian's eyes grow dark. "If I could kill that motherfucker, I would. Trust me, I would. Perhaps, I should bring you back his hands. Maybe his tongue. Would you like that?"

Laughing, this time with my whole chest. "No. Not right now, but ask me another time."

He smiles too and kisses both my hands. "You shine so brightly, darling. It shows in your eyes. Your smiles. It swirls around you, inside of you, no matter the darkness. You still shine."

I blink, butterflies starting to swirl around in my tummy.

Same, baby. Same.

My life was colorless, dark, and cold until him.

Until Sebastian.

"I need to know something," I say quietly.

"What?" he asks.

I swallow before I say, "Why the wolf?" I lift my chin towards his chest.

"I needed the reminder when the nights were dark." His intense eyes. "Every time I felt like I was drowning with how much I missed you. Every time my heart ached because of what I did… I would look in the mirror, and see you in the wolf inked on my chest. Your eyes. Your beautiful emerald eyes."

I feel tears well in my eyes.

"And the ink on your finger?" I croak out.

He smiles from ear to ear, releasing my hand and lifting his ring finger up for me to see. "I am yours. Always have been, even when I didn't know of your existence. Even then."

"Fuck, I love you." I breathe out. "I love you so damn much, Sebastian. It's not sane to love someone the way I love you."

His hand disappears under the table, and then he's holding a small box. He places a jewelry box next to my plate. Looking down at it, I ask. "More?" I shake my head at him. The man loves to spend money on us. If I didn't know better, I would actually feel like his sugar baby.

"Open it."

I do, and what I see has my heart-stopping.

A ring.

A silver band with tiny diamonds.

"I bought it in Paris, and I've been regretting not giving it to you every day since." He takes the ring out of the box, takes my hand in his, and slips the ring onto my ring finger. "Before you sass me. You should know this is not an engagement ring."

"It's not?" I look up, my eyes clashing with his.

"More like a promise ring." He kisses my hand.

"A promise..."

Nodding, he says. "I promise to never push you away when life gets hard. When bad shit happens, I will hold you tighter. I promise to always be there for you. For both of you."

I felt the sweetness of his words in my soul. "I never had this, you know." A tear falls from my eyes, and I don't wipe it away. "This joy. This type of love. I never knew it before you. You changed my life, Sebastian, and I don't think you even realize just how much. I was drowning until you breathed life into me." Looking down at the ring, then up at him. "Our love. Our love is the type I can feel in my soul, burning bright.

The type where I would know if anything happened to you because a part of me would be missing. Here," I press my hand to his chest, right above his heart. "I tried really hard to keep hating you. To stop loving you. But it was useless for me to try. When two souls are meant to be together like you and I are… that's not something you can stop." I swallow. "It's terrifying. Loving you the way I do terrifies me."

Sebastian reaches forward and traces my lips with his index finger. "Loving you, for me, feels the exact same way, darling." He says softly while his eyes are trained on my lips.

I heave a relieved breath. "Good, because I won't tolerate anything less than devotion and obsession from you," I say softly, looking into his eyes as I say it. Do I sound crazy as hell? Yes. Do I care? No, I do not.

Chuckling, "Right back at you, baby." His eyes turn heated, and then in a raspy voice, he says. "Now, come over here and show me just how much you love me." He whispers, looking deeply into my eyes.

Slowly rising from my seat, I move towards him and while Sebastian unbuckles his belt and takes his cock out, I lift my dress to my waist and straddle him.

God, I missed sex.

I missed him and it shows.

This sex would be quick, raw, and dirty. And every single bit of it is done by me.

He gives me full control.

With his heated eyes trained on me, I pull back, move my underwear to the side and impale myself on his cock.

Then, I start riding Sebastian furiously.

Threading my arms around his neck, studying his face as I fuck him. The cleft in his chin. The blueness and grayness of his eyes.

His raw beauty.

He is so handsome.

So mine.

"Oh, fuck, I'm close, darling," He hisses, leaning forward to capture one of my nipples that has slipped out, becoming available to him. I don't answer. Instead, I throw my head back and come undone with his cock buried deep inside of me.

In a matter of seconds, I feel his body become rigid, and then he is coming, too, shooting inside of my wet pussy.

Just like always, I come to long moments later when the blood finally decides to rush back to my oxygen-starved brain, with Sebastian panting under me.

His cock is still buried deep and still just as hard. "What kind of black magic have you done to me?" He asks.

I snort at that. "Nothing you haven't done to me."

Then, his hot mouth is on mine, and it feels like coming home.

Home to him.

My forever.

Chapter 32

LOVE HIM RECKLESSLY

Arianna

"You are all I'll ever need." — B

No one can accuse Sebastian Kenton of being basic because the man is extra as hell. He will never cease to amaze me. When he proposes to go all out he does it. Tonight, he decided it was the perfect night for us to go on a family date.

A family date that led him to close the Art & Tech House here in Washington. It's just the three of us.

"Oh, this is so awesome!" Ella lets go of my hand and runs toward the giant butterfly sculpture made of metal, and glass and that's decorated with white and blue lights.

It is truly beautiful, and it makes me smile. It reminds me of a beautiful blond-haired girl who dressed as a blue butterfly one Halloween night. My sister, Mila.

Nearing the giant sculpture, I snap a picture and save it to send to my sister later. I hope it makes her smile just like it did me.

"I didn't know you liked butterflies, darling. If I had known I would have purchased a butterfly garden." Sebastian says from where he standing next to me watching Ellaiza pose next to the butterfly sculpture. Turning my head, I roll my eyes, acting exasperated when I'm really not. "You would do that, wouldn't you, Sebastian?" I smile knowing that of course, the man would. Sebastian would find a way to purchase the whole state of Washington in a heartbeat, if that's what I wanted. Because that is who he is. His love language consists of acting instead of using words and, of course, opening his wallet and spoiling us rotten. Not that I mind. Not at all. Although, his sweet words and selfless acts will always mean more to me than any material item.

I feel his strong arms wrap around my waist, pulling me closer. I watch in fascination as his eyes crinkle at the corners as he gives me a small smile. Then he leans in and grates the words so close to my mouth I can taste them. "I would buy you the world if you asked me to." I believe him. "I might take you up on that offer one day, Sebastian," I whisper. And I would. As irrational as it sounds, I would love to watch this man, the man I love, move heaven and earth to make that happen for me. I truly believe if someone could make that happen, it would be Sebastian Kenton. It would be my president.

My tyrant.

He snorts in amusement. "You do that."

"Oh, my!" Ellaiza screeches, almost giving me a heart attack. Turning in Sebastian's embrace, I look to where I last saw Ella with the butterfly sculpture to find that she's gone. My frantic eyes search for her.

Where is she? My heart calms and my soul comes back to my body when I spot her tiny frame standing in front of… me. Me.

A sculpture of me to be precise.

Gasping, I step away from Sebastian, too enthralled with the sculpture made of sea glass. "How…" I croak out.

"Now everyone can see what I see," Sebastian whispers right in my ear as I feel his chest on my back. "Beauty. Elegance. Regality. You."

"Mommy, see, I told you! You're a queen! Look! Look!" My baby throws her hands in the air freaking out, while I try my damn best to hold the tears back. Damn, Baby Kenton, you've made me a crybaby.

"I see… my girl," I whisper to Ella, giving her a small smile.

With Sebastian at my back, I look closely at the piece of art made of sea glass. A piece of art Sebastian commissioned and it's now put on display for everyone to see.

It's my head, my face, my usual bitch face captured perfectly while a crown sits on top of my head.

A crown.

Once, I was mocked for my title of principessa. It was even used against me to keep me in place. Voiceless and compliant. And now… now this man, who once was my enemy, is celebrating me. Celebrating who I was and who I have become.

This beautiful man believes that I am more than I really am. I don't deserve a crown, or a title, yet Sebastian Kenton made me his queen.

A queen.

That's how he sees me.

He sees me like the piece of art in front of me.

Taking in the plaque next to the sculpture, I notice the name of the artist. V.M. The mysterious artist that's taken the world of art by storm is the creator of my piece.

Winter Storm by V.M | Materials used: Sea Glass

"No way! If you look closely, you can see tiny snowflakes and stars inside of the glass, daddy! How cool is that!" Ella presses her face to the glass, looking as enamored with the piece as I am.

"Very." Sebastian sounds amused from behind me. Turning around, I face him.

"You did this?" I ask softly.

"I did." He nods, proud of himself and cocky as ever.

"Why?"

"Because I love you." He shrugs as if that's reason enough. I guess for him, it is. Then his blue eyes shine with laughter. "And because I couldn't get a statue of you placed outside the White House. I tried, but trust me I am not giving up on that."

Crazy man…

Shaking my head in disbelief I say, "Why sea glass? The name? I-I don't know what to say…" No one has ever made me feel as beautiful, powerful, and as strong as the man before me, yet he makes me weak at the same time. I feel everything when I am with him when before I didn't feel much.

One strong arm pulls me closer while his hand falls on my belly. "The sea has always reminded me of you, darling. The moon and the stars do, as well. That's why I had the artist incorporate the snowflakes and the stars in the piece." I look into Sebastian's eyes as he continues. "The sea is where I first knew you would forever be a part of my life. I knew I loved you then, on that beach back in Malibu. I knew you were meant to be mine. Hell, I knew before then. Before I knew you, I loved you, Arianna." Thud. Thud. Thud. My heart will forever be this man's bitch. That's for sure. "Sea glass is a symbol of renewal and healing. A metaphor for life, and you Arianna Parisi have not only healed my heart but you've given me life. First, when you crash-landed into my world, and now with my child inside of you." His smile turns soft while his eyes grow intense. "You are my life. You are mine and with this piece, everyone will see what I see every time I look at you." He finishes off leaving me speechless. Because how can I top that? Ironic how I always manage to find the right words to sass someone, or when I'm writing an article for my newspaper, but I never have the right words for Sebastian. That's what this man does to me. I try to hold the tears even when I know he notices my teary eyes, I step closer to him until there's no space between us and whisper. "I'm glad you're mine, Tyrant." And I am.

"Mind, body, soul, and heart." Pinching my chin between his fingers, he forces my full attention on him. His blue eyes glitter with my ultimate favorite: possessiveness. "Say you're mine."

Sliding my palms up his chest, over his shoulders, and through his soft black hair, I rasp, "I am yours, Sebastian. Always."

"Never forget it." He breathes out and then swoops down, and I rise to my tiptoes to meet him. Our lips meet in the middle. He kisses me senselessly and I feel it down to my bones.

His love.

His devotion.

Him.

My Sebastian.

Pulling apart, I open my eyes slowly to find him staring down at me with the most breathtaking smile. The smile that tells me that all is good in our world. Because as long as Sebastian keeps smiling at me like that, no one can touch me.

No one can touch us.

"Mommy. Daddy! Look at this furry little thing. It looks like Cupcake!" Ella screeches, making us both laugh at her antics. "Can I have another dog? I think my baby sister would want a puppy!"

"No more dogs." I snap at Sebastian before he agrees because I know him. He was about to give in and get her another mutt.

"We will see." He grins, before leaning down and taking my lips in his. Then we spend an hour exploring the exhibit and taking photos of every single art piece with our two babies between us until Ella decides she has had enough fun for today and crashes in her father's arms.

***

"Don't be dramatic, Sebastian. It's not an attractive trait, you know." I inspect my nails, trying to act as if I don't find jealous Sebastian hilarious and extremely adorable.

He was on me before I could blink. One second, he was standing across the room from me, and the next, he was in my space. His face inches from mine. His short beard tickles my chest. Damn, his beard really does it for me.

I don't know if it's because it makes him look older and distinguished or because it feels really good when it's between—

"That little fucker saw me standing by you, and he had the audacity to hit on you. Mind you, you're heavenly pregnant with my baby. I should've done much worse than what I did." He turns me in bed gently until my back is pressed to his front. I gasp when I feel his hard body press against me. Everything, even the inside of his thighs, are hard. His strong, muscular jaw. His bearded mouth that started to run down the tops of my shoulders. "You enjoy seeing me lose my mind with jealousy don't you, brat?" He rasps, letting the stiff point of his tongue trail along the outer shell of my ear. "I do. So very much." I push my body back, on the edge of coming by just the contact of his hard cock between my ass cheeks. "But you are mine. That fucker does not matter. He doesn't exist in our world. None of the men that look at you as if they have the right to do so matter." He lifts my left leg higher and lines his cock up with my entrance. "Yeah, this pretty wet pussy knows she's mine." My breath catches in my throat.

"I'm yours. All of me. Every single part of me," I whisper to him, looking over my shoulder so he can see the sincerity in my eyes. "I've never been anyone else's. Never have been and never will be." That confession makes a low and sexy-as-hell growl slip from his mouth before he slides the length of his cock through my slit, coating himself in my wetness.

I'm dripping for him and the man loves it.

Loves to see what he does to my body.

"You erased every touch. Every meaningless kiss until all there is, is you. Only you," he says as he wraps his strong hand around my neck in the most possessive of ways that has me moaning loudly. "You, my darling, are all I see. All I'll ever want to see."

The tyrant sure has a way with words...

"Good. I better be all there is, Sebastian." I push back. "Now, stop talking and give me what I want."

The command has him hissing and pressing the tip of his cock to my entrance, stretching, and filling me in one quick thrust of his hips. "Yes, ma'am." He chuckles darkly, while holding my hips steady and then he is driving into me with a hard thrust, stealing all the air from my lungs.

"Oh, God," I moan, my core muscles clamping tight and my pussy closing over his cock so hard that I stop breathing. I literally can't find it in myself to do that important bodily function. Sebastian fucks me hard while gripping my neck tighter. My vision blurs, and my clit throbs.

Then his free hand comes down on my ass once more, and I draw in a sharp breath.

Sebastian fucks the same way he handles politics.

Dirty. Filthy.

He blows my mind and makes my body sing every time he touches me. Every time he is inside of me.

Sebastian follows orders and doesn't say a word. Instead, he takes hold of my hips, and pounds inside of me like a wild animal.

He fucks me as if he hates me. Not as if I am one of the most important people in his life.

The act is dirty.

Our breathing comes in rough pulls echoing in the room.

The sounds he is making only make me wetter.

After a while Sebastian's hand leaves my hips and automatically goes to the falling strands, fisting the back of my hair with such strength that I gasp and throw my head back. His free hand circles my throat, coming to rest just above my collarbone to hold me in place.

Then he holds me to him as he resumes fucking me. Using my body as he sees fit.

Last time I was in control and fucked him just how I wanted. Tonight, I surrendered all control to him after a while of both fighting for it.

Sebastian feels the moment I gave over to him, and with a deep groan, his movements became rougher and less controlled. Suddenly, the fucking turns into something more.

It is as if we are becoming one.

This couldn't be normal, this connection that we have. I'd never felt anything like this. Nothing has ever come close to what I feel every time he is inside of me. This pure, unaltered passion. This passion we have for each was something that would never, ever fade.

I am sure of it.

I won't let it.

My body gives out when the fucking becomes too much and then he is pulling me onto all fours, and starts to fuck me gently from behind.

He makes slow, sweet love to me. Driving in and pulling out, circling his hips in tune with my body, driving me insane with lust.

Every part of me is burning up for him.

Then his lips part, and I feel his soft, hot tongue run along the shell of my ear before he bites it. That's it. Not being able to take it anymore, my hand goes down to my parted thighs, and I let my fingers slip through the wet folds of my pussy, slowly moving down until I find where we are joined. I let my fingers part in the middle, with Sebastian's solid cock thrust between them. The pad of my thumb presses against my clit, and the orgasm that was building becomes urgent. My entire body is buzzing with the need to come undone for him.

Sebastian's head comes down to rest against the top of my spine, and I know he is close. Which is why I tighten my pelvic muscles and start to stroke my clit faster. "Oh, fuck. Fuck, yes. That's my good girl. Rub that pretty little clit for me." Sebastian hisses, before his hot breath explodes against my neck.

Good girl.

I've never been good. Not really. I am aware that there's little good in me but in bed and while in his arms I enjoy it.

Being his good girl.

While he does bad, bad things to my body.

A moment later, he grunts, his belly tightening, and I feel his cock start to twitch inside of me. Then, I feel his rough hand move to my breast, pinching my sensitive nipple. That's what does it, because next thing I know, I gasp as my orgasm rolls over me while Sebastian fucks me harder riding out his own release. My body bows, and the only thing that is holding me where I am, is Sebastian's tight grip on my breasts and his

cock planted deep inside of me. "Oh, yes," I breathe out, my head falling back limply against his collarbone. He hums, letting my breast go.
We lay like that, both of us trying to control our breathing for long moments. Then his hand slips back down to my stomach. "This feels like a dream. Sometimes I think to myself that I'm still in that coma and this will all fade away once I wake up." Sebastian confesses, still breathless. Hard beating fast, I whisper. "Not a dream, baby. This is real. We are real and I am here. I am not going anywhere," I place my hand on top of his as I promised him.
This is real.
The most real thing I have ever had.
Maybe the only thing real in my life.
Us.
Our family.

***

Morning sunlight comes through the window the second I open my eyes. Then, a feeling of bliss takes over me when I see Sebastian standing at the end of the bed dressed impeccably as always with a newspaper in hand. Amusement fills my heart when I think of how most men don't read the paper anymore. They just read their news on the internet but not Sebastian, no. Because he is not like most people. He enjoys sitting down with a cup of coffee to read the newspaper instead of being glued to his phone and getting his news from the internet. I, on the other hand, don't have a preference. I do enjoy both. The stupid smile on my face widens when I notice he chose a pink tie for the day. That tie has Ella written all over it, of that, I have no doubt. Then the smile drops from my face when I see the look of devastation on Sebastian's face. I also notice how he is looking through me, not at me.

Forgetting my current naked state, I move towards him. "What happened?" I can't hide the panic that takes over me. "Is it Ellaiza?"

Sebastian looks down at me and then pushes a newspaper between us. "If you wanted to break my heart, darling. This was the way to do it." My brows furrowed in confusion. I feel a pang in my chest at his tone. His words. Flipping the newspaper open, the Washington Weekly, my newspaper I read the headline.

History has a way of repeating itself... Sources close to President Kenton allege that his shady businesses, so much like his father, are the reason behind his attack outside of the Museum of Arts.

I want to throw up when I see side-by-side photos of Sebastian as a young boy being held back from his mother's dead body on the ground and the other is of his attack. A photo of Sebastian covered in blood being lifted to the ambulance before he was transported to a hospital.

This is cruel.

Disgusting.

The type of news I would have never published in my newspaper.

Never.

Even my once hate for this man wouldn't have made me go this far and stood so low.

Crumbling the paper in my hand, I take hold of Sebastian's neck bringing his face closer to mine. His body is rigid, and his stance is...cold. "I did not approve of this, Sebastian, and if you believe I would do such a thing. If you believe I would do this to you now, after everything we've been through. To Ellaiza? Then you don't know me at all." I whisper harshly, trying to make him understand. At the same time, I try but fail miserably at controlling my temper. Taking deep breaths, I notice his eyes are on mine, but it is as if he's seeing through me. He's not here but somewhere else. Somewhere dark where I can't reach him. "You did swear you would make it hurt…" His voice sounds empty.

No.

Pushing closer to him, I press my forehead to his. "I know this looks bad, but I promise you, Sebastian. I had nothing to do with this and whoever did will answer to me." I breathed out, trying to reach him. I admit, I am vindictive and impulsive most of the time, but I wouldn't go this far. I specifically ordered Nessa to trash the article. What the hell happened? Taking another deep breath, I try to cool the anger and focus on the matter at hand.

Sebastian not trusting me.

"I did wish to hurt you once as you hurt me but this is too far. This trash of an article not only hurts you, but it also hurts the girl who I love most in this world, and that's something I would never do. Never. So, you better get your head out of your ass now because we don't do this. Not anymore. Miscommunication is for imbeciles. Is not for us." My hand on the back of his neck tightens and a relieved sigh escapes me when I feel his hand gently hold onto my neck. Our noses are touching and our lips are inches away.

His hot breath caresses my face.

That is when I see it.

The pain and the doubt fade from his eyes and all it is left is love.

My heart settles in my chest.

He believes me.

His mouth might not tell me but it's written all over his eyes.

Sebastian's eyes never lie even when his mouth does.

Whoever betrayed my trust, and put my company at risk for lawsuits will pay dearly for not only that but for hurting Sebastian.

That garbage is not news, no.

That's a cruel and cheap attempt to hurt Sebastian. Not his campaign. It is a personal attack.

The country is not stupid.

They were aware of the rumors of Sebastian dealing with the underground criminals yet they still left their beds, their homes, their places of work, whatever the case was, and voted for him.

Because they believed in him.

They believed the man represented change when other straight-laced politicians who played by the book failed them. I didn't understand that before but I do now.

"I am sorry…" he breathes out, tightening his hand on my neck making goosebumps spread on my exposed skin.

"Don't ever doubt me again, Sebastian," I told him.

He gives me a soft smile before giving me a quick kiss. "I won't."

"Good," I whisper before taking his lips in mine. Kissing him like I haven't kissed him in a thousand days and then he fucks me showing me just how sorry he really is.

Chapter 33
FEAR THY BITCH

Arianna

"Love or hate me... I still live inside your head rent free." — A

One thing of value my piece of shit father taught me was that you should always make sure the people who work for you either respect you or fear you. I wanted to be different from him. I wanted my employees to respect me, and most of them do. Some even respect and fear me, and I am more than fine with that, but then there's one who clearly feels neither. Not respect nor fear.

That was my mistake.

I was so caught up in my issues with Sebastian and so consumed with hate that I slipped up. Now, I intend to rectify it.

Placing the news article that mocks Sebastian's childhood trauma down on my desk, I inhale and exhale, slowly trying to calm myself to not hurt Baby Kenton.

It's the first time in months that I've come to the office.

I didn't want to leave my little bubble, not so soon, but for him, I did.

Someone fucked with him, and that is unacceptable.

Knock, knock.

Show time. I turn my face to watch Nessa knocking on the glass door with a smile on her face. A smile that seems too damn friendly now that I am noticing it. I should have known. No one sane is that damn happy. I gesture for her to come in, and her smile falters when she sees Benjamin standing in the far corner of the room with his arms crossed over his chest and a pissed as fuck look on his face.

He is pissed.

Understandably so.

Nessa fucked with me and Sebastian. She's lucky Benjamin is not throwing her out the window right about now.

"You wanted to see me, boss?" To her credit, she keeps her voice steady and her head held high.

Leaning forward, I pick up the offending news article and throw it inside the box that's sitting on top of my desk, then I push it towards her. "I am not even going to ask why because I honestly don't care about your reasons for going against me and posting slanders about a sitting president. Just grab your things and get out." I tell her calmly, keeping my cool.

Go off on the sneaky bitch... the vicious little devil on my shoulder whispers.

Why should I go down to her level? Besides, ruining her career is more than enough.

At least bitch-slap her.

Ignoring the little voice, I keep my attention trained on Nessa.

Her eyes grow big in realization the second she catches on. She's been found out. "I don't know what you think, Aria–"

So now I am Arianna and not her boss.

Nope.

Shaking my head, I stop her, not wanting to hear her sorry excuses.

Two security guards knock on my door before entering. Then Benjamin moves towards my desk, grabs the box filled with her office things, and hands it to one of the guards.

"Gentlemen, please be so kind as to escort Miss Adams out of the premises." I tell them in a bored tone. The second I do, Nessa's victim facade disappears, and the ugly little bitch inside comes to the surface. Furious eyes with so much hate in them look from the guards back to me. How did I miss this side of her? I don't know, but it is a mistake I won't be making twice. This is the reason why I am not a woman with female friends. Truthfully, some women are worse than rats. "I wrote the truth, not a single sentence in that article is a lie." She seethes while I remain to look at her in complete boredom. Motioning to the guards to get her out, I watch as they grab both her arms at the same time she furiously shakes them off. "I'll go. The damage is done anyway." She laughs, proud of what she did.

Tsk, tsk… and here I thought she actually had a brain.

Life keeps proving to me that some humans have more air than they do brains inside of their big heads.

Rising from my seat, I button my red blazer over my belly and walk towards her. Once I am a few feet away from her, not getting too close because I won't ever put my baby at risk when this girl is clearly a loose cannon, and I don't know what she's capable of.

"You did nothing, Nessa. Absolutely nothing but make the public pity and love the man more. You tried, though. I'll give you that, but as expected, you failed. The Washington Weakly already put out a statement debunking your lies and honey…" There's ice in my tone and hate in my gaze as I carry on. "I will bury you and your career for what you did. Trust that."

She steps forward, and the guards see it as a threat, so they each move in front of me while Benjamin stands behind me, ready to intervene if Nessa pushes it. "You're a pathetic—"

Laughing coldly, I dismiss her. "Leave, and do so quietly because if you so much as cause a scandal or show your face here or anywhere Sebastian is again, I will personally make sure you don't get a second chance at life like the last time." With that not-so-subtle threat, I lean back in my seat and watch as she's escorted out of my office while everyone outside witnesses her departure. No one messes with Sebastian. No one but me. She not only tried to hurt Sebastian but my partner and friend, Quinne, too. I had Benjamin dig deep, and he found some interesting details about Nessa. For example, the last name she goes by is not her real name. Her real name is attached to Quinne's gruesome past.

A name that explains why she was so eager to help me ruin Sebastian's image. Sebastian pardoned four criminals who didn't deserve redemption in her eyes.

The girl is insane.

And she clearly messed with the wrong family.

She betrayed my trust, and what happens next, well... that's the bed she made.

She can lie and bleed in it.

"You two are one and the same..." My eyes leave the hall where Nessa disappears with the guards tailing her and turn to Benjamin. "The way you looked and sounded while handling that girl. That's how he would have done it." Sebastian, he means. I do realize Sebastian and I are a lot alike, and it works for us, even if he infuriates me fifty percent of the time. "He would have ordered me to spill some blood or call in a favor to Sandoval to handle the pricks, though."

Chuckling, "Like I would allow that girl's blood to ruin my suit or my pristine floors, Benjamin."

Rubbing my belly, I feel my kid kick, filling my once icy heart with more warmth and joy. *I can't wait to show you how to mess with people, little tyrant…*

The baby kicks again.

Yeah… you're already your daddy and mommy's baby. A little troublemaker.

Walking to my desk, I take a seat.

Nuisance resolved.

Now, we move on.

"Yeah… that's something the pompous prick would say, too." My friend shakes his head and laughs.

His laugh fills my heart with joy, too.

Opening my email, I see there's a message from my doctor's office reminding me of my next appointment. "You may leave now…" I offer Benjamin a grin.

"I love you, too, my girl." he says, chuckling as he exits my office.

Resting back on my office chair, I smile.

A real smile.

"We are loved, kid…" I whisper to my baby while looking at the clouds and sunny sky outside the window.

At one point, hate and misery plagued my heart and soul, and now… now, there is only joy. "So loved." I whisper. *So, so loved.*

Chapter 39
FEELS LIKE HOME
Arianna

"How did I get so lucky? To end up being loved by you?"

— B

I never thought it would be possible to fall madly in love with a sound, but I have. With Sebastian's and my sweet Ella's laughs. Now, this…

The distinct sound of the little heart inside of my belly has me falling in love for the third time.

My baby's heartbeat sounds like a soothing lullaby.

That's my baby's heart…

Shit, it's real now.

I have a human inside of me. A human that will split my vagina in two during labor. I am sure. Yet, it does not scare me. Not at all.

"Wow…" Ellaiza whispers in amazement from where she's being held by Benjamin. The three of them came with me to the appointment.

Sebastian stands next to me, holding my hand while I lie on the exam table. Dr. Ellis laughs at Ella's reaction while she moves the ultrasound wand over my belly.

"Wow, is right, kid." Benjamin sounds just as amazed as Ellaiza. "That's your baby brother's heart…" The big Viking whispers to my girl.

A gasp of betrayal echoes in the small room causing me to chuckle. "How could you say that, Benji!? We agreed that it's a girl!" I watch as Ella crosses her arms over her small chest and pouts while Benjamin rolls his eyes at her lovingly.

That kid better be a girl because there is no doubt in my mind that she will dress the baby in girly clothes just like she is doing to the poor mutt, Cupcake.

Sebastian's strong hand tightens around mine, making me look up at his gray-blue eyes that shine today with joy. So much joy. "Thank you, my love." The pure wonder and happiness in Sebastian's eyes make my heart skip many beats. He already is the most wonderful father, and with this baby, we both will get to experience all that we missed with Ellaiza.

Like today.

Smiling up at him, I mouth the words 'I love you', which he returns with a blinding smile on his face.

I am glad he is here to experience this with me.

The OB-GYN checkup came just in time. Since I was eager to hear Baby Kenton's heartbeat with Sebastian, Ella, and Benjamin in the room.

And that's what we did.

What an odd family we are.

"Would you like to know the sex of the baby?" Dr. Ellis asks while hitting some buttons on the machine's keyboard.

"Yes, please!" Ella screams at the same time as Sebastian and I reply with a resounding no, and Benjamin groans.

I don't want to know, because I honestly, do not care.

Boy or girl, it does not matter.

That's my baby, and all I wish is that it's healthy.

That's all.

Plus, I get a sick satisfaction in making them all wait to find out.

A bit mean? I know. But it's hilarious.

Kick.

I feel a butterfly touch in my belly.

Smiling, I think to myself. Yeah, baby. Mommy's here.

Then, while smiling, I look at the monitor that shows a grainy picture of Baby Kenton.

I can't wait to meet you.

All the heartaches throughout my life led me here.

To this moment.

To my babies.

Sebastian.

Benjamin.

My family.

When the doctor finishes, she cleans me up, and I get dressed while my chaotic little family chooses a stuffed animal, where a tiny gadget with my baby's heart sound will be placed for us to keep.

"Oh, it's so pretty!" Ella smiles while hugging the stuffed animal she chose close to her chest.

A wolf.

A white fur wolf.

Huh.

Fitting for this kid.

Finding Sebastian's gaze, I smile knowingly at him because we both know.

We both know we have come home.

We made it to the shore.

Both of us.

Chapter 35
THE FIRST LADY
Arianna

"I'm no longer freezing…" — A

"I can't believe I let you talk me into this," I murmur. Butterflies flutter like crazy in my stomach as I hold onto the President's arms, in four-inch heels and a modest beige maternity dress, while he announces his plans for re-election. Sebastian, as always, looks incredible in a Dior suit with his signature politician smile and his charming personality in full mode as he regards the raging crowd howling and screaming his name and his campaign's slogan.

It's just us two tonight. Well, us and Benjamin, of course.

After our last disastrous event together, we decided to keep Ella out of the spotlight until she was older. For now, she will stay home with her team guarding her at all times. We're not risking her anymore.

Sebastian wanted to leave me behind too, but he lost that argument. There was no chance in hell I was going to miss the opportunity to stand by his side and show both his followers and enemies that we are one and that we are stronger together.

There's no end to what we have. A bullet sure as hell couldn't.

Nothing, and no one will.

Sebastian pulls me closer to his body, and whispers in my ear. "How does it feel to know that you are the most beautiful First Lady in all history?"

I snort, "Do you see a ring on this finger, Sebastian? Cause I sure don't." I tease, smiling up at him.

"Well... I guess we need to rectify that. Don't we, darling?" His grin transforms into a full-blown ear-to-ear smile as he drops down to his knees in front of me and everyone who came out tonight to support him.

Thud.

Thud.

Thud.

My heart feels like it's about to burst out of my chest when I see him reach into his suit pocket and pull a small black box. Opening it, he reveals a one-of-a-kind emerald-cut diamond ring with several smaller diamonds around the silver band. Oh, my... It's perfect.

Our audience becomes louder, cheering and roaring, but it is all background noise as I stare down at the man that stole the heart I had so carefully locked inside my chest, making it almost impossible to reach, but he did.

He not only broke down my walls but stole my heart as well.

"Sebastian..." I breathe out when he takes my left hand in his and slips the stunning ring on my left finger. I don't miss how the promise ring he gifted me not long ago fits perfectly with the diamond ring, as if it's part of it.

A perfect fit.

I also don't miss how the smaller diamonds around the bigger one are lavender. How did he know? Once, I thought my world was black

and white…a bit gray too, but then he came along and painted it.
Lavender.
The color he chose for the ring.
"There's so much I could say to express just how much I love you, darling, but I am afraid this lifetime would not be enough. The list of all the reasons why I love you is endless, but all I can say is that I love you more than I did yesterday and a little bit less than I will love you tomorrow. Both of you." He kisses my belly with a soft smile on his face and looks back up at me with so much love and joy reflecting in his blue-gray eyes. "There's nothing in this world I wouldn't do to make you happy. I would move heaven and earth for you. I promise you that I will always be loyal, honest, and true to you. I will always fight for you. I want to spend the rest of my life with you. Only you. Always and forever. Marry me, Arianna Parisi. Marry me, and I guarantee you," he says softly. "That I won't ever leave you, and I won't ever do anything that will hurt you. Never again. I will always protect you. Care for you. Live and die for you if that's what you need from me. That, I swear to you," That part he says a little louder since the crowd around us is screaming louder.
I swallow hard because the lump in my throat is so big I can't speak.
And as if Baby Kenton senses the attention he or she makes their presence known by kicking up a storm inside of me.
Behave, little tyrant. It's my moment.
"I have one condition…" I fake seriousness, enjoying the way Sebastian's eyes narrow up at me in suspicion.
"I won't share you with anyone but our kids. I am telling you this now." He snaps. Of course, his mind would go there.
Rolling my eyes, "That I know, Sebastian." I tease him and offer him a crooked smile. He sighs as if he's annoyed, but his eyes tell a different

story. He is amused. "Go on then. What's your condition?"

I tell him the one thing I was afraid to admit to myself. "I want more kids." I do. Before, I did not even like plants, let alone children, but after Ellaiza… I realized that I wanted a baseball team of kids, if possible. A big family to love and for them to love me unconditionally.

Kids that would paint my life with different colors and bring magic to every single day of the year.

Like Benjamin told me once…

I want to create the family I didn't have growing up. Be the mother I never had. Give my children a father who would love them and protect them above all else. I want all of that with Sebastian.

Only Sebastian.

The eyes of the man I love turn soft when he gives me a crooked smile, "I don't mind one more kid."

Shaking my head, I say. "I want four." I clear my throat, then say. "Perhaps more than that. We'll see." I make myself clear.

My tyrant rolls his eyes, before he grins like a lunatic. Then he slowly stands to his full height and takes me in his arms. "Deal, darling."

"Deal, tyrant." I breathe out lovingly just before he grabs my neck gently and pulls my lips to his, kissing me savagely for everyone to see.

For everyone to witness what I mean to him and what he means to me. Everything. The world.

Breaking the kiss, Sebastian pulls back and stares intensely at me. "That a yes?"

I nod. "Yes."

Sebastian exhales loudly like he's been holding his breath this whole time. And when a tear falls from my eye, he swipes it away with his thumb before his mouth captures mine once more.

I kiss him with everything that I am and all that I have. I kiss him while tears fall from my eyes and laughter fills my heart. All the while, a kaleidoscope of butterflies invades my stomach.

Who would have thought that after so much hurt, heartbreak, and hate, I would be standing here in front of the people of the United States of America with a ring on my finger and a baby inside of me?

Who would have imagined that the man I swore war to would not only be the father of my children but my forever as well?

The owner of my heart.

My ally.

My enemy.

My tyrant.

Every-single-thing.

Sebastian is everywhere.

Like the tyrant he truly is, he took over every aspect of my life and I don't even mind. Not one bit.

Because now I know…

This is where I was always meant to end up.

We were written in the stars. It just took us a while to get it right.

But here we are.

We are happy in love.

And we are one.

One and the same.

He and I.

THE WASHINGTON WEAKLY

"The voice of a generation"

By Arianna Parisi, CEO

PRESIDENT KENTON UP FOR RE-ELECTION

Almost a year and a half before voters will cast their ballots, on Tuesday night, President Sebastian Kenton announced that he is again seeking office right after he got on his knees and proposed to me.

Now, you might ask why I am putting out an article for the benefit of my fiancé. Well, that is easy. The reason is that I am biased, as I believe most of you, the readers, are.

President Kenton is not a perfect man, just like all the forty-something presidents that have taken that office before him. Yet he has worked tirelessly to make this country better and repair the damages left behind by previous administrations, while being a single father at the same time.

The man has not only captured my heart but this country's heart, as well, with his charisma, strong leadership, and determination to move the United States into a better future.

You might also be wondering why you should believe a word I say, right? Then let me remind you why President Kenton is the better choice and why he deserves to lead the country for another four years. Here are 10 reasons why you should give him your vote.

10 REASONS TO VOTE FOR KENTON

Flip to page six to read:

EPILOGUE ONE

THE BIRTH

"My children are the very best of me." — B

Arianna

"I'm full. God, I can't breathe." I don't know what prompted me to get into this dress, but now, I am deeply regretting it. At this point in the pregnancy, I am so big that nothing fits me anymore. Nothing cute, at least, and there was no way I was going to celebrate Valentine's Day and the little tyrant's father's birthday at one of the most luxurious restaurants in Washington looking like the ugly green ogre in a dress. No way. But now with oxygen failing to reach my lungs, I know I chose wrong.

Sebastian, the big bastard, laughs at me before he shoves his hand inside his suit's pocket, takes out his phone, and types a quick message. "It's best if we go home. You'll be more comfortable."

"This is your night, Sebastian. I wanted it to be special." I ground out, annoyed.

"Whether it is at home or here, it is special, darling. You're here with me." He takes my hand and plays with the diamond on my ring.

Rolling my eyes, I try to hide the way his words make me blush. "You ever get tired of being so damn charming, Sebastian?" He shakes his head no and smiles. Thud. Thud. Thud.

My heart, his bitch, beats wildly in my chest. "Hey, baby," he says, leaning over the table and capturing my face in his hands. Then his perfect lips are on mine, showing me how much he loves me.

Only when we were both breathless and panting does he pull away with another smile.

I blink at him, unable to get my bearings for a few long seconds.

"Hey," I breathe out. His blue-gray eyes tell me he wants to bend me over the restaurant's table and do very, very bad things to me.

"You're looking at me like I'm your dessert." I point out.

He winks, "It is my birthday…."

Smiling, I kiss his lips once more. "It is… you're quite old, Mr. President." I tease.

Chuckling, he says, "You didn't seem to think so an hour ago when you were choking on my big—"

"Uhhhhh…" Oh, no. Pulling away, I look down at the floor under the table and then look back at Sebastian. "Rain check?" I smile sheepishly. My water just broke.

***

Six hours later, our child was pulled from my body and then gently placed on my chest. Baby Kenton was born a minute before midnight and came into this world screaming up a storm after splitting my vagina in half, as predicted.

Tyranny runs in this baby's blood.

"I am in awe of you, my love." Sebastian's eyes crinkle at the corners when he smiles wide, looking down at me with adoration. I must look like a mess, but I honestly could care less.

It is the only time I will allow myself to look like I most likely do.

Dripping in sweat, my hair a mess, and my makeup smeared.

I must look as if I've gone to war and survived.

And I would do it a thousand times more if it led me here.

To this perfect moment with this perfect creature lying on my chest.

"Ellaiza won't be pleased..." I murmur, looking down at the tiny human.

My tiny human.

So, so perfect, my mini tyrant.

A boy.

My son.

He has a whitish mixture of goo all over him, which is now all over my chest and hospital gown. There's even blood on my chin, but I could care less.

The nurse steps closer and starts scrubbing my son's back vigorously.

While the other two nurses assist Dr. Ellis because I tore, of course.

My baby, who is a perfect blend of Sebastian and me, was worth it, though. Worth every single tear. Every single drop of blood. Every single painful tremor.

Worth the painful burn in my vagina.

He was worth everything.

Even the long road of hurt and heartbreak that led me to him.

"She will understand and fall in love with him as soon as she sees him. You'll see." Sebastian kisses my sweaty forehead and brushes my hair back, which I appreciate. "She's a big sister now."

"She'll have him wearing a pink tutu in no time." I joke. My poor baby boy. Sebastian chuckles as we both watch a nurse approach us with a small smile on her face. "You did so well! Congratulations!"

Although her stare lingers a little too long on my baby daddy for my liking, I regard her with a small smile of my own.

"Thank you."

After that, my baby was taken from my chest, and Sebastian followed him to the corner of the room, where they weighed him and took his footprints. I can't help but smile when I see Sebastian towering over our son, looking so enamored that I am left breathless just at the sight of them. "Let's get you changed into something clean. Sounds good to you?" The nurse's assistant asked me once I was free and clear.

We do just that, and when we're done, I find myself lying back on the hospital bed, smiling wide and snuggled into Sebastian's chest. Our son nestled in the bed between us. His perfect 9-pound body fit into the small crevice between us like he was made to be there. He was perfect, albeit a smaller replica of his father. I was so beyond overjoyed that I could barely contain the happiness in my heart. The joy. The feeling of pure bliss. I lovingly counted his ten fingers. I kissed his ten perfect toes. I knew then and there that my once broken heart was capable of expanding and of loving more and that I would do anything for him. The moment I saw him, I knew I had met the third love of my life, and I would do everything in my power to protect and love him unconditionally. Bending down, I kiss his warm cheek and smile when gives me a small smile, showing a dimple just like the one that appears on Sebastian's cheek every time he smiles. "I love you, little tyrant, with all that I am and all that I have." My chest tightens when I watch my baby lift his small arm in the air. Taking his hand, I kiss it tenderly. "Royal."

"What's that, darling?" Sebastian asks as he plays with a tendril of my hair. Looking away from my baby's face, my eyes clash with Sebastian's blue gaze. "His name. Royal Amaury Kenton."

"Royal..." My baby's father breathes out before he lovingly runs a thick finger down our baby boy's face. "Welcome to the world, son. It's yours. I can't wait to witness what you do with it."

The same words he whispered to me so long ago, he now says it to the product of our love.

We've come full circle, he and I.

And what a ride it has been.

"Oh, no!" A disappointed gasp sounds from our hospital room's door making both of us look up to find a very confused Ellaiza clutching Benjamin's neck while holding pink balloons.

Here we go.

Sebastian grins at me, and I do the same.

Benjamin walks towards us with a knowing look on his face and Ellaiza hanging onto him. "Told you so, kid." Benjamin sees the baby before Ella is able to. "Damn. That's one big boy." He says loudly while cringing.

Rolling my eyes at him. "He's perfect."

"That he is, my girl. That he is." My friend smiles warmly at me.

My friend.

My partner in crime.

I will definitely name my next one after him.

"It was supposed to be a girl." Ellaiza interrupts, narrowing her eyes at her little brother.

Smiling at my girl, I tell her. "Baby girl, I would like you to meet your baby brother, Royal."

She gives Royal a once over and then crosses her arms over her chest and gives every single one of us a mean mug before tapping her chin twice, deep in thought. "I think Cupcake's skirts will fit him."

"You're not putting girl's clothes on him, Ellaiza." Sebastian tries his best to not laugh. Ella grins at her father and then at me before looking down at her little brother with so much love that is hard to miss.

That's my girl. So full of love.

Thirty minutes later, we have both our babies sleeping soundly between us while Benjamin is laid back on the chair next to the window, watching a sports game on the TV.

This is my family.

This is love.

Sebastian kisses my temple softly, and I can feel the love in that one gesture down to my soul. "I love you so goddamn much," he whispers, trying not to wake up the kids.

"I love you, Sebastian Kenton," I say quietly, brushing a kiss over his bearded jaw. He turns into me, capturing my lips with his own, as he asks, "Whose heart is this, darling?" I feel his hand on my chest where my heart beats for him.

For all of them.

Looking at those hypnotizing eyes of his that makes me feel loved beyond words, I reply. "Yours."

EPILOGUE TWO

ROYAL WEDDING

"I am marrying my best friend today." — B

Arianna

Two Months Later

My *nonna* used to say that a woman's wedding day was one of the most memorable days of her life. The happiest too, and although I am the happiest I have ever been, I can't help but feel sad, too. It all goes back to my sisters.

How I wish they were here.

I reached out to my younger sister, Mila, but she hasn't answered my texts in weeks. It's beginning to worry me. We didn't message each other every day with how busy life is now, but this disappearance act is unlike her. "There's never been a more beautiful sight." I look at myself in the mirror and find Benjamin looking at me with a smile on his face. Seeing what he sees, I smile. The off-the-shoulder, dainty yet modern lace fit, and exposed corset white wedding dress with a long train was designed by House of Arnault. Same for the stunning tulle cathedral veil. I sat down with one of Dionysious Arnault's designers and shared my vision with her, and they made it come to life. A dream of a dress that has me feeling like the most elegant and beautiful woman that's ever lived.

Conceited? Perhaps, but that's exactly how I feel looking at myself in the mirror now. Remembering that Benjamin is behind me, I turn to face him, and a smile breaks on my face when I see how terribly handsome he looks in his tuxedo right now.

My husband's best man.

"Well, you cleaned up nice." I say while walking towards him.

"Always a pleasure when you compliment me, my girl." He steps closer and kisses my forehead lingering there for a minute as if he's savoring this moment. Then he steps back with a smile that lights up his entire face, places the white veil over my face, and offers me his left arm.

Neither Sebastian nor I have families to come to celebrate with us, so we decided to have a small ceremony with just his men, our children, and our only friends.

Benjamin and Quinne.

For some, the fact that it's just us might seem sad or pathetic, but not to us. Our circle is small, and we value quality over quantity.

Interlacing my arm with his, I say. "Thank you for walking me down the aisle, Benjamin."

The Viking looks down lovingly at me. "It's the honor of my life, kid." Holding me tighter, he guides me toward the double doors which lead to the White House's Garden, where my maid of honor, Quinne, is waiting for me with a scowl on her face. "Wipe that look off your face, Jones. It causes wrinkles, you know…" I tell her in a bored tone. She replies by flipping me off and handing me my bouquet. Looking down at the arrangement of flowers, I frown. "These are not the flowers I ordered…"

I asked for white roses and got gold roses, instead.

Quinne grins, "Don't look at me. This is all your man…"

Sebastian.

Of course.

Christ, I love that man.

Turning to Benjamin, I say. "Let's go. He's waiting."

The double doors open, and as soon as I step through the threshold, music starts playing in the background.

This is it.

Forever is here.

From the corner of my eye, I watch as Shaw appears with my Ella holding onto his hand with a flower basket in her small hands. My perfect flower girl wears a lavender dress, the same shade as Quinne's maid of honor gown, with flowers in her raven curls. My sweet girl gives me a thumbs-up as soon as her eyes find me.

"You look perfect, mommy!" She jumps up and down in place before the wedding planner takes her hand and reminds her what she needs to do.

And that's exactly what she does.

With all the grace in the world, my little darling holds her head high and walks down the trail that leads to her father throwing gold petals as she goes.

Then Shaw, the big grump, takes Quinne's arm, and guides her down the aisle.

And when it's my turn, I hold my breath and let Benjamin lead me down the aisle to my forever.

And there he stands.

Perfect.

Handsome, and all mine.

Dressed in a House of Arnault tux, black from head to toe, with the most blinding smile on his face and our precious baby boy in his arms. Once I get closer to where he is standing waiting for me, he hands

Royal to Shaw, and takes my hand in his.

Benjamin and him exchange looks before my friend lifts my veil, revealing my face, kisses my cheek, and steps in place next to Shaw.

"You're a vision, darling." Sebastian whispers as we move to stand in front of the judge that is marrying us. Looking up at him, I forget there's people around us. I forget that helicopters are surrounding the White House, trying to capture the moment, and that a cameraman is standing at the far corner, filming this moment for the country to witness our ceremony.

This is our moment, but the people of this country felt like it was their moment as well. That is how much Sebastian, their president, is adored.

"And you look so handsome." I hold him tight, loving how perfect he always feels standing next to me. A perfect fit.

The officiant clears his throat, smiling warmly at us before he begins to speak. "We're here today to witness the union of Sebastian Aumary Kenton and Arianna Luna Parisi in marriage. Today, you begin a new life together, founded in love, laughter…" The officiant's voice fades into the background as I stare into Sebastian's blue-gray eyes that shine with all the love he has for me. I do hope the love I feel for him is reflected in my own eyes as he's looking at me.

Suddenly, every single memory we have shared hits me full force, replaying in my mind. The first time I ever saw him looking intimidating and so handsome at the plane track. The quiet moments we shared. Our time in Paris and in Greece. The two of us dancing while I stood on his feet. The good moments, and even the bad ones, flash through my mind, reminding me of all that is our love. Chaotic. Sweet. Hopeless. Imperfectly perfect. Strong and brave.

One of a kind.

Like a gold rose.

If death came knocking on my door, I would die a happy woman because I was loved fully and loved the same way. I learned to love with my entire heart. He taught me that.

Looking at the man I love more than life, I mouth the words 'I love you', which causes the most beautiful smile to appear on his face as his eyes shine with love. He mouths 'I love you' back to me.

"Do you, Sebastian, take Arianna to be your lawfully wedded wife and to live together as one, to treat her with love and respect, and to build a marriage that grows stronger and more loving as time passes?"

Looking at no one else but me, he says. "I do."

The officiant turns to me. "And do you, Arianna, take Sebastian to be your lawfully wedded husband and to live together as one, to treat him with love and respect, and to build a marriage that grows stronger and more loving as time passes?"

A lone tear falls from my eye, and Sebastian gently wipes it away, careful not to ruin my eye makeup. "Yes, I do."

The officiant smiles before turning to Sebastian's best man. "If you have rings, please take them out now." Benjamin hands Sebastian a ring, and Quinne does the same to me.

"These rings represent the promise of love and commitment. As you wear your ring, let it remind you of the love you feel here today."

We look at each other and no one else as the officiant continues the ceremony. "Sebastian, please place the ring on Arianna's finger and repeat after me: I give you this ring as a symbol of my love and devotion as we join our lives together today, tomorrow, and for as long as our love shall last." Holding hands, Sebastian looks into my eyes and repeats each word, and I know he means them.

Just like I do.

"And Arianna, please place the ring on Sebastian's finger and repeat after me: I give you this ring as a symbol of my love and devotion as we join our lives together today, tomorrow, and for as long as our love shall last."

I repeat each word while hypnotized by Sebastian's gaze.

"By the authority vested in me, I now pronounce you husband and wife. You may kiss your bride, Mr. President."

Sebastian does just that. He takes me in his arms and kisses me for the first time as man and wife while the people we love cheer around us.

Pulling back with lips tinted by my lipstick, he grins. "I can't wait to get you out of that dress and start working on baby number three."

I laugh into his chest before I lean back and stare up at the man I just married. I knew one thing for sure, and that was that he was my home.

I married the man of my dreams. We had two beautiful babies.

A home.

And a love that could survive anything life threw at us.

Anything.

I couldn't ask for a single thing more than I already had.

Well…

Five more babies wouldn't be much to ask. Right?

EPILOGUE THREE
HAPPILY EVER AFTER

"My mommy says I am the shit and my mommy is always right. — Ky

Arianna

"It's my turn, mom!" My youngest boy, Kyrin, screeches as he tries to snatch the globe from his twin brother, Kael's hands. This is the tale of no end every time we decide to take a family vacation twice or three times a year. My husband had the brilliant idea of allowing our kids to spin the globe to decide where our next adventure is.

Just like our oldest, Ella, did so long ago.

Since we got married, we've traveled the globe from one corner to the other. Japan, Spain, Egypt, you name it, we've been there.

Now that Sebastian has retired from politics and is focusing more on his business, on his way to becoming one of the richest men alive, we have more time to travel. There is no stopping him from conquering the world for his children. That is why he gave up politics and is working hard on creating our children's legacy and empires instead. Sighing, I put the spatula down and turn down the heat on the oven so Ellaiza's birthday cupcakes don't burn like the last time. Looking at my youngest, I can't help the smile that takes over my face. While Ellaiza, Royal, and Kael are mini replicas of their father with their black raven hair.

My littlest is all me.

Golden hair and emerald eyes.

His personality?

A hellish combination of his father and me.

The twins and Royal are eleven months apart, making them Irish twins. Turning to Kael, my wildcard child, I smile as well because as much as I can't stand half of humanity, my children will always get the best of me. Always.

Kael, like Ellaiza, has a full head of black curls and blue-gray eyes but a small button nose and full rosy lips that he inherited from me. Those are the only traits he got from me, and the rest? All his father. "Kael."

"Yes, Mother?" He smiles sheepishly at me. He's the one that is always pushing my buttons, trying to defy authority at every turn. My reckless child. Giving him a stern look, I try to suppress the smile that wants to take over my face when I see his top lip rising in a crooked grin, just like his fathers'. "You had your turn spinning the globe last time. It is your brother's turn. Now, let go of it and say you're sorry."

Sebastian's mini-me rolls his blue eyes, lets go of the globe, and grumbles and 'I'm sorry' to his twin before looking back at me with a grin. "Happy, Mother?"

The sass on this kid…

"Ecstatic." I ruffle his hair, and don't miss the way Kyrin sticks his tongue out. "Now sit down and help me decorate your sister's cupcakes." "Yes, mother." My dark-haired hellion mutters, climbing on the stool while my ray of sunshine hugs the globe to his chest, climbs up the stool, and tells me. "I love you, mommy." Kissing his blonde hair, I whisper. "I love you, too." Then I turn to Kael, kiss his head the same way I did his brother, and whisper. "*Je t'aime, Kael.*"

My heart softens when he whispers under his breath. "Je t'aime, maman." My twins are opposites in every way.

One reminds me of a warm summer day, while the other reminds me of a stormy autumn night.

But I love them the same.

Twenty minutes later, with two kids covered in pink frosting from head to toe, is when the rest of my family walks through the kitchen door. "Mom! Roman called! Say hello." My daughter screams, joy written all over her stunning face. My baby is no longer a tiny kid and almost comes to my chest at fourteen years old. I try to muster a smile for the Nicolasi kid when she turns her phone towards me. "Hey there, Mrs. K." The young man that looks just like his father greets me with a boyish grin on his face. See, I could never get on board with this friendship, and not because of who his parents are but because the kid loves to shorten my name and piss me off with half the shit he says. My girl can do better, but I am hoping this is nothing more than a friendship. Though Ellaiza treats him like a friend, who knows with kids these days. She needed a friend after her bodyguard slash friend left to take a job overseas, or so Benjamin says.

Shaw Banning, the asshole, broke my baby's heart, and for that, he better stay where he's at, on the other side of the world. Getting out of my head, I say hello to the Nicolasi kid and then take my girl in my arms, peppering her face with kisses. She never minds, not like my two oldest boys. Ellaiza is still, even at this age, a mommy's girl.

"Happy birthday, my darling." I whisper.

Looking up at me, she gives me a big smile. "Thank you, mom."

"Dad!" Kyrin says loudly before climbing down the stool and running to his father, who I now notice has entered the room.

As usual, the man steals all the air when he enters a room with his over-the-top and larger-than-life presence. Even in his early forties, the man doesn't look a day over thirty-five, apart from the small amount of pepper on his temples. He is still as handsome as the day I met him. The bastard is aging like fine wine. A fact he doesn't let me forget.

The cocky bastard.

I can't help but smile when I see my Royal standing by his father's side, dressed in a suit, looking like the miniature version of the devil. I know that is a weird thing for a mother to say about her child, but I am not oblivious to the fact that my eldest son is his father's child in every way. My boy looks at me, quietly leaves Sebastian's side, and gives me a quick hug before he turns to his brothers. He is a man of few words, my Royal, and that, aside from his green eyes, is the only trait he got from me. He is not a charmer, nor a social butterfly, and he is still perfect in my eyes. All of them are.

"Was the globe spun?" Sebastian moves towards me, takes me in his arms, and gives me a long kiss in front of all our kids, and yet none of them say a word. In this house, love is celebrated so they know their parents love each other after all these years, and we love them more than life as well.

Pulling back, my husband looks into my eyes, and I can't help but think that, even after all these years, he still makes me shiver when he touches me. The same spark is there when he is near me. The fire still burns, and I do not doubt that it always will, even when our kids grow and leave the house… our love will still remain.

Because it is us.

And Sebastian and I are solid.

Our hearts are forever intertwined.

"Not yet. We were waiting for you guys." I whisper to him.

"Did the twin tyrants argue for whose turn it is?"

Grinning. "They did."

Chuckling, he looks down at my barely there belly. "And how is my baby?"

Rolling my eyes, I say. "Our baby, Sebastian." I growl playfully.

"Our baby." he agrees, pure joy pouring out of him in waves.

"Come on. Dad! Our adventure awaits!" Kyrin yells, and I do my best to fight the urge to remind him that we don't yell in small spaces. What's the point? My kid will just argue back that there's nothing little about this kitchen. My sweet little smartass.

"Go ahead, son. Spin it." My husband smiles at our youngest child.

Kyrin spins the globe, and when he believes it's time, he stops it with a huge grin on his face. His twin, Kael, leans over to see where Kyrin's finger landed, and he, too, grins.

"Where are we going!?" Ella moves toward her brothers and then gasps excitedly. "Yes!" Looking up at my husband, I find him already looking down at me with love in his gaze. "I love our life." I breathe out, meaning it with my entire heart. This is the life I never dared to dream about because it always felt so out of reach for someone like me.

I was cold, jaded, and downright mean when I wanted, and good things don't happen to people like me, but they did.

And it is all because of Sebastian.

When he took me from a world of pain and sorrow, that's when my life started, and now years later, I am still living the life of my dreams. I wish I could go back in time and tell my younger self that it is okay to dream even when it hurts because dreams do come true.

You just have to fight for them and never, and I mean never, lose faith.

Because good things take time...

And someday did come.

For me.

For my sisters.

We won.

"I love you, darling." My husband whispers while kissing my temple.

"And I, you, Sebastian..." I breathe out, leaning on him.

Feeling his heart beating, his chest rumbles when he asks. "And in the next life?"

"I'll find you and love you just the same." I vow.

"That damn dog shat all over me. Little lady, come get this little shit." Benjamin's voice booms, ruining the moment and making all my kids laugh aloud.

Now that he's here, our family is complete.

Now, all my humans are where they're supposed to be, and that is how I know happy endings do exist.

Or happy beginnings, because for us? The Kentons? There is no ending.

Just beautiful beginnings.

***

Five months later, on a warm spring day, life surprises us once again with another pair of twins.

This time twin girls were born.

Like night and day.

Haven and Ambrose Kenton.

To Sebastian's dismay...my girls look like mini replicas of myself.

Something I'll regret later on once they're grown.

I am sure...

And The Kentons lived happily ever after…

THE END

For Arianna & Bastian.

Keep reading to find out who gets to tell their story next!

NEXT
MILA

"I never thought someone like you existed."- R

KENTON

Group Chat
1:05 PM

Kyrin: Mommy…

Mom: Yes?

Kyrin: Miss Knowles said I'm not the king of the world.

Kael: *Rolling eyes emoji*

Mom: Well, clearly she knows nothing.

Kyrin: That's what I told her! Now she's mad.

Mom: Good boy. I'll handle it.

Royal: Mom…

Mom: What's wrong? Royal: Don't freak out…

Mom: Pick up your phone. NOW.

Haven: Ro is in troubleeeee…

Ambrose: *Shocked face emoji*

Dad: Why are you all texting in class? Put down your phones and pay attention or you'll end up like uncle Banning.

Uncle B: Extremely handsome and successful? I see nothing wrong with that.

Ella: He got you there, dad.

Dad: Phones. Down. Now.

Dad: Or they'll be taken away.

Ambrose: Bye!! Love you all like Haven loves farts!

Haven: Shut up! I do not!

Haven: I am done with this conversation.

Kyrin: Hey dad… as long as you're taking our phones away…

Dad: You're not getting a new phone.

Kyrin: We will see about that…

Kyrin: *Emoji with shades on*

Kael: An old phone is better than no phone, idiot.

Mom: If I receive one more text notification while you all are in school… Dad: Well look at that. No more texts. Uncle B: And that is how is done, MF.

Dad: Why are you even on this chat, Banning?

                Dad removed Uncle B from chat.

                Mom added Uncle B to the chat.

Uncle B: Your wife can't live without me.

Dad: Do not push it…

Uncle B: I love you, too.

Mom: *Annoyed emoji*

AFTERWORD

If you made it this far... Thank you. I hope you enjoyed Sebastian & Arianna's journey. Their story will continue with their children and their empire so buckle up. PS: If you enjoyed this book, please be so kind to leave a review. Reviews help authors greatly
. Love, Adriana.

ALSO BY
ADRIANA BRINNE

UNHOLY TRINITY SERIES

Andrea : The Beginning (Unholy Trinity 1)

Lucan : The End (Unholy Trinity Book 2)

Unholy Night: An Unholy Trinity Novella

Fallon: The Madman (Unholy Trinity 3)

Cara: The King (Unholy Trinity Book 4)

Arianna: (Unholy Trinity Book 5)

UNHOLY GROUND SERIES

Throne Of Deception

ACKNOWLEDGMENTS

I, first, want to thank my readers. This would not be possible if you didn't read my words and support me like you do. I will never truly find the right words to express just how thankful I am for your support. Instead, I'll just show my appreciation by writing my stories. My Arc team. I am forever thankful for your support. Thank you for reading my books and sharing about them on social media. You guys are amazing and I hope you stick by me for many more books. Gisele, Thank you for your friendship. For talking about books with me and for all the beautiful teasers you make for me. I am so thankful for you.

Elsa, You are not only a good friend but you're the best editor. Thank you from the bottom of my heart for believing in my books. You work so hard to make them the best and all you do is greatly appreciated. I am forever thankful. Lastly, my mom. I love you. I hope you're proud of me. This one and all the ones that come next are for you. Thank you for reading, babes.
Until the next one!
Much love, Adri,

ABOUT THE AUTHOR

Adriana Brinne is a new author who fell in love with reading from a very young age but never felt brave enough to share her words with the world. She was born and raised in a tropical island surrounded by only beauty and water called Puerto Rico. She is a full-time IT tech, and, in her downtime, you can find her reading new adult by her favorites, reviewing books, and watching The Big Bang Theory. She has a love for all things dark in romance and almost every trope created except cheating and death trope. I hate them and you won't catch me writing or reading about it.

The Unholy Trinity characters are screaming to have their stories told and I plan to do so. You can expect from me all the feels, strong girls, and asshole heroes that worship them.

Printed in Great Britain
by Amazon